DEVOTION

Marianne Evans

This is a work of fiction. Names, characters, places, and incidents either are the product of the author's imagination or are used fictitiously, and any resemblance to actual persons living or dead, business establishments, events, or locales, is entirely coincidental.

DEVOTION

COPYRIGHT 2012 by MARIANNE EVANS

Contact Information: titleadmin@pelicanbookgroup.com

All scripture quotations, unless otherwise indicated, are taken from the Holy Bible, New International Version(R), NIV(R), Copyright 1973, 1978, 1984 by Biblica, Inc.™ Used by permission of Zondervan. All rights reserved worldwide. www.zondervan.com

Cover Art by *Nicola Martinez*

Harbourlight Books, a division of Pelican Ventures, LLC
www.pelicanbookgroup.com PO Box 1738 *Aztec, NM * 87410

Harbourlight Books sail and mast logo is a trademark of Pelican Ventures, LLC

Publishing History
Library of Congress Control Number: 2012933480
First Harbourlight Edition, 2012
Paperback Edition ISBN 978-1-61116-164-9
Electronic Edition ISBN 978-1-61116-163-2
Published in the United States of America

Dedication

There are three people, without whom this story would never have come to be:

Nicola Martinez. Nicola, you never fail to leave me amazed by your level of talent, commitment, and the deep affection you hold for your authors. It's an honor to work with you. I'm so blessed by your publishing savvy, support, and friendship. My wish is that every author in the world could work with an editor as wonderful as you. Your actions are always prayerful, anointed, and serve to remind me that there's a reason why our paths have crossed. I'm forever grateful for everything you do, and the beautiful person that you are.

JoAnn Carter. JoAnn, a long-ago e-mail tripped the wires for this story and ignited a holy flame in my heart about exploring the beauty that is Christian marriage—marriage that's a covenant, not a contract to be entered into then easily dissolved. You asked me to look at the idea of long-term love affairs, and the power of love and passion over time. I only pray I hit the mark in the pages of Devotion.

Steve Evans. You're my "DH"—and I couldn't be more blessed. God caused our lives to connect, and from there, remain forever entwined. You're an example to me of Christian love, selfless giving, and a heart that knows no boundaries. I can only hope to return half of the joy you've given me in our years together. Thank you for always supporting me and for taking me on a life/love adventure that I know will continue until our Lord calls us home. Plain and simple? I love you.

Praise for Marianne Evans

This is a heartwarming as well as heart wrenching romance. Readers will empathize with the heroine's struggle with her feelings of unimportance to God. Her final acceptance of the hero's love as well as God's comfort is remarkable. ~4 Stars from RT Book reviews, Susan Mobley on *Hearts Communion*

Hearts Crossing - Gayle Wilson Award of Excellence Finalist

Hearts Surrender - Christian Small Publisher Book of the Year nominee

[Marianne Evans] stories evoke a powerful response. She writes with a level of heart and Christian substance that puts me in mind of Karen Kingsbury. ~Rochelle Sanders, reader on *Hearts Key*

...the Christian message enhances the lovely romance that develops. An affecting love story. ~ 4-Stars from RT Book Reviews, Susan Mobley on *Hearts Surrender*

I love inspirational stories that show characters' struggles with real life issues and how they connect with God...a novel of outstanding fiction. I highly recommend. ~ 5-Stars from author Joanne Troppello on *Hearts Communion*

Riveting, with an amazing storyline...I absolutely could not put it down. ~ 5-Stars, Book of the Week from The Romance Studio, Brenda Talley on *A Face in the Clouds*

Other Titles by Marianne Evans

Woodland Church Series

Hearts Crossing
Hearts Surrender
Hearts Communion
Hearts Key

**Sal's Place Series
(Coming Soon)**

Search and Rescue
Beautiful Music
By Appointment Only

1

"I don't mean to push you." Kellen Rossiter lifted the collar of his dress shirt and slid his tie into place, adjusting its fall. He stared at his reflection in the bathroom mirror, knowing his words weren't entirely true.

"I know that." His wife stood next to him at the double vanity. Dressed for bed, Juliet wore a floaty nightgown of dark green satin. She moisturized her arms, then her face. Kellen paused to watch her, captivated by the graceful, automatic motions, the soul-deep beauty she carried with a complete lack of awareness. The image of her left him to ache inside.

"I miss you when you're not there." He refitted the shirt collar then double-checked the knot on his patterned silk tie. "I like hearing your thoughts and impressions, but mostly I just enjoy being with you."

Her shoulders sagged. Through the mirror, she tagged him with an apologetic glance. He had known the look was coming; she was ready for bed, after all. Plus, he knew the regret came from her heart. That's why his statement about missing her, enjoying her, had lacked any form of condemnation. Just longing. He *did* miss her companionship and the feel of her at his side.

With increasing frequency.

"We used to have fun scouting talent at the local clubs, talking about anything and everything while we listened to music. Plus, this is supposedly a great new place, and we haven't had a 'date night' in quite a while." He paused again, just long enough to look at her once more. Gentle refusal still lived in her eyes, so Kellen braced himself for her 'no thanks.'

"Sweetheart, you'll be working. I get in the way when

1

you're shaking and moving." She smiled at him, sincerely. Her eyes were so soft, a beautiful shade of deep green. "Next time, OK? I'm seriously tapped out, or I'd let you tempt me." She moved close and tucked in tight, resting her head on his chest. Kellen wrapped his arms around her, ignoring the bite of disappointment, the urge for recriminations, like: *We have no children, Juliet, nothing that ties us down. I know you're busy with a hundred different activities that help our church, our city, and I know that fills you up, but what about us? Where do we fit together?*

The thoughts launched, but with practiced ease, he shot each one down. He was being selfish. She was tired. The winter season was giving way to spring around Nashville, and she had spent the entire afternoon and evening volunteering at a soup kitchen and warming center sponsored by Trinity Christian Church, where he and Juliet were active parishioners.

"Tell you what." Juliet leaned back in his arms. The curve of her lips, that promising sparkle in her eyes, almost cured his sadness. "I'll wait up for you."

Kellen nodded. He dotted her nose with a kiss; his hands slid against the glossy fabric of her nightgown. The color highlighted her ivory skin, and turned spectacular eyes to absolutely dazzling.

He made a vow to himself, then and there, that he'd get home early.

❧

Irritation riled him as he drove north on I-65. He didn't need to do this. It would be a typical late night/early morning spent at a club, this time listening to a jazz singer. Then, if he sensed any kind of potential, he'd have to host an introductory meeting. He wasn't supposed to be taking on new clients. His roster of represented musicians was exclusive, and full to overflowing. He would have much preferred an evening at home with Juliet. At least, that's what he told himself as intimate moments came along less and less often of late. Still,

Kellen couldn't resist that tickle in his gut, the excitement stirred by the prospect of discovering something—someone—extraordinary.

According to Associated Talent's Weiss McDonald, tonight's mission to Nashville's newest hot spot, *Iridescence*, would be a slam-dunk. Beyond that, Kellen's boss had offered nothing about who, or what, Kellen would be scouting.

"I refuse to taint your perceptions with any of my own." Weiss had said, seeming euphoric. "Go. See. Report back in the morning."

A sharp ache gnawed at his heart as Kellen navigated the narrow descent to an underground parking structure. Something didn't feel right about this. He should have stayed home with Juliet.

Leaving the car, he made his way into the office building that housed Iridescence. A swift elevator ride later, the doors parted to reveal a white marble lobby, a translucent podium decorated by a deep purple vase full of vibrant colored calla lilies.

Nice, he thought. *Definitely upscale and luxurious.*

He was led to a table near the window where wall-to-wall glass revealed a Nashville skyline bursting with lights and a carpet of added illumination that went on for miles. To his left was a large, raised dais presently curtained off by black velvet. In passing, he saw a face he recognized—Jack Collins—the owner of the club. Jack's eyes went wide when he looked Kellen's way. Kellen chuckled under his breath, sitting down.

A waitress stepped up promptly. "Good evening, and welcome to Iridescence. Can I get you something to drink?"

She was young, a gorgeous blonde whom Kellen took in, and dismissed, just as quickly, though he offered a kind smile. "Tonic and lime would be great, thanks."

"Right away." Her smile and attention lingered. Kellen's didn't. Of far greater interest was Jack Collins who worked his way to Kellen's table.

"Rossiter. Good to see you." Jack touched the arm of the waitress to get her attention. "Mindy, his tab is on me."

Further impressed, the waitress gave Kellen a second long look, which again he registered, then ignored. His focus homed in on Jack, and when the owner sat down in the chair opposite, Kellen leaned forward. "What am I in for?"

Jack's smile took off like a fast ride. The man's eyes flashed like a kid with a secret. "Seriously. Weiss didn't cue you in?"

Kellen lifted a shoulder. "Mumbled some new-age nonsense about not wanting to mess with my perceptions or some such ridiculous thing. So tell me. What's the deal?"

Jack sat back and kicked out his legs, flattening his hands against his stomach. He was a sharp man, hip and artful—with an eye for what would appeal to high-end customers. "Nope. I'm glad he didn't tell you about her."

"Her?"

Jack straightened and settled his forearms on the table. "Chloe."

Lord. For whatever reason, Kellen's mind drew pictures of a platinum blonde with buxom curves and slinky lines. He sank on the inside. "I'm here to see a woman named *Chloe*?"

"Yeah. Chloe Havermill. Listen, I've gotta see to some things right now, but stick around after the upcoming set. It's her last for the night. I'll introduce you."

Before Jack could dash off, Kellen put out a restraining hand. "Hey, don't cue her in. Don't stack the deck or get her riled up that there's an agent in the house. I'm here to listen. That's all."

Jack's eyes flashed, and his posture radiated confidence. "Yeah? Let's see if that's all you have to say once you hear her sing."

The man's stance was so definitive it took Kellen aback. His interest level inched upward.

వ∞ఉ

The lights dimmed until all that remained was a centered spotlight. The curtain across the dais glided open.

Conversations and dish clatter faded as the audience turned in unison, looking toward the stage, and waiting. A rhythmic, almost tropical drumbeat, accompanied by flowing bass, signaled the start of the Sade classic, *Paradise*.

The spotlight remained trained upon a woman who put to rest every doubt Kellen had felt upon hearing her name.

A long, silver dress dotted by sequins, flowed like water over a lithe body that was graceful and fluid. Spaghetti straps revealed toned arms, a long, slender neck. A straight column of black hair moved against her shoulders. He was positioned close enough to see that her large, wide-set eyes were violet.

Violet.

When she began to sing, her voice was nothing short of smooth magic.

From the opening notes, Chloe owned the room. She expressed the mood of the piece with pitch-perfect delivery. Her passion and skill rolled off the stage, slipping around the tables, enveloping her listeners. Kellen was stunned. Like the rest of the audience, he couldn't look anywhere else. Her voice became the only thing he could hear.

It was second nature for him to size up people physically. Such was the nature of his business. Talent was the important thing, yes, but beyond that came the mysterious and elusive factors of charisma and dynamic appeal.

What was the package here? What would be the strengths and weaknesses?

A flashpoint occurred, providing an immediate answer to those questions. Quite naturally, that answer was channeled into terms any agent in the entertainment industry would understand. If Carrie Underwood had sleek, jet hair and violet colored eyes, she'd look exactly like Chloe Havermill. Chloe had the same gorgeous skin and flawless bone structure. She had the same dazzling smile. And Chloe had an innocent sweetness in her eyes, a sweetness that would provoke fierce loyalty, delight, and mega-sales.

The longer he listened, and watched, the more he stared. Captured. The corner of his mouth curved up. He felt pleasure just looking at her. That, coupled with the vocals she possessed, was an incredible intoxicant—because if this was how he felt, he was certain this was how America would feel as well.

He owed Weiss an apology for underestimation.

Kellen looked around, beginning to pay closer attention to the audience. They were enthralled. Chloe roped them in and fed their awed expectations. She drifted through smoky jazz ballad after heart-felt love song. The crowd, to a person, was completely behind her.

The set ended way too soon.

Not long after, Chloe entered the main room, accompanied by Jack. Moving through the crowd, she accepted handshakes and smiles, a few air kisses and delighted greetings while Jack led her to the table where Kellen sat. They were close enough now that Jack's guiding touch and directing head nod caused Chloe's focus to zoom in on Kellen, and it stayed put.

That's when it hit him—a lightning bolt of attraction. A primitive male response to undiluted sweetness and a beguiling manner. Chloe Havermill struck him not at all as an arrogant, entitled performer—this despite a world of talent. Kellen didn't even have time to consider his reaction before she stepped up, and looked at Jack, then back at him. Kellen stood, realizing his heart started to race, that his gesture stemmed from a mystifying call to be courtly.

Jack stepped into their elongated, intense silence. "Chloe, I'd like you to meet—"

"Chloe, honey!" Kellen's waitress stepped up and held her empty tray to the side so she could give the singer a tight hug. "Happy birthday! Been waiting all night to see you so I could say hello! It's a shame to be working on your big day!"

Chloe brushed that comment aside with a graceful sweep of her hand. "No worries. To me, this isn't work. It's a joy. Thanks for remembering, sweetie, and I'll talk to you later, OK?"

"You bet."

Kellen watched. Oh, he couldn't wait to work with this woman.

She turned back, wearing an expectant expression, waiting on Jack, who started to chuckle as Kellen's smile spread. He didn't let Jack introduce him. Not quite yet. "So, today's your birthday?"

"Yes. Yes, it is. Ah…" Chloe stumbled verbally, obviously confused about what was going on, and why she was standing at Kellen's table.

Kellen reached into the breast pocket of his suit coat and extracted a business card, making ready to hand it over while Jack tried again. "Chloe, I think you're in for a great present. I want you to meet a friend of mine."

Already she extended her hand. Kellen connected to her promptly, taking her hand in his, but not shaking, just holding on.

Jack performed the conclusion. "This is Kellen Rossiter. Kellen, say hello to Chloe Havermill."

Her eyes went wide. She breathed deep and the sequins of her dress shimmered. "Kellen. Rossiter."

Because of his hold, he felt her waver just slightly.

Jack chuckled. "Pleasantries dispensed with, I'll leave you to it." Jack speared Kellen with a look that reeked of 'I told you so.'

Chloe, meanwhile, gave her boss a fast, almost desperate look. "Can't you join us?"

Kellen pulled out the chair next to his, to distract her from Jack's exit. "I may have a tough reputation, Chloe, but contrary to industry myth, I don't bite. I'd like to talk to you privately." Kellen wanted her full focus, but he also wanted her to feel comfortable. The waitress—Mindy he recalled—breezed past once again and Kellen caught her eye. "Excuse me, Mindy. Would it be possible to order something to drink?"

"Of course. What can I get for you?"

"Another tonic and lime for me. Chloe?"

The interlude, as intended, gave her a few moments to

regroup, but she was still dazed, completely unguarded and unprepared for this meeting. "Umm...ice water works for me."

"Are you sure you don't want anything else?" Kellen resumed his seat.

"Positive. I don't want anything stronger when I feel like I've been thrown into the deep end of the ocean."

He smiled into her eyes and leaned forward across the slight space that separated them. He was charmed by her. A natural reaction, all in all. "You know who I am. I'm impressed."

"No, actually, I'm the one who's impressed." She laced her fingers together and rested her hands on the table. "Anyone with a pulse in the music industry should know who you are. My nervous stumbling aside, I'm very pleased to meet you."

The comment stunned and delighted him. Full of undisguised awe, her reply stirred a second rush of attraction that wasn't entirely welcome. Kellen wrote off the response quickly, though. After all, any man within a glance of this woman would feel just the same.

He decided to play into the moment, knowing he could easily pull back.

"Well—now that my ego is sufficiently fed" --they shared a laugh-- "Happy birthday, Chloe." He extended his business card, the one he had held since being introduced to her, and slid it across the top of the small, dark wood table. Their fingertips brushed innocently when she took possession. She lifted the card and studied the elegant, raised black lettering, fingered the heavy white card stock. But he also noticed the subtle tremble that worked through her hand.

"I'm almost afraid to ask what this means." Her voice was a quiet murmur.

"Then allow me to verify what you already know." Kellen went all business and dead serious. "What that card means is you've just been given the best present of your life, Chloe. Opportunity."

She blinked. Joy, he saw, became juxtaposed against terror. "Because?"

"Because you're talented, and because I believe you deserve a shot. I want to give that to you."

Laughter, conversations, glassware chiming—the bar sounds surrounded them while Chloe openly searched his eyes. She studied him so deep, and with such intensity that Kellen could do nothing but embrace the silence and let her, maintaining a smooth professionalism he didn't feel on the inside. His pulse rate climbed. So did a heady, intoxicating roll of heat. The woman was exquisite.

"You honestly came here to see me?"

"I honestly did. And I'm not disappointed."

Their drinks arrived. She tapped her fingers against the glass, looking down in a flustered way as she slid her hair to the side. But then she looked up and gave him a smile. Kellen felt its impact straight through to the core. "Thank goodness for that much. I'm glad I didn't know you were in the audience. I'd've botched things up for sure."

Kellen highly doubted that statement. "For just that reason, I operate below the radar until it's time to make a move. Why unsettle the waters? On the recommendation of my boss, I wanted to see you perform without forewarning or prep. I get a far more honest performance that way."

For the next couple hours, they talked about everything. She was Ohio born and bred—a singer from the day she could speak. Her preferences leaned toward country blended with a soulful style of jazz. Five years in Nashville had taken her through the doorways of a number of clubs that dotted the District; she had even played The Stage and Tootsies.

Tootsies is where Jack Collins had found her, but now a chic, more high-end atmosphere called—one that was much better suited to her elegant looks and musical style.

She warmed quickly and offered her background details with increasing ease. He appreciated that she didn't mind revealing herself because his intrigue was absolute, and he wanted to know what he was getting into by representing her.

Chloe seemed to understand that without prompting.

Before he knew it, it was almost one o'clock in the morning, and the spell shattered.

I'll wait up for you.

Kellen double-checked his watch while Juliet's promising smile, her sparkling eyes, swirled through his mind and prompted him home. "I have to leave."

Chloe moved back with a nod and a chagrined expression. "I'm so sorry if I kept you."

"You did no such thing. I've enjoyed the time we spent talking."

"Me, too. I should have been home a while ago myself."

Boyfriend? Husband? They stood, and his attention darted to her ring finger. Empty. But that didn't mean much. He'd find out more on that later. "Call my office and let's set up a formal meeting. Meantime, my team will draw up an agreement for you to look over."

"I certainly will, and thank you again."

They walked toward the rear of the club. "Where's your car?"

"In the parking structure."

The idea of Chloe walking to her car all alone in a large, empty facility didn't sit well. "Let me walk you out."

She tilted her head; he watched a dangling gold earring brush against her bare shoulder. She folded her arms against her midsection and her eyes sparkled. "Are you always so chivalrous?"

Danger flags rose—vivid red and snapping in a stiff wind. Kellen obeyed the signs and delivered a business-like nod that he tempered with a grin. "Let's just call it looking out for my future investment."

Her smile only widened. "Let me grab my purse and coat. I'll be right back."

Kellen knew that smile of hers was going to haunt him. Big time.

❧❦

Kellen arrived home to darkness and silence.

I'll wait up for you.

Juliet's words echoed through his mind and guilt slid in.

Entering from the garage, Kellen walked quickly and quietly through the kitchen. The stove clock read one forty-five. He had never meant to stay at Iridescence so long. When he'd left Juliet, he'd fully intended to make good on his promise to return home promptly.

He removed his suit coat and draped it over his arm. He tiptoed up the stairs to their bedroom, sliding off his tie, loosening the top few buttons of his shirt. No shaft of light cut a line beneath the closed door. Of course she would be asleep by now. Guilt performed its second dance when he eased open the door and crept inside.

Tucked beneath the bed blankets, Juliet slept. He didn't need the milky, dim moonlight in order to see her. He needed nothing but the memories in his heart to draw the image of her soft, beautiful features.

What had gotten into him tonight with Chloe? He needed to figure that out—but not right now. He needed to pray about it—but the time for that would come later as well—when he was more focused, and rested. For now, he wanted Juliet. With all his heart.

He moved silently to the side of the bed where she slept. He sat down carefully, fingering back the tumbled waves of her silky, auburn hair. He bent to drop a slow, lingering kiss on her cheek, willing her awake, longing for clear, sweet eyes of deep green. He snuggled gently against Juliet's neck, nuzzling her with soft kisses. She responded by coming alert slowly, turning into the ready warmth he offered.

"Hi," she whispered in a husky voice.

"Hi." He backed away just far enough to stroke her sleep-warmed cheeks with his fingertips and cup her face. Any other loose-flung thought or desire promptly evaporated. In Juliet's presence once more, he was struck anew by the precious connection he shared with her—the wonder of their love. "I'm so sorry I'm late."

She shifted beneath the blankets and feathered her fingertips through his hair. "Was it a successful night?"

Kellen fought the urge to squirm, and he battled back every image he held of Chloe. "Very. I think I've found a very gifted performer."

"I'm glad." She stifled a yawn and stretched out a bit. "I tried to stay up."

A craving took over him all at once. He held his wife, he drew her close, and they dissolved into one another, sharing a kiss deep and stirring. Loving Juliet was as beautiful as a dream, and as easy as drawing breath.

She turned toward the glow of the alarm clock, but Kellen brushed his lips against her throat and kept her from facing the hour. He took a breath and came upon the last tantalizing traces of lily of the valley perfume, a scent that would forever speak to him of Juliet. "Don't look. It's crazy late. Do you have to be up early?"

She pulled him toward her and made a happy sound against his cheek as she loosened a few more of his shirt buttons. Her fingertips skimmed against his chest. "Not *that* early."

He sank into a mix of emotions—pure, loving desire, then a longing that possessed two very distinct and potent layers. One belonged to his wife; the other belonged to the echo of a lightning strike—to a woman named Chloe Havermill. Tangled within himself, Kellen knew just one thing to be true: Juliet was the antidote. His wife was the author of his heart, and he loved her deeply. She would keep him centered. The sureness of their relationship would soothe away anything else.

First thing in the morning, he would drink in God's word like a parched man. He would return to his daily reflections and humbly, devoutly pray. Tonight, however, all he wanted to do was pour his love over Juliet like a benediction.

2

Dancing through misty, half-consciousness, Juliet burrowed into the welcoming depth of her pillow. The space next to her was nothing more than empty indentations and cool cotton, so she pulled Kellen's pillow close and stretched beneath the bed blankets. His scent filled her.

She perceived only bits and pieces of the world that slowly emerged—but all of it was familiar, and comforting. There was Kellen's almost silent tread as he moved from the bathroom to the closet. Next came the swoosh and click of hangers as he dressed. Finally she detected the crisp snap of metal coming together that signaled the end of his morning dressing routine when he placed his watch on his wrist.

Seconds later, his fingertips glanced against her cheek, drawing back a curl of her hair. The warmth of Kellen's body filled the air for a moment. When he kissed her cheek, she registered subtle spice, a more intense version of the aroma carried on his pillow. He let the contact linger, and Juliet smiled; her pulse quickened in response.

"Bye, love," he whispered.

"Bye." She turned to give him a hug, which he took in readily. A smile later, he was gone.

Well—never really *gone*.

Juliet gave up on the realm of sleep. Instead, she drifted for a few minutes on last night's memories and a sensation of happiness so rich and full it left her wanting to dissolve into the all-over contentment of being thoroughly loved.

She breathed out, her eyes fluttering closed. *Don't do it,* she thought. *Don't you dare let yourself hope. Don't even think about setting yourself up for yet another fall.*

The inner warning carried no weight. With hesitance, she tucked her hands beneath the blanket and flattened the palms of her hands gently upon her abdomen. *Please, Lord? This time. Please?*

It had felt so beautiful to be in Kellen's arms last night. There were none of the monthly mechanics. No lovemaking governed by calendars and bio-cycles. There had been nothing but love and the two of them—together.

For nearly two years she and Kellen had been trying to conceive, but with no success. During the past year, Juliet had willingly undergone a variety of fertility tests. All of them had come back normal, with no alarming results.

Relax, her gynecologist had advised kindly. *Relax and don't let your physical relationship with Kellen become a ritual of creation. Love him, and let him love you. Leave the rest to God.*

That's what Juliet liked about Dr. Jacqueline Roth. She approached her practice from a Christian perspective, and she possessed a caring, warm demeanor. Nevertheless, her doctor's advice, following empty month after empty month, became difficult wisdom to observe.

A half year ago, Kellen had undergone tests of his own. Once again, there was no evidence of an inability to conceive.

Let me give this to him, Lord. Please allow us to have, and share, a family together. You've blessed us with so much—we want to share Your love with children of our own.

Juliet rolled back the covers and kicked her legs over the edge of the bed. She sat up with a yawn then padded through the bedroom to the master bath. There, skylights poured golden morning sunshine into the spacious, modern room. As she regulated the water temperature for a shower, a sunbeam glanced against the simple, gold band on the third finger of her left hand. Her wedding band was a perfect match to Kellen's. She had forsaken the sizeable diamond ring he wanted to give her upon their engagement almost nine years ago.

"Do you know what I want instead?" Juliet had asked.

"Name it."

His eagerness, his genuine willingness to see to her happiness was a gift beyond any price. "I'd rather save our money to invest in a big home, on a beautiful piece of land, with lots of rooms and space to grow into. I want to fill it up with family and friends. I want kids, and scout meetings, and youth group get-togethers, prayer gatherings and Bible studies. I want a home full of traditions and love and God. I don't want diamonds; I want you. I want our children and the life we can build together with all the people we love."

While the memories swirled, Juliet slipped out of her nightgown and hung it on the back of the bathroom door. She stepped beneath the soothing spray of hot water, still remembering the way he had looked at her after the request—in awed amazement—as he took her hand in his, and kissed her fingertips with lingering, tantalizing strokes of his lips.

"Consider it done," he had said.

And Kellen made good on his promise. Their home was a haven of stately grace, but not at all stuffy. This was a welcoming place, full of beauty, and comfort. Kellen's lone concession to giving her diamonds was a piece of jewelry she was now never without: a fine, gold chain upon which rested a cross pendant crafted of simple and understated diamonds. It had been his wedding gift to her.

Now, if only the rest of their dreams could fall into place. Now, if only she didn't feel like she was letting him down and leaving them both unfulfilled.

Maybe…maybe…maybe…

She lathered and the water beat down. After she shampooed and conditioned, she rode her fingertips gingerly against her abdomen once again. Her eyes stung, not from chemicals, but from a sharp, deep longing that pierced a spot in her soul that contained her deepest vulnerability: the need to share her love with Kellen and their children.

Please, Lord. This time?

As fast and potent as the plea dawned, however, Juliet pushed it to the side. Out of necessity, the practice of rebuke and refusal became another ingrained part of her monthly routine. There was no other choice for them but to soldier on as best they could and ignore the gentle, well-meaning barbs from friends and family members, the endless questions about when, and if, they would ever have children...

My plans for you are greater than the storms that come, Juliet. Rest in My hands.

The words filled her, as strong and real as any that could be spoken aloud. Juliet went still beneath the strong jet of water, listening, praying for even more from the powerful, compelling voice that slid through her soul—the voice that she knew came straight from God.

She had always believed in the truth of God calling her by name, and in ways that were specific to whatever was going on in her life—be they good or bad. He was always there—but she felt called to prayer in an even stronger way today. All at once, she longed for intensive, focused time with God.

Juliet didn't have much on the agenda this morning, so she dried her hair into a wavy tumble. Black jeans and a dark green turtleneck sweater completed a casual and comfortable ensemble. She trotted down the stairs, galvanized by the scent of fresh brewed coffee. The aroma provided yet another reminder of her husband's thoughtfulness. He was always the first one out the door, so he always made sure a new pot was in place for them both.

Juliet stopped in the family room before settling in for breakfast. She picked up her Bible from an end table between the two leather easy chairs she and Kellen usually occupied and carried it with her to the kitchen. There, a teak dinette with matching chairs was tucked into the cheery space created by a spacious bay window. Sunlight burnished the room. Juliet set her Bible by the chair closest to the window and prepared herself a breakfast of maple and cinnamon oatmeal, some coffee, and an English muffin. She added a small box of raisins to the oatmeal mix, and then settled in to eat.

But before she took a bite, before she even opened her Bible, Juliet bowed her head and folded her hands in her lap. Quietly centered, she went lax and offered up a prayer to welcome in the day, and leave its progression in the hands of the Savior she loved.

Fear not, Juliet. I am with you. I am your God. I will strengthen you. I will uphold you with my right hand.

Juliet lifted her head with a hard, startled blink. Her contentment burned away when her heart rate increased. The summons, she knew, came from Isaiah 41:10, but the resounding power of it flowed through her like an alert—a warning that ate away at her soothing mood.

She coupled this interlude with the words she had claimed in the shower, and for some reason, an icy sense of foreboding skated fast and smooth down the length of her spine. What was God trying to tell her, exactly? Why did the words resound like something ominous—a promise of shelter in a storm—rather than the assurance of His grace that she sought?

This had to be about her desire for children, right? The shiver of unease she felt stemmed from an understandable anxiety about the desire of her heart, that's all.

She and Kellen had a relationship founded on solid rock—Christ's love, and a passion for one another that remained both ordained, and beautiful. Thus bolstered, Juliet returned to breakfast and her morning devotions.

3

The night spent in Juliet's arms nearly purged Kellen's mind of the specter of Chloe Havermill. This morning he had come awake in typical fashion, spooned against his wife, his arm draped at a loose, comfortable angle against her waist. Chloe crossed his mind upon leaving the house, but only in a fleeting way that was business centered and easily dismissed.

Allowing for how late he had stayed out, Kellen indulged in a couple extra hours of sleep. Now, arriving for work, he felt content and reenergized. A perfumed cloud, of sorts, had lifted from his mind, restoring clarity. He thought of Juliet, just the way he had left her, nearly dead to the world and nothing much more than a few curvy lumps beneath the blankets. His lips curved automatically.

By mid-afternoon he was immersed in work and came to realize he had only sparingly glanced at incoming e-mail, so he switched over to the days accumulation.

His heart tripped when his sifting gaze came upon the address: CVHavermill@1cadia.com. The subject line read: Thank You.

He promptly clicked open the missive, instantly resenting the hunger that came along with its receipt. Only then did Kellen realize: he hadn't followed through on his intention to pray this morning.

Kellen –

The simple words, thank you, are completely inadequate, but for now, they're the best I seem to have.

Having admired you via reputation for quite a while now, meeting you at Iridescence was pleasure enough; being given the chance to meet with you further, and discuss ways in which we might work together to ignite my career, is beyond expectation. Yes, I admit it; I woke up this morning wondering if I had stumbled into an alternate realm, or some cruel trick of birthday fate.

I'll call later today and set up our meeting, but before doing so, I wanted to pass along the addresses to my web site and a couple of fan pages a friend of mine set up.

There Kellen stopped, and he frowned. Most entertainers these days used social media to foster connections, and pull in fans, but he hoped...*really* hoped...that he wouldn't discover a bunch of risqué pictures or any kind of lewd content that would diminish the image he held of Chloe. Nothing much could top her rich innocence, and that startling degree of charisma, if she played it smart. Eyeing the links below her signature line, he decided to avoid them until finishing her note.

I hope exploring my background will help you gain a bit more familiarity. Be well, and I look forward to seeing you again. The walk to my car, by the way, left me feeling special. And protected. 1 a.m., in an all but empty parking garage, can be pretty unsettling. I really appreciated the gesture.

Chloe

He smiled when he reread the ending. Somehow, it perfectly captured the essence of the woman. Guileless, charming, and warm.

He clicked on the links, and when he caught sight of the visuals, he was glad he was sitting down. The sites weren't at all risqué. Instead, they revealed a woman who was serious about her goals and coming to the music field ready to play. Dozens of stunning performance shots along with a few casual pictures of Chloe with friends and fans chronicled an energetic woman in love with her profession who enjoyed fan interaction. He hesitated then clicked on her profile picture to enlarge it. Sparking, violet-blue eyes fairly leapt from the screen, the tilt of her head was already familiar to him as one of her mannerisms. Dressed in blue jeans and a white oxford shirt tied at the waist, she faced the camera straight on, smiling. Kellen stared. Raven hair was a cascade over her left shoulder. Sparkling earrings dangled against her neck...like he had noticed last night...

"So...what did you think? Amazing, isn't she?"

Weiss entered the office and Kellen jerked violently, mousing in sloppy zigzags to extinguish the website as fast as he could. The last thing he wanted was to get caught crushing like some kind of hormonal groupie.

Kellen cleared his throat and stretched back in his seat. "Yep, she's amazing. She's got a lot to offer."

Weiss grinned. "We gonna land her?"

Kellen steepled his fingers and studied his boss. "I've got legal working on an agreement in principal. She can have her attorney validate, and we'll move forward from there."

"I can already tell you Summit Pointe Records is going to go crazy for her. Frank Simpson—"

"Will be my first go-to with a demo." Kellen went sardonic. "You holding my hand on this one, Weiss?"

"She's going to be *mega*. It's incumbent upon me to keep tabs."

"I can tell. I'm just wondering why you feel it's necessary." Prickles of that protectiveness Chloe mentioned in her e-mail—a protectiveness that bordered on the territorial— went to work against Kellen's nerves, and mind. "I'm the one you wanted to land this performer—I'm the one you got."

"And I couldn't be more pleased. Get it done, and good work!"

Weiss left Kellen's office, and Kellen stared into the now empty entryway of his suite; his brows pulled together. This whole Chloe thing was ridiculous. What was going on with him right now?

Straightening, he slid back up to his computer and clicked the reply toggle to the e-mail she had sent. He began to type, rapid-fire, knowing just what he wanted to say.

Hey, Chloe –

Thanks for the e-mail and links. My calendar is pretty locked up this week, but next week works. That should give my legal department time to craft an agreement for you to review and execute.

I'll e-mail you the document as soon as it's prepared.

Would you be available for a meeting next Thursday? I've got ten or eleven o'clock available. In the meantime, I already have ideas about where to start submitting your demo—we'll discuss strategy when we meet.

Take care—and I'm looking forward to working with you.

Kellen leaned back and propped an elbow on the armrest of his chair. He pursed his lips as he reread his response. With professionalism and precision, he had restored the upper hand, taken the lead and dictated the terms of what would happen next—like any good agent. That small measure of control also helped him establish equilibrium. A cooling off period from the thrill of this chase would be good. In the days between now and his meeting with Chloe Havermill, he would be able to distance himself from her impact.

The next thing he did was long overdue, and necessary. He went to his office door and closed it quietly, then returned to his desk. There, he opened the second drawer on his right and pulled out his Bible. He owned several editions, but this was the one his parents had given him when he turned thirteen, and it was precious to him. It stayed with him at work because in his chosen profession, Kellen needed all the fortification God could supply.

Chloe hadn't done anything inappropriate or out of line. Neither had he. Somehow, though, this vibration of need was stirring him up and unsettling a foundation he trusted implicitly. His body hadn't betrayed him, but his heart was straying into territory that was absolutely forbidden—and signing Chloe as a client would bring them together on a continual and intense basis.

He turned to the back of the Bible where he searched an index of verses applicable to any given situation in life. Kellen ran a fingertip down the list of topics until he spotted the one he needed most.

Rebuking temptation.

He sank back in his chair and tuned out the rest of the world. Settling in, he lost himself to God's word and felt his strength of resolve slowly reemerge.

But the interlude lasted just five minutes—he knew the span of time because he clocked it on his watch when his desk phone rang, jarring him away from God's comfort and peace.

Sighing heavily, Kellen set his Bible aside and stretched forward, lifting the receiver. He shook his head, wondering if he had turned into the victim of some type of mystical conspiracy. "Kellen Rossiter."

4

The conspiracy theory gained traction in the days that followed because Kellen's carefully designed plans to establish distance from Chloe utterly backfired.

The agreement was executed and returned by her attorney, so the process of propelling, Chloe's career dominated a good part of his workload, whether he saw her face-to-face or not. Additionally, the longer he waited to see her again, the itchier he became. Images of her, which came to life in a professional portfolio she had overnighted to his attention, bombarded him constantly. Plus, for purposes of crafting a client discovery document and mapping strategies to establish her presence in the music market, he followed her social networking activities and researched her past extensively. He found her to be warmly engaging, and charming to those with whom she communicated. Authenticity rolled off her in waves.

They conversed every couple days over the phone, or via e-mail. Each instance left him with a disquieting hunger, rooted deep in a foreign and increasingly powerful part of his psyche.

By the time Thursday morning rolled around, he couldn't wait to see her.

When his assistant, Anna, notified him of Chloe's arrival, Kellen worked hard to leave those thoughts behind, but something lingered, something he hadn't yet found a way to deal with.

That something was desire.

"Hi, Chloe." Kellen stood from his desk and stepped forward when she entered his office; automatically he offered her his hand.

Her footsteps slowed to a stop when she took in the high-end décor of his office and its gorgeous view of Nashville. But then, she moved to accept the welcoming gesture. She pulled her business persona into place with a degree of speed and poise Kellen admired. She looked the part, too, wearing a stylish and flattering silk suit of light blue. She had fashioned her hair into a loosely plated braid that drew Kellen's focus to her neck, and the pulse beat that danced there.

So, he thought, *she's not quite as cool and composed as she looks. That makes two of us.*

In fact, just like the moment he had met her at Iridescence, his world turned hazy, and unstable.

When their hands slid together, he received a jolt. Absorbing the chill of her fingertips prompted him to increase the subtle squeeze of his touch and offer her a compassionate look. "Chloe, your hands are like ice."

She winced, despite the fact that his words were tempered by kindness and understanding. "Sorry. I'm not good at hiding nerves, I guess. I'm a little intimidated."

She tried to pull away from his grasp, but Kellen gave her hand a gentle shake. "Don't be." In emphasis, he kept their connection in place until their eyes met and held.

Before the moment could stir a lasting awareness, Kellen released her hand, and Chloe looked over his shoulder at the cityscape that was framed in by his office windows. She took a step away, gesturing toward the expansive display. "Would you mind if I take a peek? I'm a sucker for a view."

"Go ahead."

She crossed behind his desk and he joined her. It was a gorgeous spring day in Nashville. Cobalt skies stretched to the horizon. Sunlight sparkled off the metal and glass of the buildings that framed in downtown. Beyond it all, traffic crawled along the James Robertson Parkway and Jefferson Street Bridge. An old fashioned showboat inched its way along the blue green waters of the Cumberland River.

Kellen studied it all, considering the fact that he was

generally so wrapped up by his work he didn't take much time to savor the spectacular images that lay before him. What good was success, he found himself wondering, if none of its benefits seeped into his heart and fed his soul?

Chloe's eyes went wide; with a soft exclamation, she pointed toward a spot far below. Her gesture indicated a simple, red brick building with white accents that was an unmistakable piece of country music history. "Look! You can see the Ryman Auditorium from here!"

The expression on her face, its mix of joy and excitement, spoke to Kellen's recognition of what was lacking in his life and slid against that empty spot he had just discovered.

He laughed, enjoying her verve. "I take it from the reverence in your tone you might like to perform there one day."

She nudged his shoulder with hers. "Gee. D'ya think?" She shot him a sassy look. "The Opry wouldn't be bad, either. Think you might be able to swing that one for me, too?"

Her playful barb hit home and drew him in, so he backed off promptly, though a friendly grin stayed in place. "I'll do my best." Silence beat by. "So tell me something." Kellen ignored the view and leaned his back against the window, opting to watch Chloe instead. "What does the 'V' in your e-mail stand for?"

"Oh, my goodness. You caught that? And remember it?"

"Soon enough, you'll be paying me to catch and remember details like that." Kellen liked the way she maintained a visual hold on him. There were undercurrents of attraction from her, of an interest that dealt not in business terms, but in wants of the heart.

"I can't wait."

Deliberately, Kellen didn't respond to that, but her gaze lingered like a caress.

"It stands for Victoria," she answered. "My middle name."

Chloe Victoria Havermill. Everything about the woman struck Kellen like perfectly timed, beautifully blended music.

Her shy reply was accompanied by diverted eyes and a tint to her skin that brightened just slightly.

He fought for emotional center as he lifted away from the sill. "I love it. And now, it's time for me to start earning my keep. Let's get you started. Have a seat."

While she complied, Kellen sat down in his chair as well. "I received the signed agreement from your attorney, so I've set a few of the wheels in motion." Chloe sat back, watching. "Like we discussed, we need to start with a demo we can shop to the labels I want to approach."

Chloe held up her hands. "Wow. Hang on a second. I mean, I'm thrilled by all of this, naturally, but things are moving pretty fast. Is that typical?"

"When the talent is as strong as yours? Yes. Absolutely. Why wait around? You're ready to hit the charts. You have a gift, Chloe. That gift will take you where you're supposed to go. Have faith in that."

"I appreciate your strength of belief. It's flattering."

He ignored her subtle bout of hero worship. He needed to stay level—*objective*. "Don't be flattered. Just keep doing what you do. I know star power when I see it or you wouldn't be here." He gestured toward a beverage service tucked against the far wall of his office. "Can I get you some water, or coffee? Maybe some orange juice?"

"Juice would be great." She paused, looking up at him when he stood. "Thank you."

Kellen felt the craziest urge to reach out and stroke her cheek. He stepped away before that errant thought could possibly take hold. After crossing the room, he opened a wood paneled mini-fridge and retrieved two single-serve containers.

"So. About the demo. I want to set up some studio time for you next week." He twisted open the bottle tops, pouring juice into two glass tumblers. "You need to record some songs as soon as possible, because the sooner I can approach Frank Simpson at Summit Pointe Records the better." Kellen returned to his desk and handed her one of the glasses he carried.

Chloe, he noticed, listened attentively.

"Frank and Summit are at the top of my list because you're a perfect fit for his label. He's smart, and he's a straight shooter. He's got a fantastic company with a perfect blend of market power and production quality."

Chloe fingered her glass. Her brows lifted. "I know who Frank Simpson is—by reputation, anyway. It would be an honor to record for him."

Kellen appreciated her smarts, and savvy. She was no one's empty starlet. Once again, Chloe demonstrated solid knowledge of the music market, and a determination to succeed. "Yes, it would, but let's not let him know that until after we clinch the deal."

Chloe's mouth came open. She blinked at his tease, and then her laughter bubbled up. "Wow. That's some really great advice to keep in mind, *coach*."

Kellen looked into her sparkling eyes as she sipped her beverage and set it aside. The simple act of watching her take a drink worked on his senses. Once again, Kellen pushed the reaction aside, but doing so became increasingly difficult. He straightened and forced himself to focus. "Let me know your schedule for late next week or early next."

"I'll do that. What will I be singing?" She leaned forward eagerly.

"I have a producer I work with on demos. I'll hook the two of you up."

"Sounds great. Bring it on!"

Her face glowed, and she shook her head, genuinely dazzled, and, yes, he recognized the signs: she was enamored, too. Kellen could only watch, awed in his own way. He fed off her enthusiasm, this time ignoring the danger of falling, just a bit, for someone as winsome and appealing as Chloe Havermill.

5

"I think we're as ready for tonight's event as we'll ever be, folks. Let's wind it down and plan on reconvening late next week for a debriefing so we can review the final totals from tonight's charity gala at the clinic."

Eager to get home and indulge in a long, luxurious bath as well as some serious primp and polish time, Juliet responded to Pastor Gene Thomas's decree like the twenty or so others who gathered around a conference table at a meeting room of Trinity Christian Church: she smiled his way then assembled her file folders, pen, and notepad into a neat stack to carry out to her car.

Pastor Gene stilled their motions by continuing. "Before we scatter, though, I want to give some recognition to Juliet Rossiter who orchestrated not only tonight's event, but the development of this entire project."

Juliet cringed. She tried to push away the round of applause that accompanied Pastor Gene's kind words, but he wasn't finished yet. "The Rushton Free Clinic was Juliet's brainchild, and not only did she pour a substantial amount of funding into the project, but she also backed up monetary assistance with effort—solid sweat and muscle. Juliet, thank you for chairing the Board of Directors. God has worked through you and your team to turn Rushton from a dream into a reality. Furthermore, a dilapidated building in downtown Nashville is now a haven of hope for the underprivileged in need of both medical and emotional assistance."

A second round of applause circled the table, and Juliet leaned forward, directing her attention to Pastor Gene. "Unfortunately, you don't get off that easy. I expect to see you and everyone else at the clinic tonight, in black-tie and bling. Let's have a great time and celebrate the fact that we've all worked together to make the facility come to life. I didn't do this alone, so I refuse to take a big share of the credit, but I certainly appreciate everyone's support."

She looked around taking in the faces of the people she had worked with so extensively during the past eight months. Surrounding her were community leaders and parishioners of Trinity. Each of them was now her friend as well as her ally in the cause to provide health care to the underprivileged. A dream was now reality.

Since a family wasn't meant to be at the moment, Juliet loved pouring her energy—and her heart—into service projects like this. For now, until children came along, she felt God's call, and His pleasure, in those efforts.

When she stood, she felt a subtle tap against her shoulder. She turned and looked up into the teasing eyes of Tim Parkson. "You always so shy about accepting praise?"

She snorted lightly. "*Always.*"

"You shouldn't be. Seriously you've done a great job."

She was eager to get home but didn't want to hurt Tim's feelings with a quick brush off. She smiled at him, propping a hip against the table. "No, I just embrace the technique of effective recruiting."

"You sure didn't let any grass grow under my feet once I talked to you about volunteer opportunities here at Trinity."

Juliet laughed. "As soon as you joined, I knew I had to lasso that giving spirit of yours and put it to work!"

"Yeah—you're kind of relentless, and difficult to refuse." He studied her for a moment, and the underlying hesitance, the questions in his eyes, left Juliet puzzling. "I'm looking forward to finally meeting Kellen tonight."

Her body went tight. So that was it. Tim wondered about Kellen. It made Juliet a little sad that their paths hadn't yet crossed. In fact, after a Sunday service when he first joined, Tim stayed very close to her side during after church fellowship. Over coffee and doughnuts, they had chatted and become acquainted, and as Juliet clued him in on parish activities, she noticed the way Tim's eager warmth toned down when he caught sight of her wedding ring.

Until that point, Tim had thought she was single.

That misconception haunted Juliet long afterward. Kellen hadn't been to services at Trinity for a while now, and his absence was noticed, in a number of ways.

Juliet checked her watch, wanting distance now. Evasion. "Speaking of which, I better get home and get prepped."

"Juliet, can I speak to you for a second? It's about a media request from the Fox-TV affiliate. They're going to want to interview you tonight, and I didn't want you to be surprised by the request."

Pastor Gene's interruption was opportune, and gratefully received. Following a brief farewell to Tim, Juliet gave her full attention to her Pastor. He didn't speak right away. Instead, he watched Tim leave, then he addressed her with a kind, knowing look. "I figured I'd intervene so you could wrap up and get going."

OK, that was a strange and unexpected comment. "Ah…well…thanks…"

"He's well-meaning and kind. I just felt a call to step in."

And separate? What was going on here "What? I'm not trustable?" She framed the question like a tease, but her blood ran thick.

"You are, and I think Tim is trying to be, but with Kellen not as much of a presence here lately, I feel a bit protective …"

Though incomplete, the sentence convicted her thoroughly. An uncomfortable wobble in her stomach turned intense, an occurrence that overtook her more and more often these days. "I'm sorry about that."

Her façade crumbled, and shame burst through its holding walls. Pastor Gene touched her arm. "Don't apologize. Kellen's actions aren't your responsibility."

Juliet reared back, staring at him, now openly defensive. "You know, honestly, Kellen isn't…isn't…" Her shoulders sagged when defeat rode in. She simply couldn't find the words she needed to illustrate the feelings in her heart, but it seemed to her like Kellen was being judged, and she wanted to look out for him.

"Kellen is exactly what Trinity, and what God's kingdom, needs the most." Pastor Gene's gentle eyes and calm voice took away the sting she felt. "He's successful, charismatic, smart as can be, and he's got a heart that's tuned in to God. That's why I'm surprised by his absence lately. He's never been one to drift—and I've known him ever since you brought him here for the first time." Pastor Gene shrugged. "I married you two, and have loved watching your relationship grow. He's always stepped up and offered himself. He's genuine, and enthusiastic. I care about him a great deal. It's impossible not to. Help him see that, Juliet. Help bring him back home."

Juliet bit her lips together, because her chin quivered, and her throat went tight against on onslaught of sadness. She had been an emotional basket case lately, worrying about maintaining the happiness of her marriage, trying almost desperately to hold fast to God's hand while so many things in life conspired against her.

Pastor Gene's words rang with warning, and loving care. The confrontation, of a sort, forced Juliet to realize how adept she had become at acting. She put up a front these days, refusing to tarnish Kellen, or herself, by alluding to any kind of problems, but problems grew, regardless. Kellen was too wrapped up in work. He was straying from the basics in a number of ways, but so was she.

Juliet had gotten into the habit of covering for Kellen and burying her own needs in the work she did through Trinity Christian. It was beneficial, sure, but it was also a form of deflection. Kellen genuinely valued what precious little down time he had from his job, so he had fallen into the pattern of forsaking church on Sunday morning in favor of relaxing quietly at home and attempting to build in a peaceful stretch of time when he didn't have obligations or concerns other than stilling himself, and building up strength for the week ahead.

But Juliet knew, and Kellen used to know, that the kind of

strength he needed most came straight from time spent in God's house, in the arms of a loving faith community like Trinity.

How had he lost sight of that fact, and how had she allowed the situation to overtake them, unchecked? They were responsible to one another.

A lack of God's presence within their relationship was making a bad situation worse. Kellen had grown increasingly remote during the past several weeks, his distance intensifying to the point that only recently had she realized the blissful, passionate interlude of a month ago marked the last time they had made love. He was busy and distracted and wound up, so she gave him what seemed like some necessary space.

Was she in the wrong for that?

Pastor Gene wrapped a fatherly arm around Juliet's shoulder, seeming to decide he had said, and done, enough.

"Let's go and get spiffed up. That's going to take me hours, anyhow."

They shared a chuckle, but Juliet's heart was far from light. A corner needed to be turned. Maybe it could happen tonight when Kellen reconnected with their church friends and witnessed firsthand the results of her long hours of volunteering and service.

Lifted by expectation, holding onto a fledgling hope that their marriage might return to normalcy, Juliet strode from the church and through the parking lot. "He'll be there tonight," she murmured to herself. "He wouldn't miss it."

அ~ஒ

Kellen drove south out of Nashville, on his way to Platinum Echo Studios. Traffic willing, he'd be on time for a three o'clock meeting with Chloe and her assigned demo producer, Jason Missing. Chloe and Jason had spent the early part of the day recording, and Kellen was eager to hear the results. In addition, he had just this morning come upon a song from an up-and-coming writer that just begged for

Chloe's vocals. The title of the song was *Swing Time*, and with Chloe on lead, he had the feeling it would be a hit.

Right on time, Kellen entered the studio. Immediately his attention came to rest on Chloe. She sat before the massive, impossibly complex soundboard, but she kicked back comfortably in the padded, rolling chair she occupied, laughing with one of the technicians. She wore blue jeans, a white tank top and an open oxford shirt of purple that drew his focus to her amazing, violet eyes.

Kellen clicked the delete button on that image and approached the producer, who sat to Chloe's right. "Jason. What have we got?"

Jason delivered a smug, satisfied grin. "Pure magic. You ready to listen?"

"Absolutely." Kellen sat in a free mobile chair; he rolled into position on Chloe's left. Her smile of greeting spiked a pleasing level of heat through his system. Their gazes remained connected a beat or two longer than was absolutely necessary…

Kellen withdrew a pad of paper from his computer case and flipped to a blank page. While technicians cued the just completed recording, he claimed a pen and clicked it to readiness, registering the way Chloe leaned forward just slightly. Watching him.

The nearness of her worked a potent distraction, until the song began to play.

Kellen went still; he tuned out everything else, focusing on one of the modulator arms of the soundboard until his world zoomed in on nothing else except what he heard.

His brows furrowed.

Oh, man. Wrong, wrong, wrong.

Jason was not going to be a happy camper this afternoon.

In an operating procedure that felt as natural as could be, he started to scribble notes—notes that would only make sense to him, until the song underwent an intensive and relentlessly unforgiving review.

Synthesized her voice in the opening? Really? Pop rock instead of come-hither jazz. Why? Cheap song. Way too easy and common. Just another gorgeous female singer? No. Compelling. Mysterious. CH=Unobtainable. Image=high-end draw...? Alluring vibe needs to carry through the music...

The words poured forth. Kellen kept listening; he paused now and again to absorb the song. He chewed on the end of his pen, still completely lost to his thoughts and the music, which turned into a wholesale disappointment.

Awareness spread through his limbs in a flood when Chloe wheeled close.

Kellen realized, belatedly, she saw his somewhat provocative analysis.

She lifted her hair and tucked it to the side. She leaned against him slightly in order to even better see what he had written. Kellen didn't particularly like the rise of need her attention gave him, nor the fact that he had been somewhat revealed in his infatuation, but he couldn't refuse or stop the sensation either.

An emptiness at his core left Kellen to wonder: what was the harm in attraction? What was the harm in flirting and playing with the hot tingle of awareness and desire...?

He straightened abruptly when that thought pattern moved through him, and lent a pounding swiftness, and heat, to his body.

Into his mind echoed a one word warning and rebuke: *No.*

He turned slightly from Chloe as the song wound down. By way of added emphasis, he covered his notes with the previous pages of his legal pad. This chemical rush was as threatening as it was intoxicating. He wanted to heed what he knew was God's call. He wanted to stop this tempting vibration in its tracks.

Almost.

What would it feel like? Chloe's infatuation, her openness...it tasted delicious.

While he made the noble resolution of refusal, Kellen glanced her way. Chloe, he found, just looked at him—and into him—her eyes wide and gorgeous. Resolutions wavered.

"Well?" Jason's voice cut into the quiet that crested in at the close of the song.

Kellen shook his head and returned to his job. His verdict wasn't for Jason's consumption. Not yet, anyway. Kellen gave him a deliberately unreadable, noncommittal look. "Give me a few minutes with Chloe. I want to discuss it with her before we do an all-out review."

"Sounds good. I'll be in the break room when you're ready."

Once the door closed behind Jason, Chloe looked at Kellen with an alarmed expression. Their unspoken interplay of sensuality evaporated. "Umm...you...you don't seem real pleased. Wasn't it good?"

He could tell she was genuinely afraid she had let him, and herself, down. The display of fear melted his will to maintain apart from her. Kellen leaned forward, propping his elbows on his knees. While she watched, and waited, Kellen spoke. "Chloe, let me ask you something. Did that song speak to you?"

"Speak to me?" She drummed her fingertips against the armrest, tilting her head when she looked down at the floor. "It was fun, in a way—with spark and a beat that's catchy. I thought it would be successful..."

Her tentative response provided the roadmap Kellen needed to make his point. "I don't think this is the kind of music you've envisioned producing over the long term." She lifted a shoulder, wide-eyed. Her spirit, he could tell, was thrown open to his guidance—and that fact continued to pull at him in a way that was magnetic and powerful.

Kellen went on, trying to approach everything about her through his capacity as her agent—and nothing more. "This has nothing to do with you, Chloe. That song would sell like crazy—because of you, but not because of the music. You have the power to propel *both*."

"Me?"

"Yes, you. You're that strong a talent, and presence." The words settled between them. "That song, to me, diminished you as an artist. It was too techno-pop to play to who you really are"-- and everything he had written down, and felt, as he listened, --"you're better than that, Chloe. You're more than commercial pandering and fads. You're richly textured and evocative—that song is beneath you." He could all but hear that alluring voice of hers, backed up by a smoky saxophone or some lilting piano. She took a deep, trembling breath, and stared into his eyes. Equally provoked, Kellen diverted by consulting his notepad, only to realize once again that his analysis seemed more a poetic ode to the woman before him than a study of her musical talents.

Embarrassed once more by being so vividly exposed, he began to flip pages to a blank section, but Chloe stopped him short by settling her hands against his. "Wait a minute. Please?" Her quiet, earnest entreaty left Kellen in a place where all he could do was watch after her, and wait. She looked down and lightly moistened her lips. With careful deliberation, she paged back to the words he had written. The room suddenly went way too hot. Kellen felt tiny beads of sweat break out against his hairline and his chest...

"You see so much in me..." Her awed, sweet voice tickled against his inner ear.

Kellen's throat went parched. Chloe's hands slid against his, which remained in a tight clutch of the legal pad.

"I've never had anyone look at me"—she squirmed just a bit—"and the work I do, like you have. It's...compelling."

"Chloe..."

He spoke her name like a caution. Desperation curled through him, a desperation founded on the fact that he was happily married, a devout Christian, yet utterly magnetized toward this woman. And he had never, ever been looking to feel this way about anyone other than his wife.

Undeterred, Chloe continued, her voice a soft caress of sound. "No. Let me say this to you, Kellen." She paused for a beat. "I know you're married. I want no part in interfering. It's just that I love the way you've tuned in to me as a person and a performer. I respect you so much, and I want you to know I also respect your judgment on the song and what you want to do for me. Having you on my side is exciting and thrilling, and I want to do you proud. I want to vindicate the things you're seeing. If you lead, I'll follow. I have complete confidence and faith in everything I know you're going to be able to do for me."

In emphasis, she tilted the pad her way and openly reviewed each comment. She took them in, and the softness of her eyes, the way she lightly pressed her lower lip between her teeth made his stomach go tense and his breathing go unsteady.

"You guys through with your debrief?" Jason popped the question as he pushed through the studio door, arriving into their midst like a piercing blast of feedback.

Chloe and Kellen started, and Kellen smoothed over his uncharacteristic reaction by standing quick and going to his briefcase. From inside the front pocket, he extracted the CD of the song *Swing Time*.

"We're not crazy about it," Kellen said promptly, avoiding Chloe's pink-touched face. Kellen focused, forcing her out of his mind as he keyed in on Jason and the job he needed to do as her agent. "Jay, we're talking about image here, and both Chloe and I believe this song isn't a good fit for what we're trying to build."

Before Jason's wide eyes and furrowed brow could end in an argument, Kellen lifted the CD. "I'd like you to give this a listen. It's a little raw, and lacks the kind of polish you're going to give it in the studio, but the song is sensational. I think we can pull together an incredible orchestration and make this part of the demo we shop around."

Still a bit ruffled, Jason frowned but did as Kellen asked.

The song worked, just as Kellen hoped. By the end of the first chorus, all three of them were on board and enthused about what would come to be in the next few hours.

When they concluded, Jason left, needing to join a session taking place elsewhere in the building. Kellen packed away the CD of Chloe's work, a CD he fully intended to overnight to

Summit Pointe Records first thing in the morning. Alone with Chloe, Kellen didn't want to consider the length of time that would pass before he saw her again, so...an idea morphed into an undeniable course of action.

Kellen, walk in the spirit.

He braced against that piece of firm, but loving counsel. After all, the idea of sharing just an hour or two with Chloe in a more personal—but still very public—setting...

Walk in the spirit and you will not long to gratify the desires of the flesh.

Once again, Kellen pushed away the words. This wasn't about the flesh. All he wanted to do was ask her out to lunch. Nothing more. It's not as if he was entering into anything other than an extension of...

If you walk in darkness, you lie to yourself and live not in the truth. Submit to Me, Kellen, and the devil will flee.

Kellen steeled himself against the internal fight that was taking place at the crux of his soul. He packed up, even going so far as to keep his back to her when he very casually asked, "Would you interested in lunch sometime next week? It'd probably be a good idea for us to review the—"

"I'd love it."

She hadn't even let him finish the thought. Very slowly, Kellen turned his head. She stood across the room at a completely appropriate distance from him, but the connection between them ran hot, eager...and infinitely appealing. When he came upon her upturned lips, her bottomless, seeking eyes, his heart raced with an expectation that promptly drowned out God's voice and the call of his conscience.

6

A half-hour later, he was on the road, headed home. Removed from the influence of Chloe's presence, a sick sense of remorse washed through him. A thorough drenching of shame followed close behind.

What was he thinking, dallying with a woman—and the sanctity of his marriage—this way?

Kellen pounded a fist against the steering wheel of his car, wincing at the pain, and his own stupidity. Every sensory preceptor in his body went to work against him, calling to mind the way Chloe had looked at him, the way she had playfully but thoroughly challenged him, about the static electricity snapping between them...then there was the lunch date.

Worlds away from the present moment, Kellen unlocked the front door of his home and stepped into the foyer, eager to spend some time in peace and quiet with Juliet and get a handle on the tumult of his emotions. Restful time in the company of his wife would set his world on its proper axis once more and restore his peace of mind—and heart. Then, he'd cancel lunch with Chloe. Any other option left him sick inside.

I'm a better man than this. I'm a better husband than this. What's happening to me?

He'd pray tonight. In-depth. He had tried to do so at odd times during the past several weeks, but never at long enough intervals, and without fail, as soon as he'd drift into God's embrace, the world would encroach, as if the devil himself were bent on interfering. Well, not this time. He'd pull his Bible from the headboard of their bed and fall into the Word—

with Juliet as a prayer partner. He wanted this turmoil to cease.

When Kellen looked up, he nearly dropped the car keys, his phone, and the day's stack of mail, right there on the shimmering gray marble floor of the entryway.

Before him stood Juliet, resplendent in a knee-length dress of pale pink silk that swirled around her legs. The color added warm emphasis to the skin of her neck, the discreet V-shaped neckline drew his focus to the cross she always wore—her signature piece. Humble though it was, it belonged to them both. It was his wedding present to her, the reminder of which took the slow, sure tip of a pin strike to his heart. Kellen closed his eyes for an instant but fought back the urge he had to coil in on himself.

Juliet's hair was pulled back slightly, into loose curls that trailed down her back. She looked gorgeous, and the impact of her sparkling eyes left him breathless.

Guilty, too.

In an attempt at spiritual and emotional reconciliation, Kellen realized nothing—and no one—not even Chloe—captured him like his wife. He was being a fool. Wreaking havoc, just like God had shown, and warned. He needed to straighten up promptly.

Juliet looked down, regarding her ensemble, right to the shoes, and she didn't look confident; she seemed puzzled. "You're staring. Is this OK for tonight?"

OK? She was a vision. Was she becoming that unused to his pleasured approval? Kellen licked his parched lips, falling in love with her all over again. No one he had ever met possessed such sweetness and unfettered light. That's what had drawn him to her in the first place.

"You're absolutely breathtaking. Where are you headed? I was really looking forward to being with—"

She gaped at him. "Where am I headed? Kellen, are you serious?" The mood between them took a sudden and heavy nosedive. "You're barely home in time to change and get out the door."

Her leading, expectant look didn't help any. He was as blank as an empty canvas. So, he shrugged, openly confused while he awaited the brush strokes of her explanation.

Juliet's shoulders sagged. Her eyes went cloudy with sadness and disappointment. Her lips trembled just slightly when she turned away from him, toward the hall table, where she began to assemble and switch a few items from her every day purse to an evening bag. "It's the benefit opening of the Rushton Free Clinic."

He remembered now, and he felt miserable for forgetting. Juliet's defeat and sorrow hit him far worse than her anger ever could have.

"As the largest contributors to its creation, we're expected at the gala."

The very last thing in the world he wanted to do was hobnob at a charity function, but they were obligated, and he couldn't believe he had neglected to recall the culmination of a project that had driven Juliet for months now, and meant so much to her.

"Can you give me ten minutes to climb into my tux?" He infused the request with as much enthusiasm as he could, but he was worn out—at every level. The day had been typically long, and residual shockwaves from Chloe's presence still worked through his system. He was, at present, a tapped out mess, sinking deeper and deeper into an extremely dangerous quagmire.

Plus, Juliet saw right through him. She nodded, giving him a quick, shallow smile before returning her focus to assembling her evening bag.

Kellen dashed up the stairs, intending to make amends by double-timing his way into black-tie clothing.

⊰⊱

Juliet applied a glossing of lipstick, fighting the sting of tears. Kellen's cell phone began to vibrate and slide across the top of the hall table where he had dropped it next to his car keys. He had forgotten about tonight, and that took a bite straight out of her heart. She had been excited about the gala all week, looking forward to the success of seeing a project through to completion—a project that would benefit hundreds of thousands of displaced families in need of medical care.

But, typical to a growing pattern, they hadn't discussed the benefit recently—or anything else of import. She was beginning to feel like she just didn't matter anymore. Her efforts to create something of value, something of her own that had meaning and spirit felt insignificant now.

She ignored the call alert, and Kellen's phone went quiet and dark. She sighed, looking at her reflection. She felt out of sorts and out of her element these days. Burdened. The zesty expectation that had accompanied her throughout the day evaporated into a wisp of fast-vanishing fog.

Kellen's phone vibrated once more. Concerned that someone might need to get in touch with him on an urgent basis, she picked up his phone and turned toward the stairwell, intending to deliver it to him. She puzzled at the text that scrolled across the top of the lit-up home screen.

The demo session 2day was like a dream! Tks 4 being there. Looking forward to lunch nxt week. C

Previous to that text was ID information on the missed call that had come in just moments ago. The person's name, whom Kellen had obviously included in his contact list, was Chloe Havermill.

C.

Juliet's stomach lurched violently then wobbled against a rush of strong, hot nausea. She rested a hand against her abdomen, willing herself to settle and go still. Nausea was hitting her more and more frequently of late. Further proof of how unsettled and sad she had become.

Kellen had been talking about this Chloe woman a lot lately. He was enthused by her level of talent and had eagerly signed her on as a client. So the demo session is what had occupied his time this afternoon. And lunch was coming up?

Juliet swallowed back a lump of emotion, wishing her

heart would stop racing, wishing her imagination wouldn't run away with her just because she was trapped by a feeling of inadequacy. Sure, they needed to get to work on their relationship again, but she refused to be a clingy alarmist and go off the deep end when her marriage to Kellen had always been so strong and full of mutual caring. Kellen's world revolved around many such women. Never had she been given a cause to doubt him. Why would working with Chloe Havermill be any different?

Juliet closed her eyes, going dark against the answer that instantly came to her mind: because *Kellen's* different. Because *you're* different.

It was like she had told Pastor Gene this afternoon, Kellen's mood, his focus, had changed lately. Increasingly intense and withdrawn, he seemed overwhelmed, and that was completely out of character.

She climbed the stairs and opened the door to their bedroom. Kellen sat on a padded bench at the end of their bed, tying the laces of his dress shoes. Juliet stood in the entryway for the briefest of moments, taking him in. She had never seen such a handsome man. Thick waves of dark brown hair framed an olive-skinned face with strong lines and a squared jaw, deep-set, compelling eyes of darkest brown capped by a smile that had always sent her heart into a free-fall of dizzy pleasure...

Moving through the room, she joined her husband and handed off the phone. She drew in a deep breath, trying hard not to fall into suspicions and doubts. "Your phone is kind of going crazy. I thought someone might be trying to get a hold of you about something important."

"Thanks."

She watched him review the call, and the text. He didn't react; he slipped the phone into the breast pocket of his tux jacket and stood, walking to the dresser where he hunted, presumably, for a pair of cufflinks.

"I'm ready to leave whenever you are."

He kept his back to her. The lack of reaction, the too-smooth deflection, only served to tear additional holes in the fabric of her confidence and the resolution she had made to stay calm. Still, reaction or not, Juliet knew Kellen's nuances well enough to recognize the intensity he carried, the tightness that shadowed his movements.

He tried to hide the fact that something was going on, but Juliet wasn't fooled. And that something, she feared, was not going to be good. For either one of them.

❧❧

The Rushton clinic was located in one of the older buildings of central Nashville. As he drove up, Kellen took note of the large wooden sign, oval in shape, fastened to the front of the red brick exterior. He stopped the car at a double-door entrance thrown open to admit the evening's visitors.

After leaving their car in the care of a valet, he escorted Juliet inside. In an automatic gesture, he kept a guiding hand against the small of her back while he took in the results of her work. The interior was beautifully appointed—fresh and newly refurbished. Recessed ceiling lights shone down upon a hand-painted mural of rolling green hills, wildflowers, and trees that covered the top portion of the walls. Patient seating was complimented by end tables full of magazines and topped by thick, leafy green plants. A small tropical-style aquarium and child-sized tables with plastic crates of toys nearby polished off the décor. Directly opposite the entrance was a reception area backed by rows of metal shelving for patient files.

Kellen was beyond impressed. Juliet had been instrumental in bringing this project from concept to fruition, and the end result was amazing. He watched her, his regard unnoticed as she accepted a few ready greetings and hugs.

Her focus didn't stray from him for long though. Excited and eager, she led the way through the waiting room. "Come on back and see the rest!"

Sliding carefully past the close press of wait staff and

visitors, Kellen followed her lead. They walked through a doorway that led to the second half of the clinic. Here, exam rooms and offices formed a circumference.

"There's Pastor Gene, and Tim." Juliet tilted her head to indicate a small group of people who mixed together not far away. When they stepped up, Juliet initiated a prompt introduction. "Kellen, I'd like you to meet Tim Parkson. Tim, this is my husband, Kellen Rossiter."

"Tim, it's good to meet you." They exchanged cordial nods and a handshake.

Juliet slipped her arm through Kellen's, and her fingertips weaved through his; the fit was perfect. "In addition to being part of the clinic team, Tim's a new parishioner at Trinity, and the newest member of our weekly Bible study group."

"I've been hoping we'd get to meet, Kellen," Tim said. "I have to compliment Juliet. She's incredible, and she's done a fantastic job getting this clinic off the ground."

Tim's comment served to remind Kellen of how long it had been since he had gone to church with Juliet and cued him in further that her faith remained strong, and important—important enough that its roots had grown far and deep despite his recent neglect and failure to do the same with his walk with God. His own roots needed to return to nourishing soil, and he knew it.

The recognition was disturbing.

"Tim found out what I was doing and volunteered his services." Juliet gave Tim a grateful look. "We're very lucky to have his help."

Tim shook his head and arched a brow. "I've said it before, but it bears repeating. You missed your calling. You're an exceptionally gifted salesperson. I was contributing before I even knew what hit."

Juliet slipped a stray curl of hair behind her ear. She ducked her head and blushed. "Sure, sure, sure. You recognized a need and you're helping. I appreciate it, and so will the families who come here for medical care."

"What is it you'll be doing, Tim?" Kellen regarded the

man. Tall. Blond hair and blue eyes. Same age group as himself and Juliet. He possessed an appealing, bookish vibe. Steadiness. Maybe it was his own guilty conscience that did the prodding, but Kellen found himself looking at Tim's ring finger. It was empty. That caused Kellen to frown, given the easy, comfortable way Tim related to Juliet.

"I'm a psychologist. My work here will consist mostly of counseling teens in crisis. It's my specialty." He glanced at Juliet. "You don't have anything to drink yet, Jules. Can I get you something?"

"I've got that covered," Kellen cut in smoothly. "We just arrived, and I wanted the tour first, so we ignored everything else." Tim stepped back, and tension eased from Kellen's shoulders. Mission accomplished. "Juliet, I'll be right back."

At the bar, he retrieved two flutes of champagne then rejoined his wife, handing her one of the crystal glasses. She moved away from the people closest to her and turned toward him, cutting them off from the group so she could speak to him exclusively.

Her eyes sparkled more beautifully than the golden liquid that burst with life. "No tonic and lime tonight?"

"Absolutely not."

Tim had moved on, thankfully, and Kellen used the private moment to stroke a fingertip slowly down her jaw line. "This is a celebration."

He could have sworn she lit up, from the inside out. He tapped his flute against hers and they prepared to sip.

Unexpectedly, Juliet tilted her glass away; a teasing glint enlivened her eyes. "You realize, of course, that you've trusted me to handle a glass of champagne."

Kellen widened his eyes in a display of mock horror. "What was I thinking?" Juliet giggled, and the sound played like a song through his heart. He regarded her tenderly. "Champagne changed my life, you know."

This time Juliet's eyes went wide; she gasped playfully. "Really? What a coincidence. It changed mine, too." They shared a private smile, and Juliet winked at him. "Thank you, by the way."

"For what?" Kellen looked around. "This is all you, love, and I'm incredibly proud." He shifted slightly, wanting to alleviate the discomfort he felt for letting her down. "I'm sorry about what happened earlier."

She nestled close. Her expression went soft, and full of forgiveness. "That's OK. I know you've been busy, and you were tired. But I also want you to know I couldn't have done any of this without you, and your support." She kissed his cheek, then looked deep into his eyes, whispering, "You're the most impossibly handsome and charming man. I'm a lucky woman." She glanced back at Tim. "And...he means well, you know."

Kellen didn't bother stifling a smirk. "Obviously."

Juliet rested her hand on his arm and gave a light laugh. "I like that even after eight years of marriage you still get jealous."

Over the top of Juliet's head, he looked Tim's way. The man was deep in conversation with a few members of Trinity—Pastor Gene included. "I'm not worried. For example, he doesn't know how much you prefer Juliet to Jules."

"True. And you've never called me Jules. Even at the beginning."

"I never will, either."

She watched him, waiting to see where that statement might lead.

"Your name is poetry. I'll never shorten it. I love it too much as is."

Desire rippled through the air and encircled him, moving straight from her soul into his. "I've missed you so much lately."

The words escaped in a quiet rush, giving voice to the ache he sensed within her. It had been way too long since they'd made love. A need for connection, for intimacy, swirled around them, but Kellen was finding it difficult to handle physicality with his wife right now. His heart was leading him to a place where he felt unworthy of sharing her body and spirit in such a sacred way.

"I'm sorry for that, too, Juliet." He wanted to elaborate, knew he needed to elaborate, but the words just wouldn't come. Tonight, he would find a way. Tonight he would revere her and touch her the way he always had, in the way that had always come to him so naturally.

Perhaps she sensed his confusion. When he didn't continue right away, her brightness of demeanor went a little dim, but she kept on smiling, and kept on trying. Mentally, Kellen scrabbled for purchase—and failed.

She ended the moment by tucking her arm smoothly through his, directing them toward a group not far away. "Let's do a lap of the room."

ॐ

As the party progressed, Kellen and Juliet mixed and mingled—sometimes side-by-side, sometimes making their way to separate groups. In those moments, Kellen found he couldn't keep his eyes off her. Her energy and passion for the project transformed into a radiance that not only drew people to her, it filled the room. She possessed a star power all her own, and that recognition claimed his focus, feeding a fresh and unexpected sense of wonder about his wife.

Kellen made ready to rejoin her, but first he wanted to grab a glass of ice water. The clinic was crowded now, packed with VIP's, and the heat level inched upward.

Had he been too disconnected from her to realize the seamless way she had pulled this entire venture together? The busyness of her life, a level of busyness he had come to resent of late, made a lot more sense to him now. The recognition didn't make the distance any easier to reconcile, but he looked at his wife's world through a revised and very vivid frame of reference.

While he waited for his beverage, Kellen turned to watch her lean close and whisper to a nearby guest, then others approached and she performed introductions, touched an arm or two in a natural show of affection.

The dress she wore shimmered, flowing around her legs, capturing the dim overhead lights. Her hair danced around her shoulders. Swept into his observations, Kellen watched her chat with members of Rushton, answer some questions, and accept comments from guests who happened by. She tucked a wave of hair behind her ear as she leaned in to listen to a party attendee amidst the noise level of a full-throttle party.

"She's a remarkable woman." Reluctantly, Kellen turned away from watching Juliet when Pastor Gene stepped up and offered the compliment. "Furthermore, I like it when a husband watches his wife with such open adoration."

"I'm amazed by what she's accomplished. This has been a great night. Congratulations."

Pastor Gene placed a drink order; he started to chuckle while his gaze traveled to the spot across the room where Juliet stood, now bathed in television lights. Microphone at the ready, a reporter seemed to be asking her questions. "Look how natural she is with the media. Wish I could say the same. I just finished an interview for *The Tennessean* and can state without question that I'm not cut out for the spotlight. Too nerve wracking."

Kellen laughed in commiseration, but then he noticed something that caused him to go utterly still. Juliet gestured for Tim to join her. He stepped up to Juliet's side, and it looked like he began to answer some questions for the television crew as well. Once the interview concluded, the news team faded into the crowd. Juliet and Tim exchanged a long look, then burst into laughter, high-fiving. Juliet's laughter carried to Kellen, unmistakable to him despite the mix of a hundred other conversations and background party noise.

When the pair shared a short, tight hug, Juliet's flushed cheeks and bright smile spoke eloquently of a woman thoroughly enjoying herself and in her element.

"Kellen? Are you OK?"

Kellen snapped alert, remembering he wasn't alone. He'd been caught gaping, and since he had to force his muscles to unwind, he was pretty sure had also been caught frowning at the vignette.

He couldn't reply. Instead, thoughts of Chloe crowded in. Images of her moved through his mind and slayed his conscience. Emotional turmoil refused to let him rest and find enough peace to establish balance. His heart, his wife, and the woman he couldn't seem to shake combined against him, and Kellen didn't know how to escape the chaos.

Pastor Gene had known him for nearly nine years. The man had counseled Kellen and Juliet before their marriage, and remained a trusted advisor and friend, so Kellen braved it up enough to come a little bit clean. "I've been thinking about how many Sunday services I've missed lately."

The statement wasn't meant to placate, either. The evening shocked Kellen into realizing how much goodness he had missed, or simply ignored, during the past several months. No wonder his heart was in such turmoil. He was slipping away from God, his faith, and his marriage. Watching Juliet provided another solid wake up call to the distance his physical and emotional absence had caused between them. Juliet had continued to bloom within the love of the Trinity family. The result was pure radiance.

Meanwhile, what had straying away from fundamentals done to *him*?

Pastor Gene followed the path of Kellen's gaze. He stepped into the breach caused by Kellen's silence with a nudge and an intent look. "Tim is new, and he's eager. He's been tireless about his efforts to get this clinic going and become part of Trinity. Juliet's only focus is you, though. Always has been." The words sunk in. "I'm sure she misses you being with her at church, too, Kellen." Another pause fell between them. Kellen could almost feel Pastor Gene testing the waters. "You've always been one of the guys I rely on to help motivate and energize our parishioners. You've always participated, and I'm grateful for that. You have the gift of sincerity and magnetism, and those are tools God can put to great use. I've missed seeing you at Trinity, too. The men's fellowship group hasn't been the same without you lately. You're important."

Used to be, Kellen felt like saying. *Pastor Gene, if you could see the inner workings of my heart, you'd be shocked and horrified. I used to react so self-righteously when I read stories in the Bible about those who transgressed and stepped into what they knew were bad choices. Look at me now. Why am I finding it so difficult to rebuke what I know is wrong?*

Pastor Gene didn't condemn. He didn't need to. The kind, gentle reminders accomplished the objective of prompting Kellen back home, to his faith.

And his marriage.

A chilly bead of condensation skated down the side of Kellen's glass, then his fingertips. Genuinely contrite, he nodded, staring at the glistening lines of moisture instead of Pastor Gene. "I'm sorry for that absence. I'll be there Sunday. I'm looking forward to it."

He meant it, too. The conversation with Pastor Gene ended when Juliet approached, still aglow in the success of the evening. Her gaze touched Kellen with an intimacy and depth of feeling that worked supernatural warmth through his soul. Pastor Gene moved on as Kellen took hold of Juliet's hand and kissed her cheek.

"Tim saved me from making a total fool of myself," she exclaimed. "The reporters started asking about psychological studies and therapy programs being offered. I had no idea what to say! I was terrified!"

"I was watching. You seemed smooth as satin." Kellen fingered back a few tumbled curls of hair from where they swung against her shoulders. Longing drenched her eyes in a visual so acute he was left speechless.

"I love being together like this," she whispered.

Kellen regarded her intently for a moment. "Me, too."

Juliet nodded and settled her hand gently against his cheek. "Let's make an effort to keep connected like this, OK?"

Kellen took a breath, nodding, praying they could. "That's what I want, too. It's important."

"It's just…" Juliet fingered the slender strap of her evening bag, where it hung on her shoulder. He could tell she fought to find the right words. "We're so blessed, Kellen."

He struggled for a moment as well, but found a smile. When it dawned, he hoped it would slide straight into her heart. She deserved that—and so much more. "You honor me, and us, every day, Juliet."

She rose up on tiptoes to feather a light, easy kiss against his lips. "I'm so glad you're mine."

Kellen shoved back the stomach-sinking double standard in which he was tangled. He never, ever wanted to hurt Juliet. She was precious, and he loved her deeply. Furthermore, the commitment they shared to one another was absolute. *Until now.* The words infiltrated, a pair of creeping villains that left Kellen angry about where his life and his heart were headed.

All along, he had figured he could work with Chloe in a professional setting and walk away from her each day.

He had grossly underestimated her impact.

7

"Tell them to take the offer up by two or it's a no-go." The next day, Kellen wandered the length of his office, headset in place as he conducted—and hopefully concluded—a sticky bit of telephone negotiating.

"Kellen, you're a shark. There's no way Landfield Records can agree to that. Thom Knapp is good, but—"

Kellen shrugged. "Then I'll let Thom know. Caulfield Group loves the deal. They want him."

He let that bit of coaxing information dangle. Kellen stuffed his hands into the pockets of his crisply pressed black slacks. He looked out the window behind his desk. Far below, life swarmed in the form of people in motion, traffic inching along. In the distance, he spied birds in flight, and tiny cotton-ball clouds that sailed across the sky. He caught sight of the Ryman. The music icon called to mind Chloe and her delighted reaction at seeing it from this perch high above. He stopped a wistful smile in its tracks.

The phone silence lengthened, but Kellen was in no hurry for the decision he already knew was coming. He was as sure of it as his next heartbeat.

"Two percent additional and we go to contract?"

Kellen's smile spread slowly. That translated to roughly an extra two million dollars to his client. Not a bad day's work. "Two and you'll have a messengered contract before the close of business. Let's get Thom producing, touring, and recording again. We want this buttoned down as much as you do."

"Yeah. For a price." Kellen heard computer key-clicks in the background and could only imagine that Jeff Cox, who represented Landfield Records, was already tapping out a notice to the label's top brass to inform them Thom Knapp was staying put. Kellen knew better than anyone that keeping their current triple-platinum contemporary rock artist on the label's roster was of vital importance. Then came the final answer. "Ship the contract."

"Done, Jeff." Kellen paused. "You won't regret this. That's why you're doing it. You've made a good investment."

A sigh traveled the length of their connection, then a wry, grudging chuckle. "We better not. He's got to keep performing."

"Agreed, and absolutely."

The call ended and Kellen removed the earpiece, stretching his arms above his head. His suit coat was off, draped against the back of his chair. His white cotton shirt and gold patterned tie completed the ensemble with necessary polish. After all, in the entertainment industry, image was everything.

The Knapp contract had been simmering back-and-forth for over a month. Now, Thom could stay at Landfield Records, which is what he wanted to begin with. Landfield was where his career had been born. Now he'd receive a reward for his loyalty and success.

Yep. Not a bad morning at all.

Still, Jeff was wrong about one thing. Today's deal wasn't about price tags and dollar signs. Not completely. Sure, he fed off the excitement of the chase to land great talent, but it also tasted great to emerge on the winning side of tough negotiations. He took care of his clients because they took care of him.

Perhaps that was another part of what had him mixed up about Chloe. Did his feelings have something to do with a protective instinct he couldn't seem to resist?

The thought circled him around to what needed to be done in that regard. He expelled a hard breath—leaned forward and eyed his phone. There was no sense putting it off. He needed to call her and cancel their lunch date...*appointment*... he amended internally. Kellen reached for the receiver; he shook his head. Standing, he reinserted his earpiece, already knowing he'd need to pace off excess energy during the course of this call. Why did the idea of hearing her voice have his heart hammering in his chest?

Kellen started to dial. Cancelling on her would be easy enough—he could call on any number of worthwhile, legitimate excuses...

The office intercom buzzed, jarring him, leaving him to growl beneath his breath. Next came the voice of his assistant. "Kellen?"

"Hey, Anna. What's up?" Kellen remained standing, fisting his hands on his hips. With care, he schooled his voice to smooth courtesy.

"I've got Frank Simpson on hold, and he said it's urgent that he speak to you. He called just as you hung up with Landfield."

Kellen's heart started pounding all over again, for an entirely different reason.

"Transfer him in, Anna. Thanks." Kellen picked up on the first ring. "Frank. How are you?"

"This one is going to cost me as it is, Rossiter. I already know that—but so help me, if you put me in the middle of a bidding war to land this woman for my label, I swear..."

Succinct to the point of being abrupt, without any form of preamble, Frank Simpson performed a tirade that was half-serious, half-humorous. The president of Summit Pointe had clearly heard Chloe's demo. Kellen looked at his watch and did some quick calculating. Overnight shipping would have delivered the CD by eight o'clock in the morning. Not even an hour and a half later, the man had already listened to *Swing Time*. Better yet? He was openly hooked.

Kellen walked the space behind his desk. "I take it you're interested in meeting her."

Frank Simpson's chuckle was laced with a sardonic undercurrent. "Don't gloat. It's beneath you."

"I'm not gloating. I'm simply asking if you're interested

in—"

"Monday, four o'clock. Who's my competition on this girl?"

"Frank, c'mon now. Do you really think I'd tell you that?" On the inside, expectation caught fire and spread with wild abandon. *You don't have competition, Frank,* Kellen thought. *Your record label is exactly where she belongs—it's a perfect fit.* But he played it cool. "I need to check schedules. Let me call you right back."

"Don't keep me waiting, Rossiter, because I'm about to bet the farm you already knew I'd be calling the minute I heard her voice—and the song is fantastic. Posturing aside, she's a phenomenal talent."

"Give me an hour to confirm the meeting."

"Done."

When he disconnected the call and removed his earpiece, Kellen let out a short, satisfied whoop. He laughed and clapped his hands together to punctuate the moment. All of a sudden, he was grateful he hadn't cancelled lunch with Chloe.

He couldn't wait to tell her the news.

8

"Hey, Chloe." Kellen joined her at the restaurant table, where she sat perusing a menu. He bent to kiss her cheek before even thinking about it. He froze for half a heartbeat afterwards but refused to allow himself to second-guess a simple, innocent gesture of welcome and affection. He moved past the moment quickly, though the satin of her skin lingered in his mind.

"Hey, Kellen. How are you?"

Bursting to tell you what just happened, he thought, but he wanted to draw out the anticipation...just for a few minutes. "I'm running behind. Sorry if I kept you waiting."

"Don't even think about it. I wasn't here that long." Chloe was breezy and friendly—on the surface. In her gaze, he detected an unmistakable degree of deeper pleasure. She unfolded a menu and watched while he claimed the seat across from her. She propped her forearms against the table and leaned toward him. "I have to admit, I was people watching."

"People watching?" He could hardly contain himself about the phone call, but he opened his menu as well and reviewed the selections. "What caught your eye?"

"Before *you* came in?"

Kellen's head jerked up, and Chloe's lips curved in a teasing way. Teasing or not, Kellen was hit so hard by the words he almost forgot about Frank Simpson.

"Do you see that older couple over there?" Chloe continued, her tone quiet and conspiratorial. She glanced toward a table not far away from their window seat at The Palm Restaurant. "He just handed her a rose and a present. I think it's their anniversary, or her birthday or something. He kissed her hand, and she blushed." Chloe shook her head, returning her focus to the menu. "That long together, and she blushed. I want a man who still treats me like a princess and still makes me blush when I'm in my golden years."

Unsettled by that chain of thought, Kellen wanted to change the direction of this conversation—quickly. "I don't blame you." He pulled out his cell phone. "I've got something brewing, by the way."

"Oh?"

He nodded, studying his contact list as he scrolled through names and numbers. "What's your schedule like for late Monday afternoon?"

Chloe shrugged. "I have to be at Iridescence, but not until six o'clock or so. Why?"

"Good deal. Hang on a second." Kellen activated his desired call, and then focused on her, letting his grin and eagerness shine through. "Frank, it's Kellen…um-hmm…yeah, with almost thirty minutes to spare. We're on. Four o'clock Monday…yep…see you then."

Chloe's eyes widened when she absorbed his side of the conversation—and its implications. He ended the call, and she clamped a hand across her mouth. Her hand dropped weakly. "You can't possibly be serious," she murmured.

"I'm not the one who's serious. Frank Simpson is."

"Don't tease."

Kellen snickered. "I'm not, Chloe. He called me almost immediately after receiving your demo."

Their server approached. While they placed an order for surf and turf and Caesar salad, Kellen noticed the way Chloe steadied herself and absorbed the shock of the news. As lunch progressed, they shared plans and strategy for the meeting. The more they relaxed over a delicious, leisurely meal, the more they laughed. The more they laughed, the closer they became. In a natural evolution, their conversation strayed from strict work boundaries to personal questions and getting to know one another outside the parameters of being a singer and an agent. Doorways to the personal, and to deeper knowledge of one another, slowly swung open.

"Tell me about your wife. I noticed her picture on your desk when we met at your office." Wearing an expectant expression, with no pretense or guile, she opened up Kellen's own version of Pandora's Box.

Kellen forced panic aside. Discussing Juliet...with Chloe...would *not* be an optimal direction for this luncheon. "She's...everything." Kellen shrugged, looking into the near distance. "She's beautiful. Inside and out."

Silence rode in. "I noticed that in the photo. Somehow, I'd expect nothing less." Chloe's smile bloomed, and she settled her elbows on the table, resting her chin on her folded hands. The direct impact of her eyes robbed him of breath. "How long have you been married?"

"Almost nine years."

"I'm impressed."

"Nine years is impressive?"

"Sadly, yes. In this day and age anything over five years has become long-term commitment."

He could tell she was only half joking. Kellen shook his head, and didn't buy into her lighthearted tone. "I don't see it that way. Talk to me about impressive and long-term once we've hit the forty- or fifty-year mark—maybe like that couple you were watching at the next table. *That's* impressive."

Chloe regarded him in silence for a moment. She picked up her fork but didn't start eating again right away. "Your wife is a lucky lady. And *you're* lucky." Chloe stopped pushing the food around and settled back in her chair. "I'm on the dating wheel, and I have to tell you, it's nothing short of crazy and disheartening."

"I don't envy you having to deal with it, but I can't imagine you having difficulties. You're successful, you're attractive, and you live in a world full of interesting people and ample opportunities."

"Yes, Kellen—*very* interesting people." With an arched brow and a pointed look, she let those words, and their meaning, settle in between them.

Prickles of pleasure, and fear, danced along his skin. Kellen reared back and lifted his hands. "Come on. Seriously."

"First of all I am serious, but you're a perfect case in point. You're handsome, charming, and interesting—but you're married. Others I've met are, say, freshly broken up with a girlfriend, or I find out they're pursuing me out of a misplaced sense of fame and the glamour of being with a singer. Then there are the ones who are simply too shallow to look beyond outward packaging to what lies beneath." She shrugged. "Like I said. Crazy."

"Don't lose faith, Chloe. I've always held to the belief that everyone has a second half, a person created just for them, by God. You'll find your way to that person."

The words were meant to reassure and deflect her obvious interest in him. Kellen set his utensils aside and wiped his mouth on a linen napkin that he resettled across his lap.

Chloe ate a bite of salad while she studied him intently. "Do you really believe that?"

"Yes, I do."

She seemed subdued. "You really believe God works that closely in our lives? That personally?"

"With all that I am." He looked at her squarely now, reinforced by the belief system he had held onto his entire life. For both their sakes, he wanted to make that point clear.

"I envy you that level of conviction. I suppose I believe in a supreme being—in a creator of the universe and all that, but to me, that entity feels remote. Inaccessible. I don't see God, or whatever, as being that deeply involved." She chuckled. "After all, I'm sure He's far too busy to trouble Himself over my simple comings and goings. You might say my beliefs are more spiritual than God-centered."

Oh, Chloe, Kellen thought, *you're searching, but you're misguided...and being with you is a wonderful opportunity to evangelize—something I'm normally able to do without even thinking about it. Instead, when I'm near you, I wander into a place that offers an intoxicating thrill but scares me to death because it stems from a spot in my spirit that's not aligned to God, and what I know to be true.*

While his thoughts roiled, Chloe smoothed a subtle wrinkle in the tablecloth. Kellen rested a hand on top of hers to still the nervous gesture. "Then take a closer look at the life around you, Chloe. Find what God is showing you in the life you live and the gifts He's given you. You'll discover a whole different world. A better world. Believe me. The reason you feel remote is because you haven't found Him yet, that's all. He's as close as your next heartbeat, but you have to want Him there first. He doesn't enter where He's not invited."

When the waiter approached to check on their satisfaction with the meal, Kellen noticed the way Chloe watched him, the curiosity and attentiveness, the attraction she tried to mask. Despite his convictions, he was in danger here, and he knew it, because in her eyes he detected a new and even more powerful level of emotion.

Chloe looked at him as though he were the one who held the answers she sought, but Kellen knew better. Right now, he was nobody's role model, and he recognized unequivocally that only God had the answers Chloe needed to find.

"You make a very compelling statement for your faith."

Kellen directed his gaze to the water goblet he retrieved. He took a long gulp to compose himself and to quench the intimacy of her focus.

With a fork, she picked at the remains of her meal. He saw the motions for what they were—distraction. He pulled the napkin from his lap, setting it on the table. He leaned toward her, tilting his head until he earned her attention and she looked up. He sank into her eyes with no effort whatsoever.

"What's wrong, Chloe?"

She took a breath and looked away. The fall of her hair obscured his view of her face, but she tucked it over her shoulder. "I'm sorry for seeming so awestruck. That's not the vibe I want to give you. Really. But you're a pretty knock-em-out type of person."

Once again, she worked through him like a potion he couldn't resist. He knew she was vulnerable to him. He longed to deepen the intimacy of the moment. He wanted to take hold of her hand, draw her closer—and closer still…

Kellen. No. Do not regard a woman lustfully, lest you commit adultery in your heart…

God's irrefutable and powerful voice prompted him to keep in place, but doing so was tantamount to torture. God's presence was firm, though. A glimmer of sunlight beamed through the nearby window, shimmering against the metal of his wedding band. In response, trying hard to rebuke his desires, Kellen closed his hand into a fist, deliberately protecting the symbol of his commitment to Juliet.

Yet, here he sat, confused and transfixed by a compelling woman.

A short time later, lunch concluded and a leather folio rested on the table that contained their settled bill. They stood and Kellen moved into place from behind, promptly taking custody of her coat. Holding it open, he waited, absorbing a glance and a beat of affected silence from Chloe before she tucked her arms inside and adjusted the fit. When she began to reach up, intending to lift her hair free of the collar, Kellen took the initiative.

Something inside him, something heretofore inaccessible, wavered mightily when straight strands of black satin slipped through his fingers. The scent of her drifted to him, full of a subtle and provocative spice.

Chloe took a long look back at him over her shoulder, and Kellen moved away but kept a guiding hand against the small of her back when they exited the restaurant.

Desires and appetites not in keeping with My truth will wreak destruction in your life, Kellen.

Kellen steeled himself, jarred again by God's prodding voice and his own knowledge of right versus wrong. At that precise moment, Chloe happened to tilt her head in his direction, capturing his gaze. She smiled into his eyes in a way that was so bright and so ripe with meaning and admiration it electrified his senses. In that instant, Chloe reached a spot of his heart that he had closed in a willing resolution to any other woman but his wife.

9

Kellen needed to straighten up.

As he had said to Pastor Gene at the Rushton benefit, it had been way too long since he attended services at Trinity. That was a fact he could easily address. When he took enough time to examine his jumbled feelings, he knew he needed to find respite, and peace, for his mind. God alone would give that to him, and today presented a great starting point. A return to worship, then a Sunday afternoon spent with Juliet and her family at her parents' house would work against Chloe's siren call.

In the bathroom Sunday morning, Kellen double-checked his appearance in the mirror while Juliet moved fast through the entryway. She breezed by and opened a cabinet drawer. There, she hunted and pecked for makeup supplies. A second or two later, her eyes tagged his in the mirror.

Kellen answered the unspoken question. "I thought I'd go to church with you."

"Really?"

The smile that burst across Juliet's face forced Kellen to realize how much this meant to her.

"I know it's been a while. I've slid into bad habits. With my Saturday nights taken up by events, and talent scouting, it's been easy to ignore the church schedule so I could sleep in, or enjoy a day without any obligation except rest. That's wrong. I told Pastor Gene I wanted to make a change, and I mean it."

"It's not really a day of rest when it doesn't encompass God." Juliet's quiet remark cut into his thoughts. They lacked any form of condemnation, but her point hit home all the same.

"You're right, love."

Kellen knew what was what. He knew he needed to absolve his moral weakness—a weakness that intensified each time he found himself in Chloe's company. That's what drove him to church today. Juliet's delighted reaction was an added bonus.

"I'm glad you'll be there." Juliet gave him a lingering hug, a quick, sweet kiss. Kellen's heart twisted. He felt trapped. Trapped and divided. Today would help him change. He felt sure of it.

ॐ

Kellen's simmering disquiet held no power at all against the contentment that swept through him when he walked through the doors of Trinity. Walking into church felt like coming home—a welcome oasis of peace that threw a blanket of comfort over a world of turmoil.

The weekend's scripture readings focused on Jesus's time in the desert—Christ's physical and spiritual hunger following a forty-day fast in the desert.

"Naturally," Pastor Gene exclaimed to the congregation, "that's when the devil steps in, and a face-off occurs." He walked the main aisle of the church, pulling a thick piece of string from the pocket of his slacks. "Temptation is insidious, isn't it?"

Kellen shifted uncomfortably. Pastor Gene fingered the string. "Seldom does temptation just step up and smack you over the head all at once and pull you under. That's too obvious. Too easily rebuked."

Kellen's body heat pulsed upward...and upward again. Contentment funneled away.

"More often than not," the pastor continued, "it hits you at your weakest points. It starts small, and it builds." He tied a few simple, loose knots in the string. Shrugging, he loosened the knots and brought the string back to its proper smooth line. "If you work at it, temptation can be overcome. Never avoided, mind you, but overcome. Unless you step away, or become neglectful."

While he spoke, Pastor Gene once again fashioned a series of knots. "We kid ourselves into believing one slip up won't matter. Even two or three can be managed." He pulled more knots into place, in rapid-fire motions, with harder, tighter pulls this time. "We'll be OK. Everybody does it. It's the norm. Why should I be different from everybody else? Sin won't get the better of me—giving in won't matter. Not really. I can beat it."

At the end of his litany of excuses for sin, he lifted a messy ball of tight twists and kinks. Kellen nearly gasped, thoroughly convicted. "Brothers and sisters, let me warn you. If you hold to that belief, you'll end up just like this. Life will become a complicated flurry of half-truths, evasions and sadness. It will lead you away from the joy and peace Christ longs for, for all of us."

Thankfully, Juliet remained riveted by the sermon, unmindful of his reaction. Kellen wanted to lurch from his seat and run away. He wished, desperately, that he could charge fast down the aisle of the church and leave behind this glaring condemnation of his recent behavior.

"But let me warn you about something else, friends. Don't issue too harsh a judgment." Pastor Gene's declaration resounded through the church. "Sometimes experiencing the harrowing results of deepest sin will drive us back to God in ways so powerful it's nothing short of a miracle. That's why Christ also lived a life of forgiveness and welcome to those who live in true and authentic repentance." He lifted the twisted, contorted ball of string again. "Sometimes it's the miracle, and sometimes temptation barricades us in forever. The choice? It's ours. It was Christ's, when the devil showed Him everything, and offered Him everything. What Christ knew—knew with the surety of being God's own Son—is that He already *had* everything. All the love, all the glory, all the kingdoms of the world; all imaginable peace and joy were within His grasp already. These all came from His Father—and from embracing the mission Jesus completed to build a bridge between a fallen humanity and Heaven's gate."

Shame covered Kellen. He removed his arm from its usual comfortable perch against the back of the pew, where it could skim along Juliet's shoulders and connect the two of them. The gesture, now, felt too intimate. He was unworthy of her.

Sinful thoughts, an errant heart, left him unable to reach out to Juliet and draw upon the strength of their marriage and commitment to one another. Kellen couldn't avoid the wedge that was being shoved between them. He fidgeted once again. Juliet turned her head, looking at him with curiosity.

He couldn't even find a way to fake a reassuring smile, so he looked down, unable to focus on the service and the holy, usually calming peace of being in God's sanctuary. He twitched his wrist so he could discreetly check his watch. Another fifteen or twenty minutes and he could escape.

Worship entered into a segment of musical reflection. While the congregation stood to sing praise to God, Kellen could hardly focus on the song or the words that scrolled past on the projector screens above the wide altar. Conversely, Juliet seemed to tune in completely, swaying a bit to the strains of a Nicole Mullins song. Kellen watched as she followed the words, and seemed to take in the lovely pictures that accompanied.

Could he hide? No. Not much longer. Kellen fought to smoothly maintain the spot next to his bride. A heart-threatening, painful crossroads stretched before him, and it was going to be the most difficult pathway he'd ever traveled in his life.

��

"So, when are we going to hear the pitter-patter, guys? C'mon! The whole family is looking forward to expanding! Kellen, you gotta get with the program, man."

Kellen's blood pressure rose. He tried to ignore his

brother-in-law Peter, tactfully deferring a glare and an exasperated groan, but he couldn't help thinking *so much for a day of rest.*

When he glanced at Juliet, she gave him an understanding look and mouthed *sorry.*

Kellen's return smile was weak, but it came from a spot of sincerity. None of this teasing and needling was her fault, after all. He passed by, giving her arm a squeeze on his way to the living room where he could tune in to whatever sports event was playing on TV. He'd take anything but this. As he left the kitchen, his phone buzzed softly, and then vibrated against his belt.

Between the main rooms, the hallway was empty. He braced against the wall and puffed a heavy breath as he extracted his phone and checked caller ID. He had received a text from Chloe. That surprised him—they really had nothing to discuss until they met at Summit Pointe Records—but there was no mistaking the pleasure he felt hearing from her.

He glanced around quickly, ensuring privacy before he entered into his messages and read *"Sry 2 bug u on a Sunday but the excitement can't b contained! Wish it were Monday already. Can't wait 2 c u…we'll take this opportunity by storm! C"*

Suddenly, he could all but feel her around him, and he didn't object to her Sunday intrusion whatsoever. Rather, it enticed him away from all the negativity that kept searing him and took him to a place that was beautiful, and exciting.

Given his present mood and circumstances, Kellen couldn't wait for Monday either. He clicked the reply toggle and began to work the keyboard. *"You bet we will. LOLing @ ur enthusiasm. Love it - keep it coming. I'll call u later 2 review some thoughts."* He typed *"Miss u"* but seeing the words glowing back at him on the screen caused his pulse rate to hitch. Had he really just entered that? In a hurry, he struck the delete key until the last two words were erased.

He clicked send, but then he stood there, in the quiet of the hallway, thinking about what he had almost done—what he was dangerously close to doing. Hitting backspace didn't change the fact that the statement was true. A simple electronic communication from Chloe had left him aroused at every level and completely engulfed in his feelings for her.

And Juliet.

Where was God in this situation? Why didn't He ease this discomfort and help his confusion go away?

"Uncle Kellen, come here!" Eight-year-old Max Taylor, the son of Juliet's sister, Marlene, and her husband, Peter, bounded into the hallway, on a collision course with Kellen's legs. In fact, young Max wrapped them in a hug. The youngster started to jump up and down, grabbing Kellen's hand. "We're playing Wii Tennis in the family room! Be on my team, OK? You *rock* at Wii Tennis! Let's play!"

Max's gleeful bout of recruiting worked magic. Kellen cast a fast look over his shoulder, toward the kitchen where he knew Juliet worked on food preparations with her sisters.

Emptiness and sorrow rode toward him with thundering hoof-beats.

10

So, when are we going to hear the pitter-patter, guys?

Juliet stood at the sink, rinsing vegetables for her sisters to cut into pieces for cooking. Deliberately she kept her back to them. Marlene's husband was the tease in the family, and Peter meant well, but sometimes, teasing hit upon raw nerves.

After drying her hands, Juliet took a pained breath and settled a palm against her abdomen. There were times when it physically hurt to feel hope bloom and grow. There were times when it physically hurt to want something so desperately, to sense it within your grasp, only to know that in a single moment of time, with a fateful, irrefutable signal from her body, all the dreams and wishes of her heart could shatter into oblivion.

Today, though, she continued to hope. Today, she kept a building recognition to herself. After all, recent physical symptoms might turn out to be nothing.

Or then again…

She'd been so keyed up lately that delays in her monthly cycle might be expected. Her dreams of having Kellen's child, and finally realizing that culminating, solidifying act of their relationship held so much power she might actually be psyching herself into a place where she experienced literal queasiness at odd times during the day, or those occasional prickles of soreness in her breasts.

For now, Juliet was too afraid to make an appointment with her doctor and find out for sure. While dashing around town during the past week running errands, she'd strode past the pregnancy test kits at a local drug store and her entire body went jittery. She paused there when a flood of anticipation—visions of everything that might come to be—washed through her spirit. That's when she walked away.

There was hope in not knowing.

In the meantime, she wanted to make a point with her sisters. Just in case this month ended like all the others. She carried a strainer full of cleaned vegetables to the kitchen counter so they could continue cooking preparations. "Y'know? I really do wish y'all would lay off Kellen and me with regard to the whole having kids thing. It's not fun for us, OK? And we don't need the added pressure."

Marlene and Bonnie paused from seasoning the pork loin to give her a startled look, then an apology. When everyone returned to work, Juliet noticed the way the two women shared a brief, expressive look of concern. Juliet waffled on the inside. She had snapped at them, and they didn't deserve it. She knew she was being defensive, but she couldn't help herself. The topic was too much of a hot-button.

Everything was so frustrating between her and Kellen right now. Nothing seemed appropriately centered in their lives, and that left Juliet empty and afraid on a number of levels. His continuing distance was disturbing, so was his reaction to being at services today. A family would break the pattern of Kellen burying himself in work. Family would return him to the Kellen she had fallen in love with and the Christ-centered relationship they had forged from the beginning.

Until recently, they could do no wrong. His career had hit a crescendo of success some five years ago, and so had their marriage. They were driven toward God, and Kellen used his power in the entertainment industry to focus on Christian artists and their genre of music because he believed in it passionately. The venture had been a resounding success for Associated Talent, and Juliet had loved the ride. Kellen's focus on like-minded people kept him solidly grounded, and freed enough of his time to dedicate to children and the family for which they both longed.

The plan seemed so perfect. Why was God saying *No*?

Why, recently, did Kellen seem so removed from their relationship? Why did work claim increasing portions of his time? Why did he continue to drive himself harder, branching out to promote artists in other genres? Why wasn't enough, enough?

Juliet nipped at her lower lip, stemming her negativity with the fact that he enjoyed his nieces and nephews so much, and despite the pressure of hearing *pitter-patters* Kellen remained a total sport about these monthly Sunday dinners and family visits. He claimed to enjoy being with her family and backed it with his actions—like now, with Max. Through an opening in the wide corridor of the hallway, she could see and hear the mounting ruckus of a Wii game taking place in the den. Kellen's laughter and encouraging shouts could be heard just as clearly as the kids'.

That made Juliet smile. Kellen's parents were based on the West coast. Juliet liked to hope her family here in Nashville filled a bit of the hole in his heart that was created by logistical distance.

If their inability to conceive continued, how else could that hole in their hearts be filled? They hadn't talked much about the issue and its alternatives—like adoption or foster care. There simply hadn't been time. These days they were both too busy for that kind of in-depth discussion. More and more often it seemed as though she and Kellen were married yet running in opposite directions.

That needed to change.

Against the linen fabric of her slacks, she slid gentle fingertips against her stomach. Once again, Juliet pondered the miracle that might...just *might*...be taking place inside her body right now. Wistful joy filled her as she pondered the idea of receiving a perfect answer to her most heartfelt prayers.

For now, though, she kept everything to herself—private and guarded against the unsettling pattern of her marriage, and the hopes that would be crushed if the new life she hoped for wasn't meant to be.

A short time later Juliet and her sisters were starting to

mash potatoes when she happened to glance out the kitchen window. Kellen walked slowly along the far edge of the backyard, taking a phone call. His shoulders were hunched against a bit of a breeze, and his free hand was stuffed into the pocket of his slacks. He smiled frequently and nodded from time to time as he carried on his end of the conversation.

For some mysterious reason, nostalgia perhaps, the image of him sent her tumbling backwards in time, recalling the moment they had met.

Almost nine years to the day, she thought. It amazed Juliet how much time had passed, and how quickly. She still recalled the details of that night so vividly.

Her roommate at the time, Tami Oaks, had passed along an opportunity to make some extra money by helping out a catering company with an understaffed party event. A member of the wait staff had come down with the flu, so Juliet accepted the assignment. She had just graduated from the University of Tennessee, and although she had landed a job that made decent use of her business/marketing degree, she had college loans to pay off. Plus, she was freshly indoctrinated into the world of rent, utility, and car payments. The idea of working with her friend, plus the prospect of earning some extra cash, spurred her to don black slacks, a white blouse and black bowtie.

"OK, so, the record label is Infinity. Tonight is all about their upper echelon hosting a meet-and-greet session for prospective talent." Tami furnished the information as they went to work in the kitchen area of a private home owned by Jamison Arellio, president of Infinity.

Tami and Juliet stacked their appetizer trays with salmon canapés, fresh shrimp, and spinach and brie in artichoke hearts. Tami looked up, adjusting the waistband of her white apron. "There's going to be lots of sexy singers, talent scouts, and label execs, so look lively. You never know what might happen!"

Juliet made sure her tray was artfully arranged and visually appealing. The food smelled great as a variety of aromas wafted through the kitchen. "Tami, only you could turn a catering assignment into a love connection."

"JJ, I swear. It'd take an act of God to get you to even *stumble* across Mr. Right, let alone latch on to him for good! You need to get out more and mix and mingle!" JJ was Tami's favorite nickname for her, a combination of the initials of Juliet's first and last name.

The massive, formal living room was packed with people. Music played at a moderate level. Groups shifted and changed like rays of light splitting across cut crystal. Luxury abounded—in the clothing, jewelry, and style of the attendees. Conversations and laughter filled the atmosphere with appealing warmth.

Juliet didn't mind keeping to the background. For efficiency's sake, she had fashioned her long hair into a sleek ponytail, and the standard-style uniform kept her from drawing any overt attention. That was fine. Getting a chance to people-watch at an event like this kept her happily occupied, and the rest of her focus stayed firm on making sure she didn't wobble her tray or drop anything.

Just before the call to a sit-down dinner came a request for champagne service. Apparently, Jamison intended to make a toast. Activity in the kitchen went into overdrive as bottles of Cristal were popped open. Flutes appeared and were filled in a rapid-fire, assembly line motion.

Juliet followed Tami into the living room with a laden tray.

On the second round of champagne deliveries, she approached a group of about six people, offering a serving. Tami stepped up as well, and in the end they were both left with extra flutes.

Intending to return to the kitchen, Juliet spun too fast, and crashed directly into a tall, hard body that featured a broad chest, a crisp white shirt, and an expensive-looking silk suit of royal blue.

Now doused by Cristal.

Toppled glassware rolled and bounced on her tray. Juliet

squeezed her eyes shut and winced, wishing to high heaven that the elegant parquet floor at her feet would simply come open and swallow her whole. Really. Anything but this.

The impact of the collision nearly sent her backwards, but the tragic recipient of her clumsiness reached out fast and took hold of her arms. He steadied her with grace and ease. "Are you OK?" he asked.

Only then did she dare open her eyes. She nearly spilled the tray all over again. Before her stood, without question, the most handsome man she had ever seen. What made him handsome wasn't so much his looks as something that flowed from the depths of his eyes, something within his confident carriage—which he maintained despite being drenched in champagne.

"I am *so* incredibly sorry," she whispered.

The man just smiled, continuing to look into her eyes, his brows pulled together slightly, as though he were intrigued.

Oh, Juliet, get a grip, she chided herself.

She licked her lips and groaned. "I can't believe this. Please let me do what I can to make amends..." Doing so would probably cost every cent of the money she had earned tonight, but she would gladly see to the cleaning and care of his shirt, tie and suit.

"Sir, I'm so sorry, and JJ, are you OK?" Tami handed the man a clean, white linen napkin, thank goodness.

He began to brush off excess moisture, but kept looking at Juliet, which caused Juliet to go flush and look away in horrified embarrassment. "JJ. What exactly does that stand for?" He continued to work at the stains on his suit.

"Juliet Jenkins...in case you want to file a suit in small claims court."

The man laughed in an understanding way, seeming to take the entire situation well in hand. "I think we can avoid litigation. No real harm done. Now...if this had been red wine, we might have a problem."

The guy was unbelievable. He still had the bulk of the evening ahead, full of networking and dining, and he was acting like a champ despite the fact that she had nearly demolished his attire. But even in his drink-spattered state, he looked fantastic.

Juliet shuffled her feet, wishing she didn't blush so easily. "Thank you for being so gracious. I'm a catering rookie, obviously, and I couldn't be more apologetic—or mortified."

"Don't be. It's all good." The man settled his napkin on the tray that Juliet now held with two hands, keeping it in her grip as though her life depended upon it. "I'm Kellen Rossiter." His focus returned to her, and Juliet's heart thundered at his intense perusal. His lips curved, and Juliet couldn't help admiring their full, supple line. "I'd shake your hand, but..." He gave a teasing shrug, and then the grin flowed into a smile. The smile did her in—a beautiful thing to behold. Large and warm, it left no doubt that he teased her out of sincere humor and shared folly, not to demean or needle.

"I think I better keep hold of my tray instead." She sounded breathless but didn't berate herself much over the fact. Her poise was utterly destroyed anyhow.

Kellen's suit began to dry into somewhat rumpled lines as the party progressed, but he kept tabs on her for the rest of the night. She felt the touch of his gaze every time she entered the dining room to serve. At the end of the party, Juliet noticed the way he lingered around the entrance to the kitchen.

Even Tami noticed his interest. "Would you please just *go*? Go talk to him! He's waiting for you, JJ. Talk about the best meet-cue ever!"

"Right. Try most humiliating!" Juliet's hissed retort belied her nervousness. At last, she ran out of reasons to evade. Unfastening her bowtie and apron, she pulled them both away then pushed through the swinging door of the kitchen.

And there he stood, focused on her. "Hello, Juliet."

He didn't use the nickname of JJ or the frequently used short version of Jules. Coming from Kellen, in that rich, low voice of his, her full name sounded lovely. Her breath caught and a light-headed, spinning sensation took over. She couldn't fight it. This guy was as attractive as could be, and he had been nothing short of a prince. Maybe, just maybe, God *had* interceded tonight...

She smiled at him. An enticing warmth bloomed across her shoulders, moving fast up her neck, then her cheeks. "Hi, Kellen." She squared her shoulders and lifted her chin. "I'm glad to see you. I absolutely insist in paying for the dry cleaning bill."

He shook his head firmly, just staring at her. Unsettled, enchanted, she realized he kept quiet on purpose. Awareness settled in. So did attraction—in a large, heavy dose. She perched her hands on her hips and arched a brow at him, refusing to give him too much of an upper hand.

"Then how can I make amends?"

"I leave town the day after tomorrow, so I don't have a lot of time, but I'd like to take you to dinner."

Take her to dinner? As recompense for dumping a tray of drinks on him? "That's not exactly making amends."

"It is to me." He stepped a bit closer, closing the space between them, but not encroaching too much. "Do you like to dance? I'd love to check out the Wild Horse Saloon."

The suggestion stirred delighted expectation. The Nashville institution was one of her favorites for great food, drinks, and the hilarity of attempting to line dance. "You're serious about this?"

"Very much so."

His presence pulled at a ticklish, sensitive place in her belly. She nodded her acceptance. Reaching into the breast pocket of his suit coat, Kellen extracted a business card and held it out to her. He maintained possession for an extra beat when she tried to claim it. "My cell number is on there. What's yours?"

He pulled out his phone and entered her information promptly when she recited her contact information. "You don't know me," he said, as he keyed in digits and letters, "so I understand completely if you want to meet me there." Their eyes tagged once more. "Does that sound OK?"

She appreciated the gesture to her privacy—even though

she sensed it to be unnecessary. They agreed to meet at Wild Horse the following evening at seven o'clock.

There, over pulsing music, fun atmosphere, and flashing lights, they shared a dinner of charbroiled shrimp served atop barbeque-spiced grits. Kellen, she discovered, was a music agent on the rise with Associated Talent, one of the largest entertainment representation agencies in North America. The firm was on a mission to expand its portfolio of country music performers, hence his trip to Music City. His boss had sent him to Nashville, charged with the task of scoping out some of the bigger-name venues for live music and to connect with label execs.

"I'm absolutely in love..." Kellen took in a forkful of food while the sentence dangled. His eyes sparkled at her as he slowly chewed the bite. Juliet laughed, waiting...and waiting. "...with your accent. You're a native?"

"Tennessee born and bred, y'all." She answered with an exaggerated twang.

Kellen didn't laugh as expected. He went still, studying her in a way that was disarming. Juliet began to fall head over heels, at a speed that took her on a crazy, seductive thrill ride. The recognition caused her to shift on her stool at the high table where they sat. She slipped a slice of hair behind her ear. What captivated her most? The fact that this charismatic, suave man seemed equally drawn to *her*.

"Why me, Kellen?"

He shook his head, obviously surprised by the question. "What do you mean?"

Juliet tucked her hand against her neck, sliding her fingers beneath her hair. She shot him a playful, teasing look. "Come on. Surely my question can't surprise you that much. You could have had a date with any woman at that party."

"Luckily, I ended up with the only one who captured me." The intensity of his words lingered. Juliet dipped her head, hiding her delight at his unabashed interest. "Please understand something clearly, Juliet—that's not a line. I'm dead serious." He took a moment to study her, and Juliet felt beautifully exposed. "I'm not a drinker. I never have been. But last night, when I saw you handing out champagne, I finally had an excuse to meet you. I was coming from behind, and all I wanted to do was grab a flute and introduce myself. I didn't even intend to drink it. I only wanted to find out who you were."

She slid into the depths of his eyes and settled there quite comfortably. "It would seem God intervened."

"Without a question."

His serious, emphatic tone made her heart race. Juliet nearly teased him about being mighty smooth in the first-date department, but somehow, the idea of joking with him stalled. Kellen wasn't making light of this evening together, therefore, neither could she.

"Anyway—this is my first trip to Tennessee. I've only been here for a week, but I like Nashville a lot. It's got a great atmosphere." His comment prompted her to nod with the pride of a hometown girl. It also showed that Kellen understood a need to move away from the intensity of the moment. Still, Juliet was lost to him. She edged forward, leaning on the table, watching him as he spoke. His chestnut brown hair was a wavy, tantalizing fall against his white shirt collar. "I hope this scouting mission will be a success. A pair of VP's here in Nashville retired recently. Taking over their portfolios and helping grow the business out here would be a great project to take on."

"You might land here permanently?"

"If the president at Associated Talent feels I've earned my spurs, it's a possibility."

Her heart lifted into a swooping, delicious soar. Following a shared smile they focused on their food, then explored a few likes, and dislikes, some personal histories and family sketches.

"Tell me about your family." Kellen's urging left her to consider the fact that he had a way of listening that let Juliet know he was deeply interested in what she had to say. He didn't just listen to her, he took her in with his eyes, with the brush of his hand as he settled it next to hers. The slight tilt of his body toward hers made her feel exclusive.

"I have two sisters. Marlene and Bonnie. How about you?"

"I'm an only child."

The conversation stilled for a moment as she searched his eyes—and he seemed to welcome the gesture. "Marlene is the oldest—and she's always been our protector." Rather than interject, Kellen waited for more, watching after her as he dug a fork into his seafood and grits. Juliet did likewise, but eased into the conversation. "She's my hero. Smart and sweet and pushy and loving."

Kellen studied her, but then he looked away. He studied the ebb and flow of the crowd that continued to build as the night deepened. Juliet wondered. Was he uncomfortable? Had she said something wrong, or—

He looked back soon enough, though, and resumed an easy, comfortable demeanor, but Juliet got a sense something deeper rode beneath the surface.

"And are you the middle child?"

Although his eyes lit with a teasing playfulness, Juliet catalogued his mannerisms and came to the conclusion that Kellen might be a bit lonely—yearning for connections like the ones she took for granted. "That would be Bonnie. Actually, I'm the youngest."

"You're lucky."

"I am?"

Kellen nodded. "I always felt kind of alone. I have wonderful parents, but there's something about the connection you have with siblings and extended family that's really special."

Juliet propped her elbow on the table and rested her chin in her hand. "They drive me crazy sometimes, but, yeah, I wouldn't trade them for the world."

Kellen nodded. She noticed the way his eyes fixed on a slim, gold bracelet that skimmed against her wrist. "Being around people makes me feel less alone. Does that make sense? I love the interaction and building relationships. I've always loved the things most people dislike—for instance, those times when you have to break the ice, or start conversations with strangers, or work a room at a party or a business function." He took a few bites of food, and Juliet couldn't wait for what he'd say next. "I guess that's part of how God kept me from feeling alone—He programmed me to enjoy being with others."

His bold declaration of faith won him access to even deeper reaches of her heart

A short time later, the action on the dance floor won their attention. They were seated at a table on the second floor of the restaurant that overlooked the wide-open space below. People filled space as the music cranked up.

"When I found out I was coming here, I promised myself I'd attempt some line dancing." Kellen stepped from his stool and offered her his hand. "You game?"

The prospect sent a bubble of delight bursting through her body. A guy—a Christian guy—who wanted to give line dancing a try? This date kept getting better and better. "You bet I am. And I admire your bravery, seeing as how I certainly didn't display much grace last night."

He helped her down from her stool and led the way to a nearby stairwell. "You were just fine, love. Truly."

Love. Juliet melted at the natural, easy way he issued the endearment. The look she gave him in answer, she was sure, spoke volumes about the workings of her heart.

On the dance floor, Kellen caught on quick. They laughed when they made mistakes and high-fived when they nailed sequences. Once the music changed to a slow ballad, Kellen didn't miss a beat. He took her gently by the waist and held out his other hand, waiting on her to accept or refuse. She stepped into the circle of his arms without hesitation, letting him lead her around the floor to the strains of *There You Are* by Martina McBride.

Juliet closed her eyes, and enjoyed. His skin smelled wonderful—with a subtle trace of spice from his cologne. His warmth enveloped her. "I love this song."

He paused, leaning back so he could study her face. "Me, too. A person who enters your life, and remains within it, like an answer to prayer."

"I like how strongly you profess your faith."

"It feels good." He shrugged. "I wish I could be more forthright about my faith, but the entertainment industry, the media, isn't very kind to believers. That's part of why I'd love to end up in Tennessee. I think I'd be really happy here. The attitudes of the people I've met are much more in keeping with my own. The culture I work in back in California can be pretty brutal."

Juliet was grateful for the steady support of his arm around her, or she would have stumbled.

Kellen's brows drew together. "Did I say something wrong, or…"

"No, not at all. In fact, what you're saying feels perfectly right to me. Don't be afraid to step out, Kellen. Keep developing yourself as an agent then bring it around full-circle to what you believe in the most. Maybe God's moving you toward representing artists in the Christian music arena. Have you ever thought of that? Working in Nashville, growing country music stars, would lead quite naturally to that pathway. Maybe that's part of His plan for you. You'd be amazing. I can already tell."

This time, Kellen seemed stunned. They swayed together and Martina sang on about moons and stars…and prayers.

"How can you possibly know me that well?"

Juliet couldn't reply to that.

"In a few simple sentences you mapped out my career goals. How can that be when we've only just met…?" He shook his head as his words trailed off. "Wow."

He tucked in again, closer and tighter now. Juliet savored the way they fit together, the way a tender, emotional intimacy expanded between them.

"If I'm able to head business development in Nashville, I'd be able to focus on the genres I love the most. Working with Christian artists, like you talk about, would be the best of everything. I've always felt that way."

"Well, no wonder."

"No wonder what?"

"No wonder you were such a gentleman when I dumped champagne on you. I'm beginning to understand where you come from, and what matters to you. Plus, you can tell a lot about a person when they're confronted by a difficult set of circumstances. You were incredible."

"That accident was a blessing. Look at the results. I'm standing in the middle of one of the greatest spots in Nashville, sharing it with a beautiful lady who's even more beautiful on the inside. I'm grateful for every one of those stains on my suit."

In that instant, Juliet knew their lives had come together by a deliberate and brilliant design.

The promotion Kellen had hoped for happened six weeks later, and he focused on Juliet exclusively, in a spirit of romantic pursuit that stole her heart forever. Above it all, one thing about Kellen Rossiter stood true, the greatest test of grace, and of the goodness you can find in a person, is revealed when you see them react to being under fire. His love was authentic and true—all encompassing.

Now, as then, he enchanted her. Now, as then, he was her prince.

The subtle clatter of dishware being pulled from the shelves by her mom returned Juliet to the present moment, but she continued to watch Kellen prowl the yard and talk on the phone. She felt bad for him, knowing his escape outside was the only chance he'd have to converse in peace, and in a place where he could actually hear what was being said.

An idea dawned and she pulled a mug from the cupboard so she could fill it with water. After heating it, she steeped some orange and cinnamon spiced tea—one of his favorites, and a brand her mother stocked specifically for their visits.

Wanting to give him something warm and soothing to drink as he braved the windy elements, Juliet carried the beverage outside. Anticipating his tender smile and appreciation, she approached and began to hear bits and pieces of his conversation.

His back to her, Kellen laughed softly. "I know, right? I'm being protective. Can't seem to help it." He waited in silence, and then he laughed again. The sound was intimate. Rich. Juliet's stomach went into a nasty pitch and her muscles went tight. "Exactly, yeah. But I warn you it's going to be a quick meeting. Frank is very abrupt, and he's all business, so don't let that worry you." There was a pause. "Your humility is astounding." The tenderness—the affection she recognized— left her gritting her teeth. "Frank's totally on board. Once he meets you—well, let's just say he won't hold out long."

Just a few feet away from him now, Juliet froze. His back remained to her and the house in general. He wanted privacy. She tightened her grip on the mug. The cadence of his voice— deep and smooth—didn't strike her as strictly professional.

"I should probably head back in, Chloe." She detected his regret and started to breathe hard. Juliet nearly dumped the tea, fighting her buckling knees. Still oblivious, Kellen paused again. "Um-hmm, I'm at Juliet's parents. Kind of a Sunday tradition…" It was then that he turned. "Don't even worry about it, I don't mind hearing from you at all…" What she saw in his eyes hit her with the impact of hammer blows. In his eyes was a desire that she had only ever seen directed toward one person. Her.

Until now.

Who in the world was this *Chloe* person? Who was this golden child on the super-fast-track? Juliet had no time to school her troubled features, and when Kellen froze—so much like she just had—she knew she had caught him off guard.

"I'll, ah, I'll get back to you…I need to hang up." His verbal faltering made her blood boil because in it, his guilt was confirmed.

Kellen disconnected the call and slid his phone into the pocket of his slacks. His manner was tight, and his hands seemed to be trembling slightly. He was stumbling, and she knew it.

"I'm sorry I interrupted." Her voice was deceptively calm. The spice of orange and cinnamon swirled upward on curls of steam, reminding Juliet of why she had come outside in the first place. For him. For his comfort. Tears filled her eyes, overtaking her lashes and dribbling down her cheeks as she ducked her head and blinked furiously. "I...wanted to get you something...something warm to drink since you were out here for a while."

She had looked away fast, but not before seeing the way his shoulders slumped, the way his eyes were glossed by shame. She held out the mug and Kellen took custody. She closed her eyes, unable to bring herself to face the ugliness that had sprung up between them like grotesque shapes. Once he took the tea, she spun away, needing to leave behind the weedy tangle of her doubts as she tried to get a handle on her relationship with her husband.

Her husband.

Juliet made two steps toward the house then she felt Kellen's hand slide against her upper arm and hold on tight. "Juliet. Wait." His voice carried to her in soft entreaty.

Overwrought, she gathered another deep breath, gulping in as much air as she could before turning. "What?"

Again, her tone was deceptively calm, but it was also lifeless. She could tell at once that he struggled to cobble together some form of a reply that would explain the verbiage and tone of his call.

"I had to calm down a nervous—"

"*Bull*, Kellen." Inside and out, Juliet fumed. Her outward calm transformed into a storm. "That's *bull*. On a Sunday afternoon? During a gathering with our family? It didn't sound to me like you minded the interruption very much, and you were out here talking to her for quite a while. Was she *that* upset and worried?" She felt choked off and horrid. Sick. Part of her died inside even *thinking* of Kellen harboring feelings for another woman.

Kellen didn't release his hold on her. He bent quickly and

set the mug down in the grass. Then he held both her arms in a gentle, but firm grip. She wanted to kick the mug straight over and run away.

Fear not, Juliet. I am with you. I am your God. I will strengthen you. I will uphold you with my right hand.

The familiar words, the temperate, loving power of God's voice were all that held her in place.

"Juliet, please stop and talk to me. What did you hear that upset you so much?"

His attempt to soothe was the last thing Juliet wanted. It felt too placating. "I have a better idea, Kellen. Why don't *you* talk to *me* for a change? Why don't you tell me a little more about this Chloe woman you're so excited about? The woman who consumes so much of your time lately? Why don't you talk to me anymore with the same degree of tenderness I heard in your voice with her just now? What does she mean to you?"

He took a sharp breath and closed his eyes as though he were attempting to gain control of himself. She wondered about that, because she hadn't sniped at him. Despite the crusty tracks of her wind-dried tears, she had kept her gaze and her tone as level as possible. Apparently she had struck home with an arrow.

"Juliet, Chloe has a career-changing—*life*-changing—meeting on Monday. As her agent, I'm coaching her through an exceptionally fast and intense growth spurt in her career. She needs the guidance, and that's what she's paying me to do."

With love in your eyes, Kellen? The kind of love I've committed my life and my heart to?

"I want to believe you, Kellen, but lately…lately we've grown so far apart I don't know what to think. It scares me! We're not taking care of each other like we used to. I want to work on it, but…" She lifted her shoulders in resignation. Slipping away from his grasp, she hugged her arms against her middle.

Where an answer to their prayers just might be

dawning...

Tears welled up all over again.

Kellen moved close and very tentatively, very gingerly, loosened her arms from their clench. He drew her in tight. "I want to work on us, too, love. I'm here, and I was at church today. I'm with *you*."

His breath was warm and familiar against her cheek. Wonderful. Juliet had no idea what to do next. The tenor of his conversation with Chloe still riled her. Despite his assurances, the interlude struck her as being wrong. He had been thoroughly present to Chloe. Attentive. Since she missed those aspects of Kellen's personality in their marriage, perhaps she had overreacted. Maybe she was jealous of an innocent gesture because she missed him so much, because the way he watched out for Chloe is the way she wanted him to look out for her. For *them*.

Was the exchange as innocent as Kellen said? She had no clue. Either she was a mixed-up hormonal mess who imagined conspiracies, or her marriage was falling apart before her very eyes—with no forewarning and a gut-wrenching lack of fanfare.

"Lately," Kellen began, swaying slowly, "we've been struggling to make a way to each other through everything we've got going on in our lives. Every couple faces challenges. We'll make it through this one. Nothing changes my love for you. Nothing."

She wanted to believe him. She wanted to trust in him without even a hint of doubt. She rested her head against his chest and waited on God's voice, praying to hear just an inkling of divine instruction.

Instead of affirmation, a thought occurred to her: Kellen hadn't really answered her question about Chloe and what she truly meant to him.

11

Just over two weeks later, Chloe was back in the recording studio, this time fully contracted and engaged by Summit Pointe Records.

An added layer of speed and pressure manifested itself for Kellen when Frank Simpson made immediate arrangements for the production of a full-length album and a video for *Swing Time*, which would be her debut release. Kellen walked through the lobby of the building that housed the recording studios of Summit Pointe and paused just long enough to check in at the security desk. He was looking forward to witnessing the beginning of Chloe's official recording sessions.

During the elevator ride to the fifteenth floor, Kellen thought about the confrontation with Juliet—and that fateful Monday afternoon meeting with Chloe and Frank. The introduction between Chloe and Frank had been an unfocused, haze-shrouded disaster for Kellen. No matter how hard he had tried, he couldn't concentrate. Instead, he kept thinking about Juliet.

Fortunately, Chloe and Frank had hit it off beautifully. That made it easy for Kellen to fade back while he noted the general terms of the agreement Frank offered. Kellen had vowed to himself that he'd study the document in depth upon receipt, praying that proper focus would be restored by then.

The agreement was a slam-dunk, executed at warp-speed.

"Sometimes it falls together this quickly," Kellen had assured Chloe once she inked the contract at his office and Weiss McDonald popped a celebratory bottle of champagne.

Kellen had taken a sip and smiled along with the rest of

his team, but the champagne turned his stomach sour. All he could think about was Juliet, not a professional victory.

During the course of his career, he had worked with dozens of beautiful women. When he signed them on as clients, his sole purpose was to propel them toward a pathway of mutually beneficial success and nothing more. There had been a few times when a female client's gratitude had slid into something deeper, but with no effort at all, Kellen turned them away.

He didn't want, or need, anyone but his wife. He had married the woman of his dreams, the one God had designed for him alone. Juliet was a gorgeous, spirited woman who shared his life fully and in every way imaginable—for better and for worse. Chloe, and women like her, might be attracted to him in a superficial or physical sense, mostly because they confused the magic he worked on their careers with love. Kellen had always made sure he stayed God-centered enough, and grounded enough, to recognize the difference between love and lust.

Therefore, in an industry riddled by disposable relationships, his marriage remained rock solid.

But then had come that nasty episode in the backyard of Juliet's childhood home.

She knew him better than anyone else did; she sensed what was happening to him. The recognition left him walled in and claustrophobic. He tried to fight the attraction he felt for Chloe, but time and again, his mind returned to the woman. Time and again, he stepped across one emotional boundary, then another and another until the rules of what he knew to be right and wrong became smeared and indiscernible.

The elevator doors glided open and Kellen stepped out. Confusion beat against him from every side. Amidst escalating tensions and unfulfilled needs, the slow-building wave that was Chloe Havermill pushed to shore, gaining momentum, threatening to pull him under.

Embattled, but determined to do his job, Kellen skirted a

narrow, empty hallway and pushed open the door leading to the studio. He knew he couldn't continue to take a sledgehammer to his most meaningful relationship like this, but right now, he needed to take care of his client.

Chloe and Jason Missing greeted him, and Kellen dropped an easy clap against Jason's shoulder, glad that Frank had given their demo producer a chance to help launch Chloe's album.

"Hey, Chloe"—Jason rolled his chair forward and leaned against the mixing board—"you should show Kellen the rough cut of that scene from your video."

Chloe turned in her chair. When she faced Kellen, her eagerness reached out and took hold. He realized she held a DVD that glimmered beneath the ceiling lights as she wiggled it in her hand. "Do you want to see what we have so far?"

"Absolutely."

"Actually we've only recorded the last quarter of the song—the outdoor shots—and I have to return the DVD to Frank's office before we leave, but I couldn't wait to show you!"

Kellen moved a chair into place at Chloe's right, in front of a small, flat-screen monitor. Jason cued the video and after a quick fade in, *Swing Time* moved toward its conclusion. Framed by a cobalt sky and towering trees, the rear of a car could be seen. Tires spun in time to the music and the car peeled off straight and fast down a gravel road with Chloe's vocals accompanying. The vignette played out of a stunning woman escaping the narrow, tree-lined roadways and wooden shop-fronts of her small town life, moving forward to take on the world.

A quick camera cut later, Chloe's image filled the screen. Wind blew her hair into sexy, billowing waves. There was sass in her smile as the vocals and lip-synching ended. Then, she used a fingertip to edge down the frame of an oversized pair of sunglasses, revealing eyes that sparkled and danced. She arched a brow and delivered a slow, enticing wink. After that, she shrugged playfully and moved the glasses back into place over those captivating violet eyes.

Seconds later, the screen faded to black.

"No doubt about it. The camera loves you, Chloe."

Jason's comment had Kellen stifling a satisfied smile. He had known it all along. A platinum voice packaged in the being of a vibrant woman. Chloe turned her chair toward Jason, and they chatted about the schedule for completing the video. That launched a discussion of the songs they'd be recording today. Kellen listened, but the images he had just seen lingered, transforming into an overwhelming temptation.

He stretched an arm along the back of Chloe's chair. The gesture looked casual, but felt anything but. His fingertips nearly brushed her shoulder. The skin there beckoned, covered only by the fabric of a pale blue silk shell. He inched just a bit closer...another emotional boundary stretching before him, tickling his awareness, begging to be crossed...

Chloe kept her focus on Jason, but she leaned back just enough that his fingertips now connected with her, gliding against a few strands of satiny hair and warm, dewy skin. Now he couldn't pull away without being obvious about it. Kellen realized she was playing into the moment of contact as much as he was. He wanted to gasp for breath because his lungs screamed for oxygen, yet all he had done was touch her.

This was insane...

"The team will be reporting for duty in a few minutes. I'm going to grab a pop before we get started." Jason pushed back from the soundboard with a flourishing spin and then stood from the chair to leave. Once the door closed behind Jason, Kellen stood, and so did Chloe. Their eyes met. A silence, redolent with charged electricity, filled the room.

The vibrations sang against Kellen's body.

"You know—" Chloe started to speak, but stopped all at once and cleared her throat. She folded her arms across her chest. She looked up once again and a renewed strength flowed from her eyes, heightening the atmosphere even further—if such a thing were possible. "You're a dream weaver, Kellen."

The softly spoken words cut the thick, heavy silence, but left behind a moment of truth—a challenge unspoken but clearly identified. The words weren't about her music. Not completely.

Desire rammed home, knocking Kellen completely away from everything but Chloe. His muscles coiled into a tight spring. He fought, and felt himself slipping, sliding and losing precious ground.

"You're like a cosmic force that's come into my life and opened door after door to every wish I ever had. You have a golden touch, and that touch is making my dreams come true. I'm in awe of you."

This, Kellen could tell, wasn't a coy, flirty woman issuing deliberate provocations. She was genuine. That's what kept tripping him up. That fact made her impossible to resist.

"I've been prepared for everything that's happened with regard to my career. I've been ready to move forward as a recording artist ever since I could talk. But I wasn't prepared for you, Kellen. Not at all. I can't even think straight around you; you have that profound of an effect on me. You're all I can think about. I know that's wrong. I'm not the kind of girl who goes after married men. I'm not the kind of woman who…who…"

"Chloe, hang on—"

She refused his strident interruption by a firm shake of her head. "No. Please, listen to me." She stilled herself for a moment. "I think what drives me crazy is the fact that I know you feel it, too. I feed off every look and every touch you give. You kiss my cheek, making it appear so casual, or help guide my step, and it thrills me. I love the simple act of talking to you on the phone, and the much more profound act of sharing all of this incredible forward progress with you."

Kellen had to do something—the words hit him like shrapnel, ripping apart any semblance he might maintain of control and propriety. He stepped forward. His world was hazy at the edges, yet hyper-focused when it came to Chloe. He took her arms, and then drew her in for a long, tight hug.

Her heart thundered against his chest. She wasn't playing around; she was overwrought, and she trembled against him.

There was no escaping the fact that her reaction thrilled him.

"Let's sit down, Chloe...and talk this through." His nerves sizzled and burned. "It's something we should have done a while ago."

Kellen led her to a padded bench stationed behind the studio control panel. After they sat down, he kept close, settling an arm around her shoulders. He used a gentle touch to tip her head so their eyes were aligned. Hers sparkled, and she tried to look away, but Kellen kept her in place, refusing to let her gain distance.

"This is completely inappropriate. I *know* that. I'm your client, and I know all about professional boundaries, and why it's so important that they be respected and observed. But I've never felt this way before, Kellen. What I feel for you takes me over." She breathed out softly, their faces close enough that her breath skimmed his cheek. "Those are all the words I can give." She tilted her head, opening herself to him like an offering. "I want more from you."

The words chipped and chiseled, working through an opening in Kellen's mind that brought about cataclysmic change. He went white-hot and blind—blind to everything but the ache in his soul that yearned, unabated, for Chloe.

What would it feel like, he wondered in a helpless form of hunger, to take possession of the adoration, the freshness of attraction she offered? Just for a moment...just for a split-second of exploration and pleasure, that's all...

Suddenly he couldn't remember where time ended and began, where passion transformed into a primitive, elemental urgency of purpose. He only knew he needed this woman. He needed her open reception. He needed to know what she tasted like. He needed to know her textures. And none of it would be denied. Not this time.

Chloe's pulse beat at her slim, scented neck, drawing his focus. His gaze fell to her lips, glossy, moist and waiting. The ache intensified to unbearable. He lifted her hair to the side and angled his head with one thought only: her kiss—that sweetest, most intoxicating start of a physical connection.

His mouth literally watered at the idea of…

No.

His heart thundered. He trembled all over.

No!

That powerful voice kept admonishing him. He teetered, and he swayed. His head dipped low as he succumbed to the pull of soft allure.

Kellen. No!

The call of what he knew to be right faded to nothing against the drumbeat that pounded in his ears and obliterated all things logical and rational. The call became quite easy to ignore.

His lips touched hers and a strangled sound bubbled upward from the depths of his chest. An instant later, he sank into a kiss that sent him tumbling and spinning. The world swirled into mind-dizzying flashes of color. The kiss began with the giddy rush he had fully expected. The flavors and scents and feelings he had pined for now filled him. Her breath mixed with his, foreign and intriguing, pushing him on. Desire opened a floodgate, and he fell willingly beneath a deluge of passion that fed and intensified their connection.

A heartbeat later, the sweetness turned rancid.

A heartbeat later, the thrill turned to nausea.

A heartbeat later, the kiss turned into a moment of horror that washed over him in cold dread, wiping him completely out of the moment.

When he jerked away, with his breaths threatening to convulse into gasps and heaves, Kellen realized that, not only had he committed a grievous wrong, he and Chloe were no longer alone.

Jason stood framed in the half-open doorway, watching the proceedings with wide eyes and a sense of awkwardness that filled the space of the studio. The producer's gaze bounced back and forth between them. "Umm…I…I can't believe it...I almost made it to the kitchen and realized I forgot my security pass." In quick, stuttered motions, Jason grabbed his magnetized access card from the lip of the control panel. Following a hasty—"Ah...see you in a bit..."—he was gone.

Kellen wanted to disappear into oblivion. Heartbreak and self-loathing clawed at him until nothing was left except sickness and regret.

Chloe stood apart from him, her head bowed, her breathing ragged.

"Kellen," she whispered, "we needed that. We *did*. We needed to stop the tap dance." Her eyes brimmed when they lifted to his once more. "Now we need to face facts. We need to face *us*...and what we feel for one another. What we've been trying to avoid—without much success—has been eating away at me for weeks and weeks." She lifted her chin. "Selfishly, I'm glad to discover you're as affected by your feelings as I am."

For the first time, her intensity of spirit morphed from that of sweet-natured ingénue to a driven and determined woman on a quest. Kellen couldn't push a single word past the logjam in his throat.

"I'm very attracted to you."

She stepped so close he could feel her warmth. This time Kellen felt no arousal or pleasure. Instead, an explosion of poison poured through his system so powerful it caused bile to churn and rise.

Chloe slid the palms of her hands very slowly against his chest. "The way I feel when you and I are together is absolutely beautiful. Now I know, it's that way for you, too."

Kellen caught her hands and lifted them promptly away. "No, Chloe."

Finally—*finally*—the voice that had resounded in his heart all along found its way into his head, and his soul. "No, it's not, and this can't, this *won't*, happen between us again. I'm married, and I just made an enormous mistake."

She blinked slowly; the fire in her eyes snapped and crackled.

"I'm to blame, and for that I apologize, but I won't step away from my wife and my vows to her, ever again. This was wrong for me, Chloe. Completely wrong."

Her features hardened slightly, going intense. "Whether you're ready to face the truth right now or not, you feel the same way about me." She gathered a deep breath and then blew out through pursed lips. "Despite that, you'll deny yourself by walking away from me?"

"Chloe—" Kellen fumbled internally, trying to properly form his emotions into words. "Chloe, it's not denial. It's that I'm being forced to discover who I am again. Who I am, and who I'm supposed to be. Who I *want* to be." He nearly reached out to her, only intending to cushion what he was about to say, but he denied the gesture. A formidable, Christ-driven strength sang through him now—but at what cost, he wondered? How would he overcome what he had allowed to happen? "I'm so sorry for what I did."

"Don't fall on the sword all by yourself, Kellen." Anger laced her words. "I was there, too. The harlot, I suppose."

"You're not a harlot. You were confused. So was I."

"I still am."

Kellen discovered that in no way was he enamored by her any longer. Like the lifting of a distorting bank of clouds, Chloe's hold over him vanished. The kiss had awakened him to the evil of errant desire, and he found himself thinking about Pastor Gene's words at church just a few weeks back:

Sometimes experiencing the harrowing results of deepest sin will drive us back to God in ways so powerful it's nothing short of a miracle.

Never, ever again could he rebuke Juliet, and his marriage. He'd make it up to her for the rest of his life and pray she might never know how wrong, how idiotic, he had been.

Kellen, My son, what you do in the darkness is revealed in the light. Hold fast to My hand, for you are Mine.

Kellen absorbed the spirited words of God's warning and blanched at what they might mean.

No, he prayed in fervor, *Juliet can't ever know about this. It was only a kiss—and I swear to You that it's over. I've truly and honestly learned, God. You know that without question, because You know my heart...and my heart resides with You, and Juliet...*

He would atone. He would atone to her, and to God, by never straying again. He'd talk to Jason and make sure of his discretion. Jason was grateful for this opportunity after all, so the man owed Kellen for a nice bump in his career. And Kellen didn't believe Chloe would betray him if he stepped away. At this point, they could leave the episode behind—bruised but still whole.

Though his mind spun with millions of ways that plan could fail, Kellen promised himself he'd do everything in his power to shield Juliet, and their marriage, from his own folly.

Darkness is defeated by the light, Kellen. Hold fast to My hand.

The words that sang through his soul felt more ominous than comforting.

Following a lengthy silence, Chloe shifted her weight, and her eyes pleaded. "I know it's easier to stay married than go through the mess of a separation, or a divorce, but avoiding me isn't going to make you happy. Neither is living life out of a sense of obligation to vows that have grown stale. Isn't that much obvious?"

Guilt, shame, and sorrow worked as one to sting his senses, because her analysis couldn't have been more erroneous. He wasn't with Juliet out of obligation or due to vows gone stale. Chloe was also wrong about avoidance. Avoiding her now is all he wanted to do—but at what cost?

Kellen's head rang with the words of God's spirit, and he couldn't recall ever being as scared as he was right now— terrified of losing everything that was most precious to him.

Seeming to sense that their privacy was limited, Chloe stepped even further away, but she kept her gaze trained on his. "Find yourself, Kellen. Find the place where your love lives. Maybe it's me." She glanced at his ring finger. "Maybe it's her. Until you figure that out, I can't keep acting like this is just work. It's much more for me. I'm ready, and willing, to let you deep into my life. I'm halfway there already, but it's not real. It's nothing more than superficial. I don't want to get hurt, and I don't want you hurt, either."

Kellen couldn't speak. He couldn't reason, and he couldn't bring himself to confront the full ramifications of what had just happened. Nothing but fragments clicked into place-- unfaithfulness, betrayal, *Juliet*.

Chloe turned and exited the studio. Kellen was sick to the core, to a degree that gnawed at his heart and ate away at his psyche like battery acid. He closed his eyes and found he had to draw a breath. Desperately. When he did, he came upon the subtle undercurrent of Chloe's perfume—jasmine and ginger. What had he been thinking? What had happened to transform him from the man he wanted, and needed, to be? What had happened to the man, and husband, he had been before meeting Chloe?

Kellen curled his hands into fists, trying to keep steady and controlled.

This was not My pathway for you. The way you chose was not My way, Kellen. Come back to Me and stand firm against the storm.

The words fell through him, full of authority and weighted by a warning that stirred chills along his nerve endings, but one thing remained certain. The kiss he had shared with Chloe, and the firm admonishment of God, had turned Kellen completely around. He had rediscovered himself. The image of Juliet's angelic face swirled into place behind his closed eyelids.

God…please forgive me. Please…please forgive me for what I've done.

12

Juliet's heel caught in a crack of the sidewalk leading into the Renaissance Hotel. She wobbled and a brief stab of discomfort surged upward from her ankle. She groaned at her own vain stupidity. Stilettos might be great looking, and leg flattering, but that didn't change facts. They were also brutal instruments of torture.

At the moment she stumbled, she felt Kellen tuck his hand beneath her elbow, lending steady support. She blew out a breath. A flush flowed outward from her heart, blossoming against her neck and cheeks. "Sorry," she murmured. "I made a really stupid shoe choice, didn't I?"

A smile spread, starting in his eyes, deepening the small, appealing crinkles that fanned out from their corners. "That's OK. It gives me an extra excuse to watch out for you. You look beautiful, love."

"Thank you." Juliet absorbed the intimacy she found in his gaze. Kellen's attention lingered on her as they walked through the hotel lobby, expressive in a way that gave Juliet a rush of feminine pleasure. Soon after entering the Music City Ballroom, though, he became focused on the crowd of clients and colleagues who began to press in around them and offer greetings.

Associated Talent was celebrating its quarter century mark with a cocktail hour followed by a sit down dinner. Since the focus zeroed in on Kellen, Juliet was content to stand at his side and enjoy watching him. She took hold of his arm and slid her hand downward until their fingers laced and went snug. He wore a dark suit with a pop of color that came from his burgundy tie and matching pocket swatch. It was his eyes that captivated her, though. Always had. Presently they sparkled with warmth and the pleasure he found in being with people. His charisma was a powerful force because it stemmed from a point of sincerity that naturally drew people in.

As one of the newest members of the AT family, Chloe Havermill would be in attendance at tonight's event, and Juliet expected to meet her for the first time. She owned up to being curious about the woman. Also, while she and Kellen moved deeper into the banquet room, Juliet regarded her high-heeled shoes with the rueful thought that she had deliberately dressed to impress and had taken great pains with her appearance tonight. Her hair was a free-falling tumble of curls. She reached up to adjust the shoulders of her black, short-sleeved sheath. She had purchased the garment a few weeks back, when the party invitation arrived, drawn by its neckline embellishment of tiny, sparkling crystals. Yes—she was *definitely* aiming for the confident, chic look.

Kellen continued to make the rounds, and eventually she broke away, taking up conversations with folks she knew from Associated Talent. Kellen returned to her side a short time later to deliver a ginger ale and chat with Juliet's group for a few minutes.

The drink was chilly, sweet, and deeply appreciated. While she sipped, Juliet smiled a secretive, private smile.

The matter of pregnancy loomed larger and larger on the horizon, and she knew her evasion of the topic needed to end. The signs were becoming irrefutable. Each morning, and now even during the early hours of the afternoon, a dizzy-hot sickness would overwhelm her. The lack of a monthly cycle continued, and so did a growing, all-over sense of being drained and exhausted. She could almost feel her body expending every ounce of energy on the process of creation and sustaining not just one life, but two.

The more time that passed, the more her fears about being pregnant evaporated. She finally allowed herself to embrace the truth her body telegraphed in the slight thickening of her waist, the added fullness of her breasts. Irrational, perhaps, but she still refused to confirm her condition via a pregnancy test. Instead, she had scheduled an appointment with her gynecologist for Monday morning, and she prayed fervently about the outcome.

Confirmation would be the answer to so many longings...

Bursting on the inside, Juliet sipped her drink again, absorbing the burst of spice against her tongue. She slid a glance toward Kellen, wishing she could tell him the news— but no way would she do that until after Monday's doctor appointment offered verification. Tonight she intended to relax and enjoy a lovely episode of mixing and mingling as she caught up with friends and Kellen's colleagues.

After a dinner of broiled salmon, fluffy wild rice and fresh fruit, Juliet excused herself from the table to pay a visit to the ladies' room.

Standing at one of the empty marble pedestal sinks, she opened her evening bag and pulled out a tube of lipstick along with a hair comb. She started to re-fluff her hair.

A set of doors separating a sitting area from the bathroom stalls swung open and in strode two young ladies she didn't recognize. They both offered her a polite nod. Juliet smiled and finished with her hair. Despite the press of bodies and humid warmth, it had held up pretty well.

The new arrivals lined up next to Juliet and began to primp as well.

"I love these parties." The woman closest to Juliet offered that verdict to her friend while she brushed on some face powder. Her cheeks were a bit too red, and she propped a hip against the sink, as though wanting to steady herself. Juliet wondered if the woman hadn't perhaps indulged in a bit too much alcohol. "They're always so rife with drama and gossip."

Her friend perked up, arching a brow while she styled her hair. "Oh? What have I missed?"

"Jason just introduced me to that new singer he's producing for. Chloe Havermill."

Juliet uncapped her lipstick, but froze for an awkward second or two when the conversation turned to Chloe. She had not been formally introduced to her yet, but she had watched the artist from a distance during the course of the night.

"Oh...yeah...I know the girl you mean. What a knock-out. She's going to be mega."

Juliet grabbed hold of enough grace to keep from sinking on the inside. Knock-out and mega were appropriate terms. Statuesque, brimming with confidence, Chloe presented a polished image. She was decked out in an appealing pale blue satin dress that covered modestly, but emphasized a perfect figure.

"No doubt. Jay's really excited to be working with her, for sure, but man did he have some scoop!"

"He better be careful about scoop mongering—he's just entered the big leagues. He's so lucky to be producing at Summit."

"No doubt—but I know I can tell *you*."

"Of course!"

They laughed...a little too loud. "Well, it's like I said, non-stop drama. Apparently Chloe is getting way too friendly with her agent."

Juliet froze. *What?* She clung to the edge of the sink and squeezed hard. Obviously these two had no idea they were standing next to the *wife* of Chloe's agent. They continued to freshen up and never even looked her way.

"What makes him say that?"

"He *saw* them together! He actually *caught* them—*kissing*." Juliet's neighbor turned fully toward her friend, apparently enjoying the moment of revelation. "He said it was pretty steamy, too. Kicker is Jay tells me the guy is *married*! And a *Christian*!"

"Wow."

More giggles followed as they disappeared behind stall doors. Juliet's world rocked back and forth—then back and forth again. She kept carefully still, trying to right her equilibrium, but it was no use. Meanwhile, the two twentysomethings continued chatting.

"Yeah, amazing, huh? I mean, can you believe that? Getting caught in the act?"

Juliet sagged against the wall to her left. Cool ceramic tile chilled her bare arm. She swallowed hard. Her head felt heavy as a boulder, and her chest had gone way too tight. She hitched a gulp of air that did nothing to nourish her lungs.

"Clandestine trysts aside, the one I feel sorry for is his wife. I wonder if she's with him tonight. Seriously, the poor thing."

"Yeah—I mean, once a cheater, always a cheater, you know?" Juliet heard a tongue cluck and sigh from inside the second stall. "I'll have to notice who she is when we get back to the party."

The enthusiasm of these two gossip girls threw Juliet over the edge of reason. She covered her mouth with a shaky hand, pressing her fingertips against her lips to keep from screaming. Silence and a couple of flushes passed by. The women washed and nodded once more to Juliet, not detecting her discomfort whatsoever as they left.

Ambushed, Juliet wished she could tumble out of this hideous nightmare, grab Kellen, and run away. Her legs refused to budge. Suddenly, they were the consistency of hardened cement.

All at once, her stomach rolled violently and clenched, beginning a severe rebellion against the fish dinner she had consumed. She dashed into the nearest stall, thanking God for the small mercy of a now empty facility. She slammed the door closed, locked it and crumpled, dropping to her knees the instant before her stomach emptied.

Agony swept through her, escaping on a weak, broken groan.

Being completely honest with herself, she had to admit: she had known something was wrong all along. She had known since that dinner at her parents' house.

Kellen. Chloe. A kiss. Perhaps even *more*. Her *husband*. The man who held her heart in his hands, who knew its every dip and curve and had sworn, before God, to love and honor her forever and always...

A cheater. Betrayer.

The heaves that followed went dry and only served to jolt her body, sending her head into an explosion of intense, pounding pain. She needed aspirin, immediately. Juliet rose on trembling legs and exited the stall, stumbling to the closest sink. She dry-swallowed a pair of aspirin caplets and did her best to clean up, wishing like crazy she could splash cold water across her face—anything to cool the fever she felt. That wouldn't do, of course. For now, she had no choice but to choke everything back and put on a brave—utterly false front. She had no choice but to somehow deal with the world that lurked beyond the doors of the bathroom.

As a fool.

Precious Juliet—I hold you in the palm of My hand. Go forward in My love...the love that surpasses all understanding and destroys all boundaries, all limitations.

On one level, the affirmation of those holy words lit her soul and helped her remain tethered to reality. On another, she raged. *Oh, yeah, God?* She wanted to scream. *Then prove it! Take me out of this nightmare! Lift me away and make it all go away! How could this possibly happen? Please, I beg of you, Lord Jesus, please don't let this be real.*

She straightened, and made the mistake of looking at her reflection in the mirror. She nearly lost it all over again. Her skin was splotchy; her eyes were way too bright and tinged by red. Hurried and scrambling, she brushed at the lines in her soiled makeup to blend it back into place; she swiped her fingertips beneath her lashes to eliminate the runny traces of black mascara.

One labored step, then another...and another. She pushed herself to keep moving, shoving open the door of the restroom to rejoin what now felt like an over-loud, over-done gathering of people with only one goal in mind: ego, fame, power-mongering and monetary gain at the expense of everything else.

The glitter-drenched world Kellen inhabited suddenly felt like the threshold of darkness and evil and held within its grip the worst form of heartbreak she could possibly imagine.

❧❦

Where was Juliet?

Kellen scanned the room, missing the natural fit of her at his side. Intending to reconnect as soon as he grabbed some dessert, he paused at the buffet line, in front of a gurgling fountain of waving chocolate. Nice thing was that Juliet had always been comfortable mixing with the people at Associated Talent. She befriended people easily, and he was so proud of his wife. He was grateful to return to even footing in their relationship. Tomorrow would be a restful Sunday wherein he could attend church services then spend an entire day in peaceful quiet with Juliet.

One of the worst mistakes he could have ever made had transformed into a means by which to change, and reassert the best parts of his soul.

He lifted a bone china plate and plucked a foursome of strawberries from the towering display. One-by-one he coated the fruit chunks with chocolate, intending to offer a few to Juliet. The idea left him to smile; he knew she'd love the treat.

The idea of sampling one of the morsels prompted him to coat an additional berry and pop it into his mouth right away. Kellen savored the bittersweet flavors.

"So, here's something I never knew about Kellen Rossiter. He's a bit of a slob."

Kellen flinched at the sound of Chloe's light, teasing voice, but he turned politely, giving her an inquiring look.

She moved close enough to stroke a fingertip against his chin, right beneath his lower lip. Apparently, a droplet of chocolate had ended up decorating a spot just beneath his mouth. The ease of Chloe's gesture caused alarm bells to ring. Before he could react, she swiped the droplet away.

Her gaze remained steady and probing.

Kellen moved away by two generous steps. "Chloe, don't." In deference to their surroundings, the command came out soft and discreet, but no less emphatic.

Chloe turned away as well, to swirl a pair of fresh berries beneath the chocolate fountain and settle them on the plate she held. Seeing her, being in her company, filled Kellen with steel-strength resolution. An instant later, he made a decision that would lead him even farther from Chloe. Weiss McDonald could assign someone else to handle her career development from now on. Kellen would make it official as soon as possible, but in a more appropriate setting.

A slice of precious, scripture-based encouragement came alive in his mind from the book of James. *Submit yourself to God. Resist the devil, and he will flee from you.*

"What does your schedule look like on Monday?" Kellen asked.

"I'm open."

"Let's plan to meet in the morning. Nine-thirty or ten o'clock would be good—my office. We need to talk." Her gaze tagged his, her eyes soft and expectant. Kellen shook his head. "Nothing has changed, Chloe. The meeting is about your career, and where it needs to go. Nothing more."

Chloe gave him a speculative look and tossed her head to shake a wave of shimmering jet hair across her shoulder. "I'll be there."

Kellen gestured toward a nearby group of AT executives Chloe needed to meet. Introductions would also bring about separation. "I want to find Juliet, but first let me introduce you to—"

"Kellen?"

From behind, Juliet's summons stopped him in his tracks. He turned, smiling at the sound of her voice—but then he got a good look at her. His smile froze on his lips and his pulse started to thunder and push. She was pale. Although she hid it well, she trembled. Kellen quickly set the plate of fruit aside.

"Juliet?" Alarm skyrocketed once he crossed to her.

"I need to leave," she whispered. "Now."

He took hold of her arm, because she looked as though she were about to collapse. He nodded his understanding and slipped an arm around her waist. She went taut and unyielding against him. Kellen had no idea what to make of that reaction.

Chloe stepped up just as Kellen made the first step toward leading Juliet away; his client was openly curious. "You must be Juliet Rossiter. I've been looking forward to meeting you." Chloe smiled and extended her hand, likely unaware of Juliet's quiet and desperate plea to leave the party. Kellen cringed when Juliet's complexion faded further, if such a thing were even possible.

What had happened?

He watched Juliet paste on a smile and accept the gesture of Chloe's extended hand. "You must be Chloe Havermill. I've heard a lot about you. Welcome to Associated Talent." Quickly, with a sense of desperation Kellen alone could sense, she looked into his eyes. "I'm sorry to seem rude, but I'm not feeling well, and I really need to leave."

"Let's call it a night." Kellen addressed Chloe in a businesslike manner. "I'll see you Monday morning."

છ°ન

"Juliet—please talk to me."

Kellen's gently spoken request settled between them. She propped her head against the leather seat of their car and closed her eyes. "Kellen, just get me home. I don't want to talk. Not right now. I'm sick and I need to get my feet back under me. Somehow."

The last word faded. She took in a deep, shaky breath. Flashes of street light revealed her features from time to time, and he grew increasingly concerned. She was shutting down and completely remote. Were those tear-tracks that cut a glimmering path down her cheeks?

It cost every cent of his restraint, but Kellen respected her request for silence and distance. The last thing she needed right now was pressure—no matter how well intended. She kept her eyes closed, but Kellen longed to offer her comfort. More confused than ever, he sped home. He reached for Juliet's hand only to discover it was ice cold.

And she promptly pulled away.

13

Juliet stared out the windshield of her parked car, looking at the medical office building through an onslaught of rain. She swallowed back terror. She choked back dizziness and nausea trying to carefully and deliberately even out her breathing, hoping to fight off an onslaught of sickness that sent searing heat through her veins and left her ears to ring.

This is it, she thought. *I already know what's coming, and yet all of this seems surreal to me now. Unfathomable.*

Then there was the thick, heavy downpour. Naturally, it would rain in an unforgiving deluge. How fitting, she thought, that this oppressive cascade would pour down on what should have been one of the happiest days of her life. And Kellen's. The coming moments should have been the culmination of everything beautiful and precious between them.

Some would look at the rain as a benediction, like holy water, or a blessing of sorts. Juliet shook her head. No. Not this time. Instead, buckets of water crashed down in laden sheets that only served to distort her view and color her world a deep, depressing shade of gray.

Sunday had stretched out with long, unforgiving arms, yet somehow she had survived. Numbness had coated her spirit all day, an anesthetic that helped her shut down and exist, but not cope. Every time she tried to push through the fog of shock, pain exploded through her body.

She had no idea what to do about Kellen's infidelity. She had no ability to grasp it and figure out what to do next. She was grateful that physical illness had delivered an excuse to simply lie in bed and gain much needed latitude—and space—

from her husband. He didn't question her listless behavior or her request for solitude. That wasn't going to last long, though.

Her only thought, her heart's sole emphasis, remained fixed on this moment alone.

Releasing a strangled moan, Juliet clutched the steering wheel but went otherwise weak. Her shoulders sagged beneath an enormous, invisible weight. She dipped her head until it rested upon the padded leather surface of the steering wheel.

The chain of her necklace bumped against her chin and tears fell down her cheeks. Coming aware, she gulped and gave a hiccupping sigh, fingering the gold chain that was so familiar to her, worrying its pendant—the cross crafted of diamonds set pave—the piece she always wore because it was so precious to her.

Juliet held tight to the cross, squeezing the emblem until, once she pulled her hand away, its imprint remained upon her palm.

"God," she beseeched in a whisper that filled the empty car, "*please.* I beg you, *please.* I'm not in denial. I'm not unaware of all the signs my body is sending me. What's about to be confirmed, though—I won't survive it on my own. It'll take a miracle to make everything right. It'll take Your power and nothing less. Please help me. Please."

The sleek, black face of her Movado watch caught her eye. It was time. Further delay would make her late for her appointment. A thundering pulse increased. She opened the door, extended a compact umbrella and stepped outside. Her legs wobbled. Her ears started to ring even louder, and she tried once more to regulate her breathing and heart rate.

No dice. Right now, the inevitable called.

❧❦

Doctor Jacqueline Roth took Juliet by the hand. Wearing a smile, and the standard issue white jacket and stethoscope, she assisted Juliet from a prone position on the metal examination table until she sat up, perched now at the end, her bare feet dangling.

"Congratulations!" Doctor Roth said kindly. "I'm so happy for you, Juliet. You're two and a half months along."

What followed bypassed any sense of full consciousness and instead became nothing more than a swirl of images: a prescription slip for vitamins, words about maintaining a healthy diet and exercise regimen, prompts to set up additional appointments. Through it all, Juliet felt flushed and hot. She trembled, not because she was dressed only in a lightweight cotton dressing gown. Her breathing went shallow, and she felt an ominous blood rush that left her close to hyperventilation. Her body coped with an onslaught of stress and fear, and a now familiar roil of conflicting emotions about the state of her life.

The red stains she felt spreading on her cheeks, and shoulders, the shudders she couldn't fight, gave her away to her physician. Dr. Roth eyed her. "Juliet, are you OK?"

"No...ah...I mean yeah...of course...I..." She released a breath she had held in too long while trying to come to grips. It came out sounding like a gasp.

"No, you're not. And your blood pressure was high when you checked in—but I figured that was an anomaly due to nerves. I know what you've gone through, and how much this means to you and Kellen."

Dr. Roth pulled a paper cup from the dispenser positioned above a small metal sink. She filled it with water and handed it over. Juliet struggled to stay upright and cognizant. She sipped the water, which was tepid, and not altogether soothing, but it gave her a diversion. Precious seconds to march forward into what was now a revised version of her life.

"You're not as excited about the news as I thought you'd be," Dr. Roth observed gently.

"I...I am...I just...I need to adjust, that's all." Juliet tried for a smile, but it wavered. "This is huge, for me and for

Kellen."

As though somewhat assured, Dr. Roth patted Juliet's shoulder. "Well, it's not huge yet, but it will be by the end of nine months." Juliet's answering laugh was false, but Dr. Roth didn't seem to notice. "See you in a month, and if you have any issues or any questions at all before the next appointment, don't hesitate to call in and ask. That's what we're here for."

Juliet ignored the words. She knew just one thing: she had to leave. Suddenly she felt claustrophobic. She had to find her way outside, and then to a place where she could rest in silence and pray.

OK, God. This is Your plan. You know what I'm up against. You know my heart. And Kellen's. I told You before I even walked in the door that I can't handle this. I can't survive this—not on my strength alone, and not the way things are right now. Help me!

An intense urge all but overwhelmed her. She had to get to Trinity Christian as soon as possible. The need hit with such force that it could not—and would not—be denied. There she would try to find her way into some semblance of sanctuary, and God's presence, before she confronted Kellen.

About everything.

҂ѹ

"Kellen, what are you getting at? If the case is closed, and you're turning my career management over to someone else, what more do we have to discuss?"

Since it looked like Chloe was about to bolt from his office, Kellen stood and circled his desk. Before he dropped into the chair next to hers, he turned the piece of furniture so they could be eye to eye. "I want to apologize." She bristled, but Kellen didn't let her reaction dissuade him. "I'm trying very hard to get back to where I was—to who I used to be. In order to do that, I need to apologize to you for what happened."

She blinked. Kellen saw her draw a deep breath. "Meaning *us*."

Kellen pushed away his shame. "Yes, us. And the kiss, and everything that led up to it. It was wrong on my part to move forward the way we did."

"I said it at the time, Kellen—you were hardly alone in that."

He paused to ingest her sharp reply, giving her a pointed opportunity to do the same. Did she realize the deeper meaning of what she had just said? Could she see the truth in it and make changes of her own? Just like the breakdown in his marriage, the relationship with Chloe needed to be confronted, and then absolved—for the sake of everyone involved. They needed to learn from their mistakes.

"You're a beautiful woman, Chloe. You possess an amazing talent. Don't let outside forces block you from what's good in this life. What's right and *true*."

"I think I know where you're going with this, Kellen." She shifted, seeming uncomfortable.

"Do you?"

"Yes. God. Christianity and all that. You're re-finding your roots. Great. Congratulations. I won't get in the way of that. If it's over, it's over. You may think my behavior doesn't show it, but I'm not a bad person." Her grip went tight on the armrest of the chair. She crossed her legs nervously. "I won't apologize, though, Kellen. Life is about embracing experiences with no regrets and no asking 'what if.' I couldn't help but pursue what I felt for you."

That method of thinking alarmed Kellen. "Chloe, please don't live your life that way. Your career is going to take you far and wide. You're going to come up against people and circumstances that will hurt you if you embrace a life based on pleasure-seeking instead of what's best for your overall well-being."

"That's a pretty lofty ideal, Kellen, and I'm only human. Furthermore, so are *you*."

Shame washed over him, but he couldn't relent. Her posture went rigid. Kellen answered her tense reply by remaining as calm and gentle as possible. "I know. I'm speaking from experience. If any amount of good can come from the mistakes I've made, maybe this is part of it. Don't play footsies with the devil. You won't make it out alive."

"It hurts that you think of me as a mistake."

He shook his head. "No, Chloe, you're not a mistake—the places we took our relationship were a mistake. My entire world spun out of orbit when I was around you—and that's because of me—and what I allowed myself to become. It wasn't right, and it didn't just hurt me, it demeaned my wife, and the commitment we made to one another."

"Well, you won't have to worry about me interfering with that. You want me out of your life, fine. You've got your wish. I understand why you don't want to be my agent any longer, too. It all makes sense. I'm an adult, and I'll behave like one, but I still don't understand why you're saying and doing all this."

"Because turning your career over to Weiss, so he can reassign your management, is only part of what I know I need to do. Juliet is my mission now. My marriage is my mission. But I know I've hurt you. That was never my intent, but I should have recognized—and respected—the danger you and I were falling into." Kellen gave her hand a final squeeze and looked deep into her turbulent, glittering eyes. The allure of deep violet did nothing to him now. The faultless presentation of upswept hair, a simple white blouse and teal skirt, made no impact at all. "I want you to promise me something."

"What?" Her voice carried softly, and the brimming tears fell.

"Don't ever let another man do to you what I did. You deserve much more."

❧

The instant Chloe closed the door of his office Kellen's heart flew free, trailing ribbons of exquisite relief. Every ounce of temptation she presented had evaporated. He was finished walking that tightrope across a very deep canyon in his life.

He had danced willingly into a shade of gray, even as it sent him down the wrong path…but he was finished.

Once again, he thought of Juliet. Thoughts of her led him to focus on a brass-framed photograph positioned on the right corner of his desk. He picked it up and studied the image. It was, by far, his favorite shot of her. Taken on a beach in Hawaii about three years ago, the picture captured the very essence of her spirit.

Generally she was quiet, almost shy, but captivating—and so very sweet. He savored the photograph—her sparkling green eyes, the shoulder-length hair of auburn that waved around her face and, in this shot, was lifted in a soft trade wind. She wore a blue t-shirt and white shorts. In the photo, she looked at him over her shoulder with playful spunk and a degree of love in her eyes that left him humbled and in awe.

They had celebrated their fifth anniversary by island hopping. The Hawaii trip marked the high-end of what was a joyful ride for their marriage. Those few short years ago, they had been at the pinnacle of their lives—blissfully and sincerely happy. He saw, clearly now, that time had worked its way with them. It wasn't the big stuff that had led him to the ultimate danger point with Chloe. It was a numbing compilation of their daily routine, a shifting of passion from electricity to the ordinary.

An unanswered effort toward building a family didn't help matters any. Neither did non-stop busyness meant to fill the hours, and their lives, with meaning.

I love Juliet, God. I love her completely. She's the woman of my heart. How did we grow apart? Why did we let ourselves become so methodical in our approach to one another? It wasn't always that way. Not at all.

Kellen set aside the photograph and acknowledged part of the problem. He had strayed from God. Juliet had stayed devout and active in her faith life, but with an all-consuming drive that claimed their time together, and made it easy for him to drift and focus his energies elsewhere.

They needed to work on those issues. Together.

Next, he wrestled with the idea of telling her about Chloe. Juliet was an innocent. She didn't deserve the pain he would inflict by confessing. And he hadn't made love to Chloe—he had kissed her, once, and tasted ruination. He had promptly and sincerely changed after that terrible slip and never, ever would he be swept away by another woman.

Hiding from her would be wrong, though. He knew that—but he couldn't stomach the idea of looking into her eyes and shattering the love and trust they had always shared.

No. He couldn't do it—but on the other hand, how else could he live with himself? How could he ever be completely honest with her? Yes, the truth would hurt them both, but from there, they could rebuild. He was determined to reclaim his heart, and Juliet alone knew its every contour. He'd spend a lifetime assuring her of his love.

But would she ever be able to forgive him? Would she ever be able to trust him again if he found the strength, and ability, to come clean and unburden his soul?

Nope—he just couldn't do it…

But…if he didn't…

Kellen, My son, what you do in the darkness is revealed in the light. Hold fast to My hand, for you are Mine.

The words came to him, a memory stroke that carried the fortifying touch of God's spirit. This time, he took the hint.

Kellen shoved back from his desk and stood. He looked at his watch and calculated his schedule. He had a couple of hours to spare before a conference call with AT headquarters in Los Angeles. Right now, all he could focus on was the need to fall back into God's embrace. He needed grace-filled forgiveness and God's guidance so desperately he shook.

He grabbed his coat, intending to get to Trinity Christian Church. Immediately.

14

The church space sang to Juliet in a holy silence that wrapped around her like a welcome embrace. She knelt to pray, heedless of the fact that there were no kneelers in the pews of Trinity Christian. The hard tile floor felt good beneath her knees, and somehow grounding.

"God, what did I do wrong? We didn't argue. We didn't fight. We moved forward together in our marriage. Why did he leave it behind? How was that even possible for him? How did I fail him? And You?"

She sobbed openly, speaking the words aloud, heedless of being overheard. The space was empty anyhow. She laid her head on her folded hands trying desperately to bring herself to a new understanding of her life.

My promises are unchanging truth, and life. Your faith will save you. Go forward in peace, and be cured of your affliction.

The words, the glimpse of sacred Scripture, resounded through the entirety of her being. The decree swept through her with such power she went straight, tears drying on her cheeks as she blinked, and assimilated. Had she not already been on her knees, the summons would have knocked her there like the weakened heap of humanity she had become.

She pondered. Go forward? In *peace*? How was she supposed to accomplish *that*? In prompt, near supernatural response, she received the answer.

Know that I am God, Juliet. Know that I am God.

She bowed her head, drained and empty, submitting herself as best she could. Just then, the sound of footsteps echoed down the main aisle.

"Juliet?" The call jarred her. She whipped her head

around and gasped at what she saw.

Kellen.

Kellen?

Did she simply think his name, or had she spoken it aloud? Stunned and overwrought, Juliet scrambled to her feet. In an untidy spin, she faced her husband. Just as quickly, she went weak, sinking onto the pew just a second or two after standing. She didn't need a mirror to tell her that her makeup was smeared and her hair was a mess. She knew by the heat in her cheeks that her face was flushed; her eyes were probably red from crying.

Kellen's alarmed expression confirmed every one of her suspicions. "Juliet, are you OK? Please talk to me. This is driving me crazy. What's happened to you, love?"

Love. The use of that endearment caused her stomach to churn. Anger rose and obliterated everything else. "Don't."

Kellen's confusion intensified.

"I mean it, Kellen. Do *not* call me that again. Not *ever* again!" She bit off the words; their bitter taste filled her mouth.

He reared back. Although he hesitated for a moment, he eased into the pew next to her. A mask of sorts, protective and inscrutable, now shaded his eyes.

He didn't speak. He waited on her, keeping to his corner of the pew. Juliet simmered and seethed. Just as quickly, though, the anger fled, washed away by a wave of sadness that stretched clear through to every cell in her body.

"This moment is killing me, Kellen, on so many levels. I've dreamed about it since the day we married, imagining it to be bursting with joy and anticipation. Instead, it's breaking my heart."

"What moment? What happened?" Generally fearless and confident, Kellen regarded her now in open trepidation. "I have no idea what to do to hel—"

"I'll never have another chance to say this to you for the first time," Juliet interjected, "or share this moment with you the way I had always envisioned. I'm pregnant, Kellen. I'm pregnant."

A mix of emotions swept across his face. Disbelief came first, erased quickly by joy, then the most crushing visual of all: his love, intimate and rich. It had once made her feel so precious. Despite her vocal firestorm, his reaction was everything she had prayed for. This moment should have made her heart soar. Instead, she was shattered.

"You seem shocked." The words came out sounding waspish. Juliet hated that fact, but couldn't escape the rage and heartbreak. The venom inside her needed release.

"I'm very happily shocked." His response came fast, but sincere. "We've wanted this for so long, I'm thrilled—no wonder you've been feeling—"

"I'm sure you'll remember the night it happened." Juliet cut him off once more. "It was spontaneous and heated and wonderful. Remember? There were no thoughts of anything else but each other. Or so I had believed. But if you do the math, you'll realize we conceived the night you met Chloe Havermill." She sneered at him. "After all, it's not like there's been a ton of times that we've made love since then."

He went pale. Juliet wanted to slap him across the face so hard that he'd be left marked by the strike of her hand. Why had he done it? Why hadn't he woken from whatever delusion clouded his mind? In the end, she restrained herself. Of course, she couldn't lash out. They were in church, after all. God's house. A sanctuary for everyone.

Even Kellen. Even her.

"Oh—God—"

Kellen had obviously connected the dots. The exclamation that crossed his lips wasn't a curse; it was a plea. Juliet recognized the difference yet fought to maintain enough control to remain seated next to him. "Ironic, isn't it, that I'd get pregnant the night you came home from Iridescence—and *her*. I gave myself to you freely, Kellen. Like I always have. At the time, I had no idea the man I love—the man I've loved with all my heart—had most likely been riled up by dancing sensual circles around another woman."

Kellen gasped.

Juliet plowed ahead. "Yes, I received a rather rude shock at the AT anniversary party. A couple of ladies who were probably too tipsy for their own good discussed a kiss you shared with Chloe at the studio recently. Imagine how I felt, Kellen. Just *imagine* it!"

A vein at his temple began to throb. Strain tightened his mouth and furrowed brows deepened the subtle lines around his eyes. Oh, she was hitting the mark with all kinds of poisoned darts. It felt good. And positively horrifying. Wrong. Still, she couldn't stop.

"Juliet, listen to me. That's exactly why I'm here."

His desperation reached the entryway of her spirit, but she slammed the door closed. "What are you getting at?"

"I came here to pray before talking to you. About all of this. I—"

"It's Monday morning, Kellen. Don't you have an appointment with her?" She didn't care how rude her interruptions were, and she laid mean emphasis on the word appointment.

Kellen's eyes lit, snapping with the dawn of anger. "I've already seen Chloe, and I asked for that meeting with just one purpose in mind--resigning as her agent. Go ahead and confirm it with Weiss if it'll help you to believe me."

"I'd rather eat sawdust." Juliet spat the words, unmindful of his emphatic tone. She wanted to scream at the top of her lungs. This nightmare was going to ruin her, and the relationship she most cherished. She could feel her world deteriorating.

"I'm not working with her anymore, Juliet. I don't want to be anywhere near her. I want to ask you for—"

"Gossip, Kellen. Sordid *gossip*. That's what you and I have been reduced to. That's what our *marriage* has been reduced to. I feel so much anger, and shame—at you, and at myself—that I can't even *begin* to think straight. You're looking at this pregnancy as a beginning. It's not. To me, it marks the end. And I honestly don't know how to handle that fact. I'm sick to the depths of my soul. That's *my* truth—no matter what yours and Chloe's might happen to be."

"Juliet." Kellen sucked in a breath and looked away. When his gaze tagged hers again, an ocean of sorrow bathed his deep brown eyes. "There is no me and Chloe!"

"Yes there is, Kellen, and I can't even begin to figure out how to deal with it." His pained expression rolled off the armor she had erected. "Were we that bad off? I knew we needed to refocus, and spend more time together, but I had no idea I hadn't fulfilled your life. I had no idea you had fallen out of love with me."

Kellen let out an exclamation. He nearly reached out to her but seemed to think the better of it. Good thing. Her reaction to being touched by him right now would be explosive. "I came here to pray, and to find a way to ask you— to beg you—to please—please forgive me. Forgive me, Juliet." For a few beats of silence, those words echoed. "I haven't fallen out of love with you whatsoever." A silence ensued that was hot and thick. "Believe me when I say that."

Love, Juliet discovered, possessed the sharpest of stings— stings of pain that came with no type of antidote. "I can't. I can't, and I won't, believe anything you say to me right now. You've been caught. That's all your remorse is about. And, not to be cliché and all, but your actions speak much louder than your words."

Juliet broke down all over again. She cried, but she was doing this. More miraculous, she was *surviving* this. She was actually discussing Kellen—her beloved—in the context of a relationship with another woman. At the same time, she felt God's arms propping her up and heard His sure, steady words:

Rest in My peace, Juliet. Go still and listen.

She couldn't. She beat back that piece of instruction with swinging fists, because she was nowhere near ready to rest or listen to Kellen's platitudes about seeking forgiveness. Right now, she needed action, and she needed him to hurt.

"I've been sitting here asking myself why God would bring a child into a situation like ours." Water swam in crooked circuits down the stained glass windows, bringing images of angels and disciples to eerie, distorted life. "Why would He do that?"

Visually he succumbed to the same kind of all-over shock that had enveloped her world for the past two days. The pain in his eyes transformed into a glaze of paralysis that Juliet figured was her due compensation for the betrayal he had inflicted.

"Over the past few months, ever since you started working with Chloe, our relationship nose-dived. We've drifted and existed. I know that, and I admit I was too complacent to make changes. Still, you let her *in*! You found your way to a woman who is...is..."

She nearly gagged on the words. Rain drummed down on the roof of the church in a steady cadence, like a heartbeat. A baby's heartbeat. She gave up trying to vocalize Chloe's attributes. Nonetheless, delineation took place in her mind via words that swirled into place and fed her destroyed sense of self—words like vibrant, gorgeous, enamored, and naturally, after all he had done for her, Chloe was swept away by Kellen.

Worse by far, however, Chloe fed a need in Kellen's heart that Juliet obviously couldn't. She slumped against the cool, unyielding wood of the pew. She closed her eyes and residual dampness caused her lashes to stick together. Dizziness nearly overtook her, and she wished she could fade to unconsciousness. Anything would be better than this onrush of hopelessness.

"I need to move out." The words escaped before she fully considered the idea, but the course of action turned into an escape route that grew appealing wings and lifted her to a place where she just might find a way to survive. "I'll stay with Marlene or something—somewhere—somewhere away from all of this."

Words faded at the end, just like her strength, her courage, and her resolve. She loved Kellen completely and exclusively. How could she move past that fact and create a new life without him? The idea shredded her apart inside, but she'd find a way. She had no choice now.

Juliet turned her head and looked at him tiredly. This was her best friend, her lover and now, a complete stranger. A lump lodged tight at the back of her throat.

"We can't work on our relationship if we're not together, Juliet."

"That's something you might have considered before finding your way into the arms of another woman. Apparently, we haven't worked at our relationship while we were under the same roof. What's the difference if I move out?"

He flinched.

Immune to the reaction, she ignored it. "Frankly, I don't know if we're worth it, Kellen. Not anymore. What you've done speaks loud and clear about what you feel for me now." She couldn't stand any more of this. Juliet hiked her purse strap onto her shoulder, preparing to leave with as much dignity as she could muster.

Kellen rose swiftly and smoothly blocked her exit. "I can't find a way to ask you to stay put and listen to me. There's so much I want to say, but you won't hear a word of it. I'm trapped. I wish I could help you see and understand that I know I've made the biggest mistake of my life. I know all of this in my heart, but I can't make you see it."

The words were spoken in a tender way. She sensed his regret, but his tone held a layer of challenge as well. She retained just enough strength to answer him back. "Let me ask you something. Do you regret betraying our marriage, or do you regret getting caught in the act?"

Kellen's shoulders bent and his eyes flickered when he paused and shook his head. "No matter what I say to that, you won't believe me. No matter what I do, it'll be wrong."

He had aged a decade in mere minutes. Lifting her chin, refusing to feel even the slightest degree of empathy, Juliet gathered herself once again. She tried to brush past him but for a second time Kellen stood in the way. She watched him start to reach out again, this time as if wanting to take hold of her arm. When she stepped back, he gritted his teeth and dropped his hand to his side.

"I'm going to ask you—with all that I am—please don't leave our home."

Weighted by firm conviction, Kellen's words fell through her heart but found no room to settle.

"I don't want you to leave—not now and not ever—but especially not when you're pregnant with our child. *Please.* I'll do anything you ask to make it bearable. Just don't leave."

A long, tense moment passed. All she could do was stare at him, aghast and wrenched away from everything she knew and everything she held most dear. "Kellen, how much of the chivalry you're displaying has to do with me, and how much of it has to do with the baby? Finally and at last a baby, right? Family was always our dream, and look what we've turned into as that dream comes true."

Perhaps words could hit as hard as a physical blow. If Kellen's reaction was any indication, he had been rocked backwards by the figurative punch of a fist. Her vindication at that was tempered immediately by bone-deep sorrow, and loss. Tears sprang up. She dashed them away, sick of the way they felt against her skin, sick of the weakness they displayed. She hiccupped when she tried to catch her breath.

But like a woman possessed, she couldn't stop herself from lashing out one last time. She had wanted to hurt him, after all, and she was succeeding. "I don't know what I'm going to do, and I don't know what's going to happen. I've landed smack-dab in the middle of hell, and you've ripped my heart out."

෬෬

I love you, Juliet. I wanted to say that to you countless times during that horrid confrontation. You're precious to me. You're my everything. I've made an epic mistake, but I love you.

I love you…

I love you…

The words became a chorus that played through him over and over again. Kellen stumbled blindly toward his car in the church parking lot. Rain drenched him, all but gluing his suit to his body. He couldn't have cared less. He sank onto the driver's seat of his CTS and slammed the door shut. The drumbeat of pouring water pounded against the roof and windshield.

Juliet was long gone. She had exited the church and taken off with no indication of whether she'd go home, or perhaps to Marlene's, or maybe even her parents' house. She needed to be away from him, and Kellen didn't blame her. Meanwhile, in an awful glimpse of the new life he inhabited, he had nothing left.

Kellen, I am with you. Always.

He propped his head against the back of the leather seat and closed his eyes. Water ran off his hair in cold, snaking rivers that skimmed his neck and dribbled down his back as he forced himself to go still.

"There's no way to reach her now," he lamented, beseeching the God he had refused to obey. Would He hear? Would He care? Everything Kellen knew to be true as a Christian told him, emphatically, yes. No one was beyond redemption. Even him. "She's been ambushed, God, and her heart has been laid low by my stupidity."

Turning inward, Kellen allowed his mind to go blank. Muscles and joints held too tightly in place began to uncoil, leaving him in the throes of an ache that pounded through every joint in his body.

"Please—please, Father help her learn to forgive me."

His words mixed with the sizzle and pop of the rain. His eyes stung as the unwavering truth behind them hit home and left Kellen acutely aware of everything he had lost: the sweet, unfettered sparkle of Juliet's eyes when she looked at him, the soft silk of her hand in his, her presence, in both body and spirit with a force so powerful and intimate that, after the length of time they had been together, he could no longer distinguish where he ended and Juliet began.

Until now.

The two-word condemnation wreaked havoc. He expelled a heavy breath and slouched forward. He had to get going, but the simple act of pushing a key into the ignition and twisting it felt like running a marathon. The engine purred to life and hummed smoothly. Kellen couldn't move. He didn't want to. His conference call was scheduled to start in less than twenty minutes; there was no way he'd make it on time. Furthermore? It didn't matter to him one bit.

"Forget it," he muttered to the empty space. "Forget it all."

Lead Me by Sanctus Real came on the radio, and from the opening words, Kellen sank back once more and lost himself in the lyrics and music, forcing himself to remember to breathe.

Busted up and bleeding from the core of his spirit, Kellen's tears squeezed out of the corners of his eyes and trickled down his cheeks. The song couldn't have possibly been more ordained. The piece chronicled a turbulent season in the span of a Christian marriage. He clenched his fists. The lyrics sank in and a painful swell of emotion left his throat tight. The musical illustration of a man struggling to maintain his Godly hold on life—trying to lead his wife, his children and himself toward spiritual truth—shattered his defenses like the sure swing of a sledgehammer.

It was a pure moment of God-speak.

Kellen's tears rolled harder—beads of regret that poured down his face in a way he hadn't experienced since his youth.

Husband. Father. Christian leader.

He had utterly failed…on all counts.

Dreams came true as his most precious relationship, his deepest love, unraveled. He couldn't turn the tide now. Juliet had made that clear. How could he find God's grace when he had lost a large part of what was best in his life—the faith and trust of his wife? Now Juliet paid the price for his mistakes and the battle he had lost against the devil's temptations.

Help me bring her back, Lord. I can't do this without You. Help me show her my devotion. Help me recapture her heart.

Kellen groaned after that silent prayer. He meant every syllable, but wondered. How could he ever win her back? How could she ever be free enough to trust him again? Agony transformed into a physical pain. The lyrics of the song continued to wash over him, but Kellen felt far removed from any type of cleansing and hope they might provide. Rather, he considered the moments when he had stepped away from his church and turned his back on everything he knew to be right—like the woman he had committed his love to for a lifetime, and still loved above all else.

His diversion from God had intensified the instant a starry-eyed beauty had entered his field of vision, playing a perfect stroke against each and every pressure point of his thirsty ego. He had turned away from heaven and stumbled headlong into a battle against the devil in his soul. Being a Christian didn't protect him from being tempted by the call of evil. Now he needed to reassert himself by finding his way back to his faith and Juliet—the only woman who mattered.

He decided to chuck work and go home instead. He'd call Weiss with some form of an excuse for bailing on the conference call with Los Angeles. Whether Juliet showed up or not, home is where he needed to be. When he left the church parking lot, the song concluded on a provocative declaration that seeped into Kellen's soul and found fertile soil. Kellen prayed. *Father, lead me. I can't do this alone.*

❧

He piloted home, not knowing what to expect. He drove up the driveway and spied Juliet's car in the garage. He pulled in next to her black Lexus, unable to exit his vehicle right away. It seemed like God was all but buckling him into place.

Kellen might have been a few months rusty on petitions and daily prayer, but not anymore. He recognized a call to worship when it hit him over the head, and he heeded the summons. He didn't speak; he didn't think. Instead, he listened to the silence and he bowed his head, loving the way his body went lax and receptive.

Love her, Kellen. Love her well.

Six small words filled him. They might have come from God; they might have been his dearest wish given form. He didn't know for sure, and for now, he didn't care. All he wanted in his life was to somehow make things right.

He stepped out of the car. When he cut through the kitchen, all he came upon was silence. Concerned, he headed to the entryway of their home, intending to trot upstairs and see if Juliet might be in their bedroom. Forward progress stuttered to a halt when he came upon two small suitcases parked at the foot of the stairs.

Kellen's knees started to give. He grabbed hold of the banister and remained upright. Barely. A crushing recognition pressed in on him from every side. *I'm this easy for her to leave behind. I'm this easy for her to reject.* Before self-pity could take root, before he could even shed a tear, the circle of that thought came to completion. *It serves me right. What else should I expect? After all, I rejected her first…*

Punctuating the moment, he came aware of soft footfalls on the thick, cream carpet of the stairs. When he looked up, Kellen came upon eyes of deepest green that had broken the seal of his heart forever. What had he ever—*ever*—been thinking when gazing at Chloe?

Juliet came to an awkward stop just a few steps away from the landing. "You…you're home…?"

Kellen crumbled. Something bitter and acrimonious entered his soul. "Did you think I'd go back to work? Really?"

"I don't know what to think anymore, Kellen."

He banished a growl of frustration. This was his doing—not Juliet's. Following a measured breath, he looked into those heartbreaking, luminous eyes. "You're leaving?"

"Absolutely." She descended the remaining stairs and viciously extracted the metal guide handles of the luggage. "I don't know what I want over the long term yet, but I need to figure that out, don't I?"

Devotion

"Divorce?" The word tasted rotten. Even putting that idea into the universe caused his stomach to knot.

"We're the sum of our choices, Kellen, and you've made yours. That's not a criticism. It's simply a realization I've come to with the past few months as a barometer. I'm married to—" she made a couple of air quotes "—Kellen Rossiter. But the marquee isn't what I married, and the marquee isn't what I fell in love with. My biggest fear is that when you take enough time and focus on me long enough to look deep, you'll find you don't love me anymore. I guess we changed drastically without even realizing it. Where does that leave us? What does it all mean?"

Her monotone voice undid his control system. He wanted to keep fighting; he wanted her to keep fighting, too, but she looked weakened and defeated, as though the ability to do battle just wasn't in her any more.

"You're carrying our child. Think about that! God's plan is for *us*." This time, Kellen used the air quotes. Juliet's chin wavered, her eyes sparkled, but no tears fell. It looked like she had rediscovered the determination to leave him behind, but when he explored the layers of emotion residing just beneath her steel and grit, he found nothing but sorrow.

If she was this sad about the state of their relationship, could there be enough emotion left to build something better?

He battled on. "Juliet, think about something else, too. Do you think it's mere coincidence that the night I met up against my biggest temptation, God turned me to you, and to us, so irrevocably?"

"That's where you're wrong. We should have been irrevocable from the start. From the moment we exchanged our vows. So, you've answered my question. This whole horrible mess leaves us nowhere. When I'm ready, I'll get a hold of you. Don't try to track me. Don't call Marlene, and don't call my parents. Until I can come to terms, I want you to leave me alone."

The finality of that last, tortured statement stunned him to broken silence. Before he could hazard a reply, Juliet snared her suitcases and beat a hasty retreat. She was a quiet, crushed woman.

When she walked away, when he heard the definitive click of the garage entrance door being pulled closed, Psalm 46 sang through Kellen's mind. *Be still, and know that I am God.*

He didn't want to hear holy platitudes, yet there had to be a purpose for God's prompting. He closed his eyes and softened his heart. *How can I be still when I've destroyed everything I love? She's left...*

No immediate answer materialized.

The night passed in a wretched, unnatural silence that permeated the entire house. Inconsolable, Kellen sat in the empty living room, hating the lifeless feel of the atmosphere and his life. His spirit vibrated with every accusation she had hurled; every dose of her bitterness and pain wrapped around him tight, becoming claustrophobic.

He sat in the leather chair he always occupied and stared at its twin, the mate right next to his. It was Juliet's favorite spot whenever they curled up together, chatted, shared tea, or watched television. Between the two recliners stood a table upon which rested their Bibles.

Kellen rubbed his forehead and closed his eyes against all the images of her light...and leaving.

Love her, Kellen. Love her well.

Repeat counsel from God. He sighed and sank back in his chair. Sure, the advice was great, but he couldn't find a pathway to make amends—and love her well. He surrendered for the moment and forced everything out of his mind. His gaze fell to the remote control for the television, and he decided he needed noise. Clicking on the power button, he sighed and waited while the plasma screen fired to life. He scrolled through the menu screen listlessly, glancing at movie selections until one in particular froze his fingertips on the device.

Letters to Juliet.

He tuned in to the movie, which had just begun. The story played out, and the visuals of Verona, Italy were gorgeous, but nothing much captured his attention for long except the title. Then the movie focused on a letter—a decades-old outpouring of regret over love lost—that had been left behind in a crack of the wall outside the fictional home of Shakespeare's tragic heroine, Juliet Capulet.

Kellen couldn't move past the idea. A letter of love. To Juliet. Could such a thing transform into a starting point? He had so much to say, but he knew she would never give him that kind of chance face-to-face. Not yet, anyway.

Terrified of what he was about to do, praying it wouldn't cause more harm than good, Kellen extinguished the distraction of the television and reached into a drawer of the end table. He pulled out a pen and a sheet of paper. He needed to take her heart by surprise once again—but this time in only the very best and most impassioned way possible.

15

Slow-building lark song edged Juliet awake. The fade of night into a grayish, pearly dawn roused her from a restless slumber. She turned from her side to her back. Her eyes were swollen and scratchy. Her throat was too tight, and it hurt. Both afflictions were a reminder of how much time she had spent crying. She hated to surrender the night. Its cloak had provided a shroud of protection and temporary respite from pain that hadn't lessened its choking grip by even the slightest degree.

She closed her eyes, trying to shut out the cheery noise of escalating bird chatter and thick green leaves rustling in a warm breeze. Those simple reminders of daily renewal struck her as vile.

But, by God's grace alone, she had answered the call of a new day.

It felt so odd, sleeping in the guest room at Marlene's house. Everything felt off-center, and foreign. Appropriate to the moment, she thought. *Very* appropriate.

Light increased by slow degrees filling the room. A vivid flash of red outside the open window caught her eye and she watched a cardinal dance from branch to branch in the evergreen bush just beyond the screen.

Juliet tossed to her side once more and tucked her hand beneath the pillow while she watched. Her thoughts didn't stray for long, though, and she ended up taking a walk through the past several hours since she had seen Kellen.

After leaving home, she had driven a straight line to her big sister's embrace. As soon as Marlene pulled open the front door and saw Juliet's face, she stared, scowling with instant worry. "Baby? What's wrong? What happened?" Juliet didn't answer. She didn't have to. Instead, she collapsed into Marlene's arms, right there on the porch. "Oh…Juliet…come here, sweetie." Marlene drew her into the entryway and then held her tight all over again.

A tall redhead like their father, Marlene's commanding presence and steady demeanor spoke eloquently of a firstborn child's leadership. However, a fierce, almost combative loyalty was another of Marlene's characteristics. In private, they had curled up together on the comfy, overstuffed couch in the living room. There, with steaming tea mugs positioned on a table in front of them and an afghan draped over both their legs, Juliet explained it all. Once Juliet explained the details of her breakup with Kellen, and delivered the news of her pregnancy, Marlene's tears fell, and she rested a gentle hand against Juliet's abdomen in yet another display of protectiveness.

"What a *cheat*!" Typically, Marlene pulled no punches.

"Marlene…" Automatically, Juliet threw out a note of tenderhearted warning, guarding Kellen in some small, ridiculous way from a display of Marlene's fury that he most definitely deserved.

"Don't *Marlene* me. He chucked a dagger into the heart of my sister. Brother-in-law or not, I'd flatten him if he were within reach right now!"

Juliet laughed through her tears, fortified by the support. She grabbed for a few tissues—Marlene kept a box by Juliet's elbow for obvious reasons—and blew out a hard puff of air. "Do you know what? I'd probably let you."

"OK. So I think you need to rage and fume for a bit." Marlene leaned across the space between them and took Juliet's free hand in hers. Juliet squeezed tight and Marlene answered the gesture right back. "Stay here for as long as you want, OK? I mean that. And don't keep anything in. Get it all out with nothing held back. After that, you'll be able to think clearer and figure out what comes next."

Advice dispensed, Marlene waited, and watched

attentively. At length Juliet laid her head on Marlene's shoulder and simply sank away—into a tearless, but draining sense of failure.

Not long after that, for a precious handful of hours, Juliet went to bed and allowed herself to rest in seclusion. She needed space to shatter and begin to mend.

But how was she supposed to accomplish that exactly?

Forgive me, Juliet...

Kellen's words came back to haunt her. So did his plaintive tone. She kicked them away. *No, Kellen. You need to suffer. I want you to suffer. Badly.*

But what did that say about her as a Christian wife, and soon-to-be mother? Was self-righteous indignation the answer? Would hardness of spirit give her peace? She wasn't without fault in the breakdown of her marriage, and she knew it. But what he had done was so much worse...

Juliet, sin leads to sin, no matter how big, no matter how small. Sin is evil. Beat sin with love. Love him. Love him well.

I can't, God. I just can't.

It was her answer last night, and it was her answer now.

Issuing a strident and distinctive chirp, the cardinal called and bounced from spot to spot outside the window, pulling Juliet away from the jumble of last night's thoughts and memories. She watched the beautiful bird, listless, yet captivated.

The red ones were the males, right? And didn't they mate for life? The thought, coupled with a daily dose of morning sickness, nearly left her dashing for the bathroom, but Juliet couldn't even muster the energy to get out of bed. She fought off nausea by breathing slowly and evenly through her nose. Her fire-winged visitor went stock still for a moment, and then tilted his head in a way that caused Juliet's lips to curve despite it all. As though on cue, a brown-feathered female joined the papa cardinal. Together they flitted and sang. Amazing, Juliet thought, enchanted by the vision of God's creation. They were such gorgeous birds, partners in a perfect syncopation of flight and branch dance. Seconds later, they were gone—together—and the vignette broke her heart into sharp, jagged pieces.

Sobs overtook her all at once and without warning.

Well, she had made it through ten or fifteen minutes of consciousness without tears. Maybe next time around she'd make it to the half-hour mark. She grabbed a tissue from the box on the nightstand, dabbed beneath her eyes, and blew her nose.

Juliet expelled a heavy groan. This wouldn't do. Tossing back the bed covers, she landed her feet on the floor and forced herself to stand. She padded to the easy chair positioned in a corner of the room, grabbing her robe from where she had tossed it the night before. She needed breakfast to quell the queasy roll of her stomach. Furthermore, she knew she couldn't hide out forever. She had to go home. She had to face Kellen and the remnants of her marriage. Today.

That sense of purpose didn't make pushing forward any easier, though.

After breakfast, she would go home. By that time Kellen would be at work. That would give her an entire day to prepare for...

There Juliet's thoughts floundered.

Walking to the bedroom door, pulling it open, she marched into the hallway and found the conclusion of her thought. She needed to prepare herself for this new and completely unexpected turn in her life.

৵৶

Juliet turned onto the tree-lined street, and the familiar sight of her home wove into view. Perfectly shaped pear trees and magnolias framed the white brick colonial. Fragrant petals tumbled to the ground in a carpet of pink, purple, and white.

Mercifully, Kellen's car was gone. She breathed easier at the realization, and a constricting band eased its hold from around her chest.

Inside, the silence she discovered was welcome and

comforting—until she walked into the kitchen. She intended to check the message machine by the phone. What she found waiting for her on the long, granite counter just a few feet away brought her footsteps to an abrupt halt.

Propped against a crystal vase that overflowed with fresh, pink lilacs, she spied a simple white envelope. Her name was written across the front in Kellen's bold, elegant scrawl. Her nerves tripped and an all-over ache took her under in the span of time it took her to draw a breath.

She stepped forward in a slow, measured way. The aroma of the flowers, one of her all-time favorites, called to her senses, sweet and intoxicating. They were gorgeous. Had he cut the blooms from their tree out back?

Curiosity rampant, she lifted the envelope and tucked her finger beneath the flap. She pulled out two handwritten pages, and then unfolded them, bracing against the edge of the counter to keep steady.

My dearest Juliet ~

Juliet stopped reading and froze. She grabbed for air and dropped the pages onto the counter top, stepping away and turning her back. No. She couldn't do it. The opening words alone ripped new lines in her still bleeding heart. She could almost hear the loving, tender inflections of his voice…

She paced and glanced back at the papers, trying to think of anything else to do but read them. The tri-folded sheets called to her without mercy, a beckoning she couldn't possibly resist.

Condemning herself as a glutton for punishment, Juliet stalked back to the counter and grabbed the letter. Determined to be firm-spirited and resolute, she sat at the dinette and braced herself. Girded and resolved to stay detached, she picked up at the first paragraph and began to read.

I don't even know where to begin. The words 'I'm sorry' aren't nearly enough. I wronged you—I wronged our marriage—in one of the worst ways imaginable. Words alone will never atone for what I've done. Simple words won't reassure you, and simple words won't win back your love—or your trust. I can only pray you'll stay by my side long enough for me to show you, day-by-day, the truth of what I'm about to say.

I want you and you alone. I love you and you alone. You, and our marriage, are precious to me. I can't embellish beyond that. I won't even try. As I said, words will never do. Now, only actions, the reassertion of my love for you, will turn the tide between us.

What you said to me at church is the absolute truth. Although I didn't fully betray you with my body, a foolish and misguided desire led me away from everything of deepest value in my life. Misguided desire led me to betray my truest heart, and the woman I love the most. You.

A pair of tears splattered against the corner of the pages she held, spreading a dark stain that blurred a few of the words Kellen had written. Juliet dashed the back of her hand against her cheeks and fought hard to continue.

Juliet, it has always been you. From the moment I met you almost a decade ago, you've held my heart. I'm sure that seems so hollow a statement right now. After everything we've shared, that kills me inside.

Juliet had to stop there. She was overcome. The words had become indiscernible and her vision refused to clear until she wiped excess moisture away. Again. After blowing out a puff of air, she covered her trembling lips with the press of her fingertips and forced herself to finish his note.

I traveled too fast, swept up in a life that separated me from God, and you, without me even realizing it until I hit a sheet of black ice that I never saw coming. God alone can mend me back into the man I was, the one you fell in love with. Dealing with the fallout of your pain has left me broken inside. Damaged. Why? Because I'm keenly aware of what my wasteful stupidity has done to you—an innocent who certainly didn't deserve what you received from me. You offered trust. I gave you betrayal. You offered love. I gave you quick-handed deceit.

I write you this note because, for now, the idea of looking into your eyes as I speak these truths tears me up inside to a degree that I know I would never be able to express myself fully, or effectively. That direct a conversation, right now, would take me to a place where I wouldn't be able to communicate the depth of what I feel.

So, you may ask, what exactly do I feel right now? Mostly, I feel shame, and loss. In you—in us—I held beauty. In a heartbeat, I wrecked it, and I realize I never should have set foot outside the love we share, and the marriage we treasure.

I hope your faith and heart will be strong enough to give us a second chance. But know this, no matter what your answer may be, I'm after you. I'm after you with everything I am, and I won't quit pursuing you until you let me back into the deepest parts of you. I don't expect quick redemption, only a chance.

There are a million ways I can spin the words I'm sorry, but there is only one thing that will bring us back to what we were. Me. I need to prove to you—over and over again, in action by action, in every day that you give me from this point forward—that you are the most treasured gift God ever placed in my life. You're everything to me, but that statement means nothing in the face of the wrongs I've done. Give me time to fill the hollow spot I created with what we had before—an amazing, forever love.

Scarred and imperfect, my heart is yours. It always has been, and it always will be. Can you find a way to let me try and win you back? Think about it—please.

With all my love ~ Kellen

Dry-eyed now, Juliet reread the letter—and reread it again. Entire sections of it had already taken root in her memory. By the fourth go-through she was able to recall exact passages before even reading them.

This was the man she had fallen in love with. This was the Kellen Rossiter to whom she had committed her life.

Still, despite the noble intent of his note, doubt and betrayal flooded her spirit. What if he strayed again? What if another set of circumstances conspired to draw them apart? What if he was only trying to save face for his own sake, and that of their child?

Juliet settled a hand gently against her tummy and closed her eyes. Every doubt she clung to was answered by the beautiful words he had written, and the words he had spoken at church. *We can't work on our relationship if we're not together,*

Juliet.

Her entire body tingled, a force field returning to life in a way she hadn't experienced in days. She couldn't fathom how they would begin, or how they would attempt to live together in their present circumstances—and forget about sharing a bed.

Complications wove around her, so Juliet sprung from the seat and left the letter behind. When she did, she came upon the flowers. They were so vibrant and fresh they had to have been cut and arranged by Kellen. It was a lovely, subtle gesture of thoughtfulness. She paced to the counter and touched her fingertips to the tiny, velvety blooms. Brushing against the flowers released a scent that wrapped around her with comfort and beauty.

Beauty in the midst of ashes.

That's when Juliet realized what she needed to do. She ventured to the living room and claimed her Bible from the table between her chair and Kellen's.

"Pray, Juliet," she murmured to herself as she returned to the dinette. "Pray without ceasing."

She settled comfortably in her chair, opened her Bible, and in a matter of seconds she could feel herself tumbling headlong into God's waiting arms.

16

Kellen squeezed the bridge of his nose. The instant he closed his eyes, exhaustion didn't just creep in, it thundered and tromped, and beat a painful pattern against his temples.

His cell phone vibrated, sending a wave of energy against the surface of his desk. Kellen grabbed for the device more out of ingrained habit than interest.

It was Juliet.

A rush of adrenaline obliterated the remnants of a sleepless night spent in an empty, too-silent house. He almost dropped the phone in his eagerness to engage the call. "Hey, Juliet."

He walked to the entryway of his office and closed the door with a soft, discreet click. He started to breathe hard when a long silence came as his most immediate reply.

"Hey." Her voice—at last. Kellen spun from the door and raked his fingers through his hair. She sounded quiet and somber, but what else could he expect?

"Where are you?" He spoke in quiet, tender tones. He nearly ended with *love*—because the nickname was automatic for him. He clamped his mouth shut against the endearment, but it took tremendous effort.

"I'm home."

More silence gave Kellen the chance to brace himself. "And?"

The note, Juliet. Did you get my note? Did you read it? Did it help you see anything of what I feel for you?

"I need time, Kellen."

"Take all the time you need. Just…" he angled the phone so she wouldn't hear his aching sigh. "Just…don't give up.

Not yet. OK?"

The note, he begged in silence, wishing telepathy could send his thoughts directly to her. When more silence stretched, Kellen forced himself to push on. "Where...where do you want me to go tonight?"

He heard her stuttered breathing and it made him feel wretched.

"I...I just..." Her voice wavered. "I just don't know, Kellen."

He squeezed his eyes shut, cradling the phone gently—tenderly—it was Juliet on the other end of this connection.

"Your note...it was beautiful."

Relief swept through him. At least she had seen it. At least she had read it. "Thank you."

"Don't thank me, Kellen. Thank God. You know, I've always envied those people who say they pick up their Bible, and flip at random to a verse that's in perfect tune to whatever questions they have, or whatever circumstances they face." Kellen was riveted. He could tell by the way her words began to tumble that a small dam had burst free. "Bible reading doesn't work like that for me very often. Instead, I see it as a chance to pick up on knowledge and figure out the way God wants me to live."

"That's the way I feel, too."

"Today was different. I got up this morning and found myself in Lamentations." She let out a sound that was half-sigh, half-sad chuckle. "I guess the title alone was enough to draw me in."

Kellen made no comment.

"I started reading, and I couldn't stop. I read the entire book over breakfast. It was a pretty tough exercise up until...hang on a second. I want to read it to you." A pause ensued, followed by some shuffling background noise. "Here it is. Chapter three, verse twenty-two. *'Because of the Lord's great love, we are not consumed. His compassions never fail. They are new every morning. The Lord is good to those whose hope is in Him. It is good to wait quietly for the salvation of the Lord.'*"

Kellen knew Lamentations. He recalled how those few passages of hope and promise in the middle of Jeremiah's writings were like drenching water in an arid desert of sorrow and regret. He heard Juliet close her Bible. He kept quiet while she seemed to take in a breath and regroup.

"God's mercy is new every day." Her soft voice stroked his soul, left him to burn for her all over again. "I need to live my life knowing that's the truth, but I have a lot to think about. I can't...I won't... just let my guard down and throw open my arms in welcome. I can't. Please don't ask that of me."

"I promise not to ask for any more than you can give, Juliet. I'm not going anywhere."

"Like I said, I need time."

"I understand." He clutched the phone in a death grip.

"I'm going to stay with Marlene and Peter for a while longer. I'm calling because I didn't want you to worry."

"I mean what I say, Juliet. Do what you need to do, and take whatever time you need."

"I intend to."

Kellen absorbed the hit of that sharp arrow. "I'm glad for that."

He heard her sigh. "My instinct right now is to snipe."

Again, Kellen let silence have its way. He had no response to that fact.

"That's not going to help us, and I know it. That's why I want some time. I need to find a way to live past what's happened. I've spent the last twenty-four hours straight in tears, Kellen. I'm worn out and I'm drained. I have nothing in me right now."

More arrow strikes. Kellen shut his eyes, withstood the stabs and pain. It was due compensation. "I understand. Can I at least call you to check in?"

Silence. "Yes."

Then came inspiration. "Juliet, when is your next doctor's appointment?"

"A month from now. Why?"

"Umm...I'd...like to be there with you, if that's OK." He struggled, hating this awkwardness and the fear he felt in approaching the woman he loved.

"Do you want...are you interested in finding out if it's a boy or a girl?"

His heart thumped, and he smiled. He sank into the chair behind his desk and tipped his head back. Closing his eyes, he smiled. "I'd like to be surprised, but if you want to know, I could get behind that, too. It really doesn't matter what we have if our baby is healthy and happy."

"Yeah, I know." Was that a smile he heard in her voice? He fought to keep steady. One inch at a time was fine by Kellen—so long as forward progress might happen. "I'd like to be surprised, too, I think. I'll be having an ultrasound at the appointment, that's why I asked. They won't tell us if we don't want them to."

Us. We. Two of the most beautiful words in the English language...

"I'd get to hear the heartbeat and everything?" The idea of it spurred an unequalled joy.

"Yeah."

"I'd love to be there."

Another intense, hesitant silence expanded between them. "I'll call you back with the details."

Hope whooshed through him. Sure, they were miles away from any type of a comfort zone, but maybe, just maybe, this could be a start.

17

Heavy footsteps took Juliet to her closet at home. After almost three weeks away, she was ready to come back again. Shuttling between her home and Marlene's, keeping track of clothes and supplies and avoiding Kellen as much as possible in the process was becoming an inconvenient and emotionally draining exercise. She needed to move forward.

She slid the mirrored door open and stepped inside as light flooded the interior. Listless, she began to slide hangers and explore selections. She sighed. Her motions slowed to a stop. She stared ahead blankly, seeing nothing. Weekly Bible study at Trinity Christian would begin in just under an hour. She refused to miss it. She needed the Word and the support of her church family with an intensity that bordered on desperate.

Still, a proud part of her wounded spirit rose up as well. She resumed searching her clothing options determined to come up with a beautiful ensemble. She came to a flowing, crepe skirt that featured lovely pastel hues. The waistline was elastic, so it would be comfortable to wear. She probably wouldn't show for a few weeks yet, but her regular clothes were becoming way too snug. Next, she found a lightweight silvery-gray sweater with a cowl neck that would look great with a chunky, silver necklace. She wanted to look good, but knew such appearances were camouflage, a necessary mask to cover her shame and self-recrimination. That's why she hadn't attended Bible study in weeks.

The self-imposed exile would end tonight.

Tonight, just for a short while, she wanted to reclaim some semblance of routine and her old self-confidence. She wanted to feel vital, and attractive, but realizing that she needed to affirm herself in such a way caused sadness to step in the way of everything else and shove her backward.

Juliet gritted her teeth, but continued to struggle. A pair of glossy, black fashion boots rested in the back corner of the closet. She blinked her vision clear of building tears and grabbed them. Her eyes still stung, but the tears didn't fall. She was working past them—slowly but surely.

Still, I've failed. Still, my marriage failed. Still, I try to call myself a Christian?

Doubts like that prompted her to Trinity tonight. Spending time with God would help. Juliet swallowed hard. She threw her selections onto the bed and made ready to untie and remove her silk robe so she could dress. Frustration built and quickly overwhelmed.

God, speak to me. Please, please speak to me. I don't know what to do anymore. If I come back it's like telling Kellen what he did was OK. It demeans me to admit how much I still love him, and want him. I've given him my heart—completely.

Without forethought, not knowing what would come next, she fell to her knees on the thick, plush carpeting. Eyes closed, and mercifully dry, she bowed her head and sank back on her haunches.

"Jesus, please be with me. I need you to show me a way out of this nightmare that will still keep my life in Your care and truth. I'm filled with so much anger. I feel so betrayed—but I love him so much. I always have. Help me deal with that fact and figure out what to do next, because right now I only feel pain, and all I want to do is leave everything behind. Even Kellen."

❧

As always, they took turns reading. Tonight's Gospel selection came from Mark, Chapter seven. Tim Parkson read first starting at verse fourteen. "Jesus said to them: 'Hear Me, all of you, and understand. Nothing that enters one from outside can defile that person; but the things that come out from within are what defile.'"

The next participant took over. Juliet's heart reacted strangely, pumping out an uneven rhythm. She opened her mouth to breath in, to keep air flowing and help her remain steady. Her perceptions went fuzzy, and an oppressive heat crawled through her. Beginning to function outside herself, she went numb, awaiting her turn, realizing which verse would be hers to proclaim at this roundtable.

"Juliet?" Pastor Gene Thomas's gentle prod interrupted her thoughts. She had missed her entry cue.

Nodding, she bit her lips together for a moment, and then began to read at verse twenty. "Jesus went on. 'What comes out of a man is what makes him 'unclean.' For from within, out of men's hearts, come evil thoughts, sexual immorality, theft, murder, adultery, greed, malice, deceit, lewdness, envy, slander, arrogance and folly. All these evils come from inside and make a man 'unclean.'"

The murmured words came out in a deceivingly steady manner while on the inside she crumbled. Once she finished, she kept her eyes downcast. Hidden. The words of her Bible blurred into a grayish wash. What a condemnation. Was this God's answer to her plight? Was this His answer to her troubles—the identification of folly, deceit, and lewdness? Adultery?

That last word weighed upon her as the readings moved mercifully on, and discussion began. She felt harshly rebuked for allowing her marriage to fall into decline with such blindness. Was God angry? Was she being punished somehow for not being enough for Kellen? For not registering, and dealing with, the signs of a decaying relationship?

Juliet didn't hear, or absorb, a single word of the analysis that took place. As best she could, she guarded herself against the revelations those holy words forced her to confront. Breath-by-breath she willed herself to remain distant, focusing instead on the loud, even tick of the second hand as it swept across the face of the black rimmed, white-faced clock on the wall. She needed tonight's study session to end—as quickly as possible.

Survive. Get through it. All she wanted to do was bolt for cover. *I need to keep it together. I can't allow a breakdown right now. Not here!*

Nonetheless, the readings from Mark echoed and echoed, scratching against raw cuts on her psyche.

At the end of the study, Pastor Gene closed his Bible "Does anyone have prayer petitions they'd like to offer up?"

The question was a standard concluding rite to their weekly meetings. Juliet felt like such a hypocrite. Who was she to pray when her whole life echoed the very words she had just read? She was a mess. How could she possibly uplift anyone when she was so bogged down by recriminations and a poisoning level of anger?

Worst of all, everything that had happened to her and Kellen came from the inside out. Just like tonight's readings indicated.

In preparation for prayer, Tim took her hand from the left. Wanda Samuels, a delightful retiree still spry of mind and spirit, claimed Juliet's right.

"I need for us to pray for my boss," a prayer warrior began. "He was diagnosed this week with prostate cancer, and he's going in for surgery. He's got young children, and he's so scared. He's always been healthy and strong. He needs to be uplifted."

Murmurs of prayer and encouragement ran a line through the group. Juliet fidgeted, shifting restlessly in her chair. Her hand remained warmly held by Tim. She didn't like how good it felt.

Where two or more are gathered in My name, there am I in their midst. Open your heart and see Me, precious Juliet. Come to Me broken and I will restore you.

Not here, Father! Not now! Juliet railed in silence. She kept her head low, squeezing her eyes shut tight against the whispers that slid across her soul. *Not in front of these holy people! I'm ashamed...*

She longed to be open, to reveal the brokenness God saw, but she was terrified as well, so afraid of the ugliness and sin she bore.

Tim began to speak. "I have a dear friend who has a troubled heart—problems that are clouding her natural joy and enthusiasm—her zeal for life and service to the God she loves. I don't know what the problems are. I don't even care. I just pray for her to feel the touch of Your hand, Lord. Please provide Your comfort and peace as she sorts through whatever trouble life is sending her right now."

Just like that, Tim's prayer did the revealing for her. He spoke of her deliberately, and Juliet knew it. Warm moisture tracked down her cheeks. The slow but steady release of tears soothed in an almost supernatural way. She drained away as she came to the end of herself.

She tried to pull her hand away from Tim's grasp, wanting to dry her eyes. He held on fast. A few droplets fell onto the table and Juliet panicked. Desperation returned now, and she yanked free of Wanda's hold to slide the back of her hand against her cheeks. Her head still bent, she sniffled, and a soft, uncontrolled sound flowed from her lips, straight from the depths of her heart.

The table focused on her, and Juliet felt herself sink into their loving concern. The comfort they longed to give wouldn't be denied—not even by her sense of shame and inadequacy. One by one they came to her, a circle of silent prayer support and love, an uplifting tribe of Christian witnesses.

She broke then. It couldn't be stopped. She dissolved into silent sobs. No one asked questions. Not one person pushed for more than she could provide at the moment. Rather, they simply prayed and rested warm loving hands upon her shoulders.

Pastor Gene was the only one to speak. "We don't need details, Jesus. You know them all, and You are already performing Your great and powerful works. We ask only for Your comfort to rain down upon Juliet. Bring her Your loving presence, Your peace and grace in whatever it is she faces. In Your precious name we pray."

The chorus of "Amen" sang through Juliet's very being.

❧

"Let me get that for you." Juliet remained seated at the conference table, not responding to Tim's offer. He stood and reached across her to grab a used paper plate, a nearby napkin, and her now empty beverage cup.

Would you please stop being so nice to me? Would you please stop getting in the way? I can't cope with kindness right now. She felt like screaming.

The thing was, Tim *knew* that. From the beginning, he had sensed her rage, and sadness, and heartbreak. That's what bothered her most of all. She wanted to just roll up her life and stuff it away, or at least allow herself to vanish from view until she sorted out this whole unseemly mess. Especially around a man like Tim, who always struck her as being so grounded and spirit-filled.

So, she sat in sullen confusion, wanting to let him know she wasn't exactly happy about his intrusiveness. Rather than keep her feelings bottled up, she glanced around the room, to verify they were alone, and then she stood up briskly, setting a fisted hand on her hip. "That was incredibly difficult, Tim. And, I wish you would have let go of my hand."

Tim shrugged that off and continued to pick up debris. "Life's not easy. Plus, we were praying, and emotion is a part of prayer. Why is it OK for everyone else to need prayer—and react to the power of prayer—except you?"

Juliet glared at him, even though he couldn't see it, moving through the room the way he did. She was still so riled and unsettled she couldn't think straight. Meanwhile, Tim remained steady and sure, and he turned at last to look deep into her eyes. Silence fell for a bit.

"On top of which, you know, and you've seen, that most times it's best to just let the tears fall. Let them have their way.

Doing so brings us closer to healing. Have you lost sight of that?"

Juliet could find no suitable response to that comment. He was right. There were no means by which to justify the way she had recoiled from being revealed—to Tim or anyone else who had gathered around the prayer table tonight.

"You're heartbroken, Jules. Like I said, I don't know the details. I don't have to if that's not what you want, but finding release from what you're troubled by, even if it's through tears, is necessary to your well-being." His voice came to her low and gentle, reassuringly kind. He reached for her hand and gave it a squeeze. The gesture stirred warmth against her chilled skin. "I'm a psychologist, so I know these things."

Juliet gathered herself, looking at a spot over his shoulder instead of his penetrating, knowing gaze.

"Do you have to get right home?" For the first time since the group broke up, he seemed a bit uncertain, yet determined. "Would you be interested in getting a cup of coffee?" Seeming to read her doubtful reaction, he lifted his hands. "There's nothing to worry about here. I'm talking about a wide-open, public place, lots of people. We could just talk."

His warm demeanor touched her heart all over again. She wanted to open up, to share the burden she carried. He was a psychologist, after all, as well as a fairly objective outsider to her life. This church-fostered friendship might be an answer to the ache, the longing in her heart that had led her to tears in the first place.

But by the same token, mixing socially with a man who wasn't her husband—even in innocence—swirled with the same type of dangerous temptations that had tripped Kellen. Never could she allow herself to waltz along that same pathway. If she did, the damage would be irrevocable.

Still, an analysis between Tim's calm steadiness and Kellen's exciting charisma couldn't help but be drawn. For the first time ever, she wondered about the benefits of a slow and easy day-to-day life. What would it be like to be married to a man less dynamic, but more life centering?

The answer came straight from her heart, in an instant of crystal clear revelation; because Kellen was the one she loved, and always would. Her soul had recognized its twin the instant God caused their paths to cross.

With that, she embraced the fact that a troubled marriage wasn't something to discuss with Tim, be he a psychologist or not. God had used her friend powerfully, and beautifully tonight. In coping with Juliet's greatest sorrow, Tim's prayers had helped her find her faith and God's hand once more. Now, she needed to get busy doing the work of finding a way back to the man of her heart, the one she loved. Kellen. To do that, she would need practical, trusted advice from an objective and uncomplicated source. She needed to find a way to rebuild herself without dangerous pathways stretching before her like Tim's affection and ready care.

Tim Parkson wouldn't—and couldn't—be the answer. Gratitude filled her, just the same. His intervention had opened doorways, directing her heart and intentions toward what needed to come next. Counseling—with someone she could be revealed to completely. The first person who came to mind is the one who had led the subsequent prayers of intervention tonight--Pastor Gene.

For what had to be the hundredth time, the memory of Kellen's voice rang through her mind as well. *We can't work on our relationship if we're not together, Juliet.*

That much was true as well. Was he truly as remorseful as his letter had indicated? She needed to find out. Was the relationship with Chloe honestly finished? She cringed inwardly and her stomach bucked even considering the idea. That was another question she needed to have answered, because at this point she had no idea. She only knew she must return home full time, and do what she could to resuscitate her marriage. Doing so was the only way it would have a chance to survive.

The decision came to her easily now. Tomorrow she would pack everything that had made its way to Marlene and

Peter's house. Tomorrow she would tell Kellen she was coming home permanently.

Beyond that, Juliet also made plans to call Pastor Gene and set up a meeting...as soon as possible.

18

"I need to be up front with you, Kellen, and let you know I've started to counsel Juliet as well."

"You have?"

Just moments ago, Kellen had begun his third counseling session with Pastor Gene. They sat side by side, in matching easy chairs at the pastoral offices of Trinity Christian. Kellen stopped short after Pastor Gene delivered the news.

"Beyond that, I want to assure you, as I've assured her, that anything you say here is strictly private and will never be shared. She's aware that you and I are meeting as well."

"Good. I'm glad she knows. I don't want, or need, any information beyond that. We're both trying. That's all I need to give me hope."

Pastor Gene's smile dawned. "Very good. Remember what I told you from the start—the proof of Christian character is how we rise after we fall. I want you to keep that in mind as we move forward. It may sound like a simple platitude to say none of us is without sin, and that every single one of us fails, and every single one of us needs forgiveness, but it's true. And you can be completely upfront. I don't want to be a judge, I want to encourage and support. I'm a sinner, too, and I've made some horrendous mistakes. We all do. We all will."

Kellen relaxed, crossing his legs and eying Pastor Gene. The church leader was just past middle-aged, with the kind features of a favorite father figure and a heart to match. Kellen felt good about being here, and being open. The disclaimers helped, sure, but in Pastor Gene's company, he didn't fear being condemned. Instead, he knew he was being offered a loving hand and objective ears.

"It's good to have her back home," Kellen offered, settling back in the chair.

"I'll bet."

"I know it takes tremendous trust on her part to even be under the same roof with me right now, but she's trying, and that's all I can expect."

"I think the letter you wrote was a good idea."

"I don't know. She hasn't said much about it. She's so quiet, and so hesitant. I wish I could get some kind of an idea of what she wants. I wish I knew she still cares and still has feelings for me."

"She's back home, Kellen. That says something pretty strong. You're not sharing a room, I assume."

Kellen twitched with embarrassment but fought against its power. "We both agreed to that. I'm in the spare room across the hall, and that's perfectly fine as we work things through. Really."

Leaning forward, propping his elbows on his knees, Pastor Gene delivered a piercing look rife with understanding and compassion. "Kellen, I can feel how much you want things back. You're sincere and emphatic about saving your marriage, and that's going to make all the difference. I hate to say give it time when that's the last thing you probably want to hear, but…"

Kellen picked up the thread of that dangling sentence. "But it's the truth. I know, I know."

They shared a laugh. "Here's something you might consider while you're waiting."

Kellen studied Pastor Gene in a meaningful silence.

"Don't just use this time apart to focus on Juliet. Use this opportunity to search yourself as well. Are you as fulfilled, right here and right now, as you were just two or three years ago? If not, find out why. What wreaked havoc on your peace of mind, and your marriage, and your walk of faith that led you to this point?"

Guilt seasoned Kellen's uneasy reaction to that question.

As though reading Kellen's discomfort, Pastor Gene shook his head. "I'm not talking about Chloe here. I'm talking about getting rid of what led you and Juliet to this crisis point to begin with. Think of it as getting rid of the garbage. It makes room for treasure, Kellen. What do you treasure? In the deepest part of yourself, what do you want your life to be? Figure that out and the rest will follow."

The questions formed an interesting challenge to take home and think about.

"Be thoughtful about it, and take care, but don't be afraid to raise those issues with Juliet as well. Right now, your instinct is to treat her with kid gloves because of what's happened. That's understandable, and the correct instinct. But don't be afraid to talk to her and initiate a frank—maybe even blunt—discussion. At some point during the coming week, before we meet again, make an opportunity to sit down with Juliet and talk to her about what she's feeling."

Kellen stood fast and shook his head. Stuffing his hands into the pockets of his slacks, he paced to a nearby window. Just beyond, tree leaves danced in a humid breeze. Sun beat down and the sky was a blinding blue. "I'm not so sure about that, Pastor Gene. Not yet, anyway. She's not really in a place where she wants to talk."

"Regardless, that's my challenge to you. And you're right, it might go well, or it might not. Your first conversations about getting back to where you were are bound to have some painful growth spurts, but they're also necessary." He grinned. "Sorry. I'm not letting you skip out on that one."

Kellen groaned, already dreading the idea.

"When it gets tough, remember who you're becoming. Keep faith in what you're doing *now*. Trust Juliet to see you're not just working on winning her back, like some kind of a prize. You're reforming from a point of sincerity and love that she'll have no choice but to acknowledge…in time."

Kellen turned away from the window and looked back at his pastor. "Back to that again, eh? Time."

"Afraid so. You said you're back to studying your Bible

each morning?"

Kellen nodded. Doing so provided a lifeline to sanity.

"Let me give you a few scripture passages that I think will help." Pastor Gene reached into the drawer of his desk and lifted out a pen and some paper. He began to jot down notes about books of the Bible and accompanying verses. "Beyond that, maintain whatever trust you build with Juliet by never letting it waver. If these sessions move forward in a positive way, and if both of you agree to it, maybe you could attend together. It's another goal to keep in mind."

Kellen nodded and accepted the paper Pastor Gene extended, but he didn't think either goal was even remotely achievable.

ॐ

The door between Dr. Roth's waiting room and examination area swung open. A sweet young nurse waited at the threshold with a chart in hand and a welcoming smile in place. "Juliet? You can come on back."

Nervous flutters beat against Juliet's insides. She set aside the magazine she had been paging through and stood. Seated next to her, Kellen looked up in question. "Should I come with you?"

"No, not yet. They'll call you in after my preliminary work-up and after Dr. Roth has a chance to examine me." When she walked toward the nurse, she could have sworn she felt the touch of his gaze upon her.

The visit began with a typical height/weight/blood pressure screening. The nurse didn't say much beyond typical pleasantries...until she completed the blood pressure check. At that point, she frowned. "Your numbers are still high, but we'll see what the doctor has to say when she sees you." Tapping notes into a laptop, the nurse continued. "I know your bladder is full for the ultrasound, but did you bring a first-morning sample?"

Juliet nodded and handed off a wrapped, plastic vial. A

strip-dip later, along came another frown. "Your levels are good, except for the proteins. They seem high."

Juliet's nerve endings started to skip and hum. "That's obviously not good."

"No...not if it continues, but again, you've been a patient of ours for years, and you've never had these symptoms before. We'll let Dr. Roth take a look and move forward from here, but don't get too worried at this point. These things happen, and we just need to be on top of it."

The nurse smiled in kind assurance. Instinctively Juliet placed a gentle hand against the swell of her womb. She was coming along so well and finally getting over morning sickness. She didn't want to consider the possibility of something being wrong with the baby, or her pregnancy. No way could she handle such a thing. *Be with me, God.*

Minutes later, ensconced in a small exam room that was warmed by a space heater, Juliet stripped down to her underwear and tucked her arms into the sleeves of the blue and white flowered hospital gown. Next to the exam table stood the ultra sound machine. Juliet nibbled her lower lip, trying hard not to worry.

Dr. Roth entered the room not long after, carrying Juliet's file. Lab coat snapping, stethoscope tucked into the right front pocket, Dr. Roth's commanding but caring presence filled the room immediately.

Following a brief update on Juliet's overall health, she went through her warnings. "Your blood pressure is high again, Juliet. I'm becoming a little concerned."

A chill worked its way clear through to her bones. "What do you mean?"

Dr. Roth set aside Juliet's chart. "It might mean nothing. You've always presented as a healthy, strong patient. You haven't had a history of hypertension before now, so what concerns me is what's referred to as gestational hypertension. It can lead to a condition called Preeclampsia that could lead to premature labor or developmental issues for the baby. There was an elevation in the proteins of your urine as well, which again, is something I'm going to keep an eye on. Don't worry too much about it at this point, but I'm going to keep on top of it and gauge what to do as your pregnancy progresses."

She seemed non-alarmist. That was reassuring—even if her words and the latest results of Juliet's lab work didn't quite synchronize with that measured, professional sense of calm.

Dr. Roth continued. "I'm not going to medicate yet, but I encourage you to make certain you eat well and exercise. Also, I realize this pregnancy means a lot to you and Kellen. I hope that truth doesn't have you feeling overly stressed and anxious." Dr. Roth lifted Juliet's chart once again and gave it a quick glance. "You're thirty-three which is beyond the average age for having a first child, but again, I have no concerns about that because you present extremely well. Let's see how the baby is doing to confirm everything is moving along the way it should. After that, we can discuss some plans to minimize my concerns."

Juliet shivered outright, and not because of the too-thin protection of her cotton dressing gown. "Kellen is in the waiting room. He wanted to be here for the ultrasound." Saying the words, feeling the emotion of them, made her smile in a tremulous way. "He wants to hear the baby's heartbeat."

Dr. Roth gave Juliet a wide smile and a nod. "Let's get Dad in here."

A short time later, Dr. Roth's nurse led Kellen into the exam room. His eyes darted eagerly from Juliet to the doctor, and he stepped up to the exam table, resting a hand on Juliet's arm. His fingers trembled against her skin.

"Kellen, it's good to see you," Dr. Roth greeted. "Congratulations."

"Thanks. It's good to see you, too." He gave Juliet a lingering, tender look.

The ultrasound machine stood ready, and Dr. Roth assisted Juliet to a prone position, ready to get to work. "The ultrasound exam uses high-frequency sound waves to scan a woman's abdomen and pelvic cavity, creating a picture of the baby and the placenta." Dr. Roth slid the hem of Juliet's gown up to her breasts, exposing her slightly rounded stomach. The doctor squirted a blob of clear gel onto Juliet's skin, and Juliet flinched a tad at the coolness of the liquid. Next, Dr. Roth took possession of a triangular shaped hand-held device with a metal roller-ball at the end. "I know the gel feels kind of gooey and cold, but it acts as a conductor for the sound waves."

Kellen took hold of Juliet's hand. She squeezed tight without a second thought. His eyes remained fixed on Dr. Roth's motions as she began to run the receptor tool slowly and evenly across Juliet's stomach.

"The sound waves bounce off bones and tissue returning back to the transducer to generate black and white images of the baby—and...there we are!" Dr. Roth's face split into a smile and her eyes sparkled. That reassured Juliet tremendously. She had to lie still, but she craned her neck as best she could in order to see their baby for the first time. Kellen, too, leaned as far forward as he could, taking in the images on the monitor before them. Juliet cried out softly and felt tears build.

"Wow." Juliet blinked, and she glanced at Kellen because they had spoken the word in perfect, joyful unison.

The awe Juliet saw in Kellen's eyes turned radiant, flowing from his spirit into hers. Like touching the hem of Christ's robe, Juliet experienced a stirring wave of *something*...something beautiful...that pushed beauty and joy through what was a sooty, black covering of sediment in her soul. Kellen bent his head and a stray teardrop hit their joined hands. The teardrop acted upon her heart, leaving her choked up as well.

Dr. Roth, who had probably witnessed such interactions hundreds of times before, smiled indulgently and continued on in a businesslike manner. "I see good development of the arms and spine and legs. And look...there's the heart, and it's pumping along just great." A few more swipes of the device and Dr. Roth nodded with satisfaction. "Normal head and organ growth. Your baby seems to be developing just as expected."

Recovered and enthralled, Kellen seemed to study every flickering image depicted on the monitor. Carried into the moment of discovering their child for the first time, so did Juliet. Shortly thereafter, Dr. Roth punched a few buttons on the machine; a whirring sound filled the air along with the scrape and zip of paper being printed.

"Give me just a second or two and you'll have a couple of souvenirs," she said.

While they waited for pictures to print, Dr. Roth wiped excess gel from Juliet's abdomen then helped her reassemble so she could sit up again. "We can do a 3D image at six months or so if you'd like. We can also let you know the sex of the baby if you're interested."

Kellen and Juliet exchanged knowing looks and smiles as naturally as if they weren't thrust into the midst of a marital nightmare.

"We're going to wait to find out," Juliet answered.

"Good enough. Here you go." Dr. Roth presented them with two pictures of the ultrasound images and launched into a brief explanation of what they were looking at.

"Keep in mind what I told you about your blood pressure, Juliet. Also, I want to see you in two or three weeks instead of waiting a full month. Just to reiterate, I'm not overly worried about anything I've seen, but when high blood pressure and high urine proteins are discovered, I find it's prudent to keep a closer eye on the pregnancy as it progresses. I just want to be able to preempt any problems."

The reassurance worked for Juliet, but Kellen's head snapped up, and his focus zeroed in on Juliet with palpable concern. She lost herself in his eyes before she could even stop herself.

"No worries, Kellen," Dr. Roth interjected. "Juliet and the baby seem to be perfectly fine, but I'd prefer to err on the side of caution because this is her first pregnancy. Set up the appointment on your way out, Juliet, and we'll see you soon. Come on, Kellen, we'll let her get dressed."

❧

The day was summertime perfect. Temperatures hovered at around seventy-five degrees; clear, dry air and a cloudless blue sky stretched above them. Following the appointment, Kellen had suggested they eat lunch at Juliet's favorite corner-side bistro, MaxiMia, a romantic restaurant located at the heart of Nashville's business district. There, seated at a small, glass-topped table, he drank in the atmosphere and savored the moments he had just spent with his wife...and their unborn child.

A soft breeze rippled Juliet's hair. He knew its silky-soft texture, its lavender-shampoo scent, by rote. The cardigan of her pale-yellow twin set caught the breeze just right and caused the cashmere fabric to inch down her shoulder, revealing the shell beneath—and slim, tan shoulders.

On instinct, Kellen reached out, capturing the edge of the cardigan between his first and index fingers. Using a gentle tug, he restored the material and looked into her eyes.

What he found there was in no way heartening. She looked at him with an expression of surprise at the tender gesture.

How sad was it that a small display of affection startled her?

They studied meal selections and Kellen peeked at her over the top of his menu. "Can I ask a personal question?" Juliet nodded slowly. He delivered a smile that came right from his heart, and he ached for her to feel every ounce of its warmth. "Do you have any weird cravings?"

Juliet burst out laughing, and the reaction took him by surprise. Her, too, judging by the way she quickly lowered her eyes and fidgeted. "The best thing in the world right now is celery sticks and peanut butter."

Now Kellen laughed. "That doesn't count. You've always loved celery sticks and peanut butter."

"Best protein boost there is, pal."

Did she realize she was joking with him? Did she realize her skin went a bit rosy? Did she realize they traveled the length of a marriage together—full of sharing, love, and a rich, beautiful history?

"I loved being with you today," he said.

The waitress stepped up, forestalling any kind of a reply, which filled Kellen with frustration. They placed their orders and spent long minutes pouring over the black and white images of their baby, carefully reviewing each mega-pixel, exclaiming over every discernable feature.

But, as suddenly as storm clouds on the move, Juliet had looked at him, eyes wide, seeming to realize they were straying into comfort, and intimacy. She closed up after that, focusing quietly on the crowd around them. Their food arrived and he watched her pick at her Caesar salad served with a side of crispy, fresh-from-the-oven garlic bread.

Her silent retreat continued through the length of their meal until Kellen could take it no longer.

"You know?" He spoke soft and low, discouragement slicking his words. "Sometimes I catch glimpses. Glimpses of what we used to be. And those glimpses are so beautiful they break my heart." He sighed outright and stood. "My heart is empty, Juliet. It's empty of everything but you. Believe it, or don't believe it. The choice is yours. But it's the truth. I'll go up front and settle the bill. I've got to get back to the office. I wish I could stay longer..."

She swallowed hard and looked away. "Thanks for being with me today."

Her tone conceded a level of quiet sadness that lay out in equal proportion to his disappointment at having to leave her right now. She looked at him when he cupped her chin. Vibrations of intensity rolled between them like sonic waves, mapping out the state of their relationship just as surely as the ultrasound procedure had crafted the image of their baby. A breeze, soft and warm, worked through the air. A few errant strands of hair drifted across Juliet's face, rippling against her lips. A poignant ache hit him hard. He wanted nothing more than to glide his fingertips against her cheek, and stroke back that swirling ribbon of hair.

Before the debacle with Chloe, such a gesture would have come to him naturally. Now, denied by his own folly, Kellen could only stare, and wish.

He stepped around the table, bent smoothly and decided to risk the chance of following through on the impulse. He slid a pair of fingertips against the drifting curl and tucked it back into place. Sure enough, the aroma of lavender lifted to him. Mind-flooding warmth, a solid lick of desire, went to war against the complacency he had once felt—the routine and established norm of their marriage. The shell-shape of her ear was exposed. Into it he whispered, "I miss you so much, Juliet."

She closed her eyes. Her chest lifted and fell in a telling display of emotion and a dribble of moisture squeezed free from the corner of her eye, moving down her cheek. It cost him everything he had, but he stepped slowly away. The choice to come forward now had to be hers and hers alone.

"I guess I'll see you at home." Her whispered words were shaky. Affected.

He gave her shoulder a last squeeze, all but willing her to hang on. To show some spark. To fight for the years they had invested in one another and the relationship they had been given by nothing less than God's plan—and blessing.

After paying the lunch tab, Kellen walked the few short blocks to his office building at a brisk clip, thinking and praying. *I'm following through on Your promptings as best I can, but I can only take this journey to the halfway point. Juliet has to come to terms as well. She has to let me know what she wants...and if she still feels I'm worth trusting—and loving—again.*

19

Following his most recent counseling sessions with Pastor Gene, Kellen realized the first steps he needed to take toward salvaging his marriage couldn't be toward Juliet. They needed to be toward God.

So, the first weekend after Juliet's homecoming he made plans to accompany her to Trinity. He didn't ask if he could. He didn't make a big production out of it. Simply, at nine-thirty on that Sunday morning, he made sure he was downstairs in the kitchen, ready and waiting to leave.

During her time with Marlene and Peter, Juliet had attended services, and so had Kellen. They sat together, but arrived and departed separately. That separation hurt, but he expected nothing more, so he didn't question her or add pressure to the situation.

Today would be a litmus test of sorts as to whether she would even attempt solidarity now that they were living under the same roof.

Seated at the dinette table, he sipped coffee and looked up expectantly when Juliet crossed the threshold. She wore a simple black skirt and white blouse combination that, in its simplicity, looked absolutely beautiful on her. Her abdomen was growing rounder. Her hair danced loose around her shoulders. Walking into the kitchen, she tucked an offering envelope into her purse and snapped it shut.

That's when she registered Kellen's presence and intent.

Her mouth opened slightly, and her eyes went wide. The click of her heels came to an abrupt stop against the ceramic tile, and she glanced briefly into his eyes before nervously fidgeting a slice of hair into place behind her shoulder. She paused at a counter by the sink, eying the coffee pot, which still flavored the air.

"Do you mind if I take you to church?" he asked.

She kept to her own space and opened the dishwasher. While he watched, she placed a few stray glasses inside as well as a plate and some cutlery. She kept her head down. "No, I suppose not."

She reached into a glass front cabinet above the sink and pulled down a mug. She poured herself a cup of coffee and steam curled upward from the surface. She blew at the wisps, inhaling deep of the hearty French Roast Kellen had set to brew.

"Thanks for this," she said quietly.

"No problem."

She shrugged and took a sip. "Seriously. You've always done lots of little things that mean a lot to me. I never really gave you much credit, did I? Or let you know how much I appreciate them."

Gratitude mixed with hope in a combination that was nearly his undoing. Kellen cleared his throat. "Are you in the mood for me to make us brunch after church?"

It had always been somewhat of a tradition for them to indulge in a leisurely meal after services. Typically, bacon, eggs and toast would be consumed in the restful atmosphere of their home before diving in to whatever Sunday activities awaited—family dinners maybe, or perhaps nothing more than sitting together on their patio with an extra cup of coffee at their elbows and a sun kissed, leisurely afternoon stretching ahead. Those were his favorite—the restful hours they spent talking, or just listening to the birds and the wind song that slipped through thick, heavy tree branches.

"That'd be nice."

Kellen joined her at the dishwasher. Stepping from behind, he placed his used mug inside and leaned close—for just an instant. "Two eggs, scrambled, crispy bacon?"

At his recitation of her favorite combination, she stilled. Though she avoided his eyes, Kellen felt her resistance—and her longing.

"I'd like that a lot."

❧

"The point of today's Gospel reading is this: we must decrease, that Christ might increase. The words of John the Baptist from today's Gospel reading embody the resolve that goes behind that statement. Crowds gathered around John. Followers proclaimed John's greatness. Yet it was the Great Evangelizer who said, 'He who comes after me is The One. I'm not worthy to loosen His sandal straps.' Do you see? John decreased that Christ might increase." Pastor Gene paused there, looking over the assemblage. Kellen forgot about everything else—even Juliet—and lost himself in God's message. "But how does this apply to us? How does that statement apply in the here and now?"

Pastor Gene shrugged and walked up the main aisle of the church, seeming to look into the eyes and faces of as many parishioners as possible. "Allow me to illustrate. The other day, I stood in line at a food court in the mall. That's always a fun exercise, you know…"

Laughter rippled, Kellen's included.

"Well, while I waited for my order, I happened to overhear a conversation that took place at a nearby table. Two elderly people, obviously a husband and wife, sat across from each other, sharing some Chinese food."

Smiles and a gentle flow of murmurs circuited the congregation.

"What struck me about that ordinary scene were the words I heard. The woman spoke first, talking about how frustrated she was about something and how she felt somewhat worthless, and degraded by the present circumstances in her life."

Service attendees quieted and Kellen noticed the way they now listened intently.

Pastor Gene continued. "I don't know specific details. I only know her sorrow. I waited in line for my orange chicken, and I watched her husband reach across the tabletop to take her hands in his. He looked her deep in the eyes and said, 'You're a remarkable woman. You offer so much to everyone we love. You're selfless and loving and kind.' At that point, I watched the woman's eyes fill with tears, and she shook her head, saying, 'How do you know all of this?' His answer? *'Because I know you; because I love you.'"*

Kellen noticed the way Juliet pressed her lips tightly together. She swallowed and looked down, avoiding his focus. Kellen didn't blame her for being moved. The beauty of the scenario worked through the congregation like a force field.

"Brothers and sisters, he lifted her up. He sensed her heartache and he affirmed her. He decreased that she might increase." Pastor Gene paused there, taking a long, silent survey of those in his church. "What better, more powerful reflection of Christian love, and commitment, could there be? Remember, folks, live not by word, but by deed. Live not in thoughts and wishes, but in *actions*—actions that are resolute, committed, and in keeping with the love of Christ."

The sermon concluded, and Kellen stared ahead. His world came to a standstill as the sermon spelled out a clear-cut course of action—a battle plan by which to win back the heart, love, and trust of Juliet. He clung to one objective alone, earning her back by uplifting her. No matter the difficulties ahead, he needed to treat her like a precious treasure.

If it wasn't too late.

೨∞೬

After church, Kellen prodded Juliet up the stairs of their home, requesting she change into more comfortable, casual clothing while he cooked.

"It's gorgeous outside," he observed further. "We can eat on the patio, if you'd like."

The idea enticed Juliet. She nodded her agreement before trotting up to their...she performed an automatic correction...*her*...bedroom. Refusing to fall into despair, she peeled out of her heels and nylons. She replaced her skirt and blouse with a loose fitting sleeveless shirt that floated generously over a pair of slip on Capri's. When she positioned the waistband, she registered its snug fit and draped the hemline of her shirt over the top. She really needed to do some shopping and start investing in some maternity fashions. The idea left her to smile as she wound her hair into a loose bun and clipped it into place with a claw clasp. After donning a pair of sandals, she rejoined Kellen.

The brunch he prepared was delicious.

They didn't say much while they ate. Instead, they indulged in simplicity. They savored the way a late Sunday morning warmed into early afternoon, and that was more than enough.

The section of the patio where they sat featured a glass and wicker table with matching chairs and an overhang that provided coolness and shade. Chaise lounge chairs rested atop rust-brick pavers, and Juliet drank in the serenity of the moment. She sank deep into the large, comfortably cushioned seat and closed her eyes with a sigh as summer breezes danced against her cheeks.

Her hand was draped against the armrest of the chair where she sat. When she felt the warm brush and squeeze of Kellen taking slow possession, she didn't open her eyes but she went tense.

Part of her wanted to refute him. Boyishly charming and sweet...authentic...his efforts today felt as though he were attempting to court her all over again.

She didn't want that. She wanted anger. She wanted recrimination. Most of all, she wanted him to feel the same kind of desolated pain that she battled every single day since...

She who is without sin, My daughter. She who is without sin. Unburden to the one I gave you. He waits for you, My precious child.

"Tell me what you're thinking, Juliet." Kellen never called her *love* anymore. She missed the endearment very much.

Granted, she had told him unequivocally to never do so again...but still, she missed the tenderness and automatic affection behind that treasured nickname.

"I'd rather not. It's so beautiful just to rest with you right now and..."

His hold on her hand increased. "Please. It'll be OK."

She didn't reply. The sharp, distinctive chip of a nearby cardinal, nesting in one of their trees, weakened her resolve to be standoffish.

They mate for life, right?

"I..." she choked. A sob shook through her, but she stifled the reaction as best she could because Kellen maintained steady hold of her hand. "I feel like such a failure. I feel like something...or someone...who's cheap and easily replaced. I wanted to be the one for you. To be your wife was a gift to me. Something I revered. I vowed to be the woman who would share your life, and know everything about you—all the best and all the worst. You vowed that to me, too, but you came upon someone else." She couldn't speak Chloe's name. Juliet couldn't give the woman that kind of power. "You let someone else have the key to your heart. A key I believed belonged to me alone. Why wasn't that enough? What did I do wrong? Why wasn't I enough?"

Kellen shook his head. He pressed a fingertip against her lips, the gesture willing her to silence. His fingertip trembled.

"Juliet, no. Please don't take on that burden. It's not right, and it's most definitely not fair to you."

She turned her head so his touch no longer interfered. "Don't say that. It takes two, Kellen. I know that. It takes two to make a marriage, and it takes two to break a marriage."

"I'm keenly aware. What's more? I'm *afraid*."

Kellen's quiet admission inspired her to look his way—albeit with trepidation. "Kellen Rossiter isn't afraid of anything."

"Yes, I am." His look didn't waver. "I'm afraid I've lost you forever. I'm afraid no matter what I do, I'll never get you back—or *us* back. Not completely. I'm afraid I'll never find a way to make you look at me the way you used to. Most of all I'm afraid no matter what I do I'll never earn back the automatic way you used to believe in me, and trust me."

He had a point. Juliet didn't bother trying to deny it. She propped her elbows against the tabletop and watched him—working to remain steady and unaffected by his sincerity and regret.

Kellen's posture remained strained, but he kept on going. "I made a huge mistake, and I ruined something beautiful. Something I prized. Something vitally important. How can I make amends? How can I reaffirm everything I feel for you? Is there a way, Juliet? If there is, name it, and it's done. You may not believe that right now, but it's true. I want your forgiveness so badly I can taste it." He paused very deliberately. "The words I wrote to you in that letter weren't meant to placate or gloss over what I've done. They were an outpouring from my heart. I don't know how many more ways I can try."

The words opened a doorway. The note. She had never broached the topic beyond a simple though heartfelt thank you. Kellen deserved credit for crafting such a beautiful piece. Juliet wanted to give him that, but a wounded heart still bled, making the process difficult.

"The letter." She stopped there, her throat too constricted to continue. She breathed out through pursed lips. She steeled herself and tried again. "The letter was beautiful, Kellen. That's probably another thing I should have acknowledged to you. The note you wrote to me is a large part of the reason why I can attempt to move back here, and try to let you back into...into...my heart again." He settled back and watched her. "But it's like I told you before, I can't just step past what's happened and run to you. I can't." She hauled in a ragged breath, wishing the battle to reclaim her marriage weren't so difficult and complex. A Godly, picture-perfect life, had disintegrated without her even realizing it. "We need to give this time. We're trying."

The love in his eyes, the silence he kept as he waited,

touched Juliet deeply. She saw into his spirit, and the intimacy of doing so ripped away her attempt to maintain cool control. She couldn't keep her lips from faltering and betraying the depth of her emotion.

"That's the logical answer, isn't it?" He shook his head. "Time heals all wounds. Or does it?"

His sigh was quiet—restrained—yet it carried through the fast warming atmosphere. He stood and carried his breakfast dishes inside. Juliet followed. At the kitchen sink, she passed by him, and an ocean of regret filled time and space.

Her silence punctuated the moment.

"This is exactly what I'm talking about." Kellen continued. "I wonder if you'll never know what you mean to me, no matter how many notes I write, no matter how many ways I try to reclaim your love. You'll never have the same degree of trust, and that's my fault. I'm trying to find a way to reach you, but I don't see how it can happen. You're gentle about it, but you keep shutting me out, and I don't know how to move past the barriers. Once again, though, that's my fault for blind stupidity."

The declarations left Juliet stunned. Was he so broken that he was writing them off? Not out of a lack of love, but because he viewed their circumstances as being irreparable? More confused than ever, she loaded dishes while Kellen rinsed. Frustration lifted to the surface.

"I can't help that, Kellen. I still can't get my head around the fact that beautiful women are all over the roadmap of your life. Beautiful, charming women have been part of your career from the day we met. I understand that. They're a part of your business. Never have I felt threatened. Never have you been tempted. Why her? Why now? What did I do—or not do? What was wrong with us? What changed? What happened that she turned your head—and your heart? Those are the questions that keep coming back to haunt me. They throw daggers at any attempt I make to move beyond."

Her tone had escalated. The dish loading went a bit more abrupt than she had intended. A plate landed too hard against the storage rack and split into pieces. Juliet let out a frustrated exclamation and moved in jerky motions to dispose of the broken stoneware. Kellen caught hold of her shoulders and gently turned her away from the cleanup. He cupped a hand beneath her chin to still her completely and direct her gaze to his.

His gaze held hers strong and unyielding. "She never had my heart, Juliet. What she stirred in me is an emotion I can only define as overly-excited lust. There was physical desire, but beyond that was an energy, a chemical that ran rampant when we were together...I don't know how else to explain it...suffice to say it was wrong. Dead wrong, and not at all what I truly wanted." He directed her away from the cracked dish pieces and began picking up shards of stoneware from the bottom of the dishwasher. "I've learned my lesson, but how will you ever know that for sure? There was nothing more extraordinary about Chloe than anyone else I've chosen to represent in the past. There was nothing you did wrong."

Juliet propped a hip against the island of their kitchen so she'd remain on her feet. Right now her legs were no more stable than long grass tossed in the wind. She had to cut him off. This conversation was destroying her. Just as suddenly, though, the realization dawned that they had been carried into having out this ugly situation—best to go all the way with it and try to push through. They needed to find out what awaited them on the other side of a messy, jagged mountain.

"Something obviously went lacking in our marriage that led you to her. What was it?"

Kellen dumped the ruined plate into the garbage. Returning to Juliet, he took hold of her hand and led her to the kitchenette where he pulled out a chair and urged her to sit. Taking the chair across from her, he maintained a tight hold of her hand across the top of the table. "Do you honestly think it's any one thing that leads to a situation like ours?"

A situations like ours. How clinical to distill almost nine years of marriage into *a situation.* Juliet clenched her jaw. They needed to carry through on this discussion, but doing so taxed her to the extreme. "I let you down. Somehow I must have let you down."

"You didn't let me down, Juliet. That's what you need to realize, if nothing else. I got complacent. You got complacent. To a degree, that can't help but happen in a long-term, committed relationship. Maybe we didn't put enough emphasis on being together. Maybe we didn't consciously refresh, or renew. Sometimes I think the process of daily living is more dangerous to a marriage than anything else. I got comfortable. I got lazy. I'd put you off—and you'd put me off. Not out of spite, or because we didn't care. It was simply easier that way. A routine of convenience came over us. We took on a mind-set that makes it difficult to refuse excitement, or the sizzle that happens when something new enters your life in both a professional and a personal way."

"You mean *someone*," she amended quickly, removing her hand from his. She drew up her other hand and laced her fingers together tight. Fleetingly she thought of Tim and his effect on her needy heart. Confronting herself honestly, Juliet had to admit how easy it had been to become ensnared by his ready affection and tender care…

Had it been like that for Kellen?

Very slowly, he reached forward against the space between them. "It seems the circle is complete, and we're right back where we started." He slid his fingertips beneath hers, loosening her death grip, easing her hands apart. His voice went to velvet, but that velvet was steeled by a resolve she saw clear through to his eyes.

"Juliet—all I want is a chance to show you how much you mean to me."

Tears spilled over her lashes, beginning a slow, steady race down her cheeks. He reached up and skimmed the pad of his thumb against her jaw. She could tell by his attitude the gesture wasn't meant to be seductive. This was a delivery of comfort, and an ache telegraphed by a simple and small piece of physical connection.

"From this point forward will every 'I love you' feel like

hypocrisy?" He touched her cheek now, lifting away teardrops along with small pieces of Juliet's pain. "Will every caress strike you as being false and phony? Will you always wonder if I'm thinking of someone else, even if I promise you that I'm not? All of that would be your right."

Juliet's throat jammed tight as the impact of his words struck home. She shuddered with excess emotion and gulped, but nothing much helped steady her.

"What I've done to you is my failure. I dishonored everything we built and that sickens me. That's the truth."

Just like that, Kellen shouldered the entire burden of the mess they were in. That wasn't right. Nor was it fair. Part of her recognized those truths despite the anger she felt toward his betrayal. She needed to step forward and claim her share of the responsibility. But how? Still, she boiled with anger. Still, her world was rocked by the way he had floated into the arms, and passions, of another woman.

Despite it all, Juliet knew she needed to confront the truth. She had not been a good steward of their marriage either. He convicted himself, but once again, she realized her accountability was undeniable. That fact shook her and left her at a crossroads.

You didn't step away—he did. You didn't seek out someone else—he did.

A troubling voice went to work in her mind, tempering the softness that bloomed—even as it shored up her pride and an embittered sense of self-righteousness.

Kellen moved close. In slow motion, he dipped his head. Juliet froze, assailed by a blinding panic. She didn't know what to do, or what to expect—but he didn't kiss her. Instead, he slid his lips light and slow against her damp cheeks. He absorbed her tears in a gesture so soft, so amazing, Juliet sighed before she could stop herself. Their combined warmth became something shared, full of a beautiful, stirring echo of all they had once been.

That goading voice went promptly silent.

He moved away. "If only I had known what a gift I've

been given in you. If only I had continued to look after the two of us the way I was called to by God and our vows."

Juliet closed her eyes, afraid to reveal her vulnerability, afraid to let Kellen see just how much she craved his love. She touched her cheek. Before it disappeared, she wanted to capture forever the last traces of his touch and textures. She went weak, sinking against the curved back of the wooden chair.

A new voice claimed her soul, loving and sure. *Casual behavior towards love leads to neglect. Neglect leads to demise. And the slow, steady demise of an anointed marriage is a sin just as much as the ultimate betrayal of seeking the arms of another.*

That truth sent itchy disquiet through her body. Juliet regained herself and wondered. Had Kellen's betrayal been 'ultimate'? Had he forsaken *everything* with Chloe? All indications were he had not. He had been tempted. From there he had fallen, but was the sin unforgivable? Christ's teachings—even the voice she had just heard—gave her an emphatic and immediate answer.

No.

In church, on that awful day when everything had come to a head, the first words out of Kellen's mouth were *Please, forgive me.* Wracked by pain, and the shocking sickness of being betrayed, Juliet had steadfastly refused that plea, considering it her right.

Now she wasn't so sure. What about her role in the breakdown of their relationship? Had she ever extended the same plea to Kellen for the times she had failed to support him?

No.

The awful taste of that answer resonated now, pressing down upon her like lead. Owning up to sin and negligence, Kellen kept pushing on. Despite the hostility and anger she dished at him, he persisted, showing her, day after day, in ways big and small, that she was important to him. Precious, like he said. Actions versus words.

She had to find a way to do the same.

20

Kellen retracted his umbrella and shook rainwater from the lapels of his trench coat. He pushed open one of the glass doors of the Greater Grace Rescue Mission and stepped inside. He had glanced at Juliet's calendar for the day, which was tacked as ever to the side of their refrigerator at home. Discovering her whereabouts, he decided to surprise her with a visit—just because.

Well, he admitted, not *entirely* just because. A scripture verse he had come across this morning during his daily reading of the Bible left him unsettled, and full of questions. He had poured over chapter six of the second book of Corinthians, taking to heart the words about living on God's terms, in righteousness. But then he reached a passage that stopped him short, and left him re-reading it several times over: *'Do not be yoked together with unbelievers. For what do righteousness and wickedness have in common? Or what fellowship can light have with darkness?'*

He and Juliet were both believers, so that section didn't trouble him nearly as much as the convicting words that followed. Righteousness and wickedness. Light and dark. Granted, he worked hard, and with sincerity, to leave behind the mistakes he had made, but had he embraced and honored her efforts outside their marriage? Had he been a light for her?

Juliet had always been a source of support when it came to his life outside of their relationship. Without her enthusiasm and encouragement, he never would have attained the level of success he enjoyed at Associated Talent. Kellen realized it was long past time he returned to doing the same thing for Juliet.

Light needed to obliterate the dark. How could he expect her to remain caring of his life and its many elements if he didn't consistently exhibit respect and encouragement of his own?

In the length of time it took for those thoughts to cross his mind, Kellen got a good long look at the people around him.

Street people shuffled past. Hot, heavy rain drenched their clothing, saturated feeble plastic bags clutched tight in grimy, shaky hands. A nasty summer storm blew through the streets and alleys of Music City, driving the destitute inside. The facility was standing room only for dinner and shelter service tonight.

He studied life-worn faces left craggy by desperation and anxiety. In some cases, guarded eyes roved restlessly from spot to spot, full of edginess and discomfort. Other visitors were so touched by simple acts of kindness—a welcoming touch on the shoulder from volunteers or a gentle smile—they called out gratitude and praise as they partook in an assembly line production of nourishment and compassion.

Absorbing the crowd made him stumble. A pierce-point struck his heart. So, those times when Juliet had begged off a date-night that centered more around his work ambitions than anything else—those instances when she was tired and drained at the end of the day—this was what it was all about. These people, this gathering of need, was what she worked so hard to support.

Wow.

Witnessing the people who grappled for the comfort of a simple meal humbled Kellen into awe.

He moved in a bit further and looked for Juliet. He came upon her familiar form almost immediately. He stayed put, falling into the moment of being able to watch her—and listen.

"I didn't always used to be this way," Kellen heard the homeless woman say. Juliet took hold of a long, bony hand that seemed to be gnarled from the ravages of arthritis. Juliet knelt at the woman's feet, looking up at her, into rheumy, coal-colored eyes.

"What happened, honey?" Juliet asked softly. Her face, her posture, radiated loving concern.

Even from the length of the room, odors assailed Kellen. A stench of unclean skin, decay, caked dirt and urine made his eyes water and his nose twitch. How must it be for Juliet, working hours on end, right here in the midst of it? Light and dark, he thought. Light and dark.

"My daddy? He was plant manager for an electrical manufacturer. Worked the lines and did good work. He moved his way up, he did. I even got to go to college for a couple years. Got an Associate's Degree and everything."

Juliet nodded, still kneeling, still listening attentively as she stroked the back of the woman's hand with her thumb. Kellen couldn't keep his eyes off the pair.

"I went to work in the plant when I graduated college long, long ago. It was the best option I had going since I could make good money."

Juliet tilted her head, visibly lost within the story, looking deep into the woman's face. Kellen was captivated.

The woman's overlarge, bulbous eyes filled with tears. "Then came the economic shakedown and downsizing and nothin' goin' right. Daddy didn't have a job. I didn't have a job. He got sick with cancer, and I went down the wrong road." The woman started to cry—and so did Juliet. "I did bad things. Really bad things…things…I…I…"

"Badness has no trouble stepping in when life knocks you down, does it, honey? It's an easy trap to fall into."

The woman shook her head. Long, slick brown strings of unclean hair swung from beneath a knit cap still soaked from the deluge of rain outside. Her coat was frayed and dotted by dirt stains. Kellen caught his breath.

"I strayed from God." The lady looked up, taking in the warming center. "I strayed from all of this. I did drugs. I had a daughter, and I lost her to social services. I let life destroy me. But I gotta keep tryin'. I gotta keep goin'. God keeps givin' me days, and I jus' don't know what to do with 'em. I just don't know how to hope anymore, and—and—now look at me, begging for a meal."

"I am looking at you, and you're beautiful." Juliet's intercession stilled the woman. "To me and to God. You're not alone, and you're not begging. We're here for you."

The woman's head lifted, just barely.

Seeming undaunted, Juliet continued. "You haven't strayed so far that you can't be embraced by God." Juliet took hold of both of the woman's hands now, continuing to look up at her. "After all, look where you've found yourself. You're in His arms. We're here for you because of Him, and you're getting a warm place to stay, some good food to eat, and the chance to start out fresh tomorrow...not because of us, but because of Him."

"I never thought I'd end up having to be at a place like this. I'm so embarrassed...I used to be a strong, good person..."

"You still are." Despite Juliet's subservient, kneeling position, this guest of the warming facility kept her head down; her posture remained slumped by burdens Kellen couldn't begin to imagine.

"What's your name, honey?"

"Vanetta. Jus' call me Vanetta."

Juliet stood then and sat in the chair next to Vanetta, drawing her in for a tight, long hug. Juliet whispered some words into the ear of this heartbroken, homeless stranger, but Kellen couldn't make them out. What he did know was that the woman's frail shoulders began to shake, and tears fell in abundance. Juliet kept on holding her tight, ignoring everything, it seemed, except for the woman's need to find self-worth, and care.

At last they parted, and Juliet kept a hand in place on the woman's shoulder. With the other, she lifted away the woman's food tray. "I'll be right back. Let me get you some fresh food. This has gone cold. Would you like some coffee maybe? Does that sound good?"

"Yes, ma'am."

Juliet squeezed her shoulder. "It's Juliet, honey. Juliet."

Swiping at her wet eyes, the woman offered a smile that showed yellowed teeth. "Such a pretty name. You're such a pretty girl."

Kellen stared after his wife, moved and unspeakably proud. What he hadn't grasped fully until now was that Juliet's volunteer efforts weren't about filling time. They were about affecting change—in the name of God.

∽∾

Juliet passed through the swinging doors of the kitchen. Once she knew she was out of sight of the main dining area, she sank against the closest wall. Her energy drained away. All around, the bustle of dishware being cleaned, the scrape and whoosh of oven tops being whisked back to brightness kept her from being noticed. That suited her perfectly. She sucked in a few fast, sharp breaths, trying to regain her equilibrium, but her lips trembled, just like the rest of her body.

"Hey, Jules."

She cringed. Attempting smoothness and calm, she straightened, fingering back wispy strands of hair that had come loose from her ponytail. "Hey, Tim." She grabbed a tray and dropped it against the metal guide rails. Next, she reached into a storage unit and pulled out a napkin wrapped set of cutlery. She kept her back to him, trying hard to blink back tears. Tim held her arm gently, though he allowed her to remain turned away. She started to lift a coffee mug from the nearby stack, and it rattled against the others when she trembled.

"I saw the woman you were talking to." His voice came to her, sounding calm and sure. "It looked pretty intense. Are you OK?"

Juliet wanted to give up the pretense. She finally looked toward him and shook her head. She probably reeked of transferred body odor and shared disillusionment. Ignoring everything else, she bowed her head and leaned against the support rail that held a stack of fresh food trays. She loved this program, believed in it with absolute conviction. What she had failed to consider was the draining emotion, the pain. She couldn't handle being a witness and counselor to any more heartbreak right now—not even in the name of God's nobility and the ease of another person's suffering. It simply wasn't in her. She was depleted.

"Come here." Without waiting on acceptance or refusal, Tim drew her close.

Before she knew it, the giving warmth of a hug flowed from his spirit to hers, and she felt like breaking down all over again. "I'm so sorry for how hard this is. You give, and you give, and you give. It's kind of your blessing and your curse."

Tim understood her far more than Juliet had ever realized. She wanted to slide into this moment with nothing else to consider except how good it felt to be tended to and treasured. But she couldn't. Not by miles.

She backed away fast, brushing at her damp, overheated cheeks. She sniffed. "I need to make a tray and deliver some food."

When she turned away from Tim, she looked into the face of the last person on earth she ever expected to see here.

Kellen.

21

The words *step away from my wife* didn't need to be spoken. Kellen's clenched jaw and narrow-eyed stare at Tim said it all, and sent forth a vibration powerful enough to prompt Tim to back away even further.

"She got pretty upset," Tim said, meeting Kellen's icy posture without a flinch.

"I noticed. That's why I came back here."

Tim picked up the tray Juliet had brought in. "I'll heat this and give it to one of the volunteers to eat."

"I'd still like to serve Vanetta a meal." Juliet said.

Tim nodded. "You can prep a fresh helping. The food hasn't been taken away yet."

He left, but not without a last inscrutable look at Kellen.

Wordless, Juliet turned away from her husband and braced against weakness—in all its forms. She returned her attention to the empty tray before her, fidgeting with the utensils she had deposited along the side. She heard Kellen approach, but didn't bother to meet him halfway. She was in no mood. In a gloomy rush, her entire life came at her, feeling ruined again, and her existence struck her as sorrowful, and laden by heart-wrenching compromise. The devil held her in a hammerlock.

"It seems you and Tim have become even closer. You certainly are doing a lot together at Trinity."

That low-spoken, leading observation didn't help her outlook at all. Feisty resolve pushed through a bleak surface. "Yes we are…but let me put your mind at ease. I won't do tit-for-tat. I can't. I decided, after my first week back home, that the circle of pain and wrongdoing would end. I've prayed—in earnest—to move on, and to somehow find the strength to keep tuned in to what God wants me to do...with *all* of this." She spun toward him and glared. "Tim is one of my prayer partners, but don't concern yourself with losing face. I stepped away from his hug even before I saw you. It was nothing. It was innocent."

"I know that, and I saw that for myself. Still, it hurt."

"Well, welcome to my world." In defeat, she muttered the words, her head held high.

Kellen reared back. His lips firmed into a grim line for an instant. "Touché." It occurred to her then, despite the non-stop motion of bodies through the facility, if they continued on like this, they'd garner unwanted attention. She grabbed his hand. At a brisk clip, she pulled him into a private office off the kitchen area.

Once she closed the door, Juliet took charge. "You should apologize to Tim. That standoff was uncomfortable. Besides which, the territorial card isn't one I'd suggest you play right now."

Kellen had recovered. His eyes went sharp. "Congratulations on scoring several direct hits. I'll tolerate them for now, but it's getting old. Yes, I'm jealous. Yes, I'm scared, and yes, the end result is me being territorial about you when maybe I have no right to be." He moved close, transforming into the confident man she recognized and yearned for. "But I want you to keep something very important in mind. I'm not worried one *whit* about losing face, Juliet. What I'm worried sick about, as I've told you before, is losing you for good."

She fought hard to keep from moving in, touching him. Steeling her spine, she lifted her chin. This tiny, cluttered office, full of corkboard photo displays depicting the rescue mission and its history, resonated with barely contained pain—and love.

"What worries *me* sick is the fact that I didn't realize I was losing you. Not until it was too late to do anything about it and the damage had been done...and sometimes, especially when I'm overwhelmed to begin with, it rolls over me like a tidal wave!"

Flinging the words at him, Juliet discovered humiliation still found a way to leak through her, acidic and devastating. She couldn't meet his eyes any longer, but she noticed the way he blanched. She hardened herself against sympathy.

An impasse stretched between them. Kellen pushed out a hard sigh and squeezed the bridge of his nose. The office contained a desk and the chair that was positioned behind it—not much else would fit. Within these tight confines, Juliet could have sworn she felt him in the air all around her; she could absorb him into her soul without so much as a single touch being exchanged.

"I didn't come here to argue." Kellen's quiet declaration echoed with defeat. "I didn't come here to cause you more pain." He shook his head. "I think, for now, it's best that I leave. This was a mistake, and I'm sorry."

The words drifted to silence. Stunned, she watched him struggle for a moment then turn away. Juliet shot into action and grabbed his arm. "Not a chance." When she yanked him back into place, their bodies brushed then bumped. Their eyes met and her heart rate took off. The yearning she had always felt for him intensified to the point of being unbearable, but she fought that ache with everything she possessed. "You're not getting off that easily, Kellen. Why did you come here? What's this all about? If you want to talk to me, then *talk to me!*"

Fire came to life in his eyes and Juliet nearly gasped at the wrecked expression on his face. "OK, I'll *talk to you*. This was about me wanting to support you the way you've always supported me. This was about me wanting to be part of the things that are important to you. This was about me realizing I need to build a bridge to the kind of support I used to give you before....before...*life* took over. But I can't redeem myself alone. It takes me, it takes God, and it's going to take your forgiveness. I'm only one-third of the equation, Juliet. God knows my heart. I'm trying to grasp the fact that I can be forgiven by Him because my remorse is real. The rest of it? The missing piece? It's in your hands, and it's up to you."

That revelation crashed against her with the impact of hitting a brick wall at top speed. Her jaw dropped, and she stared at him. Kellen stayed put, staring right back.

At last he stepped forward. He took loose hold of her hand. When his thumb skimmed against her wrist, absorbing the erratic thump of her pulse, she felt far too revealed. She looked down in evasion of the truth that she ached for his love—physically and emotionally.

"Let me try this again." His words were slow, tentative. "Let me start this conversation the way I meant to when I first walked in." Bearing an equal measure of hesitance, Juliet nodded but trained her attention on a scuffmark and a crease in the tile floor. "I came here to help you. I want to be part of what you're doing here. When I saw you with that woman, my heart broke. I noticed the way her story affected you. I'm amazed by the way you reach out, despite the fact that you're hurting, too."

She looked up. Inch by painful inch, her heart eased and softened of its own volition. She wanted to resist that melting swirl of surrender, but she couldn't. "It always hurts to see people in pain, people who struggle just to get by, and survive. Comfort is how I've tried to give thanks to God for the blessings He gives us and the successes we've achieved. Well. That *you've* achieved."

"The successes belong to both of us, Juliet. *Both* of us."

"I used to think so."

Kellen physically wilted. He shook his head, staring into her eyes. "God, how I want my wife back."

Standing there, facing off with him in the seclusion of the utilitarian office, Juliet forced herself to ease up as best she could. He made a point. God wouldn't ordain acrimony— from either one of them. Right now, though, she was an overwrought mess.

The unexpected touch of his affirmation gave her strength, despite the tightness in her chest. "It's becoming clearer to me that blessings are given. While we may think they're as solid as a rock, and built on forever, circumstances can build up that destroy those blessings and take them down like a wrecking ball." She paused strategically. "Like Vanetta, for example. She had a good life, an honorable life. Piece by piece it fell away from her."

She knew by the pained expression on his face that Kellen understood the underlying point she made. *Like the surrender of our marriage.*

"You've always seen to it that we never wanted for a thing. You're a wonderful provider, Kellen. This kind of activity is my way of saying thanks—to God, and to you. It feels good to give my time, and our resources, to help people who are in need. It's a grace from God, because I've looked into their eyes. I've seen the results. The gratitude, the provision and peace that a simple act of kindness can provide is a miracle to behold. We're the ones who win, as much as them."

Kellen seemed to ingest that for a moment. His gaze strayed to the entrance of the office and she watched him draw a deep, steady breath. "Is there anything I can do? I want to help."

Their eyes met and held. He was so uncertain, so out of his element. Such things were completely out of character, and the vulnerability she detected continued to dilute her hostility.

"It's not easy."

"That's OK. I don't need easy."

Juliet led the way back to the kitchen. Lined up on wall pegs were rubber aprons, just like the one she currently wore. Her gaze slid over the lines of Kellen's silk suit, the trench coat draped across his arm. Juliet grabbed an apron and handed it to him. "It can be messy work. You'll need this."

Without a second's hesitation, he peeled off his suit coat and tucked his over garments onto the empty peg. After sliding away his tie and loosening the top button of his dress shirt, he pulled the apron over his head. Juliet handed him an expandable paper hat.

Kellen's eyes went wide, sparkling with humor. "C'mon. Really?"

She giggled—deep and from the belly—it couldn't be helped. "Yes, really. Turn around and I'll tie the apron for you."

While she looped and pulled, Kellen donned the cap and looked at her over his shoulder. "It's worth wearing this thing just to hear you giggle again. I miss that sound."

The words stilled her levity at once. She fussed with an arrangement of cups and bowls that were stacked on the service counter. Kellen picked up a tray and went to work. The apron and hat didn't detract from his impact whatsoever. Juliet watched his smooth movements and familiar mannerisms as he dished up a serving of steaming meat, mashed potatoes, corn and fruit.

"If you don't mind" --Kellen glanced at her— "I'd like to give Vanetta her food. I'd like to sit with her for a bit."

"Are you sure?"

"Absolutely." He paused, apparently uncertain. "Do I just go out there and give it to her?"

"Yes. Usually, they receive their food by walking up and getting in line, but she's expecting delivery."

He spied the empty tray Juliet had just settled on the rail next to her hip. "What's that for?"

"Oh—" Startled into proper focus, Juliet gave a light, shy shrug. "I thought I'd make you a tray, too. You're probably starving by now."

"Come to think of it, I *am* hungry. I appreciate it."

She fixed the tray quickly and handed it into his care. His answering smile stirred sweetness in her heart. Stocked and ready to serve, Kellen left the kitchen behind.

A quickening pulse stirred her blood. A flow of hope worked over her. Happiness and joy—how long had it been since she felt those emotions?

❧

Tucked into a corner of the hall, staring out a nearby window, Vanetta seemed lost to the view. A gray, water-glossed world drew Kellen's attention for a moment as well. He approached her table then gently set down the two trays. Vanetta's gaze swung around and focused on him.

"Hi." He tried not to sound tentative about breaking ground with this unkempt woman. "Would you mind if I sit with you?"

Openly skeptical, Vanetta frowned. Her eyes moved from his face to the kitchen, where he could only assume she searched for Juliet. "I don' mind if you don' mind."

For some reason, that response made Kellen smile. "I don't mind at all. I'm Kellen." Vanetta looked uncomfortably at Kellen's extended hand.

"You don' gotta be all friendly like that. I'm filthy. You're a clean, good lookin' man. I don't want to get you dirty."

Kellen sat down and bumped his shoulder against hers instead. "That doesn't matter to me." He tried again, and this time she accepted his hand. When their eyes met, he found gratitude and human dignity pushing to life.

She smiled a great, gap-toothed smile. "Like the Good Book says, I guess there's nothin' so dirty God can't clean it up, right?"

Kellen laughed warmly and squeezed her hand tight. "Amen, sister."

All at once, he understood the rare and precious blessing of acceptance. Looking into this woman's face, he saw what Juliet saw. Beauty. As soft-hearted and sweet-natured as Vanetta was, there was no way Juliet would be able to refuse the needs of a soul like this. The epiphany left him in love with his wife all over again.

Emboldened, Kellen continued. "I'm just like you. I'm dirty and in need of a thorough cleaning just like that scripture verse you quoted."

In receipt of her grateful look, Kellen found it easy to ignore Vanetta's smell, the dirt, and water stains. He looked toward the kitchen area and saw Juliet in conversation with one of the other volunteers. Softness slipped through him. His heart tripped into a faster beat.

"I'm Vanetta, by the way."

Kellen jerked away from staring and directed his attention to his dinner companion. "I'm glad to meet you."

They prayed over the offering then in unison they launched into their meal. At length, she chuckled, the sound coming out more like that of a rumbling train. "I like you. You're not one of them snooty types. You're OK."

"Nah, I'm not OK, but I'm trying, just like you, Vanetta."

She shrugged and they continued to eat in a companionable silence. Kellen's attention kept straying to Juliet. He noticed the way she glanced at him every once in a while.

"You keep lookin' at her."

"I'm sorry?" Kellen took a sip of coffee, delivering an inquiring look toward Vanetta.

"Pretty lady. The one who came over here and talked to me a while ago." She pointed a long, shaky finger in Juliet's direction. "Her. You're staring at her."

Kellen didn't go flush very often, but he did right now. "I guess I am. Can't seem to help it."

"Don' blame ya.' She's something.' Can't 'member her name though." Vanetta released a frustrated sound. "I used to be so much sharper than this."

Instead of leaving her to struggle for details, Kellen decided to fill them in. "Her name is Juliet."

Vanetta slapped her knee. "That's right. Pretty name…for a pretty lady. I remember now." She looked at him hard. Then, her too-thin, angular face split into a large grin. "You got a crush on her, don't you? I can tell. I can see it in your eyes."

Kellen laughed, thoroughly enjoying this woman's company. "Since the first moment I saw her."

Vanetta sighed. "Oh…oh, I do love a good romance."

Kellen extended his left hand and pointed at his ring. "She's my wife."

"And you still look at her like that? Well, God bless ya.

God bless ya and then some!" Why did that humble, enthusiastic benediction cause him to tear up?

"And here you both are, looking after folks like me." She settled back and issued a large, heaving sigh. "Mm-mm-mm. I do guess the good Lord still puts miracle workers right here on His earth." She shook her head in wonder.

"No, Vanetta. We're not miracle workers. Remember? We're just like you."

"You're miracle workers to me, and that's that."

Kellen rested his hand on top of hers. "Trust me. We all fall short, and we all need help. All of us. You're a miracle, too."

"C'mon now. What kind of help could you ever need? You got it all."

Yes, he did. But could he continue to keep the blessing of his marriage and be allowed the opportunity to honor it all over again?

Tears sprang to Kellen's eyes once more. Humbled by Vanetta's gratitude and bolstered by her smile, he understood the fulfillment and joy Juliet experienced every time she worked here.

৵৵

When they got home that night, Kellen followed Juliet upstairs. He needed to retrieve his clothes for work tomorrow.

Juliet sat on the edge of the bed. Slowly she toed off her flats and wiggled her stocking-covered feet. The innocent image did wild things to Kellen's insides. He felt her gaze as surely as a touch against his skin, so he tried to temper himself, and divert the flood of heat that curved through him. Still, after all the emotion and heightened electricity they had shared today, he was acutely aware of her. A driving need went to work against his sense of restraint.

She watched him hang up his suit coat. He walked to the dresser and began to unfasten his cufflinks.

"I'm sorry, Kellen…for the way I treated you."

Juliet's quiet words settled into his troubled spirit. He wanted her with a passion that was undeniable—yet deny it he must. Tensing himself against a soft, enticing flow of his senses, Kellen slipped his cufflinks away then dropped them into a mahogany box. When he turned, he took in their bedroom. Juliet's bedroom now. When she had returned home, he had told her flatly and emphatically that he couldn't stand the idea of her sleeping anywhere else.

He began to slide hangers, searching for a shirt along with a suit and tie. "I deserved it."

"No, you didn't. You're not a whipping post, but that's how I treated you. It was wrong, and I'm sorry. You showed up to support me, and I snapped and threw darts. That's not going to help us. I'll do better."

Her apology called to mind something Pastor Gene had told him recently. *Make the choice to minister to her fully—then follow up that choice with your actions. If you do, God will meet you there, and you'll re-find that joy again, that connection and intimate sense of trust.*

"You did a lot more than snap and throw darts. I loved being there. Don't worry about it." Something heavy lifted away from his shoulders. "Still…thank you for the apology, Juliet."

It was all he could manage before claiming the next day's wardrobe items and leaving her behind. Avoiding her eyes, he walked away. Exiting the room, he closed the door quietly behind him.

Intimacy. He craved it with her. It wasn't just a physical thing, either. This was a working of his mind. Like stirring, masterful music, she remained with him long into a sleepless night that was beset by an ache, and a wistful sense of longing.

22

On the weekends, Kellen now made it a point to be home. He dismissed as many work-related networking and promotional events as possible, and his proximity jarred Juliet. She thought about him constantly, and weekends only intensified their connection.

She didn't want to be so edgy around him, but emotions pushed forward, increasing awareness of everything she missed about their marriage. She couldn't escape the fact that he now maintained the type of presence in her life for which she had always longed. At the same time, he didn't crowd or push. Instead, he waited patiently for her to indicate her feelings.

But that was the problem. Her feelings were such a convoluted jumble she had no idea how to move forward.

A few weeks after their visit to the Greater Grace Rescue Mission, she opted for a means of evasion so she could think clearly and focus without distraction. Following a Saturday morning shopping spree for maternity clothes with Marlene, Juliet camped out at her sister's house for the remainder of the day, baking bread.

Ever since she was little, Juliet could recall the process of her mother creating homemade bread from scratch. The task took time, and energy, but there was nothing like the smell, and reward, of fresh baked bread.

The time spent with Kellen at Greater Grace left her wanting to find a way back to even ground in their relationship. She wanted to enjoy him again, and love him again, with nothing of her heart held back. Moving forward together was all that she longed for, but the idea terrified her.

How could she cope with that level of openness again?

Once a cheater, always a cheater.

Condemnations echoed, but condemnations didn't change facts. She missed him. She longed for his touch, and the warmth of his eyes on her. She missed receiving that exclusive smile that would slip softly into her heart and saturate her with love. Mostly, she missed the impetuous way he'd step behind her and nibble at her neck, then spin her slowly around and take her on a dance that needed no music to enhance its steps.

There were huge issues to overcome, and patterns of living that needed modification, but Kellen kept trying.

For her part, Juliet could number off at least a half-dozen times when she had negated requests from Kellen to be a part of his life. Functioning separately became an easy pattern to fall into, especially as time passed.

That dangerous pattern didn't stem from a lack of feeling. That was the most frightening aspect of their dilemma. Instead, an aching, needy heart is what had led Kellen to Chloe. Combining two full and busy lives had become problematic over time. Juliet realized that now.

Seldom had the twain met.

Confusions refused to dissipate, but Juliet looked forward to the day ahead. Freshly changed into comfortable maternity slacks and a cotton blouse of vibrant peach that floated around her body, she rejoiced in the flutters and thumps of their child inside of her. Ironic that at the most tumultuous point in their lives, their dreams of a child together had finally come true. Was Kellen right? Was that God's message of hope in the chaos of their lives? She was too tangled to know any longer.

In the kitchen, midway through their bread preparations, Juliet lifted a large, stainless steel mixing bowl. Marlene stood across from her, a towel draped over her shoulder. She tossed out a dose of flour then used her hands to spread it across the countertop. Juliet dumped a freshly formed head of dough into the middle of the white, silky dust.

"I want to be healed of this whole situation," Juliet said,

continuing their conversation.

"It doesn't quite work that way, Jules. There's a lot of hard work involved." Although Marlene gave her a compassionate smile, the words minced nothing.

Juliet began to knead, and it felt good. She loved the process of pushing into the dough, rolling and squeezing, bullying it from nothingness into nourishing loaves.

"I don't know how to reach out to him anymore. I'm so full of self-doubt and fear that I'm frozen. I realize I've let him down, too. I didn't do my part to be more engaged in his life. I know that now. He stepped away, and I don't know how to get back to where we were, and make things right again." Juliet added flour to the dough and worked the heels of her hands relentlessly into the mixture, which began to yield and soften.

"You're not supposed to. Stop trying to get back to where you were. You can't. Instead, find out where you're meant to begin again. Figure out how you're supposed to move forward."

That piece of advice caused Juliet to go still. "I should have been there that night. He asked me to go with him. Did I ever tell you that? I had just gotten home from some volunteer meeting or another. You know, typical me—running, running. I don't even remember what group I was helping now."

"You need to tell him that."

Juliet bristled but figuratively bit her tongue. Defiance transformed into a hot circuit of sparks, a sweep of pain that left her wanting to lash out a fast refusal of her sister's advice. But she fought that instinct.

Marlene continued. "He asked you for forgiveness."

"Yes, he did." Juliet forgot about the dough and crossed her arms against her chest, unmindful of sticky dough clumps and flour debris. She fought acknowledging that fact because she was miles away from accepting his gesture. Yes, that was wrong—and yet—

"Forgiveness is where it needs to begin." Marlene's conclusion was emphatic.

"I see. So, he says, 'Forgive me,' and I'm the dirty dog if I don't. After what he did? Is that what you're saying? Hey, everything is great now. He asked for forgiveness and all is right with the world."

She wanted their marriage back, but admitting it felt like giving in, and accepting—without due consequence—the fact that she had been betrayed.

Remember, daughter—let she who is without sin cast the first stone...

"It's not about making a fast apology and brushing past what he did." Marlene greased pans, setting them on the counter one by one. "It's about reclaiming your commitment. Failure is human, but redemption is heavenly. Take a taste of what you had before. It might become the start of a loving, beautiful journey—if you let it happen, and embrace the chance God is giving you to return to one another." Marlene paused to lean against the kitchen counter and waited until Juliet looked at her. "Do you think this is easy for him? Do you think it's easy for him to be in the position of having to ask you for forgiveness? Do you think the road he traveled isn't hurting Kellen?" Marlene arched a brow, waiting once more.

But he deserves it! He turned his back on me and ripped a hole in my heart!

She who is without sin, daughter...

"Hey, Aunt Juliet, did Uncle Kellen come with you?"

Lifted away from God's gentle admonishment, Juliet winced on the inside and fumbled for a way to answer her nephew. Max bounded into the kitchen and started dribbling a plastic ball as he crossed to a pair of sliding glass doors that led outside to the backyard.

"Uncle Kellen had stuff to do at home today, buddy." Marlene gave Juliet a compassionate look and stepped in as a buffer. "We'll see him soon, though. By the way, what's the rule about balls in the house?"

The dribbling stopped promptly. Visually sheepish, Max's head lifted. "Sorry, Mom."

Marlene winked at her son. "Scoot. I'll call you in for

lunch as soon as the bread is in the oven."

"OK."

Head bowed, Juliet paused, clutching the edge of the kitchen counter. Oblivious to the undercurrents, Max charged into the yard, tossing the ball and kicking it with happy gusto. Alone with her sister once more, Juliet braved a reply to Marlene's question. "I know this has affected him. I know he's hurting. I also realize it's very easy to get angry at Kellen and paint him with all the colors of a bad guy, since he's the one who was tempted by someone else, but I neglected our relationship, too. I stepped away when I should have moved toward. I have responsibilities in this breakdown of ours and I know it."

"Have you ever told him that?"

"No."

Marlene took over kneading responsibilities since Juliet was thoroughly distracted. She paused from the task just long enough to deliver a penetrating stare. "Maybe it's time you did."

"I...well..." Juliet stopped speaking. She hated her own weakness, the way she yearned for Kellen. There were so many happy, beautiful memories to call upon, so many ways he had genuinely touched her heart. The note, for example...returning to church and Bible devotions...helping at the rescue mission and tolerating her cutting mood swings.

Juliet steeled her shoulders, still determined to push his love to the side for now. She busied herself scraping away excess dough from the stainless bowl. She dumped the remnants into the trash then went to the sink, intending to wash it clean.

"I, well, *what*?" Marlene toweled off her hands and shot out a restraining hand so she could hold Juliet in place.

Juliet expelled a frustrated sound. "I don't want to feel good around him."

"He's not leaving you much of a choice, is he?"

Juliet glowered. She moved to the sink and squirted dish soap into the bowl before turning on the hot water. "Feeling good around Kellen makes me feel like I've given in and accepted what he did."

"Oh, baby. Don't let it. It shouldn't. Feeling good around him, when he's working so hard to redeem himself, and earn your forgiveness, is simply a reflection of the love you feel. And the love he feels, too. That hasn't changed. You love each other. Time to start dealing with it."

Marlene's challenge brought Juliet to a standstill. Juliet nipped at her lower lip; her brows tightened into a furrow. "I can't shake him. He haunts me like a dream, but he sliced me like a nightmare. Everything about him, about us, used to be open and free and effortless. Now part of me wants to stay closed off. I don't want to let him get that close to me again. I can't afford to let myself be that vulnerable to him again. It's killing me inside because all I want to do is get rid of this emotion—"

"You want to get rid of the *pain*. Big difference." Marlene's very direct interruption prompted Juliet to forget the running water that filled the mixing bowl, the building soapsuds. "You want to release all that ugliness, not the emotion. Let's be clear about that."

Remembering herself, Juliet extinguished the pouring water and went to work washing dishes—with a vengeance. Water crested onto the counter, along with apple scented soap bubbles. "Maybe."

"The crux of the matter right now, as I see it, is the fact that you're not just hurt by Kellen. You're hurt by the fact that you were blindsided. That your marriage, which had always been such a beautiful model of what Christian relationship should be, fell apart."

"Nice."

"Actually it's not nice at all. But it's *true*." Marlene used a dish towel to mop up the overflow of water.

"I know, I know, and I've said as much to Kellen." More like *sniped* as much, she admitted to herself. Rather violently, Juliet dumped water and soap from the bowl into the stoppered sink so she could continue washing dishes.

"You're refusing to forgive Kellen, and you're refusing to forgive yourself. It takes two to build, and two to destroy, a relationship."

Juliet gasped. "Nice one, Marlene. Slam me with that when you know how badly I'm struggling! I've admitted I need to accept my share of the blame!"

Marlene grabbed a fresh drying towel. After she tugged the bowl from Juliet, she let a calming beat slide by. "You haven't admitted as much to Kellen. Think about what you've been saying. You said you should have been there. You said he wanted you with him. You said he wants you in his life, and that he's always included you in his functions. If you ask me, that's not the pattern of a sleazy guy on the prowl for available women. The first step forward is reaching out. Have you made an effort to include him in the goings on of your life?"

"He's too busy! He would have said no!" But he had shown up at the mission site...

Marlene shrugged. "I'm not so sure. I think if you had made the consistent effort, he would have been there. Point is, now, you'll never know for sure, will you?" Marlene propped a fisted hand on her hip. She arched a brow while Juliet stared, and stewed. "Gee, are those light bulbs I see going off over the top of your head?"

Juliet snorted. "Do you ever hold back the punches?"

"Nope. Not when it comes to you, Jules. You're my baby girl. Always have been, always will be."

"You're such a mom."

"Yep." Stillness returned, along with quiet understanding. "Do you still believe you and Kellen were ordained to be together?"

Juliet pondered that question for a moment. "That's what I want to believe. Right now, I just don't know. I'm back and forth and up and down like a yo-yo these days. One second I miss him so much it physically hurts. The next I get so angry I want to just chuck it all and say, fine, it's over. I take it out on him constantly. Either I shout and rage or I go all wistful and sentimental. Take your pick."

"Your reactions are understandable, Juliet. But while you sort things through, ask yourself this, is Kellen trying?"

"Yes." Juliet didn't hesitate. His efforts couldn't—and shouldn't—be denied. Even in the face of her pain. Still, she wanted to hurl the pot she scoured straight across the room, because at the same time, she had legitimate doubts about what prompted his efforts. Her emotions surged. "But by the same token, what I am right now for Kellen Rossiter is a problem that needs to be solved."

"Fair enough. But is that *all* you are to Kellen Rossiter?"

Juliet glared at her sister and dumped a milk covered mixing cup into the water. "He wants me back. He wants our child. He's trying to solve a problem, and he's trying to negotiate. That's what he does best." She shrugged. "To be honest, that's part of what I love about him. Thing is, I can't fall back into place just because *he* says so!"

"Hmm."

"What?"

"Well, it's interesting that you don't use the word love in the past tense. That's telling. As telling as the circumstances you just described." Marlene's posture softened. She stepped forward and gave Juliet a tight hug. "If he's trying as hard as you say he is, then give a little. Help make amends. Doing so is what Christ would want and expect of us. Like I said, Juliet, you love him. You can't deny that."

No. She couldn't. But she couldn't deny the fear, either.

She wiped the counter, where a few more water splatters and dough clumps remained, needing to be washed clean. So much like her entire relationship with Kellen.

Marlene swept her hand into place on top of Juliet's, stopping her nervous motions. "He loves you, too. That's another truth you can't escape."

Juliet wilted.

She rested her head on Marlene's shoulder and tried to regain herself.

Juliet, precious one, the Spirit I have placed within you is far greater than the world around you. Do not fear. Rest. Rest in Me.

"I'll try." The whispered words passed through clogging emotion and laden tears. Juliet's eyes fluttered closed in utter exhaustion.

Shaky though her answer was, it wasn't just delivered to Marlene. It was delivered to God Himself.

23

Juliet yawned and trotted down the stairs from her bedroom, intending to enjoy some coffee and make a piece of stomach-settling toast for breakfast. She looked forward to sampling the fruits of her labors this past weekend with Marlene...on a number of fronts.

Tingling with an equal mix of apprehension and anticipation, she settled a hand against her well-rounded midsection, subconsciously snuggling with the baby. The idea nudged a grin into a full-blown smile and calmed her nerves.

By design, she rose early enough to catch Kellen before he left for work.

She entered the kitchen, and sure enough, he sat on a padded stool at the tall counter between the sink and dinette. His back was to her, but from her angle she could see that his black leather Bible was open, and he was reading. A mug stood at his elbow, and she noticed a piece of paper towel next to his mug. Upon it rested a half-eaten slice of the bread she had made. The vision of nourishment and peace stroked her heart.

"Morning." The word crossed her lips, sounding hesitant. Her smile trembled a bit, paying a visit to the land of uncertainty. She wanted to work past that now—somehow. *God, show me the way. Help me.*

Kellen turned toward her. He shook his head and let loose a rich laugh. Sunshine streamed in through the large bay window, burnishing the dark waves of his hair. "Unbelievable."

Juliet was taken aback by the unconventional reaction to her arrival. "What's unbelievable?"

"God's timing. Your timing. Come here for a second." She approached and Kellen slid the Bible toward her. He tapped the open page with his index finger, indicating a chapter of Proverbs. "This is what I was reading when you walked in. Tell me that's not God's voice at work."

Juliet stood close. The enticing blend of sandalwood and spice cologne welcomed her to the side of her husband as he directed her to Proverbs 31:30.

"Charm is deceitful and beauty is vain; but a woman who fears the Lord, she shall be praised." She read the words aloud. A moment or two after she finished, during a silence that fell comfortably between them, the deeper, more personal meaning dawned.

"I've learned that proverb the hard way—but I've learned it." His earnest expression and the direct clarity of his eyes sanded down the edges of her hurt.

Juliet embraced the tender atmosphere between them, continuing to simply look at him.

Kellen had never been ashamed of turning to God— despite his chosen profession, and despite his sin with Chloe. Even though the world in which he moved looked down on faith and outright declarations of Christianity, he did everything he could to stand on his core beliefs and promote them as well.

But then came Chloe...

That voice of doubt kept creeping in, hitting her hard. This time, for the first time ever, Juliet didn't fight thinking about the woman.

Kellen might consider Juliet to be the woman of faith in that selection from Proverbs. He might also see Chloe as the one whose charm and beauty had deceived his heart. In part, the analysis rang true, but Juliet forced herself to look deeper. She needed to execute ownership of her marriage. Responsibility.

While thoughts tangled and swirled, Kellen leaned in carefully. He kissed her cheek, lingering over the connection. Juliet didn't pull away. Instead, her lashes fluttered. She closed her eyes and gave herself permission to fall just a little bit...

"Did I tell you?" he murmured. "You are such a beautiful mother-to-be."

His gaze traveled slowly against the length of her. Juliet's reactive squiggle earned a loving smile from Kellen.

"Thanks. I'm starting to feel pregnant, that's for sure. It's a lot more comfortable to be in maternity clothes."

Kellen's fingertip grazed against the hem of her blouse. "I like the new look."

At that moment, the baby began to kick. Juliet jumped, and Kellen grabbed her arm in steadying support. "What's wrong?"

Panic laced his voice.

She smiled assurance into his eyes and lifted his hand from her arm, placing it instead upon the spot where he might feel the baby move. "I'm fine...but it seems we're percolating an NFL caliber kicker..."

It didn't take long for the baby to slide and shift and kick again, rolling against the gentle pressure of Kellen's flattened palm.

"How amazing..." His eyes were closed, his words a prayer of awe. Juliet kept her hand over his. She hoped their unity, their shared warmth, might transfer to the tiny, vibrant life bursting just below.

She savored the moment until their baby settled.

"What's up for you today?" He sat down to finish his bread and coffee.

"I have a doctor's visit in a couple of hours; then I'm seeing Pastor Gene this afternoon."

Even the mention of counseling didn't build too heavy a cloud over the moment. Kellen's brows went up, and he turned to her once more. "Do you feel like having lunch together?"

This initiation into their day felt so normal, so luxuriously routine. Juliet nodded her acceptance, her smile filling her face without a second of hesitation.

❧

"I still can't believe I left my purse at your office."

"No worries. Will you be late for your appointment?"

Juliet angled her wrist and checked her watch. "No, I'm fine. I've got plenty of time. Still, I feel like the clichéd absent-minded professor."

They stood side-by-side in a mirrored, dimly lit elevator. Kellen chuckled at her comment, maintaining a guiding hand against the small of her back. Lunch had just concluded and they returned to Associated Talent. He felt lighthearted, savoring the miraculous way they had connected today. Never again would he take such a beautiful gift for granted. The only stain on his happiness was Juliet's continuing struggle with blood pressure levels and an excessive level of proteins in her system. If the numbers didn't improve before Juliet's next visit, Dr. Roth intended to begin a round of medication.

A bell chimed and the elevator doors slid open to reveal a marble lobby trimmed with mahogany wood accents. They rounded a corner where a manned reception desk stood sentinel in front of a sitting area framed by plush area rugs and comfortable leather chairs.

Kellen froze when he realized Chloe Havermill occupied one of the seats. He wove his fingers tight against Juliet's hand and drew her close.

Chloe spotted them, and stood promptly. "Hi, Kellen." Her smile was welcoming, but a tad strained.

He couldn't be rude and brush past her, but that's exactly what he wanted to do. "Hey, Chloe."

Juliet's reaction hit him instantly. She literally shrank against his side, though her face remained friendly and smooth, her smile in place with beauty and perfect timing. He wondered what that graceful display of class cost her on the inside.

Kellen stepped up to his former client and shook her hand, but he quickly included Juliet, keeping her as close as he could. "Juliet, you remember Chloe Havermill."

"Of course I do." The women shook hands as well.

"Congratulations on the success of *Swing Time*."

"Thanks so much. It's good to see you again." Chloe reacted warmly, but her gaze traveled to the unmistakable swell of Juliet's pregnancy. Chloe's lips wavered and she blinked, but in an instant, that reaction passed, and she looked at Kellen and Juliet with nothing more than a friend's admonishment and curiosity. "You have news to share, it seems. Can I offer you my congratulations?"

Kellen felt Juliet's grip go tight against his hand. Next, the fingers of her free hand wrapped slowly around his forearm. She wasn't being possessive, he realized. She was completely displaced and uncomfortable, looking for a means of steady support.

"We're expecting." Kellen focused on Chloe but kept hold of Juliet, all but willing her to read his thoughts. *Don't fade away and step back on me. Don't feel threatened. You're the one I want. You're the one I'm fighting for—with everything I have to give. Our marriage and our child is what I want more than my next heartbeat.*

Chloe's demeanor remained bright, but Kellen recognized the slight tautness of her shoulders, and her stiff stance. "How exciting. When are you due?"

"In a little less than four months," Juliet replied.

"A Christmas baby, perhaps—how great." Chloe's gaze trained on Kellen. "Congratulations again."

Although the only thing he wanted to do was bolt and run, and protect Juliet as best he could, an amazing thing happened when he looked into Chloe's eyes. There was absolutely no sizzle. No trace of a spark. Not even a whisper of the driving, heady attraction that had led him so close to spiritual annihilation.

"Are you here for a meeting?" Kellen asked.

Chloe nodded. "With Ryan Douglas."

Ryan, Kellen knew, was now Chloe's agent. He was about to wish her well and conclude this uncomfortable and unexpected encounter when a doorway opened into the lobby.

"Kellen—I thought I heard your voice. I've got...oh...I'm

sorry. I didn't mean to interrupt."

Never had the sweet, eager face of his assistant, Anna, been so welcome. Kellen turned swiftly from Chloe. "We were just wrapping up. What's going on?"

"I've got In His Name Productions on the line. They have preliminary action items about securing Tyler Brock to participate in their Christian music festival. When I heard your voice, I trailed you. Sorry to just jump right in."

Anna was sorry? Kellen wanted to give her a big, fat raise. "Don't apologize. I'll grab the call." He nodded at Chloe and steered Juliet gently toward the hallway leading to his office.

Kellen thought about the Scripture verse he had read this morning—the proverb about charm, beauty—and deception. He considered the ways in which a Godly woman was so precious and realized the verse wasn't meant to speak only to him; it was meant to comfort and strengthen Juliet as well— for this very moment.

He only hoped she might recall its wisdom and cling to its comfort.

∂∽∾

Juliet held it together.

She snagged her purse. Before leaving and letting Kellen resume his business day, she gave him a perfunctory hug good-bye accompanied by a smile she didn't truly feel. By that time, the lobby was empty and she escaped from Associated Talent without further delays or awkward interactions.

It's not that she was angry with Kellen. Chloe's arrival to meet with her agent certainly wasn't Kellen's fault, and Chloe had every right to remain engaged as a successful artist of Associated Talent.

Juliet knew all that—but reasonable thought patterns didn't keep her heart from shredding. She had been forced to look straight into Chloe's stunning eyes...heard her speak with the lips that had touched Kellen's. Juliet had been left with no choice but to extend a hand of courtesy when she actually wanted to slap the woman straight across the face and run away. Playing nice with the one who had all but destroyed her marriage left Juliet devastated. She stumbled into her car and closed the door. The insulation didn't help. She gasped for air. Ricochets of pain zinged against her nerves.

Every noble ambition, every faultless desire to move forward kept meeting up against tribulation. Is this how the rest of her life and marriage would be? From this point on, would she be forced to endure an endless cycle of reoccurring pain and doubt?

Juliet posed the question to Pastor Gene at her counseling session that afternoon, and she did so amidst tears that rolled big and warm down her cheeks. She dabbed them away with tissues, but they kept on coming.

"Every time I feel like we've made progress, reality steps in and slams me down. I don't know what to think. Kellen has returned to worship. We're doing everything we can to embrace God and pray together, and rebuild. But then the world rushes in and steals what precious little peace we can find. Kellen has told me he thought he was looking after his well-being by grabbing a few extra hours of rest rather than going to church. I never fought him on it. I gave in, and tried to be supportive, and understanding. Now I know better. What could possibly be better for him—for both of us—than time spent in communion with God?"

"Nothing." Pastor Gene's answer came instantly, but he didn't condemn Kellen. There was comfort to be found there. He leaned forward in the chair across from Juliet, planting his feet and propping his elbows on his knees. "Here's something I'd like you to consider." He paused until Juliet focused on him. "Evil isn't ever going to give up, no matter how strong your faith. Evil isn't ever going to stop fighting. In my opinion, that's part of what you're coming up against. The closer we get to God, the harder the devil tries to tie us up." He grinned. "Look at it this way. You must be doing something right, because it seems you and Kellen are ticking off the prince of evil."

They shared a laugh.

"You've both grown from the problems you face, Juliet. You've emerged from a period of complacency and routine, and if you can find the way to openly and freely forgive, you'll both emerge stronger than ever."

"I pray for that every day." Her soft words faded to silence.

Pastor Gene settled back against his chair; his gaze was steady. "Is Kellen the same man he was six or seven months ago?"

Juliet didn't answer right away. She thought about her answer. "No. He's changed."

"For the better?"

Juliet sighed, and nodded.

"That says something. Furthermore, I don't think he's getting away from this episode unscathed. Do you?" He waited for a moment, until Juliet shook her head, keeping her eyes diverted.

She tried and tried to find a way to hang on to the anger, but doing so was difficult now—nearly as difficult as letting it all go and beginning her relationship with Kellen on even ground, completely renewed.

"Keep at it," Pastor Gene concluded. "Don't give up. Big changes are happening, and God will meet you there. I promise."

24

Kellen's cell phone buzzed. He launched the call, eyes not straying from the spreadsheet he constructed. "Kellen Rossiter."

"Hey, Kellen. It's Mom."

This was a pleasant surprise. Kellen promptly ignored his quarterly report to Weiss McDonald providing per-client-income calculations and revenue percentages. "Mom—hey!" He turned away from the computer. "I'm not used to hearing from you in the middle of the day. How are you doing?"

"Great—just got back from the craft store."

He chuckled. "Indulging your scrapbooking passion again?"

"Always! Dad even came with me, but I had to reciprocate by helping him do some work in the yard." Another laugh followed. "Anyway, we got to talking."

"About?"

"Mostly about how much we miss you and Juliet."

"Well that sentiment is definitely mutual. Strange that lawn work would lead you to that connection."

"We were wishing for your muscle and pruning skills."

"I'm horrible at horticulture and you know it."

"What can I say? We're desperate."

"You must be." He stretched back, relaxing into the tone of the call. It warmed him to touch base with home.

"So, back to you and Juliet. We were wondering, do you think you might be able to indulge us with a visit sometime soon?"

Just like that, relaxation blew into pieces of shrapnel. Kellen cringed. It had been way too long since he had been to

Los Angeles...but...a trip? Now? With Juliet?

Were it not for the shambles of his life, a trip to California would have already taken place, or been in the works. The request wasn't unexpected. Unintentionally, his silence stretched. "I'm not trying to put any pressure on you and Juliet..."

Kellen rubbed at a sudden muscle knot between his neck and shoulder. "I know that, Mom. No worries."

"With the baby arriving in a few months, your lives will be changing. You probably won't be traveling for a while, so we thought we'd float the idea."

The knot moved from his shoulder to his stomach. "You make a good point. Flying with babies isn't always fun." How was he supposed to handle this situation?

"Then, I looked at the calendar and went all nostalgic."

Kellen propped an elbow on the desk. He picked up a paperclip, fidgeting. "What do you mean?"

"Well, with your anniversary coming up, Dad and I thought it would be fun to celebrate with dinner at The Skyline Club."

Kellen bent the paperclip over his thumb, channeling nervousness into the flimsy piece of metal until it snapped. His nine-year wedding anniversary was three weeks away. Kellen knew the date loomed, but he hadn't found a way to deal with it yet. Out of necessity, he focused on one goal alone--recapturing the heart of his wife.

Confronted with the prospect of celebrating his marriage, Kellen realized he couldn't refuse his parents. Furthermore, he could use an afternoon in LA to touch base at the headquarters for Associated Talent. Any other work-related issues could be handled remotely. Logistically, nothing stood in the way. Emotionally, however, he looked down upon a deep and dangerous chasm.

How would Juliet react to the idea of vacationing together, and celebrating a troubled marriage in the process? He couldn't possibly answer his mom's request without asking Juliet first.

"Let me get with Juliet. Can we call you back tonight?"

"Absolutely. Are you sure you don't think I'm being a meddlesome mother?"

Despite turmoil, affection poured forth in a deep laugh. "Never. Talk to you in just a bit."

"Sounds great, honey. Love you."

Excitement laced her tone. That helped Kellen do what needed to come next. Ending the connection to his mom, he reengaged his phone. He auto-dialed Juliet and she picked up on the second ring.

"Hey, Kellen."

The sweet, gentle lilt of her voice left him to tingle and ache. "Hey, lo...Juliet." He winced, wishing desperately he could call her *love* again. Fortunately, she didn't seem to catch his stumble. "I just hung up from my mom. Do you have anything going on tonight?"

"No, actually I'm just starting dinner." She took a sharp breath. "Wait a minute...is everything OK with May and Jack?"

"Yes—yes. They're perfectly fine. Don't worry."

"Oh...good."

Her relieved exclamation melted him. He loved the fact that she cared so much about his parents. If their marriage didn't survive this nightmare, how would he ever explain it to his folks? Kellen braced and shut down that circuit of negativity.

Juliet continued. "Tell me what's going on out west."

"We can talk over dinner. The upshot is, they'd like us to come out for a visit in the next few weeks—before you're too far along to travel—"

"Oh...ah..." Her discomfort returned and Kellen sighed. "We need to think about this, Kellen. Really. I'm not sure..."

Her words drifted off. Kellen stepped into the void. "We'll figure things out—together." He emphasized the last word and was met with a moment of contemplative silence.

"OK. Thanks for letting me know."

"I didn't want you to be blindsided if she calls you. Plus, I figured you'd want some time to think it over."

He heard her breathe softly. "I appreciate that. I'm not trying to be difficult. I'm just confused, and I—"

"Juliet, you don't even need to say it. I understand. I'll see you in a few hours."

Kellen hung up. He didn't know whether to rejoice that she hadn't rejected the idea out of hand, or weep bitterly over the losses he continued to endure.

☞☜

Over dinner, Juliet listened while Kellen rehashed trip particulars.

"I'm concerned about you—and the baby. I'd feel better about taking a flight if you were cleared by Dr. Roth. She's concerned about you."

The subtle spices of basil, garlic, and tomato sauce warmed the air around the dinette. Seated across from Kellen, she looked up after scooping a fork full of eggplant parmesan from her plate. She arched a brow and offered a teasing smile—a ghost of what they had once been able to share so effortlessly. "I'll call her tomorrow, but I'm not an invalid. I'll be fine."

She ate, and the serving dissolved against her tongue. Anxieties crested in. After savoring the bite, she pushed at her romaine salad, refocused on her plate rather than Kellen.

"You're under enough stress," he observed, and he sighed. "You don't need this."

"Neither one of us *needs* this, but we can't beg off, and we certainly can't alarm Jack and May by telling them what we're going through—not when we haven't even figured it out for ourselves yet."

She looked up as Kellen set aside his fork and knife. His shoulders sagged, and Juliet experienced an itch to reach out, to soothe a gentle hand against his arm and lend comfort. She didn't allow that emotional entrée. Instead, she leaned back in her chair, building a buffer of physical distance.

"Maybe there's a purpose here. Maybe we need to look at this trip as a chance to catch up with your parents and get away from our routines for a while. That might help us."

He regarded her steadily, his mouth a firm line. "You're sure you're on board?"

"Kellen, I love your parents. Loving them has always been an extension of the love I feel for you. Refusing their offer wouldn't be right. It would send up all kinds of red flags."

"I agree, but what about our anniversary? That's going to be—difficult."

Juliet slumped. "The anniversary will come at us no matter what we do or where we are." She speared some greens dashed by raspberry vinaigrette. "It'll just be a quiet dinner, with two people we love. It might even make the day more comfortable than if we were just...you know...*here*..."

The awkward phrasing couldn't be helped, but pain touched Kellen's eyes and left Juliet feeling bad. "We can make this work," she added. "We *have* to. They're my family, too."

25

Once plans were finalized, Juliet felt like two weeks passed in a hurry. They were set to spend a week with Jack and May and the visit would conclude with a sumptuous dinner to celebrate Kellen and Juliet's ninth anniversary.

During the drive to the airport, Juliet kept quiet. She noticed Kellen went introspective as well, though his mouth was taut. The subtle lines around his eyes were more pronounced as well, revealing his stress. His fingertips thumped restlessly against the gearshift on the console between them.

She looked out the passenger window, wanting to connect with him physically. Doing so in happier days would have been natural and expected; now she was unsure. The need became undeniable. Keeping one hand tucked on her lap, she slowly reached across the leather divider and settled her hand against his forearm.

He kept his focus on the road ahead, and sunglasses shielded his eyes, but she noticed the way he worked his jaw and swallowed hard. So, she gently increased her hold, sensing he needed the contact as much as she did.

The roadmap to Kellen's thoughts was plain, a mirror of her own. Visiting California was going to be an excursion riddled by the anxiety of walking on eggshells so the elder Rossiters wouldn't sniff out any problems and become concerned.

The flight was a whirlwind, featuring a bit of turbulence over the mountains, then a descent from the heights of a sun-drenched, pure blue sky. Juliet got a bit wobbly in the stomach toward the end of the journey, but at the moment queasiness hit, she felt the baby move. The reassurance kept her focused enough to fight back a touch of illness. She tenderly stroked her swollen stomach, calming herself, and connecting with the baby.

As the sun set behind the San Gabriel's, they pulled up to Kellen's childhood home, a place that remained much the same now as it had been the first time she saw it as his fiancée.

With her hand dutifully tucked into Kellen's, Juliet followed him up the walkway to the entrance of a gracious brick colonial. Kellen's mother swung the door wide and launched into Kellen's arms with a happy exclamation. A sentimental lump clogged Juliet's throat as she released Kellen's hand and took a step backwards.

After the hug, Kellen stepped back and gestured toward their rental car. "I've got to grab the luggage. Be right back."

May Rossiter nodded and embraced Juliet. May walked her inside, roping an arm around Juliet's shoulders. "You look wonderful. How are you feeling? You must be dead on your feet after traveling."

Juliet kissed May's cheek, touched by the woman's loving manner. "I'm fine. Don't worry a bit."

Jack Rossiter stepped into the entryway. His eyes lit up and he swept Juliet into a hug. "Boy, oh boy. Just when I think you can't possibly get any more beautiful you go and prove me wrong."

Juliet kept hold of his offered arm. "You sweet talker. I've missed you, Jack." He was a silver-haired, more deeply lined version of his son—tall and lean, yet powerful in personality and presence.

Kellen entered the house, rolling two suitcases, the third piece, an oversized duffle, was slung across his shoulder. Kellen deposited their luggage in the entryway for the time being and greeted his dad with a tight embrace.

May had prepared snacks to eat, and for the next few hours, they settled in, sinking into the familiar ebb and flow of updates and memories. Juliet avoided any reference to troubles in their marriage, and they carefully masked any tensions. The amazing thing was that Juliet didn't find the exercise to be difficult. Solidarity with Kellen shined a spotlight on the best aspects of their relationship.

"...I remember coming here with Kellen for the first time, to announce our engagement. I was terrified!"

Laughter coursed the room. Juliet and May were curled up on a large, overstuffed couch. Grogginess began to steal over Juliet, but she fought it, eager to spend time with May and Jack.

"You had nothing to worry about." Jack's firm assurance prompted Juliet to smile. She exchanged a tender look with Kellen, who sat in an easy chair next to his dad.

"I'm serious," Juliet snared a carrot from the cracker, veggie, and dip tray. "I wanted to impress you, and let you know how much I loved your son. Everything had happened so quickly between us, and I kept wondering what on earth we'd all find to talk about."

Juliet ate, and Jack harrumphed. "For better or worse, keeping a conversation going has never been a problem for me."

May rolled her eyes. "You can say that again."

Juliet's gaze tagged Kellen's once again. Their fingers bumped as they both reached for wedges of cheese and a pair of crackers.

"Besides, we certainly didn't want you to get away." Jack sipped from a mug of tea then set it back down on the end table. "After all…"

"Here we go," Kellen muttered, giving his dad a playful nudge.

"She's the daughter I always wanted," sang Jack, Kellen, and May in perfect unison. Juliet blushed furiously, especially when she absorbed the intent way Kellen looked at her. His love reached out, touching her heart in every spot where she needed it most.

They stayed up late, talking until the evening ran deep and exhaustion overshadowed everything else. Juliet realized she needed to call it a night before too long so she rolled her shoulders and stretched. "If y'all don't mind, I think I'm going to turn in."

Kellen stood. "I'm pretty beat, too. Let's pick this up again first thing, OK?"

"You bet," Jack agreed. "I'm hoping you might be able to take a look at the sprinkler system tomorrow, Kellen. I've got a couple spigots along the side of the house that aren't working right."

"I'll give it a look."

Juliet squelched a grin. Kellen and Jack loved to putter, and take on whatever projects came up. Arm in arm with May, she quipped, "Two heads always being better than one, right?"

"There's always strength in numbers." May laughed and squeezed Juliet's fingertips. Upstairs, they paused at the first closed door and May opened it wide. "I've got you two set up here in the guest room, as usual. Holler if you need anything, OK?"

Juliet stared at the queen-sized bed tucked beneath a large, open window. Not far away, a sitting area and adjoining bathroom basically provided them with a suite unto themselves. Right behind her, Kellen froze, their luggage in his care.

The one thing she had failed to consider in orchestrating this trip?

She would be sharing a bed with Kellen.

26

Sleeping arrangements that had been as natural as could be for years suddenly felt brand new—and evocative. At first, Juliet stretched as much space between their bodies as possible, timid about even brushing against him, afraid of the way her mind and body might betray her deepening reception.

But the next morning, she awoke to the weight of his arm tucked against her waist. She automatically snuggled against him. The intimacy stirred her with contentment and longing instead of tension.

So, she didn't move right away.

Instead, she closed her eyes and enjoyed their connection.

"Mmm." Kellen's breath slid softly against her neck. "I've missed this so much…"

"Kellen…"

Fear hit her hard, landing in her voice, adding texture to that solitary word of warning.

Undeterred, he moved closer.

Juliet opened her eyes and watched in helpless suspense as he dipped his head. Full, beckoning lips came close, and closer still. Nestled beneath a cocoon of bed blankets and body warmed half-wakefulness, she struggled to maintain steady. She wanted him—so very much.

But…

"Kellen, we need to think, and…"

Light as a feather his lips dusted hers—not claiming, just gliding, and touching. Her blood seared through her veins, and she melted. A tender ache rippled through her body. Words fled.

"Kellen..." Once again, she breathed his name; this time in a helpless plea. Physically and emotionally she dissolved into surrender. He drew her forward, tugging gently against her waist. A pulse-beat of desire built steady and strong.

Caught off-guard and unprepared, she went blind to everything but the two of them. His love and tenderness, which she had longed for so desperately during these lost and lonely nights, was so close now. He offered her everything for which she most wished—

What are we doing?

The thought crashed in on her. So did the recognition of how far they had gone—and how quickly. Innocent physicality had left her mind spinning. Juliet fisted her hands against his chest. In motions almost drunken, she shoved Kellen and the blankets so she could tumble from the bed. Standing on wobbly knees, she cleared her throat and pushed hair back from her eyes. In quick, jerky motions, she slid on her robe.

Chloe. Cheating. Pain.

Three small words became a drumbeat that destroyed the joy of being in his arms again.

"Juliet...please come back." The quiet, sleep roughened texture of his voice, the smoke of his gaze, became more of a temptation than she could bear. He pulled back the blankets, re-opening the space she had just vacated. The simple gesture caused her legs to tremble with want. "Come back to me."

The deliberate double meaning of those words rammed home. She couldn't tolerate the nearness, the flood of emotions both beautiful and wretched. It drove her crazy to feel his warmth again, to be enveloped by his scent and the sound of his breathing and the subtle shifts and gives of his body while he slept.

But all things considered, she refused to give in. She couldn't offer him what he wanted. Her body remained tightly connected to her soul, and her soul still questioned, still doubted, and still searched.

"I can't," she murmured, grasping at the last remnants of

her willpower by a margin so narrow it robbed her of breath.

Kellen watched her, but dejection rode a pathway straight from his eyes to hers.

"Not yet," she said.

A tense silence followed. "I want you back so much it hurts, Juliet. But it'll never happen, will it?" Kellen's words echoed through the room, a muttered condemnation of himself, of her, and of all that their marriage had once been.

Defeat caused her muscles to go taut, stoking a heat that crawled against her skin. Juliet wanted to crumple up and wail. What could she say to that? How could she possibly respond? She tried to formulate an answer, but only silence held sway.

Issuing a low, frustrated growl, Kellen ripped back the bedcovers. He didn't look her way, so she couldn't read his expression. He stalked to the bathroom—and slammed the door.

Juliet winced but gasped when she heard the sound of crashing glass that resounded through the space Kellen occupied.

Galvanized, she pushed through the entrance. She tumbled into his unyielding grip, and he pinned her against the door, which slammed closed at her back.

"Stay put!" She shivered. His voice was too loud—too harsh. He stalked away, going to a space by the toilet where water spatters dotted the wall. On the floor just beneath, glass shards decorated the ceramic tile like sparkling glitter.

Apparently, he had thrown the glass against the wall in a move of abject frustration she understood completely. He squatted and began to pick up the splinters. His fast, reckless motions broke her heart. "Kellen, please, let me help you! You're going to get hurt."

"Get out of here! I don't want you to get cut!"

Juliet froze when he turned his head and she look into his eyes. Never, ever, in their time together had she seen him look so tortured, so ravaged. Had she done this to him? Had the power of his feelings so completely overwhelmed him? He was out of control—a foreign entity from the composed, smooth man she knew.

In the near distance, a knock sounded at their bedroom door. "Kellen? Juliet?" May's voice reached them, urgent and concerned. "We heard a bang, and glass breaking. Are you OK?"

Juliet eyed her husband in plaintive desperation. "Your mom," she eked out.

Kellen leaned forward and propped his head against the wall. He closed his eyes and groaned. "Sorry, Mom. The door got away from me, and I accidentally knocked the glass from the sink. We're fine."

"Let me get you a broom and dust pan."

"Don't worry about it. I've got it covered. We'll be right out."

"OK, sweetheart. Be careful of the glass."

Thankfully, May left it at that. Kellen stood and went to work all over again. His bare feet came dangerously close to a glittering pile of broken crystal. Juliet moved toward him without thinking. She sank to her knees, picking up remnants and throwing them into a small garbage pail. Her knees made contact with splinters and glass dust and it hurt. She sank into a weak heap.

Kellen leaned down just far enough to grab her wrists and lift her away. "This is *my* mess to deal with! Please, would you just leave me be?" She saw through the veneer of his sharp words to the anguish that lay beneath.

"I can't."

"Yes, you can, Juliet. In fact, you're doing a great job of it." He continued the task of picking up debris. He scooped by hand and viciously dumped glass remains into the wastebasket. Tiny glass cuts emerged in the form of thready, red smears that glossed his fingertips. He didn't even pause. "I'm at the end of it all. There's nothing I can say anymore, and nothing I can do to make things right again." He continued to shovel and toss, never meeting her eyes. "How much more can I repent? I've tried everything I know to make my way back to you."

"Kellen, I'm lost, too! I'm on a roller coaster, and it's exhausting! One second I feel fine about you and I—the next second I feel thrilled about having our baby—then this horrid black cloud comes over me, and I return to your office following a beautiful lunch together and come face-to-face with...with..."

"Chloe." The word came out sounding flat and lifeless. "Stop trying to step over the walls between us. It can't be done. We need to obliterate them. We..." He gulped. His chest worked convulsively. "No. Not we. *You* need to find a way to forgiveness, or we don't stand a chance."

Kellen groaned. He slid down the wall again, all the way to the floor and onto his backside. Drawing up his knees, he dropped his head onto his crossed arms. "I watched while you stood in the middle of that soup kitchen and hugged a man. It was innocent, and I knew it—but all I wanted to do was rip the two of you apart, so I can't imagine how what I've done has broken your heart. I wanted to put my fist through a wall I was so angry—and scared—about what I saw between you and Tim. That pales in comparison to what I did to you. I know *all* of this, Juliet. What I don't know how to do is make you believe that I love you, and always will. I'm trying to show you that I regret what I did. Beyond the way I live my life, I can't do anything more."

Before Juliet could respond, Kellen pushed to his feet and padded from the bathroom. When he closed the door this time, it was with a considerably lighter touch.

His surrender to hopelessness stayed with her long after the silence rode in. His seemingly endless supply of patience had run out—just when she was trying to come to grips with the fact that, despite everything that had transpired, she still loved her husband beyond any power or emotion she had ever known before.

27

That afternoon, Juliet decided to embrace a bit of solitude and take a nerve soothing dip in the pool.

Jack and Kellen worked on the jammed sprinkler units out front. Meanwhile, May attended a weekly bridge club gathering. Crossing through an empty and peaceful kitchen, Juliet exited the house through sliding glass doors. She was dressed to swim in a deep blue one-piece, a towel draped over her shoulders. Jack and May's backyard was a welcoming oasis, framed by hydrangea bushes, lemon and pear trees. Metal bistro tables and chairs surrounded the curves of the kidney shaped pool. Rainbow shades of snapdragons formed borders against thick green grass.

Tossing her towel and cell phone onto the closest table, Juliet performed a fast, bracing dive.

Pushing through the water provided a pleasant stretch to her muscles and diverted her attention—if only temporarily—from focusing on Kellen. She paced herself carefully, pausing every once in a while to sink deep then break through the water. She rolled onto her back and floated, humming a soft sound of approval. She closed her eyes, moving with the ebb and flow of the water, relaxing muscle-by-muscle.

"...I'll restart the system, Dad. Let me know if we unclogged the unit."

Kellen's voice drifted at first, and then intensified as he pushed through the wooden gate of the backyard.

His shadow passed across the spot where she lay, and Juliet's serenity shattered. She kicked her feet until they landed on the bottom of the pool and stood, raking back her hair and scrubbing her face. She blinked her eyes free of water, realizing he had come to a stop, watching her as he opened an electrical box not far away.

"Hey, Juliet..." He seemed surprised to see her, but then he smiled. "Every mother-to-be should look as good as you."

Though insulated by the rippling water, Juliet shivered, thoroughly aware of him. He didn't dwell for long, though. He explored the interior of a wall-mounted unit that housed the sprinkler control. Seconds later, he was gone without a backward glance or another word.

Juliet dove deep then plunged out of the water, stepping from the pool. She dropped onto a chair bathed by sunlight. Pursing her lips, she reached for her phone and keyed into her directory. She needed support. She needed to talk to the person she could most rely on for wise counsel and understanding.

"Hey, Jules." The sound of Marlene's voice soothed Juliet immediately. "How's it going?"

"Good. I just wanted to hear your voice." Juliet curved a hand against her abdomen as she stretched out her legs and soaked up the warmth. The atmosphere of tranquility lent itself to Juliet being able to go still. She tilted her head back once more and closed her eyes.

"That bad, baby?"

Marlene's tender remark caused Juliet to smile. "You're perceptive."

"How are you holding up? Honest answer."

Juliet shrugged. "I'm OK."

"Really?"

"Honest answer."

"Fill me in on what's happening behind the scenes. How are you and Kellen handling things with his folks?"

Juliet lifted her head and cast a fast glance toward the closed fence. Kellen was out of earshot, and she'd keep an eye out in case he returned to the backyard. For now, she could release some of her turmoil into Marlene's care.

"It...it's been...interesting."

"Hmm. Well—talk to me about interesting."

Through the phone, Juliet heard background noise of water running, then the *thunk* of a mug being set down. A door closed and a blip later, the familiar whir of a microwave began. The interlude gave Juliet time to think about what to say.

"Well, when we arrived yesterday, Kellen and I were shown to our room." Deliberately, she let the sentence dangle so Marlene could pick up the threads.

"You're sleeping with Kellen."

"Couldn't very well get around it."

A whoosh crossed their connection as Marlene expelled a sharp breath. "Wow. May and Jack have no idea that—"

"None. So don't even go there, Marlene. We have no choice but to hold up and make the best of it." The intensity behind those words caused Juliet to realize how edgy she remained.

"I know, sweetie, I know. Still—that's got to be so hard on you."

Marlene's gently spoken response helped Juliet calm down. "It's harder—much harder—on Kellen." Verbalizing that fact broke the dam in her heart, the one that held back all the words she most longed to say.

Birds swooped through the air, landing artfully upon tree branches laden by verdant leaves. A soft breeze, sweetened by the aroma of mixed florals, skimmed her cheeks.

"Marlene…it's becoming so hard to stay clear of him, and what we feel for each other. I can't keep being angry. It's taking up too much energy."

"Because you're fighting it."

"Why does that come off sounding like a criticism?"

"It's not. It's simply the relay of perception—from someone who's known you for just this side of thirty-some years."

"He's trying to win me back, and…and…" Tears helped blur and dim the stark brightness of the sky. "It feels so much like it used to…"

"For instance?"

"For instance, it felt so good to wake up next to him. We ended up spooned together like always, and it was beautiful."

The muffled ding of the microwave pulled Juliet back to Marlene, away from the flow of phantom sensations she carried of his body strong and sure, aligned against hers.

"Are you seeing it through? Have you let him make love to you?"

"Marlene!" Juliet hissed the admonishment and blushed furiously. She clutched the phone to her ear, looking left and right. No one was anywhere near, of course...but still...

"Well, did you?"

"What difference does that make?" Besieged by desperation, Juliet attempted to calm her racing heart.

"All the difference. If you did—if you're coming close—that means you're letting him back into the places you cordoned off after Chloe."

"*Chloe.* Thanks, Marlene. Thanks a lot. And the answer to your question is no." Bitterness conducted its debilitating and now familiar release through her system.

"Came close though, huh? The ropes and security tape are bound to come down. He's been working to reclaim your heart, and it's working. I can tell by the tone of your voice. You're worked up."

Oh my goodness. Was she *really* having this conversation? And why did Marlene's frank and unapologetic analysis cause her whole body to tingle and awaken? This was dangerous territory.

"But we didn't. I...I..." She couldn't admit how deeply their morning interlude had stirred her—not just physically, but emotionally. Why? Fear. Plain and simple. She could admit as much to herself, but not Marlene. Not yet.

"You *what*, Juliet? Are you running out of room to run? Excuses to push him away?"

Every word Marlene spoke stoked the fire of the love Juliet was rediscovering for her husband—a precious love she ached to reclaim—on every level.

"Loving him that deeply would leave me wide open to

being devastated again, and you know it."

"Honey, I *do* know it. There's just one problem." Juliet puffed out a sigh, and waited. "You're already there—whether he makes love to you or not. That's got to be leaving you aching—on so many levels." This time it was Marlene's sigh that crossed their connection. "Trust. It's going to be the last hurdle you face and the toughest one to clear—but oh, when you do…"

There was a deliberately savoring, tempting promise to the way Marlene polished off that sentence. Juliet sank against the chair, releasing an involuntary, strangled sound. The ache Marlene described assailed her with tender, knowing fingers, making her yearn to be his again, fully—and forever.

Once a cheater, always a cheater.

The words crept in, poking against the love she felt, turning into hot, sharp pinpricks against a surface no stronger than the rubber skin of an inflated balloon.

Do not be afraid, Juliet. I am with you. I am your God. I will strengthen you. I will be with you. Always.

Unexpected and immediate, God's loving voice moved through her. Her disquiet stilled. She breathed in deep and let herself accept the fact that she was falling in love with Kellen—all over again.

Juliet straightened, lifting carefully to wander through the yard—anything to expend this buildup of energy. "You know, for five measly minutes—ten tops—I want Jesus to make *me* the big sister so that just once I can turn the tables on you like this. It's really not asking for much."

Marlene laughed warmly and the intensity of their discussion diminished. "I *am* kind of awesome like that, aren't I?" She laughed again. In the silence that followed, Juliet heard her sister sip and swallow. "Don't worry. In a few months, you'll be nurturing and caring for a little one all your own. Motherhood—talk about the penultimate opportunity for table turning."

Juliet snickered. "You're mean."

"Nah. Realistic. Speaking of which, how's my little niece

or nephew doing? Bouncing around happily, I hope. Are you feeling OK?"

"He or she is quite active today. I'm doing well, so don't worry." The topic shift felt good, and leagues safer. Juliet skimmed a hand softly across her baby bump, contentment on the rise.

"Check in again when you can. I'm praying for you, Jules."

"Keep it up, OK? We need the covering."

❧

The days that followed passed in an ordinary way that somehow assured Juliet of constancy and life as normal. Kellen and Jack continued to putter at home improvement projects. Juliet helped with laundry and went on shopping expeditions with May to indulge her mother-in-law's passion for all things related to scrapbooking.

In the evenings, Jack and May went to bed early. Exhausted from traveling and emotional chaos, Juliet gladly followed their lead, generally with Kellen close behind.

A few days after their arrival, as Kellen stretched out beneath the blankets, Juliet prepared to join him. He sat with his back propped against a pair of fluffy white pillows and the wooden headboard and she stuttered to a stall. Unmindful of her hesitation, Kellen turned to the nightstand and picked up his Bible.

"I'm glad you packed this." He opened it, resettling comfortably.

"No problem. I wish I could have packed the one May and Jack got you when you turned thirteen. I know how special it is to you, but I also know that one is always with you at work."

Kellen stopped turning pages to focus on her. The warmth and affection in his eyes ran so deep it stole her breath. "Do you know what I'm growing to realize more and more?"

"What's that?" Juliet stretched out on top of the bed

covers, no longer in a hurry to click off the light and sleep. She leaned on an elbow and studied him, waiting.

"Married life is made up of so many ordinary, day-to-day exchanges and moments, like how well you know me, and how precious a thing relationship is. Marriage is about love, sure, but it's also about building the sequence and patterns and memories of a life by sharing times just like this. It's a privilege. Marriage to you is a privilege, Juliet."

Their gazes held. Juliet nibbled the inside of her cheek, touched but uncertain how to proceed.

Until an idea took root. "Know what would be a privilege to me?"

"What?"

"Praying."

Kellen had allowed himself to be revealed and vulnerable. It was her turn now.

"I want to pray for us, Kellen."

Without a word, without hesitation, Kellen set aside his Bible. Juliet sat up, and he slid his hands beneath hers and held her fingertips snug. He bowed his head, waiting. Juliet studied him for a moment, captured afresh by the timeless act of preparing to pray with him.

They had done so countless hundreds of times during the span of their relationship. Returning to prayer now filled empty chambers in Juliet's heart.

"Lord, please watch over us. Please be with Kellen and me. We ask for Your continued guidance and provision. Be with our baby. We know that You're always alive and at work in our lives. Help us remain focused on You, on each other, and on all the blessings You give. In Your precious name, we pray. Amen."

"Amen," he whispered.

Juliet turned and reached out to extinguish the light. Kellen stopped her short when he settled a hand against her arm. "Wait a second." When Juliet turned in question, he gestured toward the nightstand. "Will you hand me that?"

She followed his motion and realized Kellen wanted a

tube of cocoa butter lotion that stood by the lamp. Puzzled, she handed it to him then stretched out again.

Kellen remained seated. He began to slowly roll up her t-shirt, exposing the mound of her expanding belly. Juliet quivered, realizing his intent. This would have been so natural a thing for him to do—once upon a time. He carefully tucked down the waistband of her sweatpants and Juliet froze. His touch ticked against her nerve endings. A stirring vibration left her feeling exposed, and wistful, despite the fact that she remained modestly covered...except for the area of her belly where their baby grew.

Kellen paused, seeming to sense her tension. He looked directly into her eyes. "Juliet. Relax."

He loosened the cap on the lotion, squeezing a dollop of white cream onto his palms. Before touching her, he rubbed his hands together, warming the liquid. Juliet couldn't relax, no matter how hard she tried.

The instant his hands slid across her skin, her muscles tightened further. Shivers transformed into an all-out tremble that mixed fear, longing, and love into a saturating flood of dizziness. He focused on the circles he made, and Juliet stared at him, the tightness gradually dissolving as she sank against the pillows at her back and hot tears pricked at the corners of her eyes.

Kellen continued his tender ministrations. He didn't look into her eyes, or cause discomfort by over asserting himself. He simply worked the lotion. "I've wanted to do stuff like this for you for the longest time now." His fingers continued to move slow and gentle. The baby began to flutter within Juliet, giving an occasional kick as well. "I've missed out on so much." Kellen sighed heavily.

Juliet kept watching him.

"I've missed out on being able to simply touch you, just like this, or let our baby know I'm there in my touch, and in my voice."

There was nothing Juliet could say. She couldn't apologize for being brokenhearted. She wouldn't apologize for being devastated by the decisions Kellen had made. But she also couldn't deny him the chance to indulge a need he had apparently restrained for far too long.

Visibly enthralled by the process of touching her, and being close to their baby, Kellen continued. "I always imagined myself being the guy who'd do just this—slather cocoa butter all over your tummy to keep it soft and comfortable, or whisper silly words near your bellybutton, as if it were a microphone leading straight to our baby's heart."

He still didn't meet her eyes, but his voice went rich with longing—and regret. He bent his head, momentous love releasing in a series of tiny kisses he dotted across her abdomen. Then he whispered against her skin. "Night-night, little one."

Kellen rested his head against her, and Juliet worked her fingers slow and easy through the thick waves of his hair. She closed her eyes, and for a few precious moments, she let herself fall into her hearts dearest wish—she let herself believe this was how it could be between them...forever.

Kellen gave her belly one last kiss and turned away, sliding into place at the farthest edge of the bed. Empty inside, Juliet reassembled her shirt and waistband. She clicked off the light, leaving the room doused by a darkness that was interrupted only by the milky white moonlight that poured through the sheer draperies of the windows.

Kellen kept so much space between them that, as she drifted to sleep, Juliet figured there might as well have been a literal blockade between them.

So much love trying to burst its way through so much pain.

28

After breakfast Friday morning, Juliet came upon Kellen standing near the window in their bedroom. He propped back the sheers with an elbow and leaned a hip against the windowsill, staring out across the yards and homes of his parents' neighborhood. He was dressed for work in a suit and tie.

"You ready to leave?" she asked.

Kellen angled his head and looked at her. "I won't be gone long. I have a staff meeting, then two client meetings, so I'll be home right after lunch." Juliet nodded. He offered a smile. "Thank you for understanding. I've been distracted at work these days, so attending to a few matters at headquarters will help me re-find my footing."

Outwardly composed, a deeper exploration revealed his exhaustion. Juliet forced herself to keep inching forward. She padded quietly to the spot where he stood. She fell headlong into the clear, gentle depths of his eyes. "Are you OK?"

He shrugged.

She tucked her hand into his and held on tight. "I can tell you're drained."

"Keeping up appearances is tough." For a moment, he surveyed the space they were presently forced to share...like any happily married couple. "I wish this were real."

Before she could respond to that, Kellen blinked free of melancholy and his lips curved once more. "How about dinner tonight—just the two of us?"

Tomorrow was the anniversary dinner with May and Jack that would conclude their trip, so the idea of enjoying a meal with Kellen alone held an undeniable appeal. The emotion she saw in his eyes was translucent; his posture made it easy for Juliet to accept. "That sounds nice."

A need to forgive kept biting at her peace of mind, but she couldn't quite follow through. That didn't change the urge, though, or dim its power. She was coming close—in spite of her reservations—but nagging issues of trust remained in place like a blockade around her heart.

"What are you in the mood for?" he asked.

Unabated longing traveled the length of her body and opened the deepest, most vulnerable parts of her heart. She stepped around him until she stood between Kellen and the window. She wanted to take a battering ram to her fears, so she wrapped her arms around his waist and looked up. "Let's grab some Pad Thai."

Kellen stared into her eyes. He shook his head. "You know just how to get under my skin."

"No—I simply realize you've always been a sucker for great Thai food."

"No—meaning you captivate me, no matter what the situation, or topic." The statement set her back on her heels. Kellen didn't linger over the words. He didn't allow any kind of awkwardness to build between them. He stroked her chin with a fingertip and stepped away, offering her his hand. "I've got to get going."

❧

"Honestly, Kellen, you need therapy!"

Juliet's teasing admonishment stirred his laughter. The sound was beautiful music, she thought. Absolutely beautiful. The restaurant where they ended up wasn't far from Jack and May's house. They opted for fondue rather than Thai, which was something new and different for them both.

"About pens? Seriously?" He settled their bill with bold strokes then resumed the conclusion of their meal.

Juliet had thoroughly enjoyed the evening. The atmosphere between them transformed into something very date-like and courtly—a tantalizing echo of their best times as a couple.

"Yes, pens. Don't even try to deny it. I've known it since we met, when you paid for our check at the Wild Horse Saloon like you did just now, with a Mont Blanc fountain pen."

Throughout the evening, Juliet relaxed. Consequently, the baby danced, thumping and pushing pleasantly against her tummy. Kellen's tenderhearted ministrations left her no other option. Knot by knot, the strings that held down her heart continued to come loose and slip free. For now, any negative thoughts glanced against her mind and were quickly refuted.

Kellen's laughter bubbled over once again; he went sheepish. "Am I that bad?"

"Facts are facts." Delighted to have the upper hand, Juliet persisted. "Ever since I've known you, you've loved fountain pens." She affected a haughty air. "Ballpoint pens are unacceptable." She huffed an exaggerated sigh. "That's a direct quote from you. Ergo, you are a pen snob."

Once again, their laughter mixed. The meal wasn't quite finished, and the fondue was delicious. They had already made plans to find a similar place in Tennessee upon their return.

An enticing call toward the future.

"Man is this great." Kellen speared, dipped, and devoured a morsel of crisped garlic bread. "Have you tried the fruit yet? It's amazing." He used his fingers to lift and dip a curved pear slice into the steaming surface of the fondue, but he didn't eat it. Instead, he held it out to Juliet. And he smiled.

The smile held her in a tender embrace and she came upon the man she had always been crazy about. Intimate warmth drew her toward him. Her lips trembled as she opened her mouth to accept the offering.

He watched her bite into the fruit. His touch lingered against the corner of her mouth. A sweet, gritty texture burst against her tongue, tempered by the cream and salt of the cheese. He moved just a bit closer, surrounding her with nothing more than the power of his presence.

Juliet found it difficult to catch her breath. The love, the need she felt, crested with that much power. She loved this man, with everything in her heart, and everything she possessed. He used the pad of his thumb to wipe away a drizzle of cheese from her bottom lip.

Just like that, the moment shattered.

The gesture sent her tumbling straight back to the nightmare of watching Kellen and Chloe at that awful record party. She fell into the darkness all over again, with just as much intensity now as the moment it had happened.

A tiny drip of chocolate dotted a spot just beneath Kellen's mouth. Chloe stroked a fingertip against his chin, right beneath his lower lip. Fevered rage and sorrow took over. Juliet watched, helpless, while Chloe laid claim to the most precious piece of her heart—the piece of her very soul Juliet believed impenetrable.

"Juliet." Kellen offered the quiet summons. Then, she felt a touch against her cheek that was warm, and infinitely tender. "Juliet?"

As she returned to the present, she realized she was taking short, shallow breaths. She had clenched her hands into tightly held fists that rested on top of the table.

"Where were you just now?" A quiet urging layered the words. He slipped his hands beneath hers and gently worked them open. "Where did you go?"

She looked into his eyes. For a few heady and much-needed moments, she drifted into them and didn't think twice about the risk. After all, up to now, wasn't tonight just like the old days, before her life was divided into two very distinct eras—the era that came before Chloe and the era that came after?

Kellen was trying so hard—and not even so much trying as *acting* on the refreshed and more clearly defined pathways of his heart. The last thing she wanted to do at the moment was shame him.

"I—" After just one word, she gave up, and she shrugged.

"What happened?" Kellen wasn't the least dissuaded. He

sat next to her in the secluded, padded booth and moved close until there was no space between them. He glided his hand against her neck and traced a slow, soothing circle against its back. "Please talk to me."

What continually astounded Juliet was the fact that he knew her to the deepest reaches. Furthermore, like the Kellen of old, he seemed unafraid of tackling emotions.

But so much had gone wrong. Sadness rushed at her, diminishing the joy of the evening, but not its possibility to recapture something precious.

Wasn't that the point of staying together? Of trying?

"What you did just now—the way you touched me—it made me think about the record party." Juliet fought to keep from squirming. "I'm sorry. I don't want to bring up bad memories and ruin what we've had together tonight."

"Trust how strongly I feel for you. Whatever is bothering you, I can take it. Open up to me. Talk to me. What hurts the most is the idea of you being remote or afraid to share yourself with me anymore."

OK, she thought, *fair enough. Let's try to turn yet another corner—if we can.*

"I love the way you're so much a part of me again. As wonderful as that is, it's scary. I'm afraid. I'm afraid of being hurt again. Betrayed. I could get the rug pulled out from under me all over again."

Kellen ingested that comment. His gaze searched hers. "Juliet, find a way to let go, and forgive me. I promise…if you do, you'll only have to do it once. What happened is a mistake I will never repeat. All you have is my word on that, and I know you can't take me at my word right now, but someday, somehow, I think you'll find a way to move back into trust. Until then, I'm not going anywhere. I'm fighting for us 'til the end."

Beautiful memories, the composition of a shared life—a loving marriage—flowed into being and would not be denied.

Kellen set aside his napkin. "I have an idea." He stood and held out his hand, waiting to help her from her seat and guide her from the restaurant. "I want to take you somewhere."

The tab was settled, the meal was done, but Juliet had no idea what to expect. Confused but willing, she followed his lead.

�≫✦

Rush hour traffic had long since thinned. A mile or two rolled by in silence as they drove from the restaurant, and Juliet couldn't stand the suspense any longer. "Where are we going?"

"I'm kidnapping you." Kellen shot her a playful grin that slipped through her in heat sparks.

"Ha-ha. Seriously." Though the light was sporadic, Juliet took in his tilted brow and the teasing glimmer of his eyes. She focused on his features a tad longer than necessary.

"I'll fill in details once we get a little closer. How would that be?"

Juliet wasn't satisfied. She manipulated and prodded, savoring their interplay. While he drove, she continued to pout and push and press—not because she needed to know where he was taking her, but because it was such fun playing with him.

Their drive skirted the ocean, taking them north along the Pacific Coast Highway. Juliet brushed a fingertip against the window control button and lowered the glass until a cool, tangy stream of air flowed against her face. From the corner of her eye, she picked up on the way Kellen frequently glanced her way. Each instance felt like a caress.

"Remember our first trip to LA together?" Kellen spoke. With one hand, he guided the wheel, the other rested atop hers on the console between them.

"After we got engaged."

Kellen nodded. "And where did you want to be more than any place else?"

"Your arms." The reply didn't stem from flirtation, or a

testing of what had once been their typical, sensual, husband-and-wife banter. Her answer was blunt truth. Kellen looked away from the road just long enough to acknowledge her reply. His expression revealed his pleasure.

"Point taken and thank you."

Heat crept up her neck and cheeks.

"OK then, what was the first runner up?"

It only took a moment for realization to evolve, for joy to wash through her. "Really?"

"Yes, really."

Juliet let out a soft exclamation, covering her open mouth with her hand. She uncovered her mouth just as quickly. "You're taking me to Santa Monica Pier?"

Making good on his vow, Kellen had said nothing until the last minute. His answer came not in words, but in navigation. He pulled into a public lot not far from the expansive pier with its shimmering, colorful medley of roller coaster and Ferris wheel lights. A giant, wooden walkway stretched far into the ink black waters of the Pacific, entrée granted by an arched sign that was a national landmark.

Juliet gazed out the window. Bittersweet tears stung her eyes. Kellen didn't say much. He only asked her to wait while he crossed behind their vehicle and opened her door, escorting her from the car.

Although he kept her close, Juliet grappled for a sense of balance that had nothing to do with physicality.

Hand-in-hand they walked toward the beach and the call of pounding surf. Sea salt added zest to an intermittent breeze that skated against her arms, neck, and cheeks. Juliet kicked off her shoes so she could sink her bare toes into cool, velvety sand. Kellen took custody of her sandals.

Her gaze sidled to him. Love formed a cascade that drew her closer and closer to the man who stood attentively at her side. Stars and a blanket of blackest sky were interrupted only by the luminous face of a half-moon, a moon that painted silver sparkles against the ever-rolling waves of the ocean.

"Kellen, this is perfect." The steady rumble of cresting

water nearly covered her words.

"You came to California for the first time and what appealed to you most was the idea of seeing this spot and dancing with the waves."

"And you let me."

He released her hand and his chest rose and fell on a deep breath. "Only because after that, you danced with *me*. Remember?"

Of course she did. Too overcome to reply, Juliet looked into his eyes. They sparkled, illuminated by nothing but the moonlight. Shadows and flashes of light painted his face.

The beach stretched before them, gleaming as water ebbed and flowed. People wandered by every once in a while, wrapped up in their own worlds. Not far away, a group of kids gathered around a boom box and an active fire pit. A radio station played at soft, appealing levels. The song *This Dance*, by Five for Fighting had just begun with a haunting piano riff and lyrics that instantly stoked the embers in Juliet's heart.

"What an appropriate song." Kellen's observation moved to a silence that slid past on a sea-scented breeze. "Will you dance with me?" Juliet panicked. Kellen's posture remained resolute. "The song can't be much longer than three minutes. Give me that, please?"

He set her shoes aside and held out his hand, waiting. The silken cadence of his voice rendered any other choice impossible. She stepped into the circle of his arms as naturally as the waves that rolled inland—timeless and unstoppable.

"Look in my eyes," he requested gently.

His warmth seeped through the cold encasement that surrounded her heart. She began to relax against him. In response, she forced herself to go tense. Fear provided a barrier that was plenty effective against his tender call.

"What do you see, Juliet?" He swayed with her, spinning her across soft, even sand in motions that were smooth and graceful. She went tighter still. "It's three minutes. Just three minutes. What do you see?"

"I see you…" Navigating uncharted land, she struggled to get the words out. "I see…I see the man I fell in love with."

"Nothing about the love you see in my eyes has changed, or ever will. Keep fighting it—for as long as you feel you need to." He traced her cheek lightly as they continued to move in time to the music.

Yet another layer of her defense system crumbled, and her knees turned to liquid. She opened like a flower after the rain.

"Like I said at the restaurant, I'll keep fighting for you until we can find a way back, as long as I know the answer to just one question."

"Which is?"

"Is it still anger that has you holding back from me right now, or is it a fear of letting everything else go?"

His presence echoed in the air around them, curving around her, drawing her home. "It's both."

Kellen waited on more, guiding her along.

"The anger is colliding with the love I feel for you. The love I guess I'll always feel for you. The anger doesn't seem to be winning as many battles these days."

"But still, you're afraid I'll betray you again."

Tears sprang to her eyes. Very slowly she nodded. "Trust is delicate."

"Yes, it is."

She swallowed back a lump of emotion. "Still…I should have been there, that night, at Iridescence. I never meant to let you down. It's my responsibility to take care of our marriage as much as it is yours. I messed up, too. If I had been with you, you might have looked at Chloe, considered how successful she could become, and that would have been the end of it."

"That's true. When you and I are engaged with one another, no one comes close to you." He brought them to a standstill. "But, Juliet, you can't be with me all the time, and I know right from wrong. I never should have let her in. You're the most precious part of my life." He settled a hand briefly against her mounded stomach. "You and our baby, that is."

Waves pounded, water sparkled, drawing her gaze for a

time as he resumed their dance. She rested her cheek against his chest. His warmth, his beating heart, the scent of him filled her. She lifted her head to look up once more. "It's your turn, Kellen. When you look at me…what do you see?"

His smile broke like a sunrise. "I see a miracle—one I don't deserve, but one that was gifted to me by none other than God Himself. That's what I've always seen. "

"Kellen—" She went dizzy and she trembled.

He drew her in tight and nuzzled her cheek, leaving her to sigh with a pleasure she couldn't contain. "Shh…it's just another minute or so…"

His lips skimmed against her throat. Juliet dissolved; she tipped her head back to encourage the caress. She quivered with anticipation. Kellen stopped their dance. He stood steady as he glided a hand against her neck. "Just for now, let go. I won't cross boundary lines. I won't hurt you."

After that, he didn't hesitate. He held her fast and dipped his head to claim her lips. Juliet cried out softly, knocked completely away from reality, away from everything but Kellen. Gradually he deepened the kiss, sighing into her mouth. His breath filled her spirit and she weakened to the point where Kellen alone held her up.

Juliet felt as though she were floating, suspended in a world so beautiful it rendered her under its spell. She melted into him, never wanting to leave this moment behind. The connection between them felt too wonderful to banish into a world of what used to be. She wanted this—and him—forever and always.

Dazzled and out of breath, she hung back from him. The pattern of love she discovered in his eyes rocketed her even further off balance. The music faded but intimacy evolved.

"Kellen, I know I need to forgive you. I *know* that. Seventy times seven and everything else…" Her voice wavered. "I'm trying, but I'm *so* afraid…"

"I know you are. What I want you to know is this: I am, too. And I know what I'm about to say may seem trite after what I've done, but you're what I treasure. I won't betray that truth ever again. Doing so has come close to ruining me."

How could she answer that? Kellen had asked for her forgiveness long ago—from the start, really—leaving the control and decision up to her. More and more she felt compelled to surrender, and allow him all the way back in. Resistance continued to thin away as Juliet moved toward a hard-won but very real sense of forgiveness—a forgiveness they both needed to deliver and accept in order to move forward.

Eventually she had to find a way past the fears Kellen acknowledged and say the words aloud.

29

October twentieth. For Juliet, it wasn't just the date of their wedding anniversary, it was a day of reckoning.

Kellen's parents had asked to meet them at Skyline, and gifted them with limousine service to and from the restaurant. Reservations were just under an hour away.

She slid her feet into a pair of silk nylons and smoothed them up her legs, pulling the waistband into place over her stomach. At a little over six months along, she felt increasingly large and wished she had purchased the thigh-high variety of stocking. Kellen entered the room unexpectedly, startling her. Clad only in a satin slip, she jumped up from the bench and turned away quickly. Moving to the jewelry pouch she had settled on the dresser, she diverted herself with the task of choosing a few pieces to wear.

"I'm sorry. I thought you were finished. I just need to shave."

Nodding, she slipped out a double strand of pearls. She still needed to finish with her hair and makeup, which meant she would have to join him in the bathroom. There, at the sink, Juliet struggled with the clasp of her necklace.

"I can get that for you." Kellen stepped from behind. His fingers moved warmly against the back of her neck.

He slipped the ends from fingertips that had gone suddenly shaky. Juliet stiffened, and then promptly wondered why. This was innocent. Chivalrous. Kellen fastened the gold clasp, concluding the moment with a slow, deliberate caress of the back of her neck. OK...maybe *not* so innocent...but definitely thoughtful.

He rested his hand lightly against her shoulder. Their

gazes tagged in the mirror, but Kellen's features revealed nothing.

"Thank you." She diverted her gaze and exhaled softly, opening a drawer to extract a few cosmetics she had stored there. While she whisked on mascara and brushed a light layer of rose color onto her cheeks, Kellen shaved in smooth strokes that drew her attention away from her makeup application. The shared routine struck her as being so familiar—so *right*.

Finally, he stepped away from the sink and slid past, full of a just-showered scent that pulled at her insides. Before leaving, he paused. He lifted the glass atomizer she had just set down—Lily of the Valley. He uncapped the top and sniffed. The evocative gesture tweaked her senses.

"You've always known just how to wear perfume. You keep it subtle and intriguing—not overpowering. I've always loved your scent."

She blinked. Pleasured warmth slipped through her. He reached for a hand towel hung on a rack next to the sink and slid it from the hanger. Shaken, Juliet polished her hair with a comb. She stood before him in silence and noticed the way his gaze tracked to the spaghetti straps of her slip, which rode against her shoulders. She could almost feel his touch against her bare skin, the smooth stroke of his lips along her neck...

Kellen swiped the towel against his damp cheeks, then beneath his chin. After re-hanging it, he left.

Nerve endings on simmer, Juliet finished primping then returned to the bedroom. She stood at the open entryway of the closet wrestling with love and fear. She slid hangers in fast succession until she came upon her choice for the evening—a black wool dress with a rippling hemline that would float around her legs and ankles. Despite being maternity wear, a discreet 'V' in back gave the dress a feminine flare that Juliet loved. A pair of low-heeled black suede pumps finished off the ensemble.

Before rejoining Kellen, she gathered herself for a moment of prayer. Centering herself in still silence, she gave God the control for tonight's anniversary dinner. She'd need His grace and guidance in order to see it through.

❧❧

Juliet stood next to Kellen in the elevator. He pushed the button for the fifteenth floor and a rapid ascent took them to the Skyline Club, where Juliet's parents were members. The familiar scent of his sandalwood cologne surrounded her in an appealing cocoon, but Kellen maintained a respectful distance. Juliet admired anew his willingness to keep from crowding and pushing.

The doors whooshed open to reveal the glass-walled restaurant and an explosion of cheers and music shook the air. "Happy anniversary!" A unison shout rose up.

Juliet gasped and pressed a hand to her chest. *No...no, no, no...*

She snapped her head to the left, taking in Kellen's reaction. His mouth opened. His eyes went wide with shock. He moved close and drew her in protectively as they stepped forward into an unexpected sea of at least fifty family members and friends. Juliet's parents broke from the crowd to step forward first, laughing and clapping.

"Congratulations!" Ellen Jenkins enfolded Juliet in a hug. Kellen came next.

"Are you surprised?" Adjusting the knot of his blue silk tie, Juliet's father, Max, tugged his suit coat into alignment and offered Kellen a handshake. Juliet absorbed Kellen's shell-shocked expression and imagined it matched her own.

"Very much so, Max. This is...wow...this is amazing," Kellen told her father.

"We could have waited for you to hit the ten-year mark. That would have been more traditional, but why do the ordinary?" Ellen linked arms with Juliet and her mother led the way forward. People began to crowd and call out, offering quick, congratulatory greetings. Marlene and Bonnie were in attendance with their families—Juliet forced in a number of deep breaths, trying to somehow regulate her heart rate. She waved occasionally. She smiled as expected. On the inside, she went numb.

"May pulled this off without a hitch!" Juliet's mother spun and an organza skirt of pale blue drifted around her legs as she hugged them both once more. "Oh, I hope you enjoy the party, kids! It's all for you!"

Disoriented, Juliet relied on Kellen's guidance as they entered the enthusiastic circle of loved ones. Before Juliet could sink into anxiety, Marlene moved in and tugged her away from the crowd toward a secluded corner of the club. Kellen followed Juliet's father and Marlene's husband to the bar.

"Baby," Marlene whispered, "I am *so* sorry I couldn't prepare you for this."

"Marlene, it's OK. I understand. This whole situation is Kellen's and mine to contend with, not yours. Don't worry about it."

Marlene turned Juliet so they were eye-to-eye. "Since when is an anniversary a mess to contend with? You're both trying. I keep telling you, give a little, Jules. Don't be so afraid of loving him. Let him in."

Juliet considered the electric interlude they had shared in the bathroom just a short time ago. Edgy needs and longing hit her insides with sizzle strikes. "Kellen and I are trying. Let's leave it at that." Juliet's blood ran thick, pumping through her veins in a hot, congested flow.

"OK, I will. Just…let tonight be a blessing. Forget about the problems. For the next few hours focus on why you married him in the first place. The people in your life who love you the most have put a lot of thought into this party. Let yourself enjoy it."

Kellen stood across the room within a cluster of their friends. Joyful noise carried to her, all of it brought together by the celebration of their wedding anniversary. Kellen didn't seem to be paying too much attention to the conversation at hand. Instead, he watched her. When Juliet captured his gaze, a tickle of awareness danced along her skin. For an instant, she surrendered to his intimate regard. Memories crested in—memories of sleeping next to him, of slow dancing with him on the beach, of the kisses they had shared.

As a cocktail hour kicked into full swing, Kellen and Juliet teamed up to make the rounds. After that, lights flickered and wait staff appeared; both gestures called party guests to their assigned table spots for dinner.

Before long, the succulent flavors of filet mignon, russet potatoes, and a vegetable medley burst against Juliet's tongue.

"Remember how nervous you were the night before the wedding?"

Kellen and Juliet exchanged a smiling look in response to her mother's question. Juliet nodded. "I remember trying to sleep, but I couldn't. Instead I laid in bed, thinking about how strange it was that it would be my last night sleeping at home, in my bedroom…that the following day, I'd be married."

"I remember the night Kellen asked me for your hand."

Juliet looked at her father; wistfulness swept in.

"You were celebrating your birthday," he continued. "He flew in to surprise you and take you out to dinner. Remember that, Kellen?"

"Like it was yesterday." Kellen sliced into his filet and sidled Juliet a measured, tentative glance. His uncertainty called to her protective, tender instincts.

Juliet's dad stretched back in his chair and issued a rumbling chuckle. "As usual, Juliet, you were taking forever to get ready for your date. While you primped, Kellen asked me to sit with him in the living room for a minute so we could talk. I knew, from the ashen color of his skin, that he was nervous." Laughter rounded the table. "He told me he had spent more than enough time away, and he promised if I gave him my permission to marry you, he'd not only be your partner, but he'd take good care of you and love you for the rest of his life. Those were some pretty lofty and romantic words, but he's lived up to the promises far better than most, eh?"

Juliet fought the lump in her throat and lowered her

lashes. She tried like mad to find a way to respond to her father's innocent observations. A thundering heartbeat and lack of suitable words kept her frozen solid.

"Nobody's perfect, Max, least of all me, but I love her more now than I ever have."

Juliet exhaled, awash in gratitude for her husband's reply. "Thank you, Kellen. What a beautiful thing to say."

"It's the truth."

A depth of meaning lent texture to his words.

"You came home walking on air, young lady." Ellen sipped from her goblet of red wine. "I'd never seen you so happy."

Of course, 'The Engagement Story' had been told countless times during innumerable family get-togethers. Still, warmth touched a spark to Juliet's heart. She *had* been happy. During the span of their marriage, Kellen had lived up to his vows without hesitation.

Until...

Chloe's stunning image materialized, but Juliet braced hard against negativity. Taking Marlene's advice, she refused delivery on all thoughts but the celebration of their marriage.

New York-style cheesecake was soon delivered. Upon each linen-covered table, servers placed silver trays divided into thirds that were laden with warmed strawberries, blueberries and peaches—the mixtures were poised to be drizzled over tall, creamy wedges. Next came small, chilled bowls heaped with whipped cream. As guests created individual masterpieces and dug in, May Rossiter stood and tapped her knife gently against a water glass.

"While we enjoy dessert, Juliet's sisters unearthed a bit of history we thought you'd enjoy. Can we dim the lights, please?"

The restaurant went dark, illuminated only by the flickering glow of crystal encased votive candles wreathed by burgundy hued baby's breath and white sprigs of lily of the valley. The play of light against rose colored china and white tablecloths created a dramatic and lovely effect.

At the back of the room, a video screen lowered against the wall. Seconds later, a DVD began to play and scenes from their wedding day came to life.

Juliet eked out a soft cry. Kellen didn't turn toward her. Instead, he watched the video. Beneath the table, his hand strayed to her knee, and he offered a supportive squeeze. He kept his hand in place to perform a steady, comforting caress…but his gaze never left the screen.

The montage of their wedding began at Trinity Church, as family and friends assembled in the pews. There were brief glimpses into the bride and groom preparation areas—like Jack Rossiter clasping Kellen's hand in a solemn gesture that spoke volumes despite the hubbub of groomsmen slipping on ties and suit jackets and struggling with boutonnières. A quick cut showed Juliet's dressing room and a visual capture of the moment when her mom gently lifted a layer of the bridal veil over Juliet's head and settled it into place. Despite the deflection of light gauze that covered her face, Juliet exchanged a long, glittering-eyed look with her mother.

The processional and ceremony followed. In the end, Kellen and Juliet exited the church wearing beaming smiles. Enthusiastic cheers filled the air as their guests lined up and launched white balloons tied by burgundy and black ribbons into a flawless, cobalt sky.

Juliet watched, enrapt, but her stomach ached from clenching her muscles so tight. She settled her hands protectively against her abdomen and discovered it was as hard as a rock. Alarmed burst through her—as did the pain of a subtle contraction. The nervous shift in her posture was slight, but Kellen looked at her in concern. She shook her head quickly, returning her attention to the video. Her gesture silently willed him to do the same.

On screen came snippets from the reception. Kellen and Juliet stood on each side of Juliet's grandmother, their arms around her slim, almost frail shoulders. In honor of their chosen honeymoon destination—the Mexican Riviera—the elder Jenkins looked into the camera with a jaunty grin and waggled her fingertips as she began to croon. "Ooooh, Mexico...I never really been but I'd sure like to go...Ooooh, Mexico..."

James Taylor music had never sounded so sweet. Juliet fought against a swell of emotion. "Oh, I miss you, Nana...." Juliet whispered. Nana Jocelyn Jenkins had died of heart failure the following year.

In laughter through tears, Juliet watched the progression of the garter toss—the way she had perched upon a chair in the middle of the dance floor, her lace and satin dress a billowing cloud of white all around her. On screen, she nipped her lower lip and squiggled happily, full of bridal glow as Kellen kissed his way slowly up her ankle and calf, toward his goal of the hidden piece of satin positioned against her lower thigh. Her feet, one of which he held like a treasure, had been adorned in shiny, white patent heels...

Juliet felt every touch of his lips, every dewy skim of his breath against her skin. He had taken his time about the task but finally slipped the blue and white lace garter down her thigh, then her knee, then her calf, teasing her with his eyes and his smile once he pulled it free.

The wedding-couple dance that followed nearly did her in. They swayed together, murmuring to one another, tucked together perfectly. Even from the distance of nearly a decade, she recognized Kellen's reverence toward her, a loving protectiveness that left Juliet to ache. In so many ways, he was just the same. There was no way to deny that fact despite the pain left behind by the mistakes he had made.

The mistakes they *both* had made.

Her tears flowed free. The saving grace of that reaction was that several of their tablemates were in the same boat.

Kellen leaned close. "I'm sorry, Juliet. I had no idea this was going to happen." His whispered words helped settle her nerves, and he appeared to be equally taken aback by the magnitude of the anniversary celebration.

At the same time, his words brought her back to a troubled reality. She needed, and wanted, that reality to change. She could make change happen by opening herself once again in unconditional love, and trust—by offering him her wholehearted forgiveness, and asking for his in return.

"This is nothing to be sorry about, Kellen. It's our *anniversary*."

Emotional hills and valleys peppered this night spent traveling the streets of their marriage.

30

"So the trip to California was a success?"

A few days after the party, Kellen sat in the easy chair across from Pastor Gene's desk at Trinity Church in the midst of a counseling session.

"Yes, we're making progress, but it's still an up and down ride. I feel like we're close to being back to what we were, but I also feel like there's something missing, some ingredient to the recovery process that I've overlooked somehow."

"Recovery, even when progress is made, still requires slow steps and a lot of patience. From what you've described during our last few meetings, she's getting the message. If the seeds are replanted, all you can do is continue to nourish them."

Kellen pondered that. He crossed his legs and stared across the room. "She's definitely trying, but right now, forgiving me is beyond her ability."

"Perhaps, for now. But there's something else she might be struggling with that you haven't mentioned yet."

Kellen frowned. "What's that?"

"Have you considered the fact that Juliet might also be struggling with the issue of asking you for *your* forgiveness as well as offering hers in return?"

Kellen reared back. "What? No. That's just crazy. Why would Juliet need my forgiveness? I'm the one who—"

"Kellen, hear me out." Pastor Gene edged forward against the desk. His brows lifted a few inches. "Marriages don't succeed or fail in a vacuum. It's a partnership. It's dual caring, dual commitment and dual *accountability*."

"Don't blame her for my mistakes." Kellen bit the words.

He clenched his hands against the armrests of the chair.

But then came a memory. The sound of Juliet's voice, soft—touched by the cadence of the south, drifted through his mind and into the mix of his emotions.

I never meant to let you down. It's my responsibility to take care of our marriage as much as it is yours. I messed up, too.

Kellen's brows pulled together and his hands relaxed.

Pastor Gene stretched back in his chair and steepled his fingers. "Did something hit home?"

Kellen looked at the man, chagrined.

Pastor Gene continued, "You're struggling through some of the most delicate territory there is in a marriage—the idea of free will in a committed relationship. You've both come to realize that love doesn't just depend on you, or on her. It depends on *both* of you and the choices you make as a couple to stay together—and in love—despite everything life throws your way. Love is a very deliberate choice, no matter what mistakes either one of you may make."

Kellen stood in a brisk motion and paced. He came to a stop in front of a painting that depicted a calming, earthy woodland scene. Ideas rolled through his mind. There were so many things in his life that didn't fit properly at the moment. He had nearly destroyed the most precious relationship in his life. Despite material success and the kind of professional accolades most men might envy, these days his job struck him as empty—void of divinity. Worst of all, he had stepped away from his personal relationship with God, and look where it had gotten him.

He wanted to make changes.

Like a form of acid, the deterioration of his values had eaten away at everything he knew to be most important.

Well, the truth was coming back to him now. He wanted to reassert himself as a tool meant for God's use. He belonged to God, wounds and all. God loved him fiercely, wounds and all. The very idea stirred a holy fire in his spirit.

"Take a long, hard look at your life—and hers." Pastor Gene's voice cut into the silence Kellen had allowed to build.

"Meaning?"

"Meaning figure out what led you to this point to begin with."

Kellen expelled a hard sigh and walked back to the chair in front of the desk. He slumped into it. "That much is obvious."

Pastor Gene shook his head. "Once again, let me advise you to move past Chloe. That's not my point. You've beaten yourself up enough about the mistake you made, and you're regretful. You moved past that error in judgment. Furthermore, you're *forgiven*. Accept that grace. Then, with revised perception, look at what changes need to be made to your life. What can you make better? More fulfilling? What drew you and Juliet apart?"

Kellen had touched upon the root causes already, but what were the remedies? With Juliet, he shared a strong faith that enriched every aspect of their lives. From there, they both loved service. Giving their time and support to activities they felt strongly about further strengthened their bond to one another, and the God they served.

But into that idyll had crept circumstances they couldn't seem to control.

To correct that, he could...

Kellen straightened abruptly.

"Kellen?"

He ignored Pastor Gene's call and stood, awash in an instantaneous and potent rush of adrenaline. He held up a hand and started to pace again. "Hold on a second..."

Pastor Gene kept his questions to himself, but Kellen felt the man tracking him as he stalked across the room.

Could it possibly be this easy? Had the answer come to him this quickly—with such certainty?

Return to me.

God spoke and anticipation prickled; an epiphany ignited.

"Kellen, are you all right?" Pastor Gene sounded alarmed.

"I'm OK—just stunned. I think God's leading me toward some of the answers I need."

"Oh?"

He paused at the window of Pastor Gene's office and looked outside, at a nearby park full of people taking advantage of a sparkling autumn day. Kids flew through the air on swings, propelled by pushes and gravity. Others glided down slides or ran the perimeter of the playground. Parents watched from their seats on nearby benches.

Kellen turned back to the church leader and counselor, propping his shoulder against the windowsill. "You're absolutely right. Identifying mistakes has been easy, but I've spent so much time trying to work past the things I've done wrong that I never really looked for solutions. You've helped me focus on that fact. You and God…"

His words trailed off. A smile split his features. Crystal clear, Kellen saw a pathway to his deepest wants and needs—and he couldn't wait to begin the journey.

∂∞

Kellen stopped at the desk of his assistant. "Anna, I need you to print off a copy of my client rundown, with full contact information, as soon as you can, please."

"Not a problem."

If she found anything unusual in the request, she didn't show it. Kellen went to his office and closed the door—not typical for him—but nothing odd enough to stir excess curiosity.

The timing here had to be perfect. He needed to carefully line up his plans and participants before following through on the plan that had bloomed.

Not much time passed before a soft knock sounded at the door.

"Come on in, Anna." Tentative steps led her toward his desk.

"Here you go." She handed over a stack of paper a couple of inches thick.

"Thanks."

She nodded and turned to leave. "Do you want the door open or closed?"

"Closed, please."

Her brows knit, but she did as he asked. Kellen tuned out everything but the call sheets.

Over the next hour, he twiddled a pen and edited the list of names, circling some, crossing out others. The deletions came a lot easier than he thought they would. Surprisingly, each name he cut lessened the weight on his shoulders—and his soul. By the time late afternoon hit, he was unbound, floating on relief...and expectation.

This exercise was long overdue. He had carried enormous burdens and allowed them to pile up—brick by brick—without even realizing it until the weight overwhelmed everything else.

The papers now spread across his desk had crowded out his love for Juliet, his family and friends—even his devotion to God. The freedom he found in claiming grace from the ashes of that mistake was a sensation more beautiful than anything he could have possibly imagined. The life changes to follow were nothing more than detail work he entrusted completely to God.

At last he set aside the pen and breathed deep. He closed his eyes and relaxed into stillness. The next part of his newly found pathway would be a bit harder to traverse, but equally liberating. He needed to tell Juliet, then Weiss McDonald, that he intended to resign from Associated Talent.

31

Juliet huffed in relief when she deposited a load of grocery bags onto the kitchen counter. She glanced at the phone and message machine on the counter and noticed a red message light flashing. She depressed the play button.

"Kellen, it's Weiss. I've been trying your cell for the past couple hours with no luck, so I thought I'd try you at home. I know you had to get to an appointment, but I'm not letting this go. Call me back. We can work something out. Let's dive into this thing and think it through before you make any final decisions. We need to make time to discuss the bombshell you delivered."

The sound of a phone being hung up ended the message. Juliet cocked her head, resting a hip against the counter. Kellen was avoiding Weiss's calls? Kellen had dropped a bombshell?

Brows furrowed, she stared ahead at packages of food needing to be stored. Prickles danced against her arms and down her neck when she went about stashing away the week's foodstuffs.

Kellen burst through the garage entrance an hour later. Juliet was seated on a tall stool at the kitchen island paging through a clothing catalogue she'd pulled from the day's mail delivery.

"Juliet?" His energy instantly filled the kitchen. He tossed aside his computer bag, so lit by excitement she was momentarily taken away from misty imaginings of a wardrobe that didn't feature pants with expansion panels and billowing maternity blouses.

"Hey...you're home early." She prepared to stand, but

Kellen had already trotted to her side, capturing her in a hug.

"Stay put. Actually, I'm glad you're sitting down."

Baffled, Juliet gestured in the direction of the fry pan on the stove where their dinner entrée of breaded pork chops had been set to sear. "I need to turn the meat…and—"

"I've got it."

Kellen retrieved the tongs she had set on the stovetop and fussed over the food for a moment. The aroma of onions, garlic and sizzling pork intensified, drifted through the air on curls of steam.

He claimed the stool next to hers and stilled himself—as though in prayer. Seconds later, he tilted his head and gave her a long, intent look. "Are you ready for this?" Juliet nodded, perplexed. "I want to leave AT."

Juliet jerked slightly. Her stomach freefell as though she had just leaped off a cliff. "Wh…what?"

"I told Weiss my intention, but nothing's official until I have your support, because it'll be an enormous life change." He took hold of her hand. "But it'll be good, Juliet. *So* good." He paused, and she soaked in the happy flash of his eyes. "I *want* to do this. Branching off on my own is something I've always wanted to try, and there could be no better time than now. I've got the means and the skill to build the kind of agency I've always dreamed of…doing the type of work that's most meaningful to me, the kind of work that's a lot more in tune with who I am, and who I want to be."

"You'd walk away?" Despite his lofty ideals, she couldn't quite grasp the idea. "I'd never ask you to do that, Kellen. Don't give up who and what you are. Don't give up what fulfills you and brings you joy. Are you sure about this?"

"Juliet, music brings me joy. My faith brings me joy." He shook his head. "Most of all, *you* bring me joy. You and the family we're creating. In order to be true to myself, I have to refocus. The thing is, I've *never* felt better."

Enthusiasm rolled off him in a circuit of energy that Juliet could taste in the air all around them. He slid off the chrome barstool and strode across the length of the kitchen.

When he stopped, he looked her straight in the eyes. The look dug deep, pulling every ounce of love she felt straight out of her heart and into his possession. "To answer your question, the only thing I've ever been more sure of is asking you to be my wife."

His comment led Juliet to a moment peppered by nine years' worth of love and meaning.

"You," she whispered, "in charge of your own company. Heading up a roster of clients who hold to the same principals we do." She imagined her smile told him what he wanted to know even before she concluded. "I like it, Kellen. I like it a lot."

The temperature indicator beeped on the oven, cutting into a lingering silence. A batch of croissants was laid out on a metal sheet ready to be baked. Before Juliet could lift from her stool, Kellen went to the counter and slid the tin tray onto the top shelf of the oven.

After double-checking the chops, he reclaimed his stool. "I went to work for a while after my counseling session with Pastor Gene today. Before I met with Weiss, I pulled the Bible from my desk. Over the years, I've kept notes about what verses to turn to when I face difficult situations. Today I came across a verse that...well, wait...hang on. I want to get the quote just right."

Kellen dashed from the kitchen and returned seconds later with his Bible in hand. He flipped through the pages. "Listen to Ephesians, chapter two, verse eight. *By grace you have been saved, through faith; and this is not your own doing. It is the gift of God.*" His gaze speared Juliet and he arched a brow. He thumbed the pages once more. "Then came this one, from Proverbs, chapter twenty four. *By wisdom a house is built, and through understanding it is established; through knowledge its rooms are filled with rare and beautiful treasures.*" His gaze returned to Juliet's and he shook his head, his features full of the childlike wonder of rediscovering and redefining the gifts he had been given. "Those verses point straight at us, Juliet. Being wise will lead me to the treasure of your love, and our baby, but wisdom must include my role as an agent, and provider for our family as well."

He closed the book and slid it against the slab of cool, granite counter they shared. Juliet's throat stung. Never had she loved him more.

"No matter what happens in the days ahead, I won't go back to the emptiness I embraced before," he said.

"It'll be hard work, Kellen, but you're right. It'll be *so* worth it."

He made an affirmative sound. "If clients want to follow me, fine. If they don't, that's fine, too. If Weiss wants to raise a stink about me leaving, let him. I'm ready for the battle. If I have to start from scratch, with nothing but moxie and hard-won experience, I'll make that work, too, because God will meet me there. That's His promise."

Resting her hand on top of his, Juliet watched, and marveled. His excitement morphed into a contagious entity that stirred her heart. "Very true. And if you hang on to that fact, we'll be fine."

"Both of us?"

Juliet lifted his hand. She settled it against the spot where their baby grew. "All of us."

Kellen kissed both of her cheeks. Standing, turning fast, he let out a whoop of happiness. "What do you think of The Rossiter Agency? Is that a good name?"

Juliet laughed, tears streaked down her cheeks.

"I haven't been this excited in years." He slid a hand against her waist to draw her down from the stool and pull her close. "This career change is going to be like premium fuel in a better engine. It'll be smaller, but it'll be smarter, and a whole lot more meaningful. Not just for me, but for my clients, and for the legacy I want to leave to our baby." Once again, he rested a gentle hand against her womb, drawing light circles. "I want goodness back, and goodness doesn't come from more, it comes from God. It comes from following the call He places on our heart."

Kellen leaned forward and kissed her lips, claiming her

mouth with a softness that caused Juliet to sway and nearly slide to the floor. "I'm behind you, Kellen, with all that I am."

"That's where you're wrong, love. You're not *behind* me. You're *next* to me. *Always*. Please, please know that." Unmindful of her increasing reaction, Kellen trotted to the exit of the kitchen. "I'll be right back. I'm going to give Weiss a call and make it official. That'll get him off my back. Then, there are a few client meetings I want to set up right away. I need to find out who's brave enough to take this journey with me." At the threshold of the kitchen, he turned back. "I love you, Juliet."

She wavered once more, knowing she needed to remember how to breathe. When his smile spread, she gave up any semblance of pretenses and launched into his arms. Kellen spun her in a wide, dizzying circle. She thought of completeness and heavenly grace, knowing she found both elements right here in his embrace.

Like a diamond flash, he was gone. Juliet listened to him bounding up the stairs, to his office most likely. At that moment, she realized fresh tears rolled down her cheeks, fast, warm and fat.

Liquid joy.

32

Up to now, Kellen had functioned within a world full of people who thought nothing of saying just the right words, at just the right time, with no other ambition in mind than personal gain and the manipulation of good favor. He used to be able to tolerate it, figuring such was the nature of the beast he rode. If he could promote the genres he loved, he figured the struggles were worth it.

Tyler Brock, on the other hand, represented every positive element of the entertainment industry. Christian to the core, governed by his beliefs and nothing else, Tyler had been a client of Kellen's for nearly five years. Beyond a client/agent relationship, Kellen valued the man's friendship, insights and most of all his strength of heart.

The folks at In His Name Productions had stepped forward to finalize a great opportunity for Tyler, the details of which had solidified with perfect timing because Kellen had an offer of his own to make to the singer.

Tyler Brock didn't live far away—they both called Franklin home. So, the following night, Kellen made a quick call to Tyler during his evening commute. Assured that his client was available for a chat, Kellen diverted to the farmhouse where the Brock family lived.

A half hour later, they were seated side-by-side on a long, wooden porch swing, sipping sweet tea and swaying slightly as nighttime rode in on pastel skies and shadows gone long against the hills and valleys that surrounded Tyler's home. The air was cool, bordering on nippy, perfumed by the last of the heartiest summer flowers that rimmed the front walkway.

Tyler was Detroit born and bred, but a decade in the

south had refined his natural gentility and propensity to take life slow and easy. Tall, with sand colored hair and striking features, he was the full entertainment package. He was boyishly playful; his clear green eyes were compelling. Best of all, he moseyed into life. He didn't push, bully, and shove. He followed God's path in faith and trust. That faith and trust had led the musician to phenomenal crossover success that remained firmly grounded in Christian roots. Plus, he maintained an amazing love affair with his beautiful wife Amy.

Kellen enjoyed the peaceful ambiance, but he was also eager to cut to the purpose of his visit. "So, in my capacity as your agent, I have to ask. How do you feel about performing at the LA Memorial Coliseum in a few months?" Kellen cast his friend a grin then took a deep pull of his refreshing, sugar and mint spiced beverage.

Tyler's brows shot up, revealing pleasured surprise. He stretched out his legs. "Seriously?"

"Um-hum. You've been invited to perform at In His Name Productions' annual *Days of Praise*, which I'm sure I don't even need to tell you is their three-day extravaganza of contemporary Christian music."

"I went to it once. It's amazing. Amy and Pyper will flip. Zach's just a baby—he won't have a clue—but, man, what an opportunity."

Pyper was Amy's daughter from a previous marriage. Four years ago, Tyler had officially adopted Pyper, giving her his name along with the entirety of his heart. Last year, the Brocks had welcomed baby Zachary into their family.

"What would your advice be, as my agent and all?" Tyler's question drew Kellen back to their conversation.

"Don't walk—*run* to California."

They burst out laughing. From inside the brightly lit house came the sound of a sweet voice raised in tune to the strains of a melodic piano riff Kellen recognized at once as the Twila Paris classic, *How Beautiful.* Pyper was practicing her passion—music.

"My protégée," Tyler remarked with quiet pride.

Kellen listened intently while the youngster sang. "She's fantastic."

"She's ten years old and sounds like she's twenty. She's got amazing natural talent."

"And intuition." Pyper's music carried through the open front door. Pyper nailed the song, ten-years-old or not. "She's such a beautiful girl."

Tyler let out a harrumph. "You're tellin' me?" He shook his head, seeming to go within himself for a moment. "She's such an innocent, but she's already determined to enter the entertainment field. I'm not sure if I'm ready for such a thing. It's a brutal industry."

Kellen listened expectantly, realizing their conversation edged close to the territory he longed to explore.

"I mean, when did it all become so corrupt? There's such a beauty in music, especially the kind of music that becomes part of your personal soundtrack. There's beauty in well-made movies that take you to a time and place you'd never get to experience otherwise."

"That's very true."

Tyler lifted his shoulders in a big, questioning shrug. "So tell me why it's all so greed infested. Why is the entire industry so immoral, and awash in ideas that broadcast life styles and messages that rip away the fabric of everything that's good, and right? Why?"

Kellen blew out a sigh, keeping the swing in motion with a push of his foot against the floorboards of the porch. Inside, Pyper launched into a sassy version of *Paved Paradise*. "The simple answer is money. The more complicated answer is ego. It gives people a taste of almighty power when millions of people hang on their every move."

"Maybe so, but that pattern is nothing more than a dirt stain on something that could be beautiful."

"Amen." Kellen paused deliberately. "Know what bothers me about that scenario? I'm part of the problem."

Speaking the words aloud, to someone he implicitly

trusted, afforded Kellen the chance to test their weight and feel. And impact.

"What do you mean by that?"

Kellen didn't focus on Tyler's shocked tone. Instead he came clean. "I fuel that issue by always pushing for more. By scoring big deals for my clients and rejoicing in their monetary and career successes because I share in it. That leaves me culpable."

Tyler watched him for a time, his expression unreadable. "Y'know, when you first signed me on as a client, and for a couple of years after that, you were on fire for the arena of Christian music. You still are—don't get me wrong—but ..."

When the sentence dangled and Tyler leaned forward, sparing him a probing look, Kellen battled the urge to squirm. He didn't need a compass. He realized what was what. He maintained and genuinely cared for his stable of Christian artists, but various forms of jazz and soul music had taken the industry by storm. Music like Chloe's. His focus had splintered.

Juliet's beautiful features centered and focused in his mind.

"It's the thrill of the hunt with you," Tyler observed.

Kellen frowned and shot his friend a sharp look. "More like the thrill of the find. Of discovery."

Tyler grinned. "Are you forgetting? I've been on the receiving end of your pursuits. It's the hunt *and* the chase, pal."

"And the *find*," Kellen battled back. "Establishing a worthwhile artist in a worthwhile home."

Despite their intense banter, Tyler's affection shone in the warmth of his eyes and the width of his smile. "What I'm saying is, remember to keep fighting for the Christian message. Nothing else matters—and that's what led me to sign on with you in the first place."

True enough—and fair enough. Kellen stared out across the darkening expense of Tyler's yard. He scuffed his feet and ducked his head, concerned about wearing his truest heart and emotions out in the open.

"Kellen—are you OK?"

Kellen nodded.

"Oh, c'mon. Stop being the cool guy for half a minute and say what's on your mind. After all, avoidance isn't working, now is it?"

The blunt though gentle challenge snapped through Kellen's restraints. He found himself unable to maintain outward appearances, that deceiving sense of 'cool' to which Tyler referred. Instead, he wanted to be known. "I've opted to make a pretty drastic change."

"Like?"

"Like leaving Associated Talent."

Kellen slid a glance toward Tyler, who would have made a fine poker player if his smooth, unruffled appearance were any indication. Then the words didn't just come, they poured. "I can't get into minutia, so please don't ask me to. Suffice to say my life has changed, Tyler. I don't like the direction it was headed. The work I do is a large part of that issue. I've risked the foundation of my life in order to savor the hunt you talk about and chase after success. Doing so has left a horrible taste in my mouth."

"I won't badger. Just remember, nothing's beyond God's repair."

"I'm clinging to that truth with all that I am." In the ensuing cricket song and leaf chatter, Kellen remained still.

Tyler's brows puckered; his expression edged toward concern. "Tell me what you can."

"During the past several months I've come close to losing everything I value the most. Namely Juliet."

Tyler kept the swing moving. "Y'know? Amy and I? We've always enjoyed and admired you and Juliet. The two of you share something special. I knew it from the moment I saw you together at that record label networking party years ago. Remember that?"

Indeed Kellen did. A wispy fog of memories curved through his mind. Those were much happier, less complicated times. "Yeah—and the feeling has always been mutual."

"So what's the deal?"

"The deal is this: I messed up." In automatic defense, he lifted his hands. "Please don't ask for more than that right now. All I can say, from the depths of my heart, is that I'm fighting my way back—not just as an agent, but as a husband and a Christian."

"And?"

"And that's meant a big shift in emphasis. Therefore, I have an important question to ask you—agent to client and strictly on a professional basis." Tyler nodded amicably and waited. "Would you...do you...have the faith to stay with me if I start an agency of my own?" Tyler didn't react or say anything right away. "The agency would be smaller, and laser focused, driven by what I love the most—Christian music and maybe even Christian-centered movie production if God sees fit to make that calling a success."

"How does Weiss McDonald feel about this?"

"We've already hashed out a separation package. My contract with AT is specific. I'm free to recruit and retain any client I brought to AT on my own. Those assigned to me by Weiss or the team in Los Angeles are untouchable." Fierce determination skated through him. "That's fine by me, because guess what artists I brought to AT? Christian artists. The ones I want to keep."

Tyler leaned forward on his knees, studying the yard. "So you've learned the lesson I've grappled with for ages."

"Which is?"

"The idea that less is definitely more."

"Precisely." Silence reigned.

"Kellen, I hired you, not Associated Talent. I placed my career in the hands of a man I respect and trust, not a company name." Tyler extended his hand. "I'm in, and I congratulate you on making a smart choice."

Was it this easy? This refreshing? It wouldn't be like this every second, and not in every instance, but meeting with Tyler affirmed Kellen's choices. He shook Tyler's hand and nodded.

"Your backing will probably enable me to win over the majority of artists I most want to keep."

Tyler shrugged. "If I can help, great, but that doesn't hold weight in why I'm doing what I'm doing. I have faith in what God is laying out. You have faith in His actions. From where I sit, that's a win-win situation. You're a great agent. Nothing changes the talents God gave you in that regard."

"That means a lot to me, Tyler. It gives me the confidence to see this through."

"Then make it happen."

In that moment, Kellen caught glimpses of all that might come to be...

By nothing else but God's grace—and unwarranted mercy.

33

Juliet's most recent visit to the gynecologist wasn't altogether positive. She remained healthy. The baby continued to develop and grow, but protein levels in her system had increased slightly, straying well into the high territory. Her blood pressure was under control, thanks to Methyldopa, but when Doctor Roth factored in Juliet's increasing bouts of Braxton Hicks contractions, the decision was made to increase her checkups from bi-weekly to weekly as concerns remained in the battle against preeclampsia.

Safety measures aside, Juliet had never felt better. She knew the best thing to do was continue on with a healthy diet and exercise routine. She also had to believe an improved emotional outlook helped her efforts to stay strong.

For that reason, she hauled herself out of bed early a few days after Kellen's announcement and slipped on a pair of cotton shorts, a sport bra, and a loose fitting sleeveless shirt. After strapping on a pair of running shoes she trotted outside, fashioning her hair into a high ponytail to keep it out of her way.

She pressed her hands and forearms flat against the brick wall of the garage, stepping away until her body was at an angle to the structure. Suitably braced, she stretched her thighs and calves. Next she stretched gently and slowly from the waist, extending her arms above her head.

Minutes into her warm up, Kellen joined her. Dressed in similar athletic fashion, his unexpected arrival tripped her senses. In passing, he smiled into her eyes and glided her ponytail softly through his fingertips. She loved the sensation of tingles his quiet gesture stirred.

Looking up at him, she felt shy and wistful. "Hey."

"Hey." Kellen stretched by leaning against the garage as well and pulling up on his right leg by gripping his foot. "Do you mind if I join you?"

"You can *try*," she sassed. She offered a teasing glance that held no restraint or fear. No doubts.

"Oh, I see. So *that's* how it is. A *challenge*?"

Juliet arched a brow, cocking her head in a playful pose. She winked at him.

During that heady instant, she stored the image of him, locking it in her heart to pull out and savor whenever she wished. He was tall, lithe, and absurdly handsome. His olive skin was kissed by sunlight that performed a golden dance through the mahogany waves of his hair.

Without warning, Kellen tugged her into the confines of the garage. He backed her against the wall and claimed her lips, taking her on an electric kiss that moved fast and steep, lifting her up into a beautiful, perfect spiral. Body and soul she caught fire for him as the longings she had held in check, the ones she had banked over and over again, burst into life. She clung to his shoulders.

Kellen's sigh danced against her skin. She sagged against him, weak and submissive—truly welcoming. She trembled when he resumed a kiss that sealed her heart to his completely.

For the first time in months, that was OK. She fed off him and his love the way she always had, and the moment felt like coming home.

A cool breeze skated over her skin, awakening her senses even further as Kellen moved back just a bit, outlining her face with the long, lush stroke of his fingertips. One look into his heavy-lidded eyes and her mind spun. Openness and love lived in their depths.

"Juliet...thank you for continuing to try. I want you back. All the way back. I'm grateful we're coming so much closer now." He slid a fingertip slowly against her lips. His eyes tracked the motion, darkened and deep. Juliet dissolved into an all-over ache and released a quiet exclamation of pleasure. "When I say that, I'm not just referring to this." With a gesture of his head, he indicated their intimate position. "I'm talking about every aspect of our relationship. That brings me so much happiness. *You* bring me so much happiness."

"Kellen…" She could barely whisper his name. Wrapped in his arms, she tucked in tight, savoring the warmth and solid security of being held deep in his embrace. The moment brought to mind an image—that of a precious treasure being protected and guarded by a noble warrior.

He inched away. "Let's jog."

The gentle way he parted from her caused Juliet to quiver. "I couldn't run right now if I tried." Attempting to catch her breath, she remained a lax, dazed semblance of herself.

Kellen answered with an intimate look that wreaked havoc on her nerve endings. He gave her arm a tug. "Come on. I'm not letting you off the hook that easily."

Regaining her bearings, Juliet let out an exaggerated whine. "I'm pregnant you know. I need to be treated with kid gloves and stuff."

Kellen stretched his arms over his head while he moved away, trailing laughter. "You're seriously going to play the pregnancy card?"

"Yep." Juliet's heart felt so light it carried her away. She fluttered her lashes, openly flirting when she brushed past, and then took off like the wind…or as close to the wind as her heavily encumbered body would allow.

Kellen caught up easily but she could tell he kept to a deliberately temperate pace. Juliet stole glances at him every now and then as they ran. Marlene was right. Physical surrender would be the last barrier they crossed, and when they did, it was going to be a return to everything beautiful between them.

Fully renewed by his love, Juliet accepted and anticipated what was to come.

&∽&

Kellen monitored Juliet carefully. Their strides were steady and smooth, but slow enough that she could maintain a healthy workout without risk of injury or overdoing.

She kept up like a champ, and his mind drifted. If he could drink from the air around them, it would taste of freedom, goodness, and second chances. Second chances he should never have needed to claim in the first place.

But that, as Pastor Gene might say, was the past, so instead of negativity, he focused on the sacrificial forgiveness and salvation of Christ. God's own Son saw to a full and sins-forgotten reconciliation when life was embraced anew, with sincere contrition. *Therefore, if anyone is in Christ, he is a new creation; the old has gone, the new has come.*

The words from 2 Corinthians, chapter five, verse seventeen, reverberated; Kellen lifted his face to the morning sun and praised God silently as he moved slightly ahead of Juliet on a winding, narrow pathway that cut through a municipal park near their home.

Still, he tracked her peripherally, enjoying the vision of her glistening skin, the rosy tint of her cheeks and her soft puffs of breath as they continued to run.

Fellow joggers blew past, offering silent nods. Despite the deepening chill, families dressed in sweatshirts and jeans scrambled and jumped, enjoying Frisbee games, dog chases and ball tosses. One family in particular caught Kellen's eye—one he could easily associate with himself and Juliet in times to come. The mother pushed a stroller one handed. Mom and Dad, meanwhile, held hands with their second child, lifting him up and swinging him intermittently while they walked along and chatted.

He couldn't wait to hold his son or daughter.

The thought no sooner dissipated than Juliet slowed, unexpectedly and dramatically. At first, he noticed the way she wobbled a bit but didn't pay that much mind since this portion of the running path was a little uneven. Nevertheless, instinct drove Kellen to decrease his speed and aim for Juliet just as she stopped completely, heaving and bending down to grip her knees. She fell forward, but he caught her before she hit the ground. Her breathing was erratic and her body felt tight and rigid. Kellen became an anchor when she toppled against him in a stiff, dead weight.

She continued to gasp, losing the fight for air.

"Juliet?" He rubbed her back, guiding her off the path and onto a patch of grass near a tree where he could prop her up or lay her down if necessary.

Her body wouldn't bend, so he laid her out prone. It felt to Kellen as though she were in the throes of a seizure. Her eyelids fluttered crazily, and she tried to speak. "Ke...I ...can't...I..." She heaved and heaved. "...can't breathe..."

Kellen yanked his cell phone from the pocket of his shorts. He made ready to dial 9-1-1 while panic swept through him. Still, he didn't want to scare Juliet. He rubbed her arm then settled his free hand against her rounded stomach. It was unyielding and constricted. He gulped. *The baby. My wife...*

"Juliet, I want you to listen to what I'm saying. Focus on me. Focus on my voice. You'll be OK. Your blood is rushing and your lungs are tightening up. Anxiety will feed whatever is making you go tight. Close your eyes and feel your body, muscle by muscle. Focus on relaxing. Let it pass..."

Though he kept his tone soothing and calm, Kellen dialed emergency services while he tried to coach her through the crisis. An operator answered promptly and recorded his location assuring that help was nearby and on the way.

Juliet shuddered. Her eyes glazed over. Kellen's panic increased. He continued to touch her, doing whatever he could to lend comfort.

She sipped air in tiny, shallow bursts that sounded like nothing much more than horrific rasps.

"Baby—" Her eyes fluttered. She stumbled over the simple word. Her head sank onto his shoulder as she lost the battle to stay conscious, but at least she was drawing in air— bit-by-bit. Kellen became frantic, not knowing what to do. Tears raced down his face as her body went lax and she slid toward unconsciousness.

"The baby will be fine. Just rest. And breathe. We'll get you to the hospital." Could she even hear him? Sense him? No matter—Kellen kept the tone of his voice smooth and assuring. Terror grabbed his chest and held on fast.

Dear God, no. Not, now. Please help her! Please help us!

And please, dear God, help our baby!

Minutes later, the sound of approaching siren whistles split the air.

34

"Juliet has been wheeled into pre-op. You can scrub in if you'd like, but indications warrant an emergency C-section. She's gone into labor, but she's lapsing in and out of consciousness and won't be able to deliver naturally."

The curtained off cubicle Kellen occupied was a space he couldn't wait to vacate. He sat next to the empty spot where Juliet's gurney had been stationed just moments ago. He shifted uncomfortably in a metal chair covered by sticky, green vinyl. Slouching forward on his knees, he raked his fingers through his hair. He wanted to cut loose with a tormented sob. He wanted to sink to his knees and pray with every ounce of energy he possessed.

Instead, he forced himself to focus on the doctor's diagnosis—on medical procedures that might save Juliet's life—and the life of their unborn child. Ripping his heart from his chest would be preferable.

"We've paged Doctor Roth," the physician continued. "She's on her way in. Meantime, there are several factors that seem to be working against Juliet right now—for example, her inability to remain conscious, and our inability to stop the contractions. Fortunately the initial seizure hasn't been followed by additional episodes."

"But what happened? Can you explain why this overcame her so quickly? She's healthy and I watched her during the course of our run. She was fine. I swear she wasn't overdoing it or I would have—"

"I understand, Mr. Rossiter. There's nothing you or Juliet did wrong. According to your wife's chart, Doctor Roth has been monitoring some factors that affected her pregnancy."

"Yes."

"The issues she faced led to a condition referred to as preeclampsia."

"Yes, I'm aware of that, but she's been taking care of it."

The doctor nodded. "Unfortunately there are instances when preventive measures won't stop the condition from occurring. Think of it this way, the *pre* in preeclampsia are the measures Doctor Roth took as she monitored Juliet's pregnancy in order to prevent eclampsia, which is the type of seizure that can lead to unconsciousness, and premature labor—just like Juliet is facing today."

Kellen's mind went into a sickening tailspin as he attempted to process the terms and information.

"That's another reason we need to deliver the baby as quickly as possible. We want to get both mom and baby out of danger. As you know, we've tried to stop the contractions with no success."

Kellen stared helplessly at the man. This ER doctor demonstrated a level of patience that had probably been honed by years of witnessing crisis pregnancies just like this one. That was fine enough, he supposed, but this was *his* child. This set of circumstances was tied to *his* future.

"I just don't understand how she could turn so critical so quickly. She's a healthy woman. She's strong."

"But that's only part of the issue, Mr. Rossiter. Let me see if I can explain." Following a few screen touches to the tablet-style computer he held, the doctor tilted the screen toward Kellen. On it was depicted the diagram of a uterus with various notations and directional arrows. "In most cases, preeclampsia begins when the placenta doesn't grow the usual network of blood vessels deep in the wall of the uterus. The only cure, if you will, is delivery of the baby. Juliet has been healthy, the baby has also seemed to develop well, but the seizure acts as a type of endgame that forces delivery of the baby before the mother's—and baby's—life is endangered."

"But that birth will come almost seven weeks too soon."

While Kellen tried to grasp that fact, the ER physician

continued. "Doctor Roth indicated she's about ten minutes away. Why don't you follow me to the OR, and we'll get you prepped?"

Kellen lifted from the chair and followed the doctor's lead. The attending doctor hadn't responded to his comment, and that told Kellen a lot. No matter what he witnessed in the moments to come, it would become part of the tapestry of his life. No matter what happened next, his marriage to Juliet and the bond he would form with his as-yet unborn child would be forever changed. The colors of that tapestry were up to God—be they woven in dark hues, with deep, saturating colors, or bright and vibrant with the shades of new hope and joy.

35

Flashpoints lit Juliet's pathway to consciousness. First came the ghost of a debilitating bout of nausea that had hit her like a fist to the stomach. Next came the recollection of hard, biting contractions and stiffness that had overridden her entire body. She remembered trying to brace against the sickness, pain, and paralysis—the way every bit of effort she possessed had gone into remaining conscious. The last thing she recalled was stumbling then sinking onto blessedly cold grass. Blackness had inched inward from there. Velvety peace and freedom had pulled her into an inexorable surrender—and she had felt Kellen's arms around her.

Fighting her way back to the present, Juliet tried to open her eyes. Black turned to gray then went way too bright during the attempt, so she gave up. She tried to lick her lips. The effort was beyond her, because her mouth was dry, metallic tasting and gritty.

"Kellen..." The single word wouldn't be denied, even though the act of speaking burned against her parched throat. A breath of air slid against her exposed left arm and in an instant—just like the moment when she had lost consciousness—she felt him at her side. She turned her head just slightly and groaned, forcing her eyes open this time, no matter what.

And Kellen was right there. Juliet watched him lean close and lower the guardrail so he could sit next to her. "Hey, love."

Beneath bed blankets, her right hand strayed to her stomach—considerably shrunken and blooming with pain. Realization struck her all at once. "The baby—"

"Shh...shh...she's fine. She's fine." Soothing her quietly, Kellen kissed her forehead, taking his time, lingering.

"She?" Juliet's heart hammered so hard she could have sworn it vibrated against the thin white bed sheet.

"She. Brittany is in the NICU."

Before he could continue, Juliet's chest began to heave. Brittany was the name they had decided on if their baby ended up being a girl. Tears sprang to her eyes and poured down her face. "No! That can't be! It's too early. She's going to be in trouble—"

Once again, Kellen hushed her tenderly and edged in even closer despite the complication of IV bottles and clear, plastic lines attached to her secured left arm. "She needs some time for her lungs to develop so she's going to be here in the hospital for a while, but she's fine."

Juliet sobbed, verging on hyperventilation. Kellen stroked her hair. He looked deep into her eyes. "Please relax. Be still— breathe in slow."

"I have to see her. Now." Juliet started to sit up, ready to bolt. A burst of pain speared straight through her, stemming from her midsection. *Heaven above, help me,* she thought, *I've been through a Caesarean section—major surgery.*

Kellen pressed her back gently into the pillows. She relaxed, but only a trace. "I can hardly move."

"Give it time."

"You promise me she's OK?"

"Yes, I promise. The nurse will come and get you when the doctor authorizes your first walk. It shouldn't be long. You'll get to see her in just a bit. Right now you need to rest."

Juliet's lips quaked.

In words and soft touches, he ministered to the gaping hole in her heart. She forced herself to uncurl from the onslaught of tension until silence was broken only by the sound of her breath evening out.

"We need to trust," he continued gently. "We need to keep faith."

Juliet nodded but went adrift nonetheless.

"Will you pray with me?" he asked.

Prayer was exactly what she needed. Kellen took hold of her unencumbered hand, and Juliet experienced a flow of much-needed peace. Her grip tightened on his fingers and she nodded. For a moment, Kellen closed his eyes in silence…perhaps assembling the right words.

"Jesus, thank you." He bowed his head close to hers. "Thank you for already knowing what we face. Thank you for already going to work for us, and for Brittany. You know our hearts and our fears. You know the plans You have for us. Thank you for carrying us through the storm. Uphold Juliet as she heals. Keep Brittany safe in Your hands as she continues to grow. Be with the doctors and nurses who are caring for them both, and keep us calm and steady in the truth of Your word— that in You is our help, and in You is our strength."

"Amen," they murmured in unison.

At last, Juliet found she could relax.

കൈൾ

"Mrs. Rossiter? How are you feeling?" A squat, middle-aged nurse entered the hospital room a couple of hours later, rousing Juliet from a nap. The woman sported a uniform top bursting with pastel colors.

"I feel like the baseball instead of the bat."

The woman—Rayleen according to her laminated ID badge—answered with a bubbling laugh. "I hate to break it to you, sweetheart, but it's about to get even better. Are you ready to take a stroll?"

Brittany. *Finally*, Brittany. Juliet firmed herself and nodded. "You bet I am. Straight to the NICU, if possible."

"I assumed as much, and I think that can be arranged."

The process took some time. When Juliet tried to sit up and scoot her legs out of bed, a burning sizzle struck home against the line of her incision. The pain intensified when she landed her feet on the floor. Once she hobbled to a crouching stand, she gasped. "Oh. My."

Rayleen took hold of Juliet's shoulder in an offer of steadiness. "Yeah—the first time is the toughest. You're doing great, but you need to straighten up nice and tall for me. Don't be tempted to baby yourself, because you need to move around and get your body back in tune. If you're slow and careful, you'll be just fine."

"Even though I feel like I'm about to come apart at the seams?"

"Yep—and I promise you won't. You're stitched together a lot better than you may think. C'mon and slide your feet into those slippers right there on the floor next to you. They have extra grips at the bottom, so be careful."

Before long, despite the odds Juliet would have stacked against it, she shuffled down the main hallway with Rayleen at her side. Any kind of movement felt akin to a marathon right now, but Juliet pushed ahead. Fine beads of perspiration dotted her hairline and the back of her neck while she continued to creep along. She had just one goal in mind, and nothing would keep her from it—seeing her daughter. Juliet smiled in anticipation. She would have run to Brittany if possible.

Inside the wide open space of the NICU, at least half a dozen incubators hummed; nurses jotted notes, spoke quietly. Their movements were a ballet of sorts—confident strides from baby to baby, smiles and warm words exchanged with several visiting parents. Monitoring personnel appeared unruffled despite the myriad of crisis points that surely occupied the lives of each precious soul they monitored.

Juliet looked to the right when she heard a familiar voice—Kellen's—whispering tenderly. Of course he would be with Brittany. Instantly her pains and tiredness decreased. She inched slowly toward them.

"Hey there, Britt." He slipped his hand very slowly into a protective glove that stretched into the clear, sterile unit where their daughter lay. Silent and unseen for now, Juliet watched. "It's your daddy again, sweetheart. I just got back from having some dinner. Are you hungry? Are you doing OK?"

Since Kellen blocked her view, all Juliet could see right now were fleeting images of their daughter—a flash of stretching legs, fluttery motion as Kellen's fingertips danced against Brittany's body. Juliet moved forward by slow degrees, not making a sound.

"Do you recognize my voice yet, little angel?" Kellen continued to touch her, and whisper. "Because I want to tell you something. Kind of our first daddy-daughter secret." He paused there, as though listening for Brittany's reply. Juliet lifted a hand to her clogged throat. Her lips quivered at the heartbreaking, though perfect vision of Kellen and their struggling daughter. "Some daddy's, they want a little boy at first. They want someone to play ball with, and coach, and horse around with. Well here's our secret, Britt. Not me. I wanted a little girl."

His fingertips continued to move in time to the rise and fall of Brittany's lungs, matching the tempo of her heartbeat Juliet had no doubt. "Because if you turn out to be even half as incredible as your mama, you're going to be a blessing to everyone around you. I promise to protect you, and love you, with all that I am…and your mama and I will always do our best to show you that even though we're not perfect, there's nothing Jesus can't make right, and there's nothing He won't do to keep you close to His heart. We learned that lesson together, Brittany, and we'll teach you that truth, too."

Juliet struggled for control over her emotions, brushing away tears as she stepped up to the incubator. "She'll never know a better father than you, Kellen."

He rose fast and offered an unsteady smile. A single glance into his red, full eyes told her he was choked up. He assisted Juliet toward the stool he had just left behind.

Kellen cleared his throat gruffly and kept an arm around her shoulders. "Come here and say hello to your daughter."

It only took a glance, a millisecond, for Juliet's entire universe to shift. A never-ending love settled in and took irrevocable hold of her heart. She absorbed her fill of their squirming, striving child, and she sank against the clear, tube-shaped device where Brittany lay. "Oh...oh, Kellen...she's absolutely gorgeous. I want to touch her so badly!"

Emotion poured out in tremors and warm moisture that spilled down her face in a dance of bittersweet tears. Brittany Alexandra Rossiter was a beautiful, miraculous piece of heaven itself.

"Kellen, just look at her—she's got your hair! It's so thick and dark. And her mouth—her mouth is shaped just like a heart when she closes it and puckers up...do you see that?"

Juliet's excitement built roadways over the physical strain she bore. Love cut a direct pathway, paved in gold, between her heart, Brittany's...and Kellen's. Despite wrinkled, reddish skin and slightly underdeveloped features, despite the scary sanitation of her present home and her tiny size, Brittany remained a vibrant baby who moved with strong motions that already demonstrated a fighter's instincts.

Fear abated as Juliet overflowed with gratitude. She was a mother now and a renewal with Kellen left her undone, and rejoicing. Nothing would ever be the same again.

Praise God.

Juliet reached her hand carefully into the protective glove and she stroked Brittany's warm, quivering body. Kellen drew her tight to his side.

At that point, Juliet came to a realization. Once she recovered sufficient strength, she knew exactly what needed to come next. She knew just what needed to happen in order to bring complete closure to the nightmare she and Kellen had endured.

36

"Children chase after butterflies. They dash through the wildflowers and scrub grass, right? Following the insect from bud to bud? Think about that. They run fast, grabbing for the terrified specimen. What the youngster doesn't understand is *why* the butterfly flies away. What the child doesn't realize is that only by going still, by opening their hand in quiet receptiveness, can they draw the butterfly to perch, and rest— and trust."

Ten o'clock services at Trinity Christian Church wound down. Pastor Gene preached, inspired by the Spirit. His sermon held the entire congregation, Juliet especially, in his loving care.

It's time, daughter. It's time.

The powerful whisper resounded through her soul. For a moment, the air seized in Juliet's chest as God spoke—loud and clear.

"To conclude today," Pastor Gene continued, "I pose a question, and a challenge. First, the question. What are you fighting today? What's the struggle in your life?" He walked along the front curve of the altar and held up his hands in warning. "Now don't rush to answer those questions. Think them over carefully, and prayerfully. Take a minute to listen to God. Are you being called? Is there a prompting voice in your heart that's telling you to move forward? If so, then bow your head, and *listen*."

Juliet squirmed against the hard, wooden pew. From the moment Pastor Gene asked the congregation to listen to God, a convicted and prodding spirit worked through her. Above the sounds of harmonious piano music and Pastor Gene's quiet summons came the voice that had guided and upheld her since the battle for her marriage began.

Forgive and be forgiven.

Fitting, she thought, that God's authority would be reasserted as she acknowledged—and released—how close she had come to rebuking the covenant of her marriage. The devil had stepped into the silence of her relationship with Kellen and gladly attempted a coup.

Forgiveness needed to happen. Forgiveness presented the final link in what she knew *must* be done.

Juliet squeezed her eyes shut. Her heart hitched and stuttered. She nearly lifted from her seat, itching to obey...but...but...

Speak forgiveness aloud, Juliet, to the one who owns your heart. He whom I designed and delivered to you. Seek forgiveness in return.

Soft and gentle, loving yet powerful, the voice of her Savior refused to be denied. Juliet's fingertips jerked unsteadily when she reached for Kellen's hand and took hold. Automatically he began to stroke the back of her hand.

Pastor Gene continued. "Maybe it's addictions, job struggles, health issues, relationships in chaos, letting go of pain. Whatever it is, you're not alone. God is there. God is where you are, right here, and right now."

I love you, precious one, with an everlasting love...and so does he.

She swallowed. She bowed her head, her hair forming a curtain between her and Kellen. Still, she felt the touch of his questioning gaze.

A long paused ensued. "Now, the challenge. If you feel led, I invite you to come forward. Members of the pastoral staff are joining me at the altar. Let us pray with you. Let us listen to you. Give yourself a chance to hand the battle over to God before you try to continue on by yourself."

Kellen leaned close, slid back her hair with his free hand and looked into her face. "Juliet? Are you OK?"

Once again, she nearly stood, but the stronger part of her wavered. Her legs shook so hard she couldn't quite lift up from the pew. She couldn't look at him, either. This moment would be cataclysmic if she followed through, and she knew it. "I...I want..." She couldn't quite complete the request, though it filled her heart completely.

"Juliet...what do you want?"

Tears stung her eyes but didn't fall. She pushed herself to take in air. "I want you to come with me, Kellen. Come up with me, please. There's something I need to say to you, and God has to be there when I do. Will you come with me to the altar?"

She stood before he could answer. Her legs still trembled, but then she looked at Kellen while he nodded and slowly rose. Her attention rested on their joined hands and a supernatural power claimed the moment. She couldn't resist this call to reclamation. Now that she had made the first step forward, she didn't hesitate to continue.

Associate pastors had assembled. Despite the longer line in front of Pastor Gene, Juliet waited for him. He had counseled them both. He would understand this moment like no one else.

Confused, Kellen followed her toward the front of the church. "Are you sure you want to wait for him? Are you up to it?"

"Yes, absolutely." She touched him with a smile, bolstered by his concern. Only two weeks had passed since Brittany's birth, so she tired easily, but right now, she felt fine. Brittany was holding her own and continued to improve. Doctors expected her to be released within a couple weeks.

The closer they came to the spot where Pastor Gene stood, the more Juliet shored up her courage, knowing anxiety was the devil at work. With Kellen at her side, with her hand secure in his, she continued forward until at last they stepped up to Pastor Gene.

Offering them a welcoming smile and a nod, he encircled them both with his arms and they bowed their heads. "Precious Lord, thank You"—Pastor Gene began—"thank you for the love I feel, and the journey this couple has taken toward one another, and toward You."

A vibrating silence ensued. Juliet took over from there. The words needed release so desperately they all but poured from her. "Kellen, you've come so far, and you've reemerged into the man I love, and always will. I want to commit to you my desire to do the same. I want to become, and remain, the woman you love. In order for that to happen"— she blew out unsteadily— "I need to ask you to forgive me. Please forgive me for the moments when I let you down, and didn't support you the way you needed, and wanted." At that point, she needed to see his eyes, so she lifted her head and tears began to fall.

Within the three-way prayer circle, Kellen leaned toward her and kissed her tear-moistened lips. "Completely forgiven. Completely. I swear to you now—I swear to you forever— you're the most precious blessing God ever gave me. I will never, ever betray you again." As Kellen spoke the words, as the reverence of them took her under, Juliet closed her eyes. "I promised you that in marriage, in front of God, in front of our family. I broke that vow, but my prayer remains that you'll continue to trust me, and believe in me. Please, let me have the gift of your love all over again."

"You already have it. I promise. I forgive you, too— sincerely, and with all that I am."

Juliet was drained, grateful for the physical support both Kellen and Pastor Gene provided. Tears continued to fall, and Kellen released her just long enough to brush his thumb slowly beneath her eyes. His touch felt so beautiful and comforting.

"A second chance is all that matters to me," Kellen concluded. "I can't live in happiness without you."

They reassembled their circle in a tight hold. "You make miracles happen, Lord." Pastor Gene spoke. "I've seen it in the way Kellen and Juliet have determinedly reclaimed their marriage, and the love they share. All of this, we know, comes straight from You. Thank You for the faithful provision of Your hand in that which You ordain."

"Amen," came a three-way response that warmed Juliet to

the core.

❧✿

"I don't want to leave," Juliet whispered to Kellen. She sank back against the pew...the same pew, she now realized, that they had occupied long months ago when apathy, bitterness, and betrayal had nearly claimed them both.

Services had long since concluded and they occupied a now silent sanctuary. The lights had been turned off, leaving the interior bathed in milky light frosted by beams of sunlight cutting colorful patterns through the stained glass windows.

How different, she thought, from that rainy, awful day.

Now, Juliet closed her eyes against memories and let them fall away, harmless and ineffective against the happiness she felt.

"When we stood up there together, I felt like I was marrying you all over again." Kellen's declaration propelled Juliet to a level of contentment she couldn't have dreamed possible. "I'm so grateful you found a way back to me."

"You fought the battle, too, Kellen. I understand that now. You weren't alone in what happened to our relationship."

He sighed then shrugged. "I thought my faith would buffer me. In some ways it did, but not completely. I'm imperfect. I can't expect to dodge sin, or be immune from the consequences of my actions because I'm a child of God. I'm human, and frailty is part of my package, but I never, ever meant to fall away from you, Juliet."

"I didn't mean to ever reach a point where our relationship was taken for granted."

Kellen tipped his head back. For a silent moment, he looked around, taking in their surroundings. "Do you realize this is almost the exact spot where we sat the day you and I thought we had come to the end?"

Juliet rested her head against his shoulder. "Actually, I was just thinking about that."

Kellen kissed the top of her head and curved his arm against the back of the pew, around her shoulders. Juliet tucked into him and focused on the simple wooden cross suspended above the rear of the altar.

"There's no question He sheltered us through the storm, Juliet."

"Thank you for fighting for me, Kellen. Thank you for fighting for us and our marriage when I just didn't have the strength."

He lifted away then and turned. Juliet sat up, focusing on his face while he cupped her hands in his and lifted them up, sliding his lips against her fingertips. "It's like the butterfly analogy. Going still, hoping and praying, and waiting—giving it all to God and returning to obedience—was the only way I knew to give you the power to decide what would happen next. Could you find enough faith and trust to stay with me and keep from running away—even though you'd have every right?"

"I had already made that decision, Kellen—when we went running. I was ready then, and I'm ready now, to give myself all the way back to our marriage."

"And in return, know this, I'll remain the man you fell in love with. I'm going to hold on to my faith, and the strength of our love, with all that I am. Not just for you, but for me, and for Brittany. I want to create a legacy that'll show her the beauty of God's redemption and grace."

Juliet stroked his cheek with shaky fingers. "It's not about the fall. It's about the rising. You've risen again. Better than you ever were."

Juliet's words spelled out the roadway to a future that defined the new terms of their marriage: persistence, strength, and devotion.

The kiss they shared was long and slow, seasoned by their history—ripened by all of its joys, all of its passions, all of its struggles and victories. Once Kellen tempered the exchange and eased away, she looked into eyes full of love. There, she tasted the precious gift of their faith, and a relationship renewed by grace.

There, she tasted their future.

Thank you for purchasing this Harbourlight title. For other inspirational stories, please visit our on-line bookstore at www.pelicanbookgroup.com.

For questions or more information, contact us at titleadmin@pelicanbookgroup.com.

Harbourlight Books
The Beacon in Christian Fiction™
www.HarbourlightBooks.com
an imprint of Pelican Ventures Book Group
www.pelicanbookgroup.com

May God's glory shine through
this inspirational work of fiction.

AMDG

Are You Devoted?

Visit imdevoted.com

- **Prayer and devotion aids**: Delve deeper into the Christian view of marriage and gain better understanding and deeper appreciation for the covenant of Holy Matrimony

- **Discuss**: Communicate with other married (and pre-married) couples and individuals about the joys and challenges of marriage

- **Companion Workbook**: Great for Engaged couples' Marriage instruction, or for individual, couples, and group study and enrichment. (Used in conjunction with DEVOTION, the novel.)

...and More